Catharine Maria Sedgwick
Redwood: A Tale

Edinburgh University Press is one of the leading university presses in the UK. We publish academic books and journals in our selected subject areas across the humanities and social sciences, combining cutting-edge scholarship with high editorial and production values to produce academic works of lasting importance. For more information visit our website: edinburghuniversitypress.com

© editorial matter and organisation Jenifer B. Elmore, 2021, 2023
© the text in this edition, Edinburgh University Press, 2021, 2023

Edinburgh University Press Ltd
The Tun – Holyrood Road
12(2f) Jackson's Entry
Edinburgh EH8 8PJ

First published in hardback by Edinburgh University Press 2021

Typeset in 11/12.5 Baskerville and Times New Roman by
IDSUK (DataConnection) Ltd, and
printed and bound by CPI Group (UK) Ltd,
Croydon, CR0 4YY

A CIP record for this book is available from the British Library

ISBN 978 1 4744 6767 4 (hardback)
ISBN 978 1 3995 1111 7 (paperback)
ISBN 978 1 4744 6768 1 (webready PDF)
ISBN 978 1 4744 6769 8 (epub)

The right of Jenifer B. Elmore to be identified as the editor of this work has been asserted in accordance with the Copyright, Designs and Patents Act 1988, and the Copyright and Related Rights Regulations 2003 (SI No. 2498).

Contents

Acknowledgements	vii
Editor's Introduction	ix
Selected Bibliography for Further Study	xxxvi
A Note on the Text	xxxviii
Chronology of Sedgwick's Life and Works	xl
List of Characters	xliii
Redwood: A Tale	1
Appendix A: Sedgwick's Preface to the 1850 Edition	315
Appendix B: Significant Revisions for the 1850 Edition	317

The staff of the Warren Library at PBA must also be acknowledged. Interlibrary Loan Coordinator Nerolie Ceus tops the list; her professional efficiency and commitment to her work made scores of annotations in this edition possible. Reference Librarian Anthony Verdesca also provided valuable information and sources at crucial points in the process.

The editorial team at Edinburgh University Press have been supportive, positive and, most of all, patient throughout the publication process; obviously this book is as much their project as mine. I am also deeply grateful for the two anonymous readers of the proposal and the manuscript; their generous, detailed feedback shaped this edition for the better in numerous ways.

Finally, I thank my family for their support and patience. Charles Elmore and our children, Holly, Shelby and Andrew, are my loudest and most loyal cheerleaders, rivalled only by my brother John Bobo and sister Caroline Bartlett. I could never thank them enough.

Editor's Introduction

The suspense surrounding the parentage of the heroine, the intrigue supplied by the treachery of male and female villains, the freshness of the indomitable Aunt Debby, the glimpse into the eccentric sect of the Shakers, and the drama of multiple courtships: these rewards explain why nineteenth-century readers, both in America and in Europe, avidly invested money, time and emotion in *Redwood: A Tale* (1824). Featuring almost as many subplots, backstories and embedded texts as it has characters, Sedgwick's second novel was nearly three times the length of her first, and it was longer and more complex than most, if not all, previous American novels.

With her first novel, *A New-England Tale* (1822), Sedgwick had launched not only her own career as a novelist but also a whole genre of 'woman's fiction' that tells the stories of heroines 'who, beset with hardships, [find] within [themselves] the qualities of intelligence, will, resourcefulness, and courage sufficient to overcome them' (Baym 22). *Redwood* further develops that new genre, to be sure, but it also incorporates elements of the novel of seduction, the genre that had dominated fiction by American women writers in the decades immediately following the revolution. It also sets a precedent for nearly every other thematic concern expressed in Sedgwick's subsequent writings. Readers of Sedgwick's fourth novel, *Clarence; or, a Tale of Our Own Times* (1830), will find that *Redwood* is also, as Melissa J. Homestead argues, 'arguably a novel of manners' (Introduction 10). Readers who have celebrated the cheeky and defiant yet charming and ultimately virtuous Hope Leslie, the eponymous heroine of Sedgwick's most famous novel (1827), will enjoy Sedgwick's comparable portrayal of the older but equally bold Grace Campbell in *Redwood*. Grace's marriage plot, as Lucinda Damon-Bach has pointed out, prefigures that of Gertrude Clarence in *Clarence* (69), and the series of rescues effected by women in *Redwood*, particularly when two females rescue another from captivity, sets a precedent for the multiple rescues that women accomplish in *Hope Leslie*. The backdrop of American conflict with Great Britain and the theme of republican virtue prevailing over patrician privilege work well in *Redwood* and then feature more prominently her fifth novel, *The Linwoods* (1835). As for the theme of marriage in *Redwood*, the difficult choices of Susan Allen

critical editions. Today's readers can enjoy these nov-
benefit of annotations, critical introductions and other
that not only enhance comprehension and appreciation
ourage academic study. No comprehensive biography of
is yet been published, but Kelley's annotated edition of
m Sedgwick's private autobiography and journals, the
vailability of archival texts online, and the introductions
rn editions of Sedgwick's other novels have done much
contemporary readers with Sedgwick's biography and
career.[1] Therefore, this introduction incorporates only
iphical elements that relate most directly to this novel.
ι seeks to introduce new readers to the novel, enhance
experience and facilitate further study. In that spirit, this
i's first priority is to inform and inspire new readings,
though it clearly reflects my critical priorities and the reasons why
this novel continues to fascinate me. This introduction situates the
novel within Sedgwick's career, contextualises it within antebellum
US history and transatlantic literary culture, and suggests several
possible avenues for new scholarship. My goal is to spark a lively,
productive and sustained critical conversation about this ground-
breaking novel and its remarkable characters – not only among those
who are already fans and scholars of Sedgwick, but among those
who may be reading Sedgwick, or any early nineteenth-century
American novelist, for the very first time.

1. The list of Works Cited that follows this introduction includes entries for modern editions of Sedgwick's major novels, as well as several critical sources, including the only published collection of Sedgwick criticism to date, *Catharine Maria Sedgwick: Critical Perspectives* (Damon-Bach and Clements, 2003). That book also features a detailed chronology of Sedgwick's life (personal and professional) and an exhaustive bibliography of Sedgwick's published writings. Additional resources are available on the Catharine Maria Sedgwick Society website at <https://cmsedgwicksociety.org> (last accessed 18 September 2020), including a bibliography of published Sedgwick criticism that is regularly updated, a brief chronology of Sedgwick's career, links to full-text digital editions of many of her shorter works, and links to archival collections of works by and about Sedgwick.

and critics were largely positive, with enough mildly negative criticism to render the positive remarks more trustworthy and to show that they took the novel seriously. An early unsigned review in *Port Folio* called it 'the first *American* novel, strictly speaking, which has appeared' ('Review' 69). An anonymous review in the July 1824 issue of *The Atlantic Magazine* first pointed out that it had been previously claimed that 'America has never produced a female writer of eminence', then proclaimed that '[i]f the writer of "Redwood" is not the only exception, she is certainly the brightest; and we trust, that a long career is before her, of still increasing utility and fame' ('Review' 238–9). If anyone might have been tempted to go easy on *Redwood*, it would surely have been William Cullen Bryant. Not only was he a personal friend of Sedgwick and her family, but she dedicated the novel to him in 'admiration of his genius'. Nevertheless, in a long and comprehensive review in the *North American Review* in April 1825, Bryant called the novel 'a comparatively hazardous experiment' because the materials that it deals with, from the domestic life of its own era, are more difficult to manage successfully in fiction than historical events (246). His review proceeds in a balanced but ultimately positive manner, praising certain aspects of the novel while gently criticising others.

The first discussions of *Redwood* that were published in the twentieth century categorise *Redwood* as a domestic and didactic romance – the story of how the virtuous orphan Ellen Bruce finds her true identity and a sufficiently virtuous husband, while converting her long-lost father to Christianity in the bargain.[2] Such readings were useful for their situation of the novel within the tradition of nineteenth-century domestic fiction, but they were also brief treatments that did not explore the regional and political implications of the text. The separate spheres paradigm, which dominated the study of women's history and literature until at least the 1980s, interpreted women's literature within a limited sphere of home, family and domestic relationships; the relevance of fiction by women to the world of politics, policy, economics and international affairs was simply not recognised. This theoretical segregation produced readings of American women's fiction that were not wrong (on the contrary, they made important contributions to literary history and feminist literary criticism), but were rather one-dimensional. These limited interpretations neglected many of cultural and political ramifications of so-called domestic concerns and overlooked nearly all textual concerns that extend beyond the immediate personal concerns of the characters.

Since the 1980s, scholars of women's literature and women's history on both sides of the Atlantic have conclusively established that fiction by women of the late eighteenth and early nineteenth centuries regularly and seriously engages the public sphere at the same time that it explores and represents the domestic sphere.[3] My own thinking on this subject has developed in large part from studying Sedgwick's writings alongside those of Maria Edgeworth (Elmore, *Sacred Unions*). As I have demonstrated elsewhere, Sedgwick fashioned her authorial agenda to a great extent after Edgeworth's wildly successful and greatly respected example (Elmore, 'Sedgwick and Edgeworth'). As Edgeworth's works had extensively illustrated and commented on British and especially Irish political realities, so do Sedgwick's engage with the political in America.

---

2. These include Nina Baym's discussion in *Woman's Fiction* (1970); Edward H. Foster's in his very brief Foreword to a 1969 facsimile reprint edition of *Redwood*, as well as in his 1974 volume on Sedgwick that is part of the Twayne US Authors series; and Mary Kelley's in the first edition of *Private Woman, Public Stage* (1984).

3. Some pioneering works in this vein in the field of US literature include Cathy N. Davidson's *Revolution and the Word: The Rise of the Novel in America* (1986), Susan K. Harris's *Nineteenth-Century American Women's Novels: Interpretive Strategies* (1990) and Amy Kaplan's article 'Manifest Domesticity' (Fall 1998 in the journal *American Literature* and again in 2002 as a chapter in the book *No More Separate Spheres! A Next Wave American Studies Reader*, edited by Davidson. See Works Cited for publication details.

Redwood provides an excellent field for further study of this domestic-to-political manœuvre. This novel repeatedly demonstrates that personal and domestic concerns not only have their own political dimensions and implications, but that such homely concerns may, through imaginative literature, symbolically figure and communicate bold ideas that are political, national and international in scope. Certainly, *Redwood* is in some respects a domestic comedy of manners – one that rivals Shakespeare and Jane Austen by ending with a whopping five marriages – but it is set against a backdrop of deeply troubling and potentially insurmountable cultural and political tensions among a cast of characters who represent different regions and divergent social and religious practices – and it does not end happily for all of them. Moreover, *Redwood* is indeed a didactic tale, but the lessons it puts forward have less to do with sexual virtue and courtship *per se* than with individual moral integrity, friendship, cultural values, religious faith and the challenge of binding together a young nation in spite of glaring cultural differences, bitter sectional disputes and increasingly intense divisions over the issue of slavery.

Packaging and paratext

Before readers have any notion of its plot or characters, *Redwood: A Tale* presents them with five paratextual elements – a title, an epigraph to the entire novel, a dedication, a preface and an epigraph to the first chapter – that package the novel and announce its priorities.[4] These elements reveal a great deal about the novel, some of which may be lost on today's readers because conventions have changed, and all of which may be overlooked by readers who are simply eager to dive into the story itself.

From the main title, readers rightfully expect that the chief concern of this tale will be someone or somewhere called Redwood. For most present-day readers in the United States the word 'Redwood' calls up images of the huge, majestic trees in California, but in 1824 those trees were not generally known, and the Pacific coast was not even part of the US. However, there was a prominent American family with the surname Redwood at the time, known throughout New England for endowing an important library in the wealthy and fashionable city of Newport, Rhode Island. (The historical Redwood

---

4. For an additional analysis of the epigraph to the novel and the epigraph to the first chapter, as well as a more general discussion of the role of paratext in *Redwood*, see Damon-Bach, 'To Act and Transact', pp. 59–61.

family is further discussed later in this introduction.) There were other Redwood families living in the US, including in the state of Virginia, where the important character Henry Redwood is from in the novel. So, a nineteenth-century reader in America would probably have assumed that the title was the surname of the main character, possibly connected to the actual Redwoods of Rhode Island. The Redwood surname originated in Scotland and was still common in Scotland in the 1800s. The common noun *redwood* also has Scottish associations, meaning both 'the name given to the reddish, or dark-coloured, and more incorruptible wood found in the heart of trees' and 'the wood of the Scots pine' or the name of that tree itself ('redwood', *OED*). To the early readers of the novel in the United Kingdom, then, the title would most immediately have suggested a familiar surname, might also have suggested the strength and durability of the redwood or Scots pine tree, and would possibly have smacked of 'Scottishness' in general.

Not to be overlooked, the subtitle 'A Tale' is rather generic in that it is broad, but it is also generic in the sense of genre: it indicates something about the genre of the novel and about Sedgwick's writing style. In the nineteenth century, as well as to this day, the word 'tale' denotes both narrativity and fictionality. The word descends from the verb 'to tell', so it also suggests oral storytelling, as in the kind of story that might be told in conversation or perhaps written in a conversational style in a letter to a friend. In fact, though *Redwood* is 'told' by an omniscient narrator, it is also full of stories that characters tell to one another (and directly to the reader) through direct dialogue and in the form of embedded letters – a strategy that Carolyn Karcher describes as 'shared authorship' (10).

The epigraph to the novel, a quotation from the work *The Principles of Moral and Political Philosophy* by English philosopher, clergyman and Christian apologist William Paley (1743–1805), appears on the title page of both major nineteenth-century editions. It declares the folly of atheism and thus establishes on the title page that religious belief will be central to the novel. It also bestows an air of European erudition to this early American novel. On the other hand, the dedication to American poet William Cullen Bryant bestows an air of Americanness; it shouts out respect for one of the few American writers who had achieved international reputation and respect before *Redwood* was published: 'TO WILLIAM CULLEN BRYANT, Esq. in token of friendship and admiration of his genius, these volumes are dedicated by THE AUTHOR'. The dedication also contains the only reference to the author of the novel that appears anywhere in the first edition. While it admits nothing of the author's identity, it does hint that the author is American and probably a New Englander because of her or his friendship with Bryant, who lived in the Berkshire region of Massachusetts.[5]

The most substantial of these opening paratextual elements, the author's preface, reiterates and expands upon the concerns suggested by the first three. The preface is primarily a defence of novel-reading on the grounds of its educational and moral value; it also comments on the 'scanty' state of American literature at the time. Secondarily, the preface highlights the novel's religious theme, recalling the quotation from Paley, and reveals that the novel will contain an unflattering but truthful 'sketch' of the Shaker sect. Finally, it warns against American exceptionalism and unwarranted patriotism, soberly observing that America is 'no Arcadia'.

After these first four paratextual elements have established the broad themes and cultural context of the novel, the epigraph to the first chapter (which consists of an anonymous quotation of dialogue that has never been identified) narrows the focus to the description of a character – a heroine – with the exclamation 'A fine heroine, truly!', followed by the contradictory response, 'A Patagonian monster without a hint of breeding'. Who is this heroine? Is she a fine lady or is she a monster? We must read more to find out.

Thus, three central oppositions set the tone for the reading of *Redwood* even before the story begins: religious faith versus scepticism, America's virtues versus its shortcomings, and female virtue versus monstrosity. These three concerns arise from competing concepts of value and identity – value that is based on identity, and identity that is formed by spiritual, political and personal values. These values are contested in the novel through conversation (dialogue), narratorial commentary, subtle allusions and connotations, but most often through the contrasting choices that characters make and the different outcomes that result.

SPOILER ALERT: *The rest of this introduction gives away important plot details. First-time readers are encouraged to read the novel itself before finishing the introduction.*

The trope of seduction

Though *Redwood* is not properly a 'novel of seduction' because its heroine does not follow a narrative arc from naivety to sexual seduction to

---

5. For a comprehensive discussion of what it meant for Sedgwick to publish anonymously, see Homestead, 'Behind the Veil'.

ruin,[6] it does employ a seduction motif in ways that correspond to the novel's central oppositions. The word 'seduction' here may be defined as the persuasion of one person to abandon moral values, political ideals or religious beliefs by another person who offers in return to satisfy a sexual, emotional or material desire. The same character may act as the seducer in one set of circumstances and the seduced in another. For example, Henry Redwood is seduced spiritually and intellectually by Alsop, who influences Henry to cast off his moral and religious scruples and pursue atheism and libertinism. Without religious scruples to restrain him, Henry romantically seduces the orphan Mary Erwine into a secret marriage that, for all of Henry's practical purposes, is tantamount to an illicit affair. The marriage legally ends with Mary's death, but only after Henry's second seduction by Alsop has already ended it in every other way. Emily Allen is seduced in a religious sense by the charisma of her aunt Susan, though she resists sexual seduction by Reuben Harrington. Charles Westall is very nearly seduced into a loveless marriage with the beautiful and rich Caroline Redwood. Thus, while the novel as a whole does not follow a seduction plotline, the subplots, the backstories and many of the choices that the characters make along the way largely revolve around illustrating the consequences of past seductions, stemming or reversing the present-day consequences of past seductions and thwarting new attempts at seduction before future damage is done.

Role models for virtuous womanhood: Ellen Bruce and Aunt Debby Lenox

Because the three central oppositions of the novel are negotiated and modelled mostly by female characters, the theme of virtuous womanhood saturates *Redwood*, even where issues of religion and politics are foregrounded. Sedgwick focuses this pervasive theme through the lenses of Ellen Bruce and Aunt Debby, whose sustained presence and insoluble bond of friendship provide for the novel a unity and clarity of vision, despite its complex structure. One or both members of this dynamic duo appear in twenty-five of the novel's twenty-seven chapters, and usually they appear together. All the other characters, living or dead, and their subplots or backstories are related in some way to one or both of these two women.

6. The most widely read novels of seduction in the US during the 1790s included *Charlotte Temple* by Susanna Rowson (first American edition, 1794) and *The Coquette; or, The History of Eliza Wharton* by Hannah Webster Foster (1797).

Ellen Bruce is the main character and heroine of the novel; she represents female virtue and ideal American young womanhood. Given its linguistic and historical associations, her name speaks volumes about her character. The most familiar association with the name Ellen is the French pronoun *elle*, which means 'she' or 'her', but the name is also a cognate of the name Helen; both Helen and Ellen may be derived from the Greek word *ele*, meaning 'bright light'. This meaning clearly applies to Ellen Bruce, especially in relation to the role she plays in the lives of other characters, most notably in bringing spiritual light to Henry Redwood and literal light to the blind child Peggy. The word *ellen* was also a common noun in Old English, meaning strength or courage ('elne/ellen', *OED*). As for Bruce, it is not Ellen's surname but rather the maiden name of her maternal grandmother, bestowed on Ellen by her mother (Mary Erwine Redwood) to conceal Ellen's true parentage from everyone, including Ellen herself, until she either becomes engaged to be married or reaches the age of twenty-one. The name Bruce has readily recognisable historical and legendary associations with Robert the Bruce (1274–1329), King of Scotland. The name originated from a location in France from which the first Scottish patriarch of the Bruce line emigrated (Duncan). However, because of Robert's military and political victories, which resulted in establishing Scotland as an independent kingdom, the name Bruce came to be associated not only with Scottish nationalism but with strength, fortitude, honour and independence more generally – so generally, in fact, that the creators of the twentieth-century superhero Batman tapped into those associations when they named the righteously indignant man who wears the bat costume, Bruce Wayne, after Robert the Bruce (Kane and Andrae 44).

Ellen is not perfect, but she comes close. Though the text does not dwell on her shortcomings, she does have a few. For instance, while she seems to be morally offended by the institution of slavery and treats the slave Lilly with far more respect and compassion than Caroline does, Ellen finds Lilly's race physically repellent and is reluctant to touch or come too close to her. Ellen also does not resist joining in the rude laughter of those who ridicule Debby's appearance in an unfashionable dress at the Lebanon Springs hotel. While Ellen clearly has some room for growth, she is none the less her generation's model of virtue – virtue that has been carefully cultivated. She has been raised by two foster mothers, Mrs. Harrison and Mrs. Allen, who are described as virtuous Christians with complementary strengths. The narrator tells us that in their alternating arrangement of sharing Ellen's upbringing, 'there was a system of checks and balances that produced that singular and felicitous union of diversity of qualities which constituted the rare perfection of Ellen's character' (p. 91). The political undertones here are unmistakable. The term 'checks and balances' had been in wide use since the early days of constitutional debate, appearing in paper 51 of *The Federalist* and other political treatises as the fundamental strength of a republican constitution. Ellen possesses not a combination but a 'singular and felicitous *union*' of qualities which do not merely form but more significantly '*constitute*' her perfection. By playing with such easily recognisable political vocabulary, Sedgwick takes her heroine beyond the role of virtuous republican woman: Ellen may be read as symbolising the young nation, the Union, itself – not perfect but very good; still young and inexperienced, but showing enormous potential.[7]

At Ellen's side is Deborah Lenox, a single, middle-aged woman who is over six feet tall and familiarly known as Aunt Debby. Despite her masculine features, Debby's wisdom, kindness and sensitivity equal that of the heroine Ellen Bruce. Like her ancient Hebrew namesake in the biblical book of Judges, who was a prophet, a judge, a military commander and the only female ruler of ancient Israel, Deborah Lenox is known and respected for her individual courage, strength, righteousness and wisdom – and not because of her relationship to any man. Debby is introduced in the first chapter as bold and tough, with both stereotypically masculine and stereotypically feminine traits:

> Her height was rather above the grenadier standard, as she exceeded by one inch six feet; her stature and her weather-beaten skin would have led one to suspect that her feminine dress was a vain attempt at disguise, had not her voice, which possessed the shrillness which is the peculiar attribute of the woman's, testified to Miss Debby's right to make pretensions which at the first glance seemed monstrous; her quick gray eye, shaded by huge bushy eye-brows, indicated sagacity and thought; time, or accident, had made such ravages on her teeth, that but a very few remained, and they stood like hardy veterans who have by dint of superior strength survived their contemporaries. (p. 21)

The narrator's use of the word 'monstrous' here harkens back to the epigraph of this first chapter and the question it raises regarding female monstrosity versus heroism. Debby's womanhood is not a monstrous pretension but the genuine article; the novel clearly establishes early on that

---

7. Before Anne K. Mellor theorised English women writers of the Romantic period as 'mothers of the nation', Marilyn Butler had recognised Edgeworth's Irish heroines as 'strange variants of an insufficiently discussed type – the figure of a woman as a symbolic national leader' (Introduction, *Castle Rackrent and Ennui* 51).

the role of heroine does not depend on appearance. Note the heavy use of terms associated with masculinity, military service and bodily injury in the passage: grenadier, standard, stature, weather-beaten, accident, ravages, hardy, veterans, superior, strength, survived. This vocabulary might be taken from biographical sketches of aged American Revolutionary war veterans – and indeed that seems to be what Sedgwick had in mind.

The fictional Debby Lenox is at least partly based on the historical Deborah Sampson (c.1760–1826), a Massachusetts woman who was regionally famous for having disguised herself as a man, enlisted in the Continental Army and served for nearly a year and a half as a combat soldier (Young 7). After the war she married Benjamin Gannet and they had three children together ('Deborah Sampson'). In 1797 the newspaper publisher Herman Mann teamed with Sampson to publish a book relating her story, the extended title of which says a great deal about the fine line that the two of them wanted to walk between capitalising on Sampson's sensationally 'masculine' adventures on the one hand and insisting on her traditional femininity and domesticity on the other:

> *The Female Review; or, Memoirs of an American Young Lady; whose life and character are peculiarly distinguished – being a Continental soldier, for nearly three years, in the late American war. During which time, she performed the duties of every department, into which she was called, with punctual exactness, fidelity, and honour, and preserved her chastity inviolate, by the most artful concealment of her sex.: With an appendix, containing characteristic traits, by different hands; her taste for economy, principles of domestic education, &c.*

After the book was published, Sampson embarked on a lecture and stage performance tour of New York and New England (Young 201–2). When *Redwood* was published in 1824, Sampson was in her mid-sixties and living in Massachusetts (Young 264).

Contemporaneous accounts of Deborah Sampson, while acknowledging her cross-dressed combat service as extraordinary, do not describe her as masculine in appearance. On the contrary, they take pains to point out her conventionally female appearance and manners. For example, when she tried to get a military pension and was at first denied, the famous revolutionary hero Paul Revere advocated in her favour. In a letter to US Congressman William Eustis in 1804, Revere related that he had expected Sampson to be a 'tall, masculine female' when he first met her, yet found to his surprise that she was actually a 'small, effeminate, and conversable woman'. Other sources report her height as five feet, nine inches, which was above average even for a man in that era. Either way, though, Sedgwick adds at least four inches to

Sampson's height to arrive at Aunt Debby's height of six feet, one inch, which is very tall for a woman even by today's standards.

Many of *Redwood*'s contemporary reviewers deemed Aunt Deborah its most original and skilfully crafted character. Sedgwick's fellow American writer Lydia Maria Child went so far as to insist, 'If there be an artist who hopes to surpass "Aunt Debby Lennox [sic]" he may as well lay down his pencil and die' (236). Bryant highlighted her 'striking and novel combination' of qualities, including a mixture of 'masculine habits with those of her own sex' (266). Edgeworth considered the novel in an international context, noting that

> [T]he character of Aunt Deborah is first rate; in Scott's best manner, yet not an imitation of Scott. It is to America what Scott's characters are to Scotland – valuable as original pictures, with enough of individual peculiarity to be interesting, and to give the feeling of reality and life as portraits, with sufficient also of general characteristicks, to give them the philosophical merit of portraying a class. (Edgeworth, 'Letter')

Edgeworth clearly views Aunt Debby as authentically and representatively American, yet Debby also reminds her of Scott's style of Scottish characterisation. Both Edgeworth and Sedgwick emulated Scott, particularly in their historical fictions, so it is not surprising that a certain 'family resemblance' might be detected among particular characters in all three writers' works. In addition to using what she knew of the living legend Deborah Sampson, Sedgwick likely incorporated aspects of the Scottish character Helen MacGregor from Scott's historical fiction *Rob Roy* (1817), into her creation of Aunt Debby, particularly in crafting her rugged and arresting appearance. In *Rob Roy*, the first-person narrator describes Helen in terms that are both masculine and martial:

> I have rarely seen a more noble and imposing figure than that of this woman. She could have been forty to fifty years old, and her physiognomy must have formerly offered striking features of a male beauty, although her features had rather an air of harshness and fierce expression, and that we already noticed wrinkles formed there. . . . She did not wear her plaid on her head and shoulders, as is the custom of the women of Scotland, but she surrounded her body, according to the custom of the Highland soldiers. She had a [chief's] hat on her head. (Chapter 30)

Interestingly, the historical Deborah Sampson, the ancient Israelite judge Deborah and the fictional Helen MacGregor were not only soldiers but also wives and mothers, while Sedgwick's character Aunt Debby Lenox only looks as if she might have been a soldier and remains unmarried by choice. Given these variations from her models, Sedgwick seems to have wanted to intensify her character's physical toughness and the masculinity of her physical appearance, but not go so far as to make her an actual cross-dressed soldier. She emphasises the femininity of Debby's voice, her skills as a nurse and caregiver, and her usually latent personal vanity (which emerges in the description below from Chapter 1 and then again in the scene of the Lebanon Springs dinner party in Chapter 17). She does not move Debby so far in the direction of conventional femininity as to make her into a wife and mother, but she makes it clear that Debby had at least one marriage proposal as a young woman. Like Sedgwick herself, Debby has remained unmarried by choice:

> The only relic of worldly or womanly vanity which Debby displayed, was a string of gold beads, which, according to a tradition that had been carefully transmitted to the younger members of the family, had been given to their Aunt Debby some thirty years before by a veteran soldier, who, at the close of our revolutionary war, was captivated by the martial air of this then young Amazon.
>
> But Debby was so imbued with the independent spirit of the times, that she would not then consent to the surrender of any of her rights. . . . The careful preservation of the beads, and a certain kindliness and protecting air towards all mankind, indicated ever after a grateful recollection of her lover. (p. 21)

By having one of the two central female characters insist on staying single in order to maintain her independence, Sedgwick demonstrates that single life is a legitimate and in many ways desirable alternative to marriage – a perfectly good way to be a virtuous woman in America. Sedgwick was born in 1789 and remained single for life (she died in 1867). She was in her mid-thirties when she wrote *Redwood*, and she had refused at least two marriage proposals (Kelly, *Power* 27–9; Damon-Bach and Clements, xxxiv). Sedgwick would echo this theme in her next novel, *Hope Leslie*, with the choice of Esther Downing to remain single, and she would make it the centrepiece of her sixth and final novel, *Married or Single?* Though Debby and Esther are not heroines, they are important characters and Sedgwick refuses to let them be upstaged; she even ends *Redwood* and *Hope Leslie* with letters written by Debby and Esther. Thus these unmarried women share an authorial status with the novelist; they control the ending and make the final impression on the reader. The heroines get married but the single ladies get the last word.

Place and time

In her preface to the first edition, Sedgwick remarks that it is the business of 'fictitious narrative' to depict for posterity 'the passing character and manners of the present time and place' (p. 6). If we take Sedgwick at her word in the preface, then the 'present time' of the novel's publication in 1824 should be close to the time of its fictional setting, but the latter is never specified. The first sentence of the novel is intentionally vague, unhelpfully announcing the time as 'the last day of June, in the year ____'. The first clue to the approximate timing of the action occurs in the passage quoted above regarding Aunt Debby's suitor. If he proposed to her 'at the close of our revolutionary war', and that was 'some thirty years before' the Redwoods' arrival at Eton, then the events of the novel must take place thirty years or so after the war ended in 1783 – around 1813, give or take a few years. However, there is no clear indication that the War of 1812 (1812–15) is in progress during the events of the main plot. British soldiers are stationed in Canada and in the West Indies, but that would be the case to some extent in war or peace. Considering these and several other clues that arise over the course of the novel (some of which seem contradictory), Sedgwick probably imagined the action as taking place between 1813 and 1816. From the Americans' perspective, their young nation is either in the midst of a second military conflict against its mighty mother country or has recently won that conflict; either scenario would intensify the tension between proper national pride and 'narrow-minded patriotism' that Sedgwick discusses in the preface to the first edition.

As for location, most of the action of the novel happens at the Lenox family farm near the village of Eton, Vermont, but a substantial episode occurs in the Shaker village in Hancock, Massachusetts, and the final scenes take place at a resort in Lebanon Springs, New York. In fact, unlike the mysterious 'ice glen' of *A New-England Tale*, the lush forest scenery of *Hope Leslie* and the sublime Trenton Falls of *Clarence*, the geographical settings described in *Redwood* are not inherently compelling. Instead, they provide the stage for a much larger, national discourse on just about every aspect of what it means, or should mean, to be American. Without sacrificing plausibility, Sedgwick skilfully manipulates the events of the plot in such a way that this one sparsely populated region may as well be the cosmopolitan crossroads of early America. The Redwoods and two of their slaves are visiting the area from Virginia and South Carolina, the Westalls are visiting from Boston and Virginia, Grace Campbell and the Armstead clan are visiting from Philadelphia and England, Captain Fitzgerald is a British soldier stationed in Canada and visiting the resort on leave, the Shakers operate a separatist compound, Sooduck is an abandoned and embittered Native American who lives alone in the forest outside Eton. As Christopher Apap puts it, 'Sedgwick collapse[s] the immense scale of the nation into a farm in rural Vermont' (58).

Stretching the possible time frame of the setting is another strategy that Sedgwick employs for expanding its limited place. Sedgwick's deliberate vagueness in calling attention to a specific year in the opening phrase of the text, only to label that year as a blank, underscores the fictionality of her 'tale' and indicates that, even though readers can deduce the approximate time, these events might have taken place any time between the end of the American Revolution and 1824. Many characters whose stories occupy narrative space are already dead before the proper action begins, and others die before the novel ends; however, death does not stop them from influencing the actions of the living by continuing to 'speak' through letters. By playing with time in this fashion, Sedgwick further expands the diversity and multivocality of the novel, creating the impression that its range encompasses not only the entire nation but the history of the nation as well. Representatives of multiple generations, as well as of multiple classes, regional cultures, nations, races, religious creeds, political persuasions, abilities and levels of education interact extensively in this novel, negotiating the moral, political and religious dimensions of what it means to be American on multiple levels, the most basic of which is emotional.

The Shaker subplot

Redwood's depictions of any of the negotiations in this extensive list offer rich material for additional analysis, but perhaps the most fascinating is the contest of faith that occurs at the Hancock Shaker village, to which Sedgwick calls attention in the preface to the first edition and again in the new preface to the revised edition of 1850. Sedgwick was born and spent most of her life in and around Stockbridge, Massachusetts, which is only about thirteen miles from Hancock, so she was personally familiar with the community and knew some of its members. As she explains in the 1824 preface, her portrayal of the Shakers in the novel 'was drawn from personal observation' (p. 7).[8] The narrator's extensive descriptions of the Shakers' doctrines and their separatist way of life make their village the most curiously compelling

---

8. Because her portrayal of the Shakers, particularly the villainy of the fictional Reuben Harrington, drew some criticism from readers, Sedgwick softened some of language related to the Shakers in the 1850 edition but also defended her original depiction. She insists in the 1850 preface that the basis for her depiction was accurate and based on her personal observation. See the Appendix in this edition for more on Sedgwick's 1850 revisions related to the Shakers.

setting in the novel. The Shaker society features a degree of gender equality that significantly exceeds the reality of gender relations elsewhere, and its peaceful routines and generous hospitality to strangers, its deeply felt spiritual devotion and efficient methods of farming and housekeeping make it seem, in Sedgwick's portrayal, like a utopia – but, as Sedgwick warns in the preface, she has found no Arcadia in America, and the Shaker village is no exception. The Shaker characters reveal themselves to be regular human beings, subject to deception and self-deception, and Reuben Harrington is the serpent in their garden. In this way, Sedgwick uses the Shakers in a general sense to expose old-fashioned notions of America as a land where Christian denominations can thrive in isolation from one another – keeping their believers safe from the corruption and false doctrines of others – as potentially dangerous folly. In one of the paradoxes of freedom that *Redwood* illustrates, freedom to practise one's faith does not imply freedom from religious conflict – it practically *ensures* exposure to religious conflict. In the case of the Allens, religious freedom allows a husband to choose the Shaker faith, taking their children with him, while his wife remains a more mainstream Christian. Their children are in a sense free to choose for themselves, and in another sense forced to take sides. Susan Allen, the one member of that family who remains a Shaker permanently, not only causes her mother heartache but redoubles that pain by persuading Emily to become a Shaker as well.

While Sedgwick's narrator implicitly critiques the foundational theological belief of the Shaker sect, which is that their founding 'Mother', Anne Lee, was in fact the second incarnation of Christ, the Shaker doctrine of celibacy comes under more direct scrutiny and criticism in the novel. As the example of Debby Lenox demonstrates, both Sedgwick herself and the narrator of *Redwood* respect the celibate life and the institution of marriage. Both paths have their pros and cons. For the Shakers, however, celibacy was a non-negotiable requirement. Any sexual activity, even for a married couple, was deemed sinful. Those who did not want to remain celibate not only had to leave the community physically but were spiritually cut off from it. According to their doctrine, anyone who was married or involved in any kind of romantic or sexual relationship was 'in the world', not called to the truth of Mother Anne's gospel.[9]

9. While this summary of the Shaker doctrine of celibacy is drawn from general reference sources, one of Sedgwick's sources on that and other Shaker practices might have been Hannah Adams's *An Alphabetical Compendium of the Various Sects which Have Appeared from the Beginning of the Christian Era to the Present Day* (1784), published in subsequent editions as *A View of Religions*. Adams (1755–1831) lived in Massachusetts and is considered by historians to have been the first American woman to support herself through her writing. Sedgwick recorded in her journal a visit to Adams in 1826 (Kelley, *Power* 115–16).

Though the life of the Lenox and Allen families at Eton seems idyllic in many ways, the novel reveals that, like America itself, they have a bitter history of deep division. Old Mrs. Allen, whom Ellen Bruce attends to and nurses throughout much of the novel, was a wife and the mother of seven children when her husband became a Shaker, temporarily breaking up their marriage. Her granddaughter, Emily Allen, is characterised in the novel as weak-willed and confused, mostly as a result of the overpowering influence that her charismatically assertive aunt Susan Allen, an elder in the Shaker community, has exerted over her since childhood. Since the deaths of Emily's parents, her Aunt Susan has prevailed in a struggle for Emily's soul that Sedgwick portrays as a contest of loyalty within a divided family as well as a spiritual conflict within Emily over whether or not to remain a Shaker. In Chapter 5, when Emily and Susan visit Eton for the funeral of Emily's twin brother, Eddy, Susan tries to hedge Emily from any influence that members of the Allen household might have on her. The narrator describes Emily's 'thraldom' to Susan as 'the natural submission of weakness, intellectual or physical, to power', whereas Susan accuses Ellen of using 'the voice of a charmer' to entice Emily away from the Shaker community and asks, '[H]ow should I be justified if I suffered this child to be seduced from her obedience to the gospel?' (p. 62). Pushed and pulled by the house divided that is her own family, Emily herself is divided. She has not fully developed a mind or a moral compass of her own, and that makes her vulnerable. While she desperately wants to marry James Lenox but is constantly threatened by Susan that damnation would be the result, the secretly depraved Shaker elder Reuben Harrington concocts a twisted criminal scheme to trick Emily and coerce her into marrying him. Ironically, both Susan and Reuben abuse the authority that they enjoy as leaders of a gender-equal community (albeit to different extents), and the result is that Emily is becomes vulnerable to patriarchal abuse of a high order.

Freedom, captivity and slavery

Aside from contributing to the novel's larger discourse about marriage, Emily's abduction by Reuben is also a captivity narrative and one of several rescue stories in the novel. As such, it invites comparative analysis with the captivity narratives in Sedgwick's other novels, particularly those in *Hope Leslie*. Emily's captivity brings the fragile nature of freedom home to the Allen and Lenox families, challenging their security as free American citizens. Even before her abduction and physical captivity in Sooduck's shack, old Mrs. Allen considers Emily's life as a Shaker as a form of captivity – one that Susan psychologically maintains over Emily with an authoritative personality. Thus Sedgwick introduces, early in her writing career, the idea that captivity is not always a matter of shackles and prisons, and she reinforces and expands the definitions of both freedom and captivity in her subsequent fiction in many ways that scholars have not yet fully unpacked.

Though the novel includes multiple stories of seduction, Reuben's scheme is by far the most scandalous: it is not accurately a seduction at all but rather a coercive attempt at sexual enslavement. By introducing the threat of enslavement for a white woman, and subtly suggesting that there are many forms of slavery, Sedgwick draws a connection between 'free' American citizens and black slaves. On the surface, it is a mere coincidence that Emily's abduction occurs shortly after the Redwoods and two of their slaves arrive at Eton, but on the symbolic level the two incidents are clearly related. Though the issue of slavery moves backstage for long stretches, the passages where it is visible add up to a considerable portion of the novel. The story of Henry's boyhood friendship with Edmund Westall, particularly the latter's life-changing experience with the remarkable slave Africk, is dramatically recounted in a way that dominates Chapter 3 and casts an ominous shadow over Henry's conscience and over the novel itself. In Chapter 7, Caroline Redwood reports in a letter to her grandmother that one of the Lenoxes' hired farm hands is a former slave and that free blacks in the north are taught to read and write. Though the Redwoods' slaves, Ralph and Lilly, are behind the scenes for most of the text, they move and communicate with the people in the area all along. Caroline's personal slave, Lilly, emerges from obscurity to play a critical role in the main plot by disobeying her mistress and thereby bringing about the revelation that Ellen is Henry's daughter from his first marriage. In a masterful stroke of irony on Sedgwick's part, Lilly's seemingly heroic revelation of Ellen's identity, as life-changing as it is for Ellen and Caroline, is really just an unplanned consequence of her real act of heroism, which is her bold and successful escape from slavery and into a marriage of her own choice – an act of changing her *own* identity.

Sedgwick's portrayal of Lilly's courageous bid for freedom was at least partly inspired by her admiration for Elizabeth Freeman, who was the slave of Colonel John Ashley of Sheffield, Massachusetts, where she was physically abused by Mrs. Ashley (Sedgwick, 'Slavery in New England'; Weierman 123). She fled that household and sought to achieve freedom through the courts. Represented by Sedgwick's father, Theodore Sedgwick, Freeman and another slave successfully challenged the legality of their enslavement in Berkshire County Court in 1781, thereby establishing precedent for the abolition of slavery throughout the state of Massachusetts (Kelley, *Power* 16–17). After winning her freedom, Elizabeth adopted the last name Freeman and accepted a position as a domestic servant in the Sedgwick household before Catharine Sedgwick was born. Familiarly known to them as 'Mumbet', Freeman became a fully-fledged housekeeper, caring for the younger children, helping to manage the family's domestic arrangements and eventually serving as caregiver for the mistress of the house, Pamela Dwight Sedgwick, who suffered more frequent and lengthier bouts of mental illness until her death in 1807 (Kelley, *Power* 13–14, 62–3). In her autobiography, Sedgwick writes of her love for Mumbet as if she were a second mother, describing her as 'that noble woman, the main pillar of our household' (Kelley 68) and as 'absolutely perfect in service, though never servile' (Kelley 69). Sedgwick also recorded the story of Mumbet in her sketch 'Slavery in New England', published in the magazine *Bentley's Miscellany* in 1853.

Aside from her own affection and admiration for Mumbet, Sedgwick perceived and recorded Mumbet's deep understanding of the value of freedom. In 1829, when Sedgwick saw that Mumbet was near death, she recorded in her journal that

> [h]er spirit spurned slavery. 'I would have been willing,' she has often said to me in speaking of the period when she was in hopeless servitude, 'I would have been willing if I could have had one minute of freedom – just to say "I am free" I would have been willing to die at the end of that minute.' (Kelley, *Power* 125)

Freeman's story obliquely enters the narrative of *Redwood* not only by way of Lilly's courageous escape but also in a reference to the generally anti-slavery sentiments of the citizens of Massachusetts, an attitude for which Freeman's lawsuit for freedom had set the precedent:

> Lebanon is a border town, and the boundary line of New-York once passed and Massachusetts entered, Lilly was assured of the protecting hospitalities of the people of her own colour; and it had even been hinted to her, that in case her retreat was discovered, the white inhabitants would be very backward to enforce her master's rights. (p. 303)

Lebanon is not only on the border of Massachusetts, but on the border of Berkshire County, the very county in which Theodore Sedgwick had filed suit on behalf of Freeman and in which both Freeman and Catharine Sedgwick still lived when *Redwood* was published. In this way, the fictional Lilly benefits directly from the anti-slavery atmosphere of 'protecting hospitality' that the historical Elizabeth Freeman's lawsuit had established.

The issue of slavery also enters into *Redwood* through its very title. As stated earlier, a family named Redwood was prominent in the region, particularly in Newport, Rhode Island, where they had endowed a library in 1747 that remains an important cultural institution to this day. Their founder was Abraham Redwood, who emigrated there from Antigua in the West Indies. His father (the first Abraham Redwood, who had emigrated from Scotland to Antigua) had made a fortune from his plantations, which used slave labour. The second Abraham Redwood, founder of the library, was one of numerous slave traders and slave owners who lived in Rhode Island and operated slave-trading ships out of ports along its coast (Deutsch 233). He was a Quaker before the Quakers became major activists for abolition. When his Quaker group asked its members to free their slaves in 1773, Redwood refused and was disowned by the group (Davis, Part 5). Another of Newport's numerous slave traders was William Ellery Sr. (1701–64), father of the William Ellery (1727–1820) who signed the Declaration of Independence (Barthelmas 56–7); he, in turn, was the grandfather of Elizabeth Dana Ellery, who married Sedgwick's brother Robert in 1821.[10]

Though the slave-trading history of New England after the American Revolution is largely lost on Americans today, who tend to imagine the northern states as having always been against slavery, that history was relatively recent for Sedgwick and the early readers of *Redwood*; the slave trade in Rhode Island continued until a federal law completely outlawed the trade in 1807. By naming the primary slave-owning family in the novel Redwood, then, Sedgwick casts the shadow of slavery and slave-owning over the whole novel, subtly reminding readers in the north of their complicity in profiting from the institution without directly admonishing them. The 'philanthropist' who had established the Redwood Library in Newport for the benefit of that city did so with profits from both slave labour in Antigua and slave-trading out of the Newport harbour. The West Indies and its history of slavery come into play, albeit obliquely, twice more at the end of the novel: Lilly escapes with the slave of a West Indian planter travelling in western New York and Caroline Redwood Fitzgerald accompanies her British husband and his military

---

10. In spite of his father's business, William Ellery, the signer of the Declaration, was opposed to slave-trading and used his position as Newport's customs collector to thwart the efforts of those who tried to skirt laws against foreign slave-trading (Davis, Part 6). He also supported political efforts to end slavery beginning in 1785 (Pyne).

unit to the West Indies. In recent years, scholars have pointed out and begun to analyse similarly indirect strategies of alluding to colonial slavery and its financing of European luxuries in novels such as Scott's *Rob Roy* (1817) and Jane Austen's *Mansfield Park* (1814)[11] – novels that Sedgwick is known to have read.

So, is *Redwood* an anti-slavery novel? My answer is yes in spirit, both morally and politically, but perhaps not in terms of form or genre. On the one hand, it would be hard not to hear the novel's message that slavery is wrong and is worth risking one's life to escape. The story of Africk clearly prefigures Stowe's later story of Uncle Tom, and Africk himself prophesies that America will suffer a bloody retribution for the sin of slavery. Henry and Caroline discuss what Henry calls 'the curse of slavery' in Chapter 9, and Henry prefigures Stowe's later characterisation of Augustine St. Clare. Lilly's escape from slavery brings about the resolution of the main plot. Several paratextual elements also reinforce an anti-slavery theme. Paley, the English philosopher of the epigraph to the novel, was also an active abolitionist. A quotation from 'The Negro's Complaint' by William Cowper, one of the most influential English abolitionist poets, sets the tone for Chapter 3, in which Africk's story is told. All these features shout 'anti-slavery'. On the other hand, the novel might not belong in the genre of *abolitionist* fiction because it contains no calls for abolition and does not predominantly focus on any individual slaves or on the institution of slavery.

Furthermore, the anti-slavery message of *Redwood* has a lot of competition from the other messages in the novel, one of which is anxiety over the strength of the American union – the issue that kept Sedgwick herself from officially joining the abolitionist movement as the nation moved toward the Civil War. The first American readers of *Redwood* had lived through the contentious sectional disputes that surrounded the War of 1812 (including the secession-minded Hartford Convention, which had been chaired by the uncle of Sedgwick's close friend, Eliza Cabot) and, even more recently, those that had resulted in the Missouri Compromise in 1820.

---

11. For ways in which Walter Scott's oblique references to slavery and the West Indies might be interpreted, see Carla Sassi's 'Sir Walter Scott and the Caribbean: Unravelling the Silences' (*Yearbook of English Studies*, vol. 47, Walter Scott: New Interpretations, 2017, pp. 224–40). For Jane Austen's similar references and inferences, see Soon Wiley's 'Silence, Slavery, and Jane Austen: Empire in *Mansfield Park*' (*Journal of Commonwealth and Postcolonial Studies*, vol. 2, no. 1 (Spring 2014), pp. 59–74) and Moreland Perkins's '*Mansfield Park* and Austen's Reading on Slavery and Imperial Warfare' (*Persuasions: The Jane Austen Journal Online*, vol. 26, no. 1 (Winter 2005)).

Faith and reconciliation

After using a statement about the folly of religious scepticism as the epigraph for the novel, Sedgwick insists in the preface that she has 'not composed a tale professedly or chiefly of a religious nature' because she does not think that 'narrative sermons are of a nature to be particularly interesting' (p. 7). She then explains, however, how a novel can be infused with 'religious principle' without becoming a narrative sermon:

> [T]he religious principle, with all its attendant doubts, hopes, fears, enthusiasm, and hypocrisy, is a mighty agent in moulding human character, and it may therefore, with propriety, find a place in a work whose object it is to delineate that character. (p. 7)

She goes on to claim that faith is 'more permanent and more universal' than romantic love, and therefore faith has just as natural a place as courtship in a 'work whose object it is to delineate [human] character' (p. 7). Nevertheless, many of the characters and sometimes the narrator profess their own doctrines loud and clear. These range from the atheism of Henry Redwood to the severe but zealous faith of the Shakers; from the no-nonsense, Bible-quoting faith of Aunt Debby to the highly emotional, self-abnegating faith of Mary Erwine Redwood. The narrator explains that the 'checks and balances' of Mrs. Allen's Congregationalism (Calvinism) and Mrs. Harrison's Episcopalianism formed Ellen's faith (pp. 91–2), which Grace characterises as 'methodistic' (p. 267). The diversity of religious convictions and opinions, combined with the natural and believable ways that they proceed from the characters' personalities and life experiences, keeps the novel from becoming a narrative sermon.

Religious beliefs and concerns proceed from and are inextricably bound up within the personal history and emotional drama of each character's life, so that no character devolves into a phony mouthpiece for a religious opinion. Even Susan Allen, the charismatic and authoritative Shaker elder who seems so harsh in her manipulation of Emily, reveals a poignantly sympathetic side of herself when she tells Emily just how much she sacrificed to follow the precepts of her faith. As a young woman, she was deeply in love with a man who was even more in love with her, but she refused his proposal in order to maintain her celibacy and, in her view, her spiritual integrity and salvation. From that point in the novel, it is much harder to condemn Susan for wanting to keep her beloved niece from travelling what she sincerely believes to be the road to hell. The larger narrative distances itself from Susan's rejection of marriage as a respectable state of life for Christian believers, even to some extent mocking it through the scorn of other characters, but it respects the sincerity of her faith and lets her choices speak for themselves.

Though Sedgwick makes it clear in the preface that her object in writing the novel is to illustrate human character and not to write a sermon, she also states that religious beliefs and spirituality are the most profound shapers and components of human character. This fundamentally religious view informs not only the characterisations in the novel but also its structure. While Ellen Bruce is clearly the heroine and the main thrust of the narrative revolves around her story, she does not even enter the novel until Chapter 12, after the first four chapters focus almost exclusively on Henry Redwood and development of his character up to the time of his arrival at Eton. He is described as naturally sensitive and intellectually gifted – a person who generally *feels* rightly but has no guiding moral principles to form his feelings into actions. Having become an atheist while associating with libertines and reading Enlightenment sceptics such as Voltaire and Hume, Henry has not only no moral compass, but also no fear of divine punishment or eternal damnation; he alternates between periods of distraction through travel and aesthetic pleasures, and periods of depression and despondency.

The ongoing story of Henry's spiritual conversion through the steady evangelism and examples of Ellen, Debby and Charles Westall does not always occupy centre-stage, but it frames the beginning and end of the novel and unfolds consistently throughout the middle.[12] It is clear that in the quiet isolation of his convalescence he is preoccupied with guilt, regrets, and the moral and spiritual questions that accompany such emotions. Sometimes his spiritual agitation is related through narration or dialogue, but other times it is symbolised by the Bible that Ellen gives him in Chapter 12. Henry values the gift not only because of his affection for Ellen and gratitude for the care and companionship she has given him during his convalescence, but also for its content, as he reads it at the Allens' house in Eton and later at Lebanon Springs, where he is said to have the Bible 'almost always in his hands' (p. 276).

Sedgwick's depiction of Henry's 'deathbed' conversion (the characters believe that he is near death) no doubt was largely inspired by her own father's profession of faith within two weeks of his own death on 24 January 1813. In a letter to her older sister Frances Watson on 5 January, Catharine reports that, on the previous day, their father had confided to her that he 'had for many years been

---

12. My view of the centrality of Henry Redwood's spiritual conversion to the novel disputes that of Damon-Bach, who argues that his 'redemption and religious conversion are almost a footnote to the novel, tacked on in one of the book's final chapters' ('To Act and Transact' 57).

extremely desirous of making a public profession of religion' but had 'been deterred from very unworthy motives' that consisted of offending his beloved friends and relatives in the Congregational Church – which he did not want to join because he disagreed with some of its Calvinistic views. Catharine then offered to invite the Rev. William Ellery Channing, the leading Unitarian clergyman in the region at that time, for a visit; her father agreed, and the meeting took place on 9 January. Six days later, Catharine wrote to her other sister, Elizabeth Pomeroy, to report that their father had confessed his faith and received communion from Channing. This letter strikes many common chords with her depiction of Henry's deathbed conversion in *Redwood* regarding the connection between bodily sickness, knowledge of impending death and the experience of participating in her father's spiritual life in the weeks before his death:

> The performance of this duty seemed to remove the bar of reserve that opposed the flowing out of papa's heart, and he now shows that he feels his tenure of life to be very slight, and that his affections dwell on heavenly things; the Word of God, that precious gift to men, whose worth I believe is most felt in the sick-chamber, he listens to with unremitting interest. Oh, may I never be ungrateful for the blessed privilege of being allowed to watch the varying looks, and hear the tender accents of our beloved parent. Our excellent brothers are devoted, and I sometimes feel, when we are all assembled around our father, as if our sainted mother watched and approved us. (Sedgwick, *Life and Letters* 93–5)

Henry's similarly moving conversion in the final chapter occurs in the midst of the resolution of the other threads of the plot and has the effect of unifying those various threads into one interconnected story of love and forgiveness. There are two emotional climaxes in the final two chapters: the scene at the end of Chapter 26, when the newly reconciled Caroline and Ellen visit Henry's sickbed and 'peace, gratitude, and devotion' speak through his eyes (p. 304); and in the final chapter, when both daughters kneel by Henry's bed and he gives the emblematic Bible to Caroline in a gesture that foreshadows her coming conversion (which is reported in the letter from Debby that ends the novel). Both climactic scenes revolve around Henry's conversion and illustrate the core Christian principle of forgiveness.

Conclusion

Redwood may not be a narrative sermon but it is saturated with religious ideas, opinions and images that organise its various topics – politics, race, socioeconomic class, family dynamics, individual identity – in terms of forgiveness and reconciliation. The novel figures these ideals, as well as the baser resentments and prejudices that precede them, as sincere *feelings* rather than as dogmas or policy positions. As Henry Redwood's character arc amply illustrates, beautiful ideals, an elite education and even sound political insights are not necessarily sufficient to motivate righteous actions; they must be honed through authentic communication and emboldened by sympathetic relationships before meaningful transformation can occur. The novel is intentionally thought-provoking and instructive, yet it is clearly also intended to move readers with strong currents of pathos and to delight them with witty dialogue and vivid characters. As centuries of theorists have understood, literature cannot truly instruct or inspire its audience without engaging their imaginations. *Redwood* offers a wide field for future critical interpretation, but my hope as an editor is that new readers will agree with the first statement that Sedgwick's literary role model, Maria Edgeworth, wrote in response to it: 'Redwood has entertained us very much' (MacDonald 73).

Works cited

Apap, Christopher. *The Genius of Place: The Geographic Imagination in the Early Republic*. University of New Hampshire Press, 2016.
Barthelmas, Della Gray. *The Signers of the Declaration of Independence: A Biographical and Genealogical Reference*. McFarland, 2003.
Baym, Nina. *Woman's Fiction: A Guide to Novels by and about Women in America, 1820–1870*, 2nd edn. University of Illinois Press, 1993.
Bryant, William Cullen. 'Review of *Redwood; A Tale*, by Catharine Sedgwick'. *North American Review*, vol. 20, no. 47 (1825), pp. 245–69.
Butler, Marilyn. Introduction. *Castle Rackrent and Ennui*, by Maria Edgeworth, edited by Butler. Oxford University Press, 1994, pp. 1–53.
[Child, Lydia Maria Francis]. [Signed] F. 'Miss Sedgwick's Novels'. *Ladies Magazine* (May 1829), pp. 234–8.
Damon-Bach, Lucinda. 'Chronological Bibliography of the Works of Catharine Maria Sedgwick'. Damon-Bach and Clements, pp. 295–313.
— '"To Act and Transact": *Redwood*'s Revolutionary Heroines'. Damon-Bach and Clements, pp. 56–73.
Damon-Bach, Lucinda, and Victoria Clements, editors. *Catharine Maria Sedgwick: Critical Perspectives*. Northeastern University Press, 2003.
Davidson, Cathy N. *Revolution and the Word: The Rise of the Novel in America*. Oxford University Press, 1986.
Davis, Paul. 'Unrighteous Traffick: Rhode Island and the Slave Trade. In Six Parts'. *Providence Journal* (12–17 March 2006). LexisNexis, <www.lexisnexis.com> (last accessed 18 September 2020).

'Deborah Sampson (1760–1827)', edited by Debra Michals. National Women's History Museum, 2015, <womenshistory.org> (last accessed 18 September 2020).

Deutsch, Sarah. 'The Elusive Guineamen: Newport Slavers, 1735–1774'. *New England Quarterly*, vol. 55, no. 2 (June 1982), pp. 229–53. JSTOR, <www.jstor.org/stable/365360> (last accessed 18 September 2020).

Duncan, A. A. M. 'Brus [Bruce], Robert de, Lord of Annandale', *Oxford Dictionary of National Biography*. Oxford University Press, 2000. doi.org/10.1093/ref:odnb/3748.

Edgeworth, Maria. 'Letter to Rachel Mordecai Lazarus, 2 May 1825'. *The Education of the Heart: The Correspondence of Rachel Mordecai Lazarus and Maria Edgeworth*. University of North Carolina Press, 1977.

Elmore, Jenifer B. *Sacred Unions: Catharine Sedgwick, Maria Edgeworth, and Domestic–Political Fiction*. Dissertation. Florida State University, 2002.

—. 'Sedgwick and Edgeworth: A Transatlantic Tale of Emulation, Flattery, and Rivalry'. *Symbiosis*, vol. 22, no. 1 (Spring 2018), pp. 73–92.

'elne/ellen, n.'. *OED Online*, Oxford University Press, March 2020, <www.oed.com> (last accessed 18 September 2020).

Foster, Edward H. *Catharine Maria Sedgwick*. Twayne, 1974.

Gussman, Deborah. Introduction. *Married or Single?*, by Catharine Sedgwick, edited by Gussman. University of Nebraska Press, 2015, pp. ix–xli.

Harris, Susan K. *Nineteenth-Century American Women's Novels: Interpretive Strategies*. Cambridge University Press, 1990.

Homestead, Melissa J. 'Behind the Veil? Catharine Sedgwick and Anonymous Publication'. Damon-Bach and Clements, pp. 19–35.

—. Introduction. *Clarence; or, a Tale of Our Own Times*, by Catharine Sedgwick, edited by Homestead and Foster. Broadview, 2012, pp. 9–40.

Kane, Bob, and Tom Andrae. *Batman and Me*. Eclipse Books, 1989.

Kaplan, Amy. 'Manifest Domesticity'. *No More Separate Spheres! A Next Wave American Studies Reader*, edited by Cathy N. Davidson. Duke University Press, 2002, pp. 183–207.

Karcher, Carolyn. 'Catharine Maria Sedgwick in Literary History'. Damon-Bach and Clements, pp. 5–15.

Kelley, Mary. *The Power of Her Sympathy: The Autobiography and Journal of Catharine Maria Sedgwick*, by Catharine Maria Sedgwick. Massachusetts Historical Society, 1993.

—. *Private Woman, Public Stage: Literary Domesticity in Nineteenth-Century America*. Oxford University Press, 1984.

MacDonald, Edgar E. (ed.). *The Education of the Heart: The Correspondence of Rachel Mordecai Lazarus and Maria Edgeworth*. University of North Carolina Press, 1977.

Mann, Herman. *The Female Review; or, Memoirs of an American Young Lady*. Nathaniel and Benjamin Heaton, 1797. Evans Early American Imprint Collection Text Creation Partnership, 2011, <quod.lib.umich.edu> (last accessed 18 September 2020).

Mellor, Anne K. *Mothers of the Nation: Women's Political Writing in England, 1780–1830*. University of Indiana Press, 2000.

Paley, William. *Principles of Moral and Political Philosophy* (1785). Cambridge University Press, 2013 (reprint of first edition).

Pyne, Frederick. 'William Ellery'. The Society of the Descendants of the Signers of the Declaration of Independence, 2011, <dsdi1776.com/signers-by-state/william-ellery/> (last accessed 18 September 2020).

'redwood, n.'. *OED Online*, Oxford University Press, March 2020, <www.oed.com> (last accessed 18 September 2020).

Revere, Paul. 'Letter from Paul Revere to William Eustis, 20 February 1804'. Miscellaneous Bound Manuscripts. Massachusetts Historical Society, <www.masshist.org/database/326> (last accessed 18 September 2020).

'Review of *Redwood, A Tale*'. *The Atlantic Magazine* (July 1824), pp. 234–9.

'Review of *Redwood, A Tale*'. *Port Folio*, vol. 18 (July–Dec. 1824), pp. 66–9.

Scott, Walter. *Rob Roy*. Dent, 1906.

Sedgwick, Catharine Maria. *Clarence: A Tale of Our Own Times*, edited by Melissa J. Homestead and Ellen A. Foster. Broadview, 2012.

—. *Hope Leslie; or, Early Times in the Massachusetts*, edited by Mary Kelley. Rutgers University Press, 1987.

—. *The Life and Letters of Catharine M. Sedgwick*, edited by Mary Dewey. Harper & Brothers, 1871.

—. *The Linwoods; or, 'Sixty Years Since' in America*, edited by Maria Karafilis. University Press of New England, 2002.

—. *A New-England Tale; Or, Sketches of New-England Character and Manners*, edited by Victoria Clements. Oxford University Press, 1995.

—. *Married or Single?*, edited by Deborah Gussman. University of Nebraska Press, 2015.

—. *The Power of Her Sympathy: The Autobiography and Journal of Catharine Maria Sedgwick*, edited by Mary Kelley. Massachusetts Historical Society, 1993.

—. *Redwood; A Tale*. Putnam, 1824.

—. 'Slavery in New England'. *Bentley's Miscellany*, vol. 34 (1853), pp. 417–24.

Weierman, Karen Woods. '"A Slave Story I Began and Abandoned": Sedgwick's Anti-Slavery Manuscript'. Damon-Bach and Clements, pp. 122–38.

Young, Alfred F. *Masquerade: The Life and Times of Deborah Sampson, Continental Soldier*. Vintage, 2004.

Selected Bibliography for Further Study

Daly, Robert. 'Reading Sedgwick Now: Empathy and Ethics in Early America'. *Literature in the Early American Republic: Annual Studies on Cooper and His Contemporaries*, 2 (2010), pp. 131–52.

Gould, Philip. 'Catharine Sedgwick's Cosmopolitan Nation'. *New England Quarterly: A Historical Review of New England Life and Letters*, vol. 78, no. 2 (2005), pp. 232–58.

Harris, Susan K. 'The Limits of Authority: Catharine Maria Sedgwick and the Politics of Resistance'. *Catharine Maria Sedgwick: Critical Perspectives*, edited by Lucinda Damon-Bach and Victoria Clements. Northeastern University Press, 2003, pp. 272–85.

Homestead, Melissa J. *American Women Authors and Literary Property, 1822–1869*. Cambridge University Press, 2005.

—. 'The Shape of Catharine Sedgwick's Career'. *The Cambridge History of American Women's Literature*, edited by Dale M. Bauer. Cambridge University Press, 2012, pp. 185–203.

Lubovich, Maglina. '"Married or Single?": Catharine Maria Sedgwick on Old Maids, Wives, and Marriage'. *Legacy: A Journal of American Women Writers*, vol. 25, no. 1 (2008), pp. 23–40.

Machor, James L. 'Catharine Maria Sedgwick: Domestic and National Narratives'. *The Oxford History of the Novel in English, Vol. 5: The American Novel to 1870*, edited by J. Gerald Kenney and Leland S. Person. Oxford University Press, 2014, pp. 262–77.

Nelson, Dana. 'Rediscovery'. Damon-Bach and Clements, pp. 286–93.

Schweitzer, Ivy. *Perfecting Friendship: Politics and Affiliation in Early American Literature*. University of North Carolina Press, 2006.

Sweet, Nancy. 'Dissent and the Daughter in *A New-England Tale* and *Hobomok*'. *Legacy: A Journal of American Women Writers*, vol. 22, no. 2 (2005), pp. 107–25.

Van Dette, Emily. '"It Should Be a Family Thing": Family, Nation, and Republicanism in Catharine Maria Sedgwick's *A New-England Tale* and *The Linwoods*'. *American Transcendental Quarterly*, vol. 19, no. 1 (2005), pp. 51–74.

Wood, Michelle Gaffner. 'Inhabiting the Liminal: The Architecture of Single Life in Catharine Maria Sedgwick's Fiction'. *Liminality, Hybridity, and American Women's Literature: Thresholds in Women's Writing*, edited by Kristin J. Jacobson, Rickie-Ann Legleitner, Kristin Allukian, Leslie Allison, and Rita Bode. Palgrave Macmillan, 2018, pp. 125–44.

A Note on the Text

Two major authorised American editions of *Redwood* were published within Sedgwick's lifetime: the first in 1824 by Bliss & White (New York), and the 1850 version by Putnam (New York). The first edition is in two volumes with continuous chapter numbers but non-continuous pagination; the 1850 edition is in one volume with continuous chapter and page numbers. The 1850 edition included both Sedgwick's original preface from 1824 and a new preface. The current edition incorporates the text of the 1824 edition, while adopting most of the modernised and standardised spellings and punctuation that Sedgwick authorised for the 1850 edition.

By using the text of the first American edition, the current version preserves the original tone of the novel as written by the much younger and less experienced Sedgwick. However, the modernisations of spelling and punctuation will be even more helpful for today's readers than they could have been for readers in 1850; this edition therefore sacrifices some historical and linguistic exactitude for the sake of a more fluent reading experience. The new preface that Sedgwick added to the 1850 edition is included in an appendix at the end of this edition, along with a discussion of the more significant textual alterations made in the 1850 version.

To determine the present text, Rachel Sakrisson and I undertook a series of side-by-side comparative readings of the 1824 and 1850 US editions. We then used the 1850 text, with its already revised spelling and mechanics, as the base text and revised it to match all of the 1824 wording and some of the 1824 spellings.

This edition preserves the spellings of words from the 1824 edition that have maintained those spellings as standard British usage; for example, words such as *honour, practise, skilful* and *defence* retain their British spellings in this edition, even though for the 1850 edition they were changed to what had become the American standard spellings in the meantime. By retaining the original 'British' spellings, this edition accurately reflects the looser boundaries between what was British and what was American in 1824.

Other spellings, capitalisations and punctuation that were changed in 1850 are maintained here, including the now-obsolete use of quotation marks with indirect speech. This edition also maintains the use of italics from the 1850 edition, even when it seems internally inconsistent (as is the case with italicising foreign words and phrases).

Notes indicated by an asterisk or asterisks (*) are the author's original notes, those in numerals are the editor's.

All of the *errata* listed in the back of the 1824 edition are corrected here, as are other obvious printing errors from 1824 that were not listed as such at the time. The most egregious typesetting error in 1824 was the moving of one line of text to an entirely different page. One chapter was also incorrectly numbered. Others are more minor, such as the omission of single letters, resulting in blank spaces in the middle of words. All of these are corrected in the present edition, as are Sedgwick's own errors that she corrected in the later edition, including the inconsistent spelling of Eton (sometimes spelled Eaton in 1824) and the last name of Caroline's grandmother, which is inexplicably Olney in 1824 but changed to Manning in 1850.

Jenifer B. Elmore

Chronology of Sedgwick's Life and Works

1789	Catharine is born in Stockbridge, Massachusetts, on 28 December. Parents: Theodore and Pamela Dwight Sedgwick. Siblings who lived past infancy: Elizabeth (Eliza), b. 1775; Frances, b. 1778; Theodore, b. 1780; Henry Dwight (Harry), b. 1785; Robert, b. 1787; and Charles, b. 1791.
1802	She spends the winter in New York City for the first time, living with her sister Frances Watson and family.
1803	She moves to Albany, living for a time with sister Eliza Pomeroy and family.
1807	Her mother dies after years of suffering with mental illness.
1808	Her father marries Penelope Russell.
1813	Her father dies two weeks after professing Christian faith to Rev. William Ellery Channing.
1821	She resigns her membership in a Presbyterian church in New York City and joins All Souls Unitarian Church. She travels to Niagara Falls and Montreal.
1822	Her first novel, *A New-England Tale*, is published.
1824	Her second novel, *Redwood*, is published.
1827	Her third novel, *Hope Leslie; or, Early Times in the Massachusetts*, is published. Her sister Eliza dies.
1829	Elizabeth Freeman (also known as 'Mumbet'), the African-American servant to the Sedgwick family whom CMS considered a foster mother, dies.
1830	Her fourth novel, *Clarence; or, A Tale of Our Own Times*, is published.
1831	She meets President Andrew Jackson (January/February) during a trip to Washington, D.C. Her brother Harry dies after many years of physical and mental illness.
1834	She has a dispute with Lydia Child, as she was unwilling to write a story supporting abolition of slavery for the gift book that Child was editing.
1835	Her fifth novel, *The Linwoods; or, 'Sixty Years Since' in America*, appears.

	Her first didactic novella, *Home*, is published in Rev. Henry Ware's series called *Scenes and Characters Illustrating Christian Truth*. *Tales and Sketches*, a volume of her short fiction that was previously published in gift annuals, is published.
1836	Her second didactic novella is published, *The Poor Rich Man and the Rich Poor Man*, as well as her first longer work of biography, *Memoir of Lucretia Maria Davidson*.
1837	Her third didactic novella, *Live and Let Live; or, Domestic Service Illustrated*, is published, as is *Love Token for Children*, a collection of the children's tales she had previously published in periodicals and gift annuals.
1838	She becomes the primary caregiver to her brother Robert following his stroke.
1839	Her fourth didactic novella, *Means and Ends; or, Self-Training*, is published. She travels extensively in Europe (until 1840) with brother Robert and family in an attempt to recover his health.
1840	A second collection of her children's stories, *Stories for Young Persons*, is published.
1841	Her second full-length work of non-fiction is published, *Letters From Abroad to Kindred at Home*, drawn from her journals of her European travels in 1839–40. Her brother Robert dies (September).
1844	*Tales and Sketches, Second Series*, her second volume of short fiction from periodicals, is published.
1846	*The Morals of Manners; or, Hints for Our Young People*, a didactic book for children, is published.
1848	Two children's books, *The Boy of Mount Rhigi* and *Facts and Fancies for School-Day Reading*, are published. Building upon her involvement in prison reform, she becomes director of the New York Women's Prison Association.
1849	George Palmer Putnam announces the planned publication of the collected edition of 'Miss Sedgwick's Works'.
1850	Revised edition of *Redwood; A Tale* is published, as is a third collection of shorter works, *Tales of City Life*.
1853	CMS begins to write an autobiography, intended for her great-niece Alice Minot, a project that continues in 1854 and in 1860.
1854	She travels to what is now called the Midwest, visiting major cities and stretches of the Mississippi River.
1857	Her final novel, *Married or Single?*, is published.
1858	Her second work of biography, *Memoir of Joseph Curtis: A Model Man*, is published.

1867   She dies in West Roxbury, MA, on 31 July, and is buried in Stockbridge, MA.

1871   Mary E. Dewey publishes a biography of Sedgwick with a selection of her correspondence, *Life and Letters of Catharine M. Sedgwick*.

List of Characters

Henry Redwood: Virginia planter on a tour of Canada and New England.

Caroline Redwood: Henry's eighteen-year-old daughter, who has been raised by her grandmother in South Carolina.

Lilly: young slave woman who is Caroline's personal servant.

Ralph: slave owned by Henry Redwood.

Edmund Westall: friend of Henry Redwood from a neighbouring plantation; father of Charles.

Charles Westall: son of Edmund and protégé of Henry Redwood; he is studying law in Boston.

Africk: slave owned by the father of Edmund Westall.

Alsop: Henry's friend from his university years.

Mary Erwine: first wife of Henry Redwood in a clandestine marriage.

Mr. and Mrs. Emlyn: neighbours of the Westalls who hire Mary Erwine to teach their children.

Maria Manning: wife of Henry Redwood who died shortly after giving birth to Caroline.

Mrs. Manning: Caroline's maternal grandmother.

Captain Fitzgerald: British military officer stationed in Canada; he first meets the Redwoods in Canada.

Dr. Bristol: Physician in the village of Eton, Vermont, who treats Henry Redwood and the blind girl Peggy.

Deborah Lenox (Aunt Debby): sister of Mr. Lenox of the farm at Eton.

Mr. and Mrs. Lenox: owners of the farm at Eton where Henry Redwood recuperates; they have eight children, including **George, James and Lucy**; Mrs. Lenox is the sister of Mrs. Allen and the daughter of the older Mrs. Allen.

Ellen Bruce: young woman of eighteen or nineteen; as an orphan she was raised by two different foster mothers (Mrs. Allen and Mrs. Harrison).

Mrs. Allen: foster mother of Ellen Bruce and wife of Justyn Allen; mother of twins Emily and Eddy.

Emily Allen: a junior member of the Shaker Society and niece of Susan Allen; she is also the twin sister of the deceased Eddy Allen and the granddaughter of the older Mrs. Allen.

Justyn Allen: owner of a farm adjoining the Harrison's estate at Lansdown, MA; foster father of Ellen Bruce and father of Emily and Eddy.

Mrs. Allen (older): mother of Justyn Allen, Susan Allen and Mrs. Lenox; grandmother of Emily and Eddy.

Susan Allen: an elder of the Shaker community; sister of Justyn Allen and daughter of the older Mrs. Allen; sister-in-law of the Mrs. Allen who raised Ellen; aunt of Emily and Eddy.

Annie: former sweetheart of the deceased Eddy Allen; she is said to have broken his heart.

Reuben Harrington: an elder of the Shaker community.

Sooduck: Native American man who lives alone in the woods not far from the Shaker village.

Peggy: blind child who lives with her aunt near the Allens' farm at Eton.

Betty: Peggy's aunt.

Mrs. Martha Harrison: neighbour of the Allens and second foster mother to Ellen.

Mr. Robert Harrison: husband of Martha Harrison; owner of the estate at Lansdown.

Grace Campbell: young woman from Philadelphia whose uncle Richard Campbell is her legal guardian.

Fenton Campbell: cousin of Grace; he lives in England.

Mrs. Armstead: mother of William Armstead and aunt of Grace and Fenton.

William Armstead: cousin of Grace and Fenton Campbell.

Mr. Howard: friend of William Armstead.

Mrs. Norton: friend of Mrs. Armstead.

REDWOOD:

A TALE.

IN TWO VOLUMES.

VOL. I.

"Whilst the infidel mocks at the superstitions of the vulgar, insults over their credulous fears, their childish errors, their fantastic rites, it does not occur to him to observe, that the most preposterous device by which the weakest devotee ever believed he was securing the happiness of a future life, is more rational than unconcern about it. Upon this subject nothing is so absurd as indifference;—no folly so contemptible as thoughtlessness or levity."—Paley.[1]

---

1. *'Whilst the infidel mocks . . .'*: William Paley (1743–1805) in *The Principles of Moral and Political Philosophy* (1785).

TO

WILLIAM CULLEN BRYANT, Esq.

in token of friendship and admiration of his genius, these volumes are dedicated by

THE AUTHOR.

PREFACE.

THE multiplication of books is the cause of much complaint, and it must be conceded that the inconvenience is not trivial to those who are, or suppose themselves, under an obligation to pay some attention to the current literature of the day. When, however, the matter is duly considered, it will be found that this inconvenience, like most others, is not an unmixed evil, but productive of many advantages. It is not a conclusive objection to a new book, that there are better ones already in existence that remain unread. The elements of human nature and human society remain the same, but their forms and combinations are changing at every moment, and nothing can be more different than the appearances and effects produced by the same original principles of human nature as exhibited in different countries, or at different periods of time in the same country.

"Tempora mutantur, et nos mutamur in illia."[1]

As times and manners change, it must be evident that attempts to describe them must be as constantly renewed and diversified. We are aware that apprehensions are entertained by many intelligent persons, that the stores of wisdom and knowledge which have been collected by our predecessors, will be neglected and forgotten through an insatiable appetite for novelty: but we think that such apprehensions are often carried too far. The acquisitions of knowledge, wisdom, or even wit, once made, are rarely lost, except by some of those great changes which, for the time, subvert the foundations of society. The original fountains may be remote and unknown; but the river laves our fields, and passes by to diffuse its treasures among other regions; and even if its waters are lost to our sight by evaporation, they descend again in showers to embellish and fructify the earth in a thousand forms. Just so it is with intellectual treasures. Very few persons now read the works of Aristotle, and not many those of Bacon: but the wisdom

---

1. *'Tempora mutantur, et nos mutamur in illis'*: Latin, translated as 'times change and we change with them.'

which they first taught, or perhaps collected, is now spread far and wide by numerous modes of diffusion, and is incorporated into the minds of thousands who know nothing of its origin: and we may even remark that one cannot turn over the pages of a modern jest-book, or the files of a village newspaper, without meeting, embodied in narratives of the incidents of the day, the essence of the same jokes which nearly two thousand years ago Cicero related for the amusement of his patrician friends.

We have suggested these reflections with the double view of reconciling the lovers of former excellence to the invariable course of things, which ever did, and ever must, offer the present to our view in great magnitude and strong relief, and gather over the past the constantly increasing clouds of obscurity. There have been in ages past, and we trust there will be in future, individuals whose productions, in spite of all changes of time and language, will command attention and respect; but the course of things, nevertheless, has been, that as society has advanced, each generation has drawn more and more upon its own immediate resources for intellectual amusement and instruction.

If any doubt the propriety of these remarks as being applicable to the general course of knowledge and literature, they may yet be disposed to admit their justice so far as they relate to fictitious narrative.—It is the peculiar province of that department to denote the passing character and manners of the present time and place. There is but one individual[2] (whom it would be affectation to call unknown) who has had eminent success in the delineations of former periods, or what is called historical romance. "The folly of the moment" must be caught "as it flies."[3]

The attractions of novelty are too numerous and too evident to require argument or detail for their elucidation. Everyone knows that new books, and especially new novels, will be sought for and read, while those of more ancient date are disregarded. Many read them only because they are new, and to such they do not come in competition with any other description of reading, but are merely suffered to seize on a vacant hour which might otherwise be less profitably employed.

We have dwelt at so much length and with so much complacency on the advantages and merits of novelty, because we are sure that our production will have that recommendation, and we are not sure that it will have any other—it certainly will be the last new novel.

---

2. *one individual*: This seemingly vague phrase specifically refers to Sir Walter Scott (1771–1832), with the assumption that all readers, in 1824 or in 1850, would readily understand the reference. This expectation illustrates the enormous literary stature of Scott throughout the early nineteenth century.
3. *'The folly of the moment' must be caught 'as it flies'*: A variation on 'shoot folly as it flies' from *An Essay on Man* (1733–4) by Alexander Pope (1688–1744).

There are, however, some other considerations which have contributed to overcome our reluctance to appear before the public. The love and habit of reading have become so extensive in this country, and the tastes and wants of readers so various, that we cannot but indulge the hope that there will be found some who will derive amusement, if not instruction, from our humble efforts. We will, at least, venture to claim the negative merit often ascribed to simples—that if they can do no good, they will do no harm.

A few words will be sufficient to indicate the design of these volumes. We have not composed a tale professedly or chiefly of a religious nature, as, if left to the bias of our own inclination, we might possibly have done. We do not think that such attempts have heretofore been eminently successful; or that narrative sermons are of a nature to be particularly interesting. Still we are conscious that the religious principle, with all its attendant doubts, hopes, fears, enthusiasm, and hypocrisy, is a mighty agent in moulding human character, and it may therefore, with propriety, find a place in a work whose object it is to delineate that character. It is a principle of action more permanent and more universal than the affection which unites the sexes; and in the fictitious representations of human life, there can be no reason why the greater should be excluded by the less. On these impressions we have acted. We do not anticipate splendid success, but we are sure that we cannot be deprived of the consolation of having intended well. It will be an ample reward if we can believe that we have been able by our trivial labours to co-operate in any degree with the efforts of the good and great, "to give ardour to virtue, and confidence to truth."[4] Our anxiety is only for the great truths of our common religion,[5] not for any of its subdivisions.

The sketch which has been introduced of the society of Shakers[6] was drawn from personal observation. It would have been withheld if we could have supposed that it would wound the feelings even of a single individual of that obscure sect. But against this there is a sufficient security. The representation is deemed just, and it is hoped would not be thought offensive; and, besides, there is little danger that this light volume will ever find its way into a sanctuary from whose pale the frivolous amusements and profane literature of the "world's people"[7] are carefully excluded.

---

4. *'to give ardour to virtue, and confidence to truth'*: Samuel Johnson (1709–84) in *The Rambler* (no. 208 on Saturday, 14 March 1752). The full quotation reads, 'I shall never envy honours which wit and learning obtain in any other cause, if I can be numbered among the writers who have given ardour to virtue, and confidence to truth.'
5. *our common religion:* Sedgwick here emphasises that her concern is not with the Shakers' oddities, but with the shared tenets of Christianity that transcend denominational divisions.
6. *Shakers*: Officially known as the United Society of Believers in Christ's Second Appearing, this religious sect was founded in England in 1747 and began organising communities in the US in the 1780s. See the discussion of Shakers in the introduction to this edition.
7. *'world's people'*: The Shakers' way of referring to non-Shakers.

Whenever the course of our narrative has thrown opportunities in our way, we have attempted some sketches of the character and manners of the people of this country. We have done this with all faithfulness of purpose. If we have failed, we trust the failure will be ascribed, as it ought, to defect of capacity. We live in a country which is, beyond parallel, free, happy, and abundant. As such we would describe it—but as no Arcadia,[8] for we have found none. We have indeed little sympathy with that narrow-minded patriotism which claims honours that are not yet merited. Our republicanism is founded on a broad and general principle, which is opposed to all coronations. We cannot, therefore, unite in hailing our country the "Queen of the earth"[9] and our religion is too catholic[10] to permit us to claim for her the exclusive title of "Child of the skies," but we have a deep and heartfelt pride—thank Heaven a just pride—in the increasing intelligence, the improving virtue, and the rising greatness of our country. There is something which more excites the imagination and interests the affections in expanding energy and rapid improvement, than even in perfection itself, were that attainable on this earth; and therefore we will ask, what country there is, or has been, whose progress towards greatness has been in any degree correspondent with our own? Our change is so rapid that the future presses on our vision, and we enjoy it now. We heed not the sneer that our countrymen are "prophetic boasters."[11] The future lives in the present. What we are, we owe to our ancestors, and what our posterity will be, they will owe to us.

New York, June, 1824.

8. *Arcadia*: In its broadest sense, Arcadia refers to a utopian, pastoral landscape. Sir Philip Sidney's epic poem *The Arcadia* (published in full in 1593) is the most famous literary expression of this pastoral ideal in English literature.
9. *'Queen of the earth'* and *'Child of the skies'*: Both phrases are quotations from the poem 'Columbia' (1777) by Sedgwick's third cousin, Timothy Dwight (1752–1817). The poem was soon popularised as the hymn 'Columbia! Columbia! To Glory Arise', in which Dwight depicts Columbia (the US) as an Edenic force greater than Europe, with the powers of genius, freedom and science on her side.
10. *our religion is too catholic*: When uncapitalised, the term 'catholic' means 'universal' When capitalised, 'Catholic' specifically refers to the Roman Catholic Church.
11. *'prophetic boasters'*: The immediate source of Sedgwick's direct quotation, which she characterises as a sneer, has not been identified. More generally, however, the phrase means 'those who boast about future accomplishments' and echoes several Bible passages that warn against false prophecy or against boasting of things that have not yet been accomplished, particularly Isaiah 44: 24–5 and 2 Corinthians 10: 15–18.

REDWOOD

CHAPTER I.

"A fine heroine, truly!
A Patagonian monster without a show of breeding."

Anon.[1]

ON the last day of June, in the year ____, a small vessel, which traversed weekly the waters of Lake Champlain, was seen slowly entering one of the most beautiful bays of that most beautiful lake. A travelling carriage with handsome equipments, a coachman in livery and an outrider, were drawn up on the shore, awaiting the approach of the vessel. On the deck stood a group of travellers for whom the equipage was destined: a beautiful young woman, and her attendant a female slave, were surveying it with pleased and equal eagerness, while the father of the young lady seemed quite absorbed in the contemplation of a scene which poetry and painting have marked for their own. Not a breeze stirred the waters; their mirror surface was quite unbroken, save where the little vessel traced its dimpled pathway. A cluster of islands lay in beautiful fraternity opposite the harbour, covered with a rich growth of wood, and looking young, and fresh, and bright, as if they had just sprung from the element on which they seemed to repose. The western shore presented every variety of form; wooded headlands jutting boldly into the lake, and richly cultivated grounds sloping gently to its margin. As the traveller's delighted eye explored still farther, it rested on the mountains that rise in four successive chains, one above the other, the last in the far distance dimly defining and bounding the horizon. A cloud at this moment veiled the face of the sun, and its rich beams streamed aslant upon the mountain tops, and poured showers of gold and purple light into the deep recesses of the valleys. Mr. Redwood, a true admirer of nature's lovely forms, turned his unsated gaze to the village they were approaching, which was indicated by a neat church spire that peered over the hill, on the height and declivities of which were planted several new and neat

---

1. *'A fine Heroine, truly!* . . . *'*: No Sedgwick scholar to date has identified the source of this quotation, which was apparently a work that was published anonymously.

habitations. "Oh Caroline, my child," exclaimed the father, "was there ever anything more beautiful!"

"Never, certainly to my eye," replied the daughter; "but I think a carriage far less handsome than ours would look beautiful, after those little vile *calèches*,[2] and viler ponies, with which we made our *entrée* into Montreal. Oh papa!" continued the young lady, too intent on present pleasure and past mortification to notice the shade of disappointment that had chased away the animation of her father's face; "Oh papa, I shall never forget our odious little Canadian driver, half Indian, half French; the rose tucked into his button-hole,[3] the signal of one nation, and the wampum belt of the other; and then his mongrel dialect, and that 'marse donc,'[4] with which he excruciated his pony and us at the same moment, does it not ring in your ears?"

"I cannot say that my recollections are quite as lively as yours, Caroline," rejoined Mr. Redwood.

"You are such an old traveller, papa, and besides you are always thinking of something else; but it is quite a different affair with me. My heavens! you had no imagination of my misery from the moment I entered the *calèche* at la Chine,[5] until I was safely sheltered in my room at the hotel: you sat rolling your eyes around the green fields as if they were all drawing-rooms, and in every dew-drop a diamond, while I would gladly have drowned myself in the St. Lawrence!"

"Really, my dear," replied the father, his tone bordering on contempt, "I did not suspect you of any such mad designs on your own sweet person—you seemed very quiet."

"Quiet, yes, indeed, and enough; how could I help myself? But you must own, papa, that it was excessively mortifying to make our entrance into the city in such style. Grand-mama says that people of fortune should never lay aside the insignia of their rank."

"Your grandmother's jumble of fortune and rank have a strong savour of republican ignorance. I would advise you, Miss Redwood, not to adopt

---

2. *calèches*: French word referring to a type of light carriage, usually uncovered.
3. *the rose tucked into his button-hole. . .*: The rose refers the French custom of men wearing a *boutonnière,* a flower fastened into the buttonhole of a coat lapel, and the Wampum belt references the belt made out of clam-shell beads typically associated with the Haudenosaunee (or Iroquois) Confederacy of native tribes. Caroline expresses disdain for this man's mixed heritage, which is indicated by his display of both French and Iroquois customs, as well as by what she terms the 'mongrel dialect' of his speech.
4. *'marse donc'*: Colloquial rendering of the French phrase 'Marche donc', meaning 'Go, then'. French Canadian *calèche* drivers during the eighteenth and nineteenth centuries used this command to urge their horses forward. The phrase also came to refer to both the calèche itself and the calèche drivers.
5. *la Chine*: A district or quarter in the city of Montreal.

her wise axioms as rules for the conduct of your life. And you really allowed yourself to suffer mortification on account of entering the little city of Montreal, in the best mode the country provides for travellers—a place too, where not a creature knew you from any other member of the human family?"

"Ah, there, sir, you are quite mistaken; for Captain Fenwick had written to all the officers of his corps our intention of going to Montreal, and he told me that he had described me so particularly to his friend Captain Fitzgerald, that he was sure he would know me at a single glance of his eye."

"Then we are indebted to Captain Fenwick for the honour of Fitzgerald's civilities? I fancied our acquaintance with him had been accidental." The penetrating look with which Mr. Redwood finished his sentence, gave it an interrogative meaning, and his daughter feeling herself bound to reply, said, rather sullenly, "Our introduction was purely accidental; you saw it, sir, and I thought at the time, seemed quite grateful that the timely aid of the Captain's arm saved me from being run over."

"I was and am grateful, my child, for the aid which the gallant Captain's arm afforded you; though it may be that, stoic as I am, I measured my gratitude rather by the small amount of danger than the childish alarm. The frightened animal, as well as I remember, turned into another street, instead of passing by the way we were going; but this does not signify. I merely expressed an innocent surprise, that there should have been grounds for your acquaintance with Captain Fitzgerald which you never intimated to me."

"Lord, papa, it is so awkward to talk to you about such matters; I am sure I had no other objection to telling you that Fitzgerald knew all about us before he saw us."

"All about you, Miss Redwood; for I am quite a cipher in the eyes of such men as the Captain, having no other value than what results from being your adjunct. Fitzgerald was then apprised that you were a belle, and will be an heiress."

"Probably. And if I do possess the advantage of those distinctions, I am sure I ought to be much indebted to Captain Fenwick for making them known, that I may enjoy them abroad as well as at home." Mr. Redwood thought the distinctions which procured for his daughter a host of such admirers as Fitzgerald of very doubtful advantage, and would perhaps have said so, but the vessel at this moment touched the wharf, and the bustle of disembarking put an end to the conversation. The travellers having arranged themselves in the carriage, Mr. Redwood ordered the coachman to drive to the village tavern, where he said it was his intention to pass the night. A short drive carried them to the door of the village inn. The landlord was sitting on a bench before the door, alternately reading a newspaper, and haranguing half a dozen loiterers on the great political topics that then agitated the country: his own patriotic politics were sufficiently indicated by the bearings of his sign board; on one side of which was rudely sketched the surrender of Burgoyne,[6] and on the other, an American eagle with his talons triumphantly planted on a British lion. It cannot be pretended that the skill of the artist had been adequate to revealing his design to the observation of the passing traveller; or rather the design of "Major Jonathan Doolittle," whose name stood in bold relief on one side, under the shadow of the spread wing of the eagle; and on the other under the delineation of the victory, which, according to the major's own opinion, he had been a distinguished instrument in achieving. But any deficiency in the skill of the artist was abundantly supplied by the valuable comment of the major, whose memory or imagination filled up the imperfect outline with every particular of the glorious victory. The carriage drew up to the door of the valiant publican, and in answer to Mr. Redwood's inquiry for the landlord, the major replied without doffing his hat or changing his attitude, "I am he, sir, in the room of a better." Mr. Redwood then inquired, if he could obtain accommodation for the night. The major replied, exchanging with his compatriots a knowing wink, "that he rather guessed not: he did not lay out to entertain people from the old countries; his women folks thought they took too much waiting on." Caroline whispered an entreaty to her father to order the coachman to drive on; but Mr. Redwood, without heeding her, said, "You mistake us, friend, we are your own country people, just returning from a visit to the British provinces, and as we have our own servants, and shall not need much waiting on, you will not perhaps object to receiving us." The major's reluctance somewhat abated by this information, and would probably have been quite overcome, but for his desire of keeping up his consequence in the eyes of the bystanders, by showing off his inherent dislike of an unquestionable gentleman. He said they were calculating to have a training the next day, and the women folks had just put the house to rights, and he rather guessed they would not choose to have it disturbed, but it was according as they could agree; he liked to accommodate; "and if," he added, for the first time rising and advancing towards Mr. Redwood, "if the gentleman could make it an object to them to take so much trouble, he would go in and inquire."

This last interested stipulation of the major filled up the measure of Mr. Redwood's disgust; and turning abruptly from him to a good-natured looking man, who, at that moment riding past them on horseback, had checked the career of his horse to gaze at the travellers, he inquired the

---

6. *the surrender of Burgoyne*: Currently housed in the US Capitol, this painting by John Trumbull (1756–1843) depicts the surrender of British General John Burgoyne to American revolutionary forces under General Horatio Gates at Saratoga.

CHAPTER I.

distance to the next village. "That," replied the man, "is according to which road you take."

"Is there any choice between the roads?"

"It's rather my belief there is; anyhow, there is many opinions held about them. Squire Upton said, it was shortest by his house, if you cut off the bend by Deacon Garson's; and General Martin maintained, it was shortest round the long quarter, so they got out the surveyor and chained it." "And which road," interrupted Mr. Redwood, "proved the shortest?"

"Oh there was no proof about it; the road is a bone of contention yet. The surveyor was called off to hold a Justice's court before he had finished the squire's road, and—"

"Which do you believe the shortest?" exclaimed Mr. Redwood, impatiently cutting short the history of the important controversy.

"Oh I," replied the man, laughing, "and everybody else but the squire, calculates it to be the shortest way round the long quarter, and the prospects are altogether preferable that way; and that is something of an object, as you seem to be strangers in these parts."

"Oh Lord," exclaimed Caroline, "it will soon be too dark for any prospect but that of breaking all our necks!"

"Do you think," pursued Mr. Redwood, "that we shall be able to arrive before dark?"

"That's according as your horses are."

"The horses are good and fleet."

"Well then, sir, it will depend something on the driver; but if you will take my advice, you will stop by the way. It is not far from night; there is a pretty pokerish cloud rising; it is a stretchy road to Eton, and it will be something risky for you to try to get there by daylight. But, sir, if you find yourself crowded for time, and will stop at my house, we will do our best to make you comfortable for the night. If you will put up with things being in a plain farmer-like way, you shall be kindly welcome."

Mr. Redwood thanked the good man heartily for the proffer of his hospitality, but declined it, saying, he doubted not they should be able to reach the next village before the storm. He then directed his coachman to drive on rapidly; and exchanging a farewell nod with his informant, who rode on briskly before him, he sunk back into his seat, and relapsed into silence and abstraction.

Meanwhile, Caroline sat listening in trepidation to the hoarse, though yet distant threatenings of the thunder, and watching with a restless eye the fearful clouds that rolled darkly over, in their ascent to mid heaven. "For gracious sake put your head out of the coach, Lilly," said she to her servant, "and look if there is any sign of the village." Lilly could just discern the spire of a church that stood on a distant hill. "On a hill of course," replied

Caroline; "one would think these Yankees had contrived their churches for telegraphs. I am delighted, at any rate, that there is a landmark in sight. For Heaven's sake, papa," she added, impetuously turning to her father, "do rouse yourself, and look at those clouds."

"I have been looking, my child, for the last half hour, watching the fading away of the bright tints from the edges of that beautiful mass of clouds, and thinking them a fit emblem of human life. Thus we gaze upon the brilliant vapour and are dazzled with its changeful hues, till the storm bursts in fury on our heads. Hark, Caroline, how the wind sighs through the branches of the trees: does it not seem as if nature thus expressed her dread of the violence that is about to be done to her beautiful face?"

"Oh, what does master mean," inquired Lilly; "does he think our faces will be struck with the lightning?"

"Heaven only knows what your master means. Do, papa, tell Ralph to drive faster; the darkness is horrible."

Mr. Redwood soon felt that his daughter's terrors were not groundless. The clouds had gathered a portentous blackness, strong gales of wind were rushing over the lake, the rain already poured in torrents, and there were only such intervals between the lightning as served to contrast the vivid flashes with the thick darkness; the thunder burst in loud explosions over their heads, and its fearful peals were prolonged and reverberated by the surrounding hills. The horses became restive, and the coachman called to his master for permission to stop at the next habitation. This was readily granted, and the coachman reined his horses into a road that led off the highway, over a little knoll, to a farmhouse which stood on a small eminence at the right. Some rocks, a few feet in height, served as an embankment to the road on the left. The coachman cracked his whip, and the horses were pressing on at their utmost speed, when a thunder-bolt struck an enormous dead tree a little in advance of them, fired its driest branches, descended the trunk of the tree, and tearing to splinters the parts it touched, laid the roots bare, and passed off across the road. The horses, terrified by the excessive vividness of the lightning, or the flaming tree, or perhaps both, sprang to the left, and before the coachman, scarcely less terrified than they, had made an effort to control their movements, they had dashed over the rocks, and forced the carriage after them. The horses sprang through a clump of young walnuts that grew at the base of the rocks. Most happily the carriage was too wide for the passage and the axles of the wheels were caught by the trees: the sudden check given to the velocity of the motion of the carriage broke the traces, and the released horses bounded away, leaving it and its inmates in perfect safety.

The moment Mr. Redwood perceived the horses would inevitably descend the rocks, he instinctively opened the carriage door and sprung out; he fell against the trunk of a tree, and when he attempted to rise to move to his daughter's relief, he felt himself disabled, and sunk back insensible. Fortunately, the coachman, quite unharmed, flew to the aid of the mistress and maid, who were both shrieking in the carriage. "Oh, stop the horses, stop the horses!" cried Caroline.

"The horses, Miss Caroline, are gone." "Gone, but oh, Raphy, won't they come back again?"

Upon Ralph's repeated assurances that there was not the slightest danger of, or from such a circumstance, Caroline alighted, and found, to her surprise, life and limb unscathed. When she had quite satisfactorily ascertained this fact, she turned to look for her father, but when she saw him stretched on the grass, the image of death, she shrunk back appalled. At this moment she heard some persons approaching to their assistance; they were from the neighbouring farmhouses, and had been alarmed by her shrieks, which they had heard even amid the "wild war of earth and heaven."[7] "Make the best of your way, miss, to the house," said one of the men kindly, "we will bring the gentleman in our arms." Caroline followed the direction, and was met at the door by several females, who clustered about her with expressions of pity, and offers of assistance. She moved past them and throwing herself into a chair, vented her feelings in loud hysterical sobbings; while Lilly set up a most doleful cry of "Oh, what will become of us, master is killed, and the horses are gone!" The mistress of the house with a voice of authority commanded her to be still; and at this moment the men entered, bearing in Mr. Redwood, pale as death, but sensible and calm. "Thank God you are not hurt, my child," he said, on seeing Caroline, "and I am better." The door of a spare room being now thrown open, the bed uncovered, the pillows shaken up, the mistress of the house pointed to the men to deposit their burthen there. Caroline and her servant followed Mr. Redwood; but so much were they both terrified by his paleness, and the distortion of his face from the extreme pain he endured, that they were incapable of offering him any assistance. Not so the good matron and her young handmaidens. It seemed to be their vocation to act; and so efficient were they in their prompt ministrations of camphor and cordials, that he was soon in a state fully to understand his condition and wants. He said to his daughter that it would be necessary for him to remain where he was for the present, to summon a physician immediately, to ascertain the injury he had sustained, and to set his arm if the bones were, as he apprehended, displaced; against this the daughter warmly remonstrated.

---

7. *'wild war of earth and heaven'*: From Nahum Tate's 1681 adaptation of Shakespeare's *King Lear* (III, i).

His host, having overheard a part of the debate, which was conducted in an undertone, said he would call Debby.[8] "Debby," he said, "was as skilful as the run of doctors; she was a nat'ral bone-setter; at any rate, if the gentleman was not willing to trust himself in her hands, she could tell if there were any broken bones." Debby was summoned, and soon made her appearance, muttering something about the boys, boy-fashion, having left out the old mare, and she guessed she felt as much pain with her broken leg, as your quality. She, however, seemed a little softened at the sight of Mr. Redwood, who was evidently suffering acute pain, and what probably interested Debby more, bearing it manfully. "Not," she continued, "that I would put a beast's life against a man's; but she is a good creature, and a sarviceable, and it is a shame for the boys to neglect her because she grows a little old and unsightly." The boys, as she denominated two full-grown young men, who stood at the foot of the bed, exchanged smiles, as if they were too much inured to this privileged railer, to heed her reproaches. Mr. Redwood shrunk from her touch as she approached him; but without noticing his alarm, she thrust her arm into an enormous pocket, which hung on one side of her gaunt person, and extricating from its miscellaneous contents a large pair of scissors, (which one would have thought stood as little chance of being found as a needle in a hay-mow,) she cut open the sleeve of the coat with more care and adroitness than could have been expected from such an operator, and then unceremoniously tearing down the shirt sleeve, she proceeded to the examination of the arm, which she pronounced a bad business. The shoulder she said was out of joint, and a breakage into the bargain: "and do you, James," said she, turning to one of the young men, "mount Rover, and go for Doctor Bristol, and tell him to come as fast as horse-flesh can bring him, for it an't all nature can set this arm after tonight. And James, child," she added, "be careful when you take Rover out of the stable, not to hit the old mare; for beasts have feelings too."

There had been such promptness in Miss Debby's proceedings, and the family was obviously so much in the habit of obeying her orders, that Mr. Redwood had not as yet been able to interpose a question; but as James turned to execute Debby's order, he said, "Stop, young man; before you go I should like to know who this Dr. Bristol is, and to ascertain his ability to perform a delicate operation; and I must know from you, my friend," he continued, turning to the master of the house, (whom he had just recognized to be the same person who had so kindly invited him to accept a shelter beneath his roof,) "whether you can

---

8. *Debby*: Aunt Debby is based on the historical Deborah Sampson, who disguised herself as a man to fight for the Patriots during the Revolutionary War. See the introduction for further information.

accommodate my daughter and myself, while we may be detained by this unlucky accident."

Mr. and Mrs. Lenox (the farmer and his wife,) were eagerly beginning to proffer their hospitality, with the courtesy of genuine kindness, when Debby interrupted them, with saying, "Go along, James, this is no time to stand upon compliments, go like the wind; a miss is as good as a mile."

James obeyed; and Mr. Lenox said, "I believe you may trust Dr. Bristol, sir; he doctors all the country round, and in all curable cases, under Providence, he cures. He studied under Rush,[9] and has but few equals in these parts."

"No, no," said Debby, "nor in any other parts: he is a real likely man, and they an't much thicker anywhere than swallows in January."

"But," interposed Mr. Lenox, "as the gentleman is a stranger among us, it is natural, and very right that he should be mistrustful."

"Oh, quite right," replied Debby, "and rational; and I like him all the better for it; none but your parfect fools believe in anything and everybody. But it is," she continued, with the *goût* of an amateur[10] in the matter, "it is a real pleasure to see Dr. Bristol set bones; it is beautiful! There was Tom Russell, fool and madcap that he was, and bating his being a human creature, better dead than alive, that fell off from the steeple of our meeting-house; there was scarce a whole bone left in his body; and when the doctor first overhauled him, he looked dumb-foundered, for he is tender-hearted for all being a doctor; I spirited him up, and he went to work, and a quicker, neater piece of work never has been done since the days of miracles: the bones went snap, crack, like the guns of our militia boys; not quite so loud may-be, but full as reg'lar."

"God grant," exclaimed Mr. Redwood, (who had been writhing under Debby's story,) "that your doctor may not have lost his gifts, nor his skill." "No," replied Debby, "a wise man an't apt to lose either." Mr. Redwood felt a natural apprehension, lest he should not be able to obtain the aid of this physician, whose skill seemed to have inspired such confidence, and he inquired of Mr. Lenox if he thought it probable the messenger would find him at home. "Almost certain," replied Mr. Lenox, "he was here yesterday to pay his last visit to a young man who has been a long time sick, poor fellow: he died last evening." "A consolatory proof of your doctor's skill," murmured Mr. Redwood.

---

9. *studied under Rush*: Benjamin Rush (1745–1813) was an eminent physician in colonial New England and in the new republic era of the US.
10. *gout of an amateur*: 'In the manner or style of an amateur,' though in this case the word 'amateur' has its earlier meaning of 'one who admires' rather than today's meaning of 'one who is not a professional'.

Half a dozen mouths were opened at once, to explain the doctor's failure. Deborah's shrill tones prevailed over every other voice; "Our days are all numbered, man," she said, "and to all there comes a sickness that neither doctors nor doctors-trade can cure; and besides, as to in'ard diseases, there's none but your pretensioners that profess to understand and cure them at all times."

"And poor Edward," interposed Mr. Lenox, "died, I believe, of that which you may well call an inward disease, for which there is no help in this world, a broken heart."

"As much that as anything," said Debby; "at least that might be called the 'casion' of it all; and it is far easier," she continued, looking at Mr. Redwood, "mending broken bones than broken hearts."

"And far easier breaking bones than hearts," replied Mr. Redwood.

"That," said the indefatigable Deborah, "depends something upon what the heart is made of. Some hearts are tough as a bull's hide; you might as well break a rock with sun beams as break them with such troubles as snapped the cord of poor Eddy, a weakly narvous feeling creature." Mr. Redwood was suffering too severely to indulge any curiosity in relation to Eddy. All parties became silent, and remained so until the arrival of the physician, save the occasional interruption of a groan from the stranger, or an expression of sympathy from someone of the group that surrounded his bed. We may profitably fill this interval with a description of the various persons that the occasion had assembled. And first, as most conspicuous, the stranger, mutilated as he was, appeared a finely formed and graceful man, with a certain air of high breeding, which even an unpractised eye may detect in the most unfavourable circumstances. He was rather above the ordinary height, and extremely thin. His high forehead, from which the hair had receded, the hair itself,

> "Jet black save where some touch of gray Had ta'en the youthful hue away;"[11]

and the deep furrow in his cheeks, indicated that sorrow, in some of its Protean shapes,[12] had accelerated the work of time, that the fruit which youth had promised, had been blasted not ripened. His face was a history; but there were few that possessed the key by which the settled gloom of his pallid brow, and the melancholy of his fine hazel eye might have been interpreted. The figure of Deborah, supporting the elegant traveller, looked

---

11. *'Jet black save where some touch of gray Had ta'en the youthful hue away'*: From Canto IV of the narrative poem *Lord of the Isles* (1815) by Sir Walter Scott.
12. *Protean shapes*: Protean, or various and shifting shapes, taken from the Greek mythological character Proteus, who had the ability to change his outward form at will.

like the rough-hewn stone beside the exquisitely polished statue on which the sculptor has expended all his art.

Miss Debby's person, mind, and history were altogether singular. Her height was rather above the grenadier standard,[13] as she exceeded by one inch six feet; her stature and her weather-beaten skin would have led one to suspect that her feminine dress was a vain attempt at disguise, had not her voice, which possessed the shrillness which is the peculiar attribute of a woman's, testified to Miss Debby's right to make pretensions which at the first glance seemed monstrous; her quick gray eye, shaded by huge, bushy eyebrows, indicated sagacity and thought; time, or accident, had made such ravages on her teeth, that but a very few remained, and they stood like hardy veterans who have by dint of superior strength survived their contemporaries.

As Debby would not voluntarily encumber herself with any toilette duties that could in decency be dispensed with, she had never put any covering on her hair, which time had now considerably grizzled; but she wore it confined in one long braid, and so closely bound with a black ribbon, that it did not require, in her judgment, more than a weekly adjustment. The only relic of worldly or womanly vanity which Debby displayed, was a string of gold beads, which, according to a tradition that had been carefully transmitted to the younger members of the family, had been given to their Aunt Debby some thirty years before by a veteran soldier, who, at the close of our revolutionary war, was captivated by the martial air of this then young Amazon.

But Debby was so imbued with the independent spirit of the times, that she would not then consent to the surrender of any of her rights: and there was no tradition in the family that her maidenly pride had suffered a second solicitation. The careful preservation of the beads, and a certain kindliness and protecting air towards all mankind, indicated ever after a grateful recollection of her lover. On the whole, there was in Deborah's face, rough and ungainly as it was, an expression of benevolence that humanized its hard features, and affected one like the sunbeams on a frosty November day. She was an elder sister of Mr. Lenox; had always resided with his family; and was treated with deference by all its amiable members.

Mr. Lenox, as master of the family, was entitled to precedence in our description; but in this instance, as in many others, a prominent character has controlled the arrangement of accidental circumstances. He belonged to the mass of New England farmers, was industrious and frugal, sober and

---

13. *grenadier standard*: References the grenadier guards of most armies. The term 'grenadier' originally meant soldiers trained to throw grenades, but by Sedgwick's time it had come to refer to the strongest, finest soldiers in a regiment.

temperate, and enjoyed the reward of those staple virtues, good health and a competency. He was rather distinguished for the passive than the active virtues, patient and contented; he either enjoyed with tranquillity, or resigned without repining. His wife (we believe not a singular case in matrimonial history,) was his superior: intelligent, well-informed, enterprising, and efficient, she was accounted by all her neighbours an ambitious woman. The lofty may smile with contempt, that the equivocal virtue, which is appropriated to the Caesars and the Napoleons, should be so much as mentioned in the low vales of humble life. But the reasonable will not dispute that Mrs. Lenox made ambition virtue, when they learn that all her aspirations after distinction were limited to the appropriate duties of her station. Her husband and sons wore the finest cloth that was manufactured in the county of ———. Mrs. Lenox's table was covered with the handsomest and the whitest diaper.[14] Her butter and cheese commanded the highest price in the market. Besides these home-bred virtues, she possessed the almost universal passion of her country for intellectual pleasures. She read with avidity herself, and eagerly seized every opportunity for the improvement of her children. She had married very young, and was still in the prime of life. The elder members of her family were already educated and established in the world; and she had the prospect of enjoying what Franklin reckons among the benefits of our early marriages, "an afternoon and evening of cheerful leisure."[15] Her eldest son, with very little aid from his parents, had, by his own virtuous exertions, obtained a collegiate and theological education, and was established a popular clergyman in one of the southern cities. Her second son had emigrated to Ohio, and had already transmitted to his parents a drawing and description of a prosperous little town, where, five years before, his axe had first announced man's right to dominion over the forest. Two sons remained at home to labour on the paternal farm; and four girls, from ten to eighteen, diligent, good-humoured, and intelligent, completed the circle of the domestic felicities of this happy family. Both Mr. and Mrs. Lenox had the wise and dutiful habit, which, in almost any condition, might generate contentment, of looking at their own possessions, to awaken their gratitude, rather than by comparing the superior advantages of others with their meaner possessions, to dash their own cup with the venom of discontent and envy, a few drops of which will poison the sweetest draught ever prepared by a paternal Providence.

14. *diaper*: A type of fabric woven into a simple pattern.
15. *'an afternoon and evening of cheerful leisure'*: From Benjamin Franklin's letter to John Alleyne on 9 August 1768, concerning the benefits of early marriage. The full passage reads, 'With us in America, marriages are generally in the morning of life; our children are therefore educated and settled in the world by noon; and thus, our business being done, we have an afternoon and evening of cheerful leisure to ourselves.'

On the kindness of this family Mr. Redwood and his daughter were cast for the present; and proud and powerful in the possession of rank and fortune, Miss Redwood was obliged to learn the humiliating truth, that no human creature can command independence. Mr. Redwood had been all his life a traveller, and was a man of the world. He comprehended at once the embarrassments of his situation, and gracefully accommodated himself to the inconveniences of it, and in such a way, as to conciliate the favour of the good-hearted people about him. How far his daughter imitated his wise example the following pages will show.

CHAPTER II.

"A country doctor;" said Touchwood sneeringly; "you will never be able to make anything of him."

The Cynic.[1]

BEFORE the return of James Lenox with the physician, Mr. Redwood had made an arrangement with Mr. Lenox, who consented to consider the strangers as boarders while Mr. Redwood's accident should detain him at the place we shall call Eton. Some little bustle in the entry announced the arrival of the physician, and he entered the apartment followed by Caroline, who with more alarm than she had testified before, advanced hastily to her father, and said, in a tone which though a little depressed was still loud enough to be overheard by all the by-standers—"My dear father, you surely will not suffer yourself to be murdered by a country doctor: pray, pray, remember poor Rose."

"Your grandmother's lapdog? Do not be a simpleton, Caroline."

"I do not see," replied Caroline, still in a tone of eager expostulation, "how Rose, being a dog, alters the case. I am sure grandmama thought as much of her as of any friend she had in the world. May not," she added, turning to the physician, "may not my father wait till a surgeon can be obtained from Boston or New York?"

"Undoubtedly he may," replied the doctor, smiling.

"And without danger?" inquired Mr. Redwood, who seemed to have become infected with his daughter's apprehensions.

"Possibly without danger," replied the physician, "though I should apprehend not without great additional suffering."

"Better to suffer than to die," urged Caroline.

---

1. *'A country doctor;' said Touchwood sneeringly . . .'*: Sedgwick attributes this quotation to a publication called *The Cynic*, but the current editor has not been able to locate the quotation in any work of that title. Sir Walter Scott's novel *St. Ronan's Well*, first published in December 1823, has a character named Lord Touchwood and a character who is a country clergyman, referred to as 'the doctor', though it does not contain this specific passage.

"I trust your father is not reduced to that alternative," replied the physician. "Such accidents are inconvenient, but seldom fatal. Shall I, sir," he added, turning to Mr. Redwood, "proceed to the examination of your arm?"

The modest demeanor and manly promptness of the doctor inspired his patient with confidence; and ashamed of having for a moment yielded to the weakness of his daughter, he said, "Proceed, sir, certainly. Forgive my daughter's scruples—she is alarmed, and inexperienced."

"She is a dumb fool," muttered Debby; and laying her arm on Caroline's, with a force to compel obedience, she pushed her out of the room, and then with an absolute command, dispersing all but those whose assistance was required, she prepare to obey the orders of Doctor Bristol, to whom she evidently deferred as to a master operator. The physician in his turn treated her as a confidential agent; and so quietly, skilfully, and expeditiously did he perform the operation, that he fully substantiated, in the judgment of his grateful patient, all the praise that had been lavished on him. Mr. Redwood bore the operation with stoical firmness, but after it was over his strength seemed much exhausted.

His physician ordered that he should be kept perfectly quiet, and that no one should have access to the room but those whose services were necessary. He inquired of Mr. Redwood if he preferred that his daughter should stay with him. Mr. Redwood, sighing deeply, replied that his daughter was too much unaccustomed to scenes of this kind to be of any use to him; and the physician proceeded to make arrangements with Mrs. Lenox and Deborah. The result of their deliberations was that Deborah should keep this night's vigil at the bed of the sick man.

These important arrangements being made, Doctor Bristol undertook to inform Miss Redwood of her father's amended condition. She received the intelligence with less animation than might have been reasonably anticipated from the apprehensions she had expressed. "She was glad," she said, "it was all over, for she was tired to death, and wished to go to her room."

"Yes," said her officious domestic, "you are tired, Miss Cary, you look very sick; as pale as a ghost."

"Oh Lilly," exclaimed Caroline, "that is impossible, for I never lose my colour, you know;" and she ran briskly to a looking-glass, which, shrouded in gauze, and bedecked with festoons of ground pine, adorned Mrs. Lenox's neat parlour. The mirror was imperfect, and it sent back as distorted a resemblance of the disappointed beauty, as if spleen and envy had reflected the image. "Oh Lord! Lord!" she exclaimed, "it would be the death of me to see myself again in that odious glass."

"I hope not," said Doctor Bristol. "We have specifics against such dangers in this retirement, where there are few to admire, and none to flatter."

"Are all your specifics *caustics*, Doctor?"

"Oh no!" replied the Doctor, smiling very pleasantly, (for it cannot be denied that his instinctive indignation at Miss Redwood's insensibility was softened by her matchless beauty;) "no, we prescribe caustics for inveterate diseases only: for the young and susceptible we have gentler remedies."

"And your cure for vanity is—"

"Abstinence—or, a low diet often subdues the violence of the symptoms—the disease is of the chronic order, seldom cured. But do not imagine that I have the presumption to prescribe for you, Miss Redwood, ignorant as I am even of the existence of the malady."

"Your prescription, sir, would, at any rate, be quite superfluous," replied Caroline, arranging while she spoke with evident satisfaction, her dark glossy curls before the mirror of her dressing-case, which Lilly (with the true instinct of a lady's maid,) had placed before her mistress; "vanity will die of starvation in this solitude."

"Oh my dear young lady, you are ignorant of the disease," rejoined the doctor; "there is no element in which it cannot live, and thrive, and find food convenient for it. I am not much skilled in the history of classic gentry; but if I remember right, it was not the flatteries of a court or a multitude, that cost poor Narcissus his life, but a rustic, truth-telling, woodland stream: depend on it, Miss Redwood, the danger is within; and 'inward diseases,' as my friend Debby calls them, are apt to baffle the most skilful."

"That being so, sir," retorted Miss Redwood, "it may be well to reserve your skill for obvious diseases and real dangers." She then proceeded to inquire, with considerable interest, into the particulars of her father's injury; and concluded by asking how long they should be detained at Eton.

"It is impossible to say," replied the doctor, "five or six weeks; perhaps longer. Your father's recovery must depend somewhat on his previous health and stock of spirits."

"Oh, then it is a desperate case, for he has been on the verge of the consumption for these two years; and as to his spirits, heaven only knows when he had any. He has been as dull as death ever since I remember him.

"Very unfavourable," replied the doctor, shaking his head; "but a parent's melancholy must be obstinate indeed to resist the cheering efforts of a child; and I trust, Miss Redwood, your resolution and patience will be equal to the present demand on them."

"It is a demand I cannot answer, sir. I might as well call spirits from the vasty deep, as summon mine at pleasure. Grandmama always said cheerfulness was a virtue for common people—quite necessary for them. I am never melancholy, however. Melancholy only suits the old and unfortunate; and if I must remain here, I will try not to hang myself."

"A virtuous resolution, truly."

"Doctor," exclaimed Caroline, after a few moments' pause, "is there nothing going on here; nothing to keep one alive?"

"Yes," replied the doctor, drily, "from this very house there is to be a funeral tomorrow."

"Quite a diverting circumstance," rejoined Caroline. "Pray, sir, who is it that is to be buried? No one of any consequence, of course."

"Goodness is the only consequence that we acknowledge, in our rustic life," replied the doctor, gravely; "our young friend's escutcheon has no blot upon it."[2]

Caroline seemed mortified, and did not pursue her inquiries, and the physician took his leave after having repeated his orders that the invalid should be kept as quiet as possible till his return in the morning. Miss Redwood was shown into a small but very neat apartment, in which were two beds: one of them had just been arranged for her accommodation.

"This bed is for me, is it?" she inquired, turning to a little girl who was her conductor, and at the same moment negligently throwing down her hat on a neatly quilted spread, as white as snow.

"Yes, miss, that is yours," replied the child.

"And the other is my servant's?"

"Oh no, miss, that is Ellen's!"

"Well, you little thing, what is your name?"

"Lucy," replied the child, dropping a courtesy.

"Well, Lucy, ask your mother to order a bed made for my servant here."

"I can ask her," replied the child; "but," she added in a lower tone as she was leaving the room, "I guess she won't find it convenient to put that black girl into Ellen's room."

Lucy, however, notwithstanding her prediction, returned in a few moments to say that Miss Redwood's request was granted; "and you may thank Ellen for it," she added, "for mother would not hear to it till Ellen begged her." "Well, well, child, you may go now—it is all very well. I shall take care to compensate your mother, and this Ellen too, for any favours they may grant me. Lilly," she added, turning to her servant, "undress me, and make over that bed, it is not likely these people know how to make a bed. Pin down the undersheet all around as grandmama has hers; I feel fidgety tonight, and a wrinkle would disturb me—heigho! How long is it since we left Montreal, Lilly?"

---

2. *our young friend's escutcheon has no blot upon it*: An escutcheon specifically refers to a shield depicting a family's coat of arms, but in this context, this phrase means that there is no stain upon his reputation.

"Two days, Miss Cary."

"Two days! What an age it seems: two days since I parted from the divine Fitzgerald, and it will be twice that number of weeks before I see another civilized being. That old jade that told my fortune, coming down the lake, was not so much out when she said I should meet with losses and crosses; but who could have dreamed of such a cross as this? And then to think that the Craytons will get to Boston before us; and Maria will contrive to show off her French dresses first. Oh, it is too provoking! For heaven's sake, Lilly, stow away my large trunk out of my sight; it will make me wretched to see those beautiful dresses of Le Moine's all lying idle, getting yellow, and old-fashioned." Thus Miss Redwood continued to run on, half to her servant, and half to herself, till she lost in sleep the consciousness of her disappointments.

CHAPTER III.

"Fleecy locks and black complexion
Cannot forfeit nature's claim;
Skins may differ, but affection
Dwells in white and black the same."[1]

Cowper.

HENRY Redwood was a native of Virginia, that State of the Union where the patrician rank has escaped in the greatest degree, the levelling principle of republicanism. His father was a rich planter: adhering pertinaciously to the custom of his predecessors, he determined that his eldest son should inherit his large landed property. To Henry he gave a good education, and designed that he should resort to the usual expedient of unportioned gentility, compensating by his marriage for the defects of his inheritance. He was early destined to be the husband of Maria Manning, the only daughter of Mr. Redwood's sister, a rich widow who resided in Charleston, South Carolina.

Henry Redwood had originally a highly gifted mind, and strong affections; under happy influences he might have become the benefactor of his country, its ornament and blessing; or he might in domestic life have illustrated the virtues that are appropriate to its quiet paths. His father trained his eldest son in his own habits, which were those of an English country squire. Henry was left to follow the bent of his own inclinations, and possessing a less robust constitution than his brother, and a contemplative turn of mind, he preferred sedentary to active pursuits. He early manifested a decided taste for literature; he felt the beauty, and confessed the power of the moral sublime; he loved the virtues that illustrate the pages of the moralist, and he sympathised with the examples of heroism which the poet and the historian have rescued from the ashes of past ages.

But unhappily he saw few resemblances in life to these fair portraits. His father's character was of the coarsest texture; his life when not devoted

---

1. *'Fleecy locks and black complexion ...'*: From the poem 'The Negro's Complaint' (1788) by the English poet and anti-slavery activist William Cowper (1731–1800).

to the gaming table, the excitements of the race-ground, or the stimulating pleasures of the chase, was wasted in the most perfect indolence at home: his mother had been a beauty, and possessed many of the gentle qualities of her sex; but, unresisting and timid in her nature, she had fallen into such habits of unqualified submission to her husband, that she had no longer courage to assert the rights of virtue, or power to impress them on her children. Young Redwood had one friend, the son of a neighbouring planter, whom he called his good genius, and his elevated character and rare purity entitled him to this distinction. The influence of his virtues and affection might, perhaps, have preserved Henry from the errors of his after life, but their opportunities of intercourse were rare and brief, in consequence of a political animosity between their parents, and before Henry had received impressions deep enough to mature into principle the strong inspirations of feeling, he was sent to college; there, by one of those unlucky chances that sometimes give a colour to the destiny of life, he was led, first to an acquaintance, and subsequently to an intimacy, with an unprincipled man, by the name of Alsop. This man possessed plausible talents and insinuating manners; but his mind had been contaminated by the infidelity fashionable at that period, and his vanity was stimulated by the hope of adding to his little band of converts a young man of Redwood's acknowledged genius.

The unfeeling and audacious wit of Voltaire, the subtle arguments of Hume,[2] and all that reckless and busy infidelity has imagined and invented, were arrayed by this skilful champion against the accidental faith of Henry Redwood: for that faith may surely be called accidental which knows no reason for its existence, but is the result of being born in a Christian community, and of an occasional attendance at church. The triumph was an easy one. Redwood's vision, like that of other unbelievers, was dazzled by the *ignis fatuus*[3] that his own vanity had kindled; and like them, he flattered himself that he was making great discoveries, because he had turned from the road which was travelled by the vulgar throng.

In the free and even licentious speculations of the closet, young Redwood was not surpassed by any of his new intimates; but he had a refinement of taste, which, though it would not have opposed an effectual barrier to strong temptation, deterred him from associating himself with them in their gross and profligate pleasures.

---

2. *audacious wit of Voltaire, the subtle arguments of Hume*: The French Voltaire and the Scottish David Hume were eighteenth-century philosophers known for their deep scepticism regarding both religious faith and human nature.
3. *dazzled by the ignis fatuus*: Also known as will o'-the-wisp, ignis fatuus are fields of chemically produced light seen on marshy places, which seem to disappear as soon as one approaches them. Sedgwick uses the term figuratively to emphasise the false hopes that obscure Redwood's judgement.

He was sometimes disgusted, but never shocked by their profligacy. He maintained, that whatever a man called good, was good to him; and that, released from the thraldom of fearing a visionary future, he was at liberty to disengage himself from the galling fetters which virtue and religion impose, and to expatiate without apprehension or compunction in a region of perfect liberty. A little reflection, and a very short experience, taught him that these principles would dissolve society; and then, like some other philosophers, he adopted expediency for his rule of right. He found it to be impossible so suddenly to emancipate men from the slavery of prejudice; "some hundred years must pass away before the downfall of the prevailing systems of superstition."[4] The enlightened must submit, while the ignorant are the majority; and a man's conduct must be graduated by the standard of the community in which he lived.

Opinion was the rule, and ignorance the presiding deity, in this new creed. Still, Henry Redwood's reason was not quite obscured, nor his heart quite depraved. He often turned from the heartless pages of infidelity to the inspiration of virtue, and found, that while the first controlled his judgment, the latter could alone sway his affections. A virtuous action would send an involuntary glow to his cheek, and make him wish he had never doubted the reality of the principle that produced it.

Redwood was ambitious; and after having won the first literary honours of his college, he returned to his family elated with success, and proud of his superiority. He again met the friend of his youth, Edmund Westall, who, during their separation, had become a married man; and in whose family Redwood found irresistible attractions. Westall was a few years older than Redwood; and there was an authority in his example that could not well be evaded, and a persuasion in his goodness that touched Redwood's heart. He felt it like an exorcism that conjured out of him every evil spirit.

But the state of his own mind will be best shown by a letter which he wrote at this time to his infidel friend.

"Some months have elapsed, dear Alsop, since we parted, and parted with a truly juvenile promise to keep up an unremitting epistolary intercourse. And this I believe is the first essay made by either of us; a fair illustration of the common proportion which performance bears to such promises. You, no

---

4. *'some hundred years must pass away . . .'*: This quotation is a modification of an imaginary exchange between David Hume (1711–76) and Charon, the ferryman of Hades in Greek mythology, recorded in a letter composed by Scottish philosopher Adam Smith (1723–90). Hume defers getting into Charon's boat because he must ensure the 'downfall of the prevailing system of superstition', to which Charon replies, 'You loitering rogue, that will not happen these many hundred years.'

doubt, have been roving from pleasure to pleasure, with an untiring impulse, and your appetite, like the horseleech, has still cried, 'give, give.'[5] If one of your vagrant thoughts has strayed after me, you have doubtless fancied me immured in my study, pursuing my free inquiries, abandoning the falling systems of vulgar invention, and soaring far over the misty atmosphere of imposture and credulity. Or, perhaps, you imagine that I have adopted your sapient advice, have returned to my home a dutiful child, gracefully worn the chains of filial obedience, made my best bow to papa, and with a 'just as you please, sir,' fallen, *secundum artem*,[6] desperately in love with my beautiful, and beautifully rich cousin; have rather taken than asked her willing hand, and thus opened for myself the path of ambition, or the golden gates that lead to the regions of pleasure, and which none but fortune's hand can open. But, alas! the most reasonable hopes are disappointed by our fantastic destiny. We are the sport of chance; and as you confess no other deity, you are bound not to deride any of the whimsical dilemmas into which its votaries are led. Alsop, you have often commended the boldness of my mind, while you laughed at a certain involuntary homage I paid to the beautiful pictures of goodness, which some dreaming enthusiasts have presented to us, or to the moral beauty which, among all the varieties of accidental combination, is sometimes exhibited in real life.

"Have I prepared you to hear the confession, that I am at this present moment the blind and willing dupe of goodness, (I mean, what the moralists call goodness,) embodied in a form, that might soften a stoic, convert an infidel, make of you an enthusiast, or perform any other miracle?

"You have heard me make honourable mention of my friend Westall. He is by some years my elder, three or four at least. I think I never related the circumstances of our introduction to each other; I am quite certain I did not, for you would have laughed at them; they may now serve to elucidate to you my friend's character, and to account for our early and reciprocal interest.

"My father had among his servants a native African; one of those men whom nature has endowed with a giant frame, and correspondent qualities of mind. At the time my father purchased him, he was separated from his wife and two children, girls; the only boy my father purchased with him, whether because he thought the presence of the child would help to keep the father in heart, or from a transient feeling of compassion for the poor

---

5. *'like the horse-leech, has still cried "give, give"'*: From Proverbs 30: 15 (KJV).
6. *secundum artem*: Latin phrase meaning 'according to the art' or 'in accordance with standard practice'.

wretch, I know not. The wife had suffered deplorably from the voyage, and was knocked down with her two girls to a Georgian, for a trifle. You do not know my father: suffice it to say, that selfishness and habit have made him quite insensible to the sufferings of these poor devils, whom he classes with other brutes born for our service. But there was something extraordinary in the strong affections and unconquerable temper of this man. His wife and little ones were torn from his strong grasp, and when resistance was hopeless, and he turned from them, the large muscles of his neck swelled almost to bursting, and he set up a desperate howl, that made every heart quake or melt. Someone of the throng around him put his boy into his arms; the sight of him changed the current of his feelings; he soon became silent, and, a few moments after, his tears fell thick and heavy on the child. My father brought him home. He performed his appointed tasks well, but he was retired and sulky; and the smallest services that were imposed on his child seemed to exasperate his spirit. It was not many months after he came into our possession, that our overseer, a cruel, worthless dog, beat the child, who had unwarily offended him, unmercifully. The father interposed and rescued the child, at the expense of some cutting lashes on his own back, which he seemed to regard no more than the idle wind. The very night after, the child disappeared, and it was believed the unhappy father had put an end to the boy's life. The fact was never ascertained, though no one doubted it; for, as you will readily believe, my father was not very zealous to establish a truth which would have deprived him of one of his most valuable slaves. These circumstances transpired before I was old enough to remember them; but when I first heard the report of them among our domestic annals, I felt an involuntary respect for this man, who, with a spirit more noble than Cato's,[7] cut the cord that bound his son to captivity, and manfully continued to endure the galling of his own chains. Was not this a glorious illustration of the truth of our old friend Seneca's remark, that 'sometimes to live is magnanimity'?[8]

"Time passed on, but Africk (for that was the name my father had given him,) remained unchanged. I think I see him now, going to his daily task, always apart from the herd, and quite alone; his firm and slow step, the curling of his lip, which would have better become a monarch than a slave, and his fixed, downcast eye.

---

7. *a spirit more noble than Cato's*: Marcus Porcius Cato (95–46 BC), also known as Cato the Younger, was a leader in the Roman Republic who was known for his integrity. Following his death, Cato's virtue was memorialised by writers such as Lucan, St. Augustine, Plutarch and Dante.
8. *'sometimes to live is magnanimity'*: From *Ad Lucilium Epistulae Morales* (*Moral Letters to Lucilius*) by Seneca (c. 4 BC to AD 65).

"His mind, which, like adamant, had resisted the influence of time, was at last subdued by fanaticism; which, you know, like some chemical powers, will dissolve substances that no mechanical force can impress. My father (a little alarmed himself, as I suspect, by an eloquent harangue,) permitted a zealous Methodist or Moravian,[9] I am not certain which, but a member of one of these tribes of amiable madmen, to address his people. A great sensation was produced, and among the rest, Africk eagerly seized every opportunity of communication with the preacher. He had never before sought human communion or sympathy. He soon became a convert; his fierce manner was changed to gentleness; he no longer avoided his fellows; and though still reserved and silent, it seemed to me that his religion brought him back to the human family, and by uniting him to the common Father of all, restored the broken links of fraternity.

"Whether his faith had an enfeebling influence on his body as well as his mind, I know not; but his health fell into decay. The overseer complained that he kept long vigils after his daily labour; that he spent the nights, which were made to prepare him for his labour, in prayers that exhausted his spirits and his strength. My father inquired of Buckley if he had used the whip; the wretch replied that he never entered a complaint till that remedy had failed. It did no more good, he said, to whip him, than to beat the air; he bore it without complaint, and without shrinking. My father then recommended an abatement of Africk's daily food.

"That, Buckley said, he had tried till the rascal was so weak he could scarcely stand. I was present at this conference, and my nature rebelled against the intolerable oppression the poor wretch was suffering. I interposed, and entreated my father to adopt kind treatment.

"He swore at my boyish impertinence, as he called it; but it was not, however, without effect, for he recommended to Buckley milder usage. But the fellow's habits of cruelty were too firmly fixed for any essential change. It was not long after, that Africk interposed to rescue a female slave from the horrible lash of this tyrant: his fury, averted from the woman, fell with redoubled violence on Africk, till, no longer stimulated by resistance, he turned away from his silent victim, and left him to crawl (for he could not walk) to his little cabin. The following morning he was missing; the plantation was searched in vain, and I was despatched by my father in quest of him, as he deemed it probable that some of the negroes of our neighbours might have harboured and concealed him; these sort of courtesies being not infrequent among our slaves.

---

9. *Moravian*: One of the oldest Protestant Christian denominations, with roots in the Moravia region of the present-day Czech Republic.

"I went, but with the determination never to reveal, if I discovered his concealment, and to afford him every aid in my power, for my youthful imagination had been powerfully excited by his heroism and his sufferings, and neither philosophy nor experience had yet steeled my heart against the spectacle of human misery. Would to God they never had!

"I began my expedition on foot, being just then inspired with a passion to emulate the feats of some European pedestrians, of whom I had heard. I cannot remember a period of my life when some such whim did not rule the hour. I had entered on Mr. Westall's grounds, and in order to cross by a straight line to the cabins of the negroes, I left the circuitous road, and turned into some low ground, covered with pines. It soon became marshy, and almost impassable, but I had proceeded too far for retreat or extrication, and I continued to push forward through the snarled bushes and interwoven branches of the trees; the daylight and my strength were almost exhausted, and my patience entirely, when I perceived the ground harden to my tread, and pressing eagerly forward, I issued from the wood into an open space, a few roods in circumference, around which the trees grew so thick, that they formed an almost impenetrable wall, a natural defence for this sequestered retreat. To my amazement I saw before me, and just on the skirt of the wood, a rudely constructed hut; two of its sides were formed by slabs resting on the ground at one end, meeting at the top, and supported by poles inserted into two notched posts: the third side was filled by brush cut from the adjoining wood, and piled loosely together; the fourth, towards which I advanced, was quite open to the weather.

"Alsop, I had proceeded thus far in my narrative, when I threw down my pen; my fancy had restored me to this scene of my youth; I had insensibly reverted to the influences that then governed my mind, and I felt that I was exposing the offices of the temple to the derision of the unbeliever. I protest against your laugh, and your more intolerable ridicule; I know all these things are the illusions of youth and ignorance, but I sometimes think them better, certainly far happier, than the realities I have since adopted. Still vacillating, you say, between philosophy and superstition! *Amiable* superstition! I have described this spot with some particularity. It is, with all its accompaniments, indelibly stamped on my memory. As I said, I advanced towards the habitation, and unperceived by its occupants, I had leisure to observe and to listen to them. Africk was lying extended on some straw with which the ground (for there was no floor) had been strewn for this slight accommodation; his head was supported by an old negro woman; with one hand he grasped the hand of my friend, with the other he held firmly a saphie, which was suspended around his neck; his short and spasmodic breathing indicated the last feeble struggle with death.

"Edmund Westall knelt behind him, and might have been mistaken for a bright vision from another and a higher sphere, so beautiful was the combination of faith, hope, and charity, as the enthusiast paints them, in his fair and innocent face. The last rays of the setting sun entering an aperture in the wall, fell athwart his brow, burnished his light brown hair, and rested there, a bright halo, a symbol of his celestial ministry. My ear caught the broken sentence of the dying man.

"'No no,' he said, 'Mr. Edmund, I had no peace. I would have given my life for one moment of freedom. I looked for revenge. I thought of my wife and my little ones; and I could have poured out the blood of white men, till it should run like the big waters over which they brought us. But the voice of God pierced to my heart, and I was an altered man. And when I prayed that blessed prayer, that I might be forgiven even as I forgave others, the fire in my heart was quenched, and the terrible storm that had raged here (and he pressed Edmund's hand on his naked breast) was laid; and there was peace, Mr. Edmund; God's peace. I was a slave, and I was wretched, but the sting was taken away. Do not pray for me, nor for mine. I have been on my knees for my helpless ones, night after night, and all day long, and my prayer is heard. But pray for your father's land, and your father's children. Pray to be saved from the curse that is coming. Oh! (he exclaimed,) and his voice became stronger, and its deep tones seemed to bear to our ears the sure words of prophecy; oh, I hear the cry of revenge; I hear the wailings of your wives and your little ones; and I see your fair lands drenched with their blood. Pray to God to save you in that day, for it will surely come.' His voice was spent; his eyes closed, as I believed forever, and I sprang towards the bed. I then perceived that it was a momentary exhaustion; he still grasped Edmund's hand, and I noticed the feeble beatings of his heart. The old woman signed to me to withdraw from before him; and I silently took my station beside her. After a few moments, he again languidly opened his eyes and said, in a scarcely audible voice, 'I thought I was in my own land; and I heard the rustling of our leaves, and the voices of my kindred, and I was feeding my little ones with their kouskous as when the destroyers came. My spirit will pass easier if I hear the voice of your prayer, blessed young man. Pray for my master; for Buckley.' He paused; and Edmund, in a low tender voice began his supplication. At the close of each petition, Africk murmured amen; and at Edmund's fervent intercession for his oppressors, he opened his eyes, clasped his hands, and in the intensity of his feeling, half rose from the straw. The effort exhausted him; he sunk back on the breast of the old woman, and expired. She released herself from him, and then stretching her arms towards heaven, as if in acknowledgment to Him who had broken the bonds of Africk's captivity, she clapped her hands and shouted, 'He is free! He is free!' Edmund and

I laid our faces together on the straw beside the poor negro, and wept as youth is wont to do.

"Forgive me, Alsop, I have told you a very long, and it may be a very dull story, though I think not; for nothing is dull to you that is connected with the philosophy of the human mind. You will ridicule me forever having deemed of importance the particulars of a vulgar being, extinct after a few years of life, and that for the most part, passed in abject slavery; but like a true philosopher, you will with me eagerly explore the past, for the causes that have influenced my character and governed my destiny. And yet, 'poor playthings of unpitying fate,'[10] why should we be so anxious to penetrate the mysteries of a being which may cease forever tomorrow? The Epicureans were more consistent than we are; and we may learn from the author of a faith that we deride, the truest wisdom for us; 'let us eat and drink, for tomorrow we die.'[11]

"This scene has haunted my imagination; the memory of it has sometimes seemed to me like a voice from Heaven; for a long while it kept alive a dying spark of faith. I cherished it as a testimony, that God had not left the creatures he had formed to wander without him in the world: I fancied there was a supernatural ministry to the spirit of this much-injured man, that had converted his just and unrelenting hatred to forgiveness—his pride to submissiveness—and there seemed a witness to the mercy of Heaven in the gentle and tender countenance of my friend.

"Yes, Alsop, I confess it—the memory of this scene has sometimes been an impassable barrier to your infidel and most ingenious arguments.

"You know one of the boldest, as well as most charming of female skeptics, said, 'in the silence of the closet, or the dryness of discussion, I can agree with the atheist or the materialist, as to the insolubility of certain questions; but when in the country, or contemplating nature, my soul, full of emotion, soars aloft to the vivifying principle that animates them, to the almighty intellect that pervades them, and to the goodness that makes the scene so delightful to my senses!'*[12]

---

*   Madame Roland.
10.   *'poor playthings of unpitying fate'*: From *Appel à l'impartiale postérité* (1793, *An Appeal to Impartial Posterity*) by Jeanne-Marie Roland (1754–93), one of the leading intellectual women and political activists of the French revolutionary era. Though Roland supported the Revolution, in 1793 she was one of the first revolutionary moderates to be guillotined by the more radical faction under Robespierre. She composed her *Appeal* while in prison awaiting her trial and eventual execution. Ironically, she never advocated for women's political rights in her writings.
11.   *'let us eat and drink for tomorrow we die'*: This passage appears in Isaiah 22: 13 of the Hebrew Bible and is then quoted in 1 Corinthians 15: 32 (KJV) of the New Testament.
12.   *'in the silence of the closet . . .'*: From *The Private Memoirs of Madame Roland* (1793) by Roland (see note 10).

"Thus it is with me: nature, and the beautiful traits of nature we sometimes see in man, appeal irresistibly to the feelings, and force their way to my convictions.

"My purpose was, frankly to tell you my present embarrassments; but I have been led into too serious a train of feeling to proceed any farther, and certainly to let you into the arcana of my present perplexities.

"I explained to Edmund my intentions in regard to Africk. We found that we had participated in a strong feeling of compassion towards him, and this sympathy at once created a bond of union between us. This hiding-place had been contrived by Westall's people for a refuge for the runaways from the neighbouring plantations; not at all for their own benefit, for the conduct of the Westalls to their slaves was noted for its benevolent and paternal character. The retreat was kept secret from Mr. Westall (the father); for the negroes rightly concluded that he would have been compelled in honour to surrender, as the property of his neighbours, the refugees who took shelter there. The son had been conducted to the place by the old woman, who was his nurse, who knew she might safely confide the secret to his custody, and who could not believe that any case was so desperate that he could not bring some alleviation to it. We agreed that Africk's body should be conveyed during the night to the cabin of one of the negroes, and should in the morning be restored to my father.

"Before we parted from the remains of the released slave, we examined the saphie, which to his last breath, he had so pertinaciously grasped. You must know these saphies are boxes made of horn, shell, or some other durable material; they contain some charm, usually a sentence from the Koran, which serves as an amulet to keep off evil spirits. Africk had changed the object of his superstition, and the infidel charm had been expelled to give place to the following sentence, written at his request by Westall: 'Forgive me my trespasses, even as I forgive those who trespass against me.'[13]

"At Edmund's instigation, I made this the occasion of benefit to the other negroes. I applied to my father in their behalf, and found my way to his understanding by the sure and well-trodden path of selfishness. I convinced him that Buckley's cruelty had shortened Africk's life, and that the tyrant's harsh treatment of the slaves prevented half the profit that might otherwise be derived from their labour. My father, exasperated by his recent loss, readily yielded to my arguments. Buckley was dismissed, and an efficient and tolerably humane overseer employed in his place. I possessed then, Alsop, some enthusiasm in the cause of benevolence, and could have

---

13. *'Forgive me my trespasses, even as I forgive those who trespass against me'*: A paraphrase of part of the 'Lord's Prayer' of Matthew 6: 12–13. Africk has individualised and personalised this prayer, substituting the first-person singular pronoun for the original plural form.

envied, and possibly might have emulated the fame of a Howard.[14] But notwithstanding this strange confession, you need not now despair of your disciple and friend.

H. Redwood."

* * * * *

This epistle very naturally excited some alarm in Alsop for the security of his dominion over the mind of his young disciple. He wrote to him repeatedly, and received but few, and those brief replies, till about the expiration of a year, when an answer to an earnest solicitation to Redwood to accompany him to Europe, whither he was going in a public service, and to his setting forth in the most tempting manner, the advantages that he offered, he received the following letter:

* * * * *

"Dear Alsop,

"I am grateful for your interest, and convinced by your arguments that I ought no longer to doze away my brief existence in this retirement. I have obtained my father's consent to the arrangement you propose; and what is still more indispensable, an ample supply, in consideration of a promise I have given to him, that I will solicit the hand of my cousin immediately after my return.

"Alsop, I find it necessary to recollect all the arguments in favour of virtue and vice being only conventional terms, artificial contrivances for man's convenience; for conscience, conscience, 'that blushing, shamefaced spirit that mutinies in a man's bosom,'[15] tells me that if it is not so I am the veriest wretch alive. I am married to a young creature, without fortune, without connections; innocent, and beautiful, and *religious*; an odd union, is it not? I have not intimated my free opinions to her, for why should I disturb her superstition? It is quite becoming to a woman, harmonizes well with the weakness of her sex, and is perhaps necessary to it. No one but the priest (and he is trustworthy) knows our secret. My pride, my ambition, rebel against the humble condition of life to which this rash indulgence of boyish passion condemns me. If my father knew it, he would spurn me; for my marriage disappoints his favourite project, and my poor girl would provoke his most inveterate prejudices; and my mother, my timid mother, would never forgive me for presuming to offend my father: there is no tolerable alternative; the fact must be concealed for the present. Who knows but one of the tides,

---

14. *emulated the fame of a Howard:* John Howard (1726–90) was a famous British prison reformer and philanthropist.
15. *'that blushing shamefaced spirit . . .':* From I, iv of Shakespeare's *Richard III*.

which, 'taken at the flood lead on to fortune,'[16] may await me? Anything is better than to lose this bright opportunity of pleasure and advantage. Poor Westall is dead, and died with unbroken confidence in my virtue. Is goodness always thus credulous? He has committed his only son, a boy of four years, to my guardianship. I will not betray his trust, so help me God.

"Yours, etc., H. R."

Redwood had determined to keep his intended departure a secret, to save himself from the remonstrances and entreaties which he naturally expected from his abused wife. He had no intention permanently to desert her; she was residing in the family of a Mr. Emlyn, as teacher to his children, and might remain there for one, or even two years, if necessary; and in the meantime, an unforeseen accession of fortune, political advancement, or any of the thousand chances that happen to fortune's favourites, might relieve her husband from his present embarrassments, and enable him to invest her with her rights, without too great a personal sacrifice. By such and similar considerations he endeavored to soothe his conscience into acquiescence; but neither these, nor the sophistries of his friend, availed him to silence the voice of nature within him that incessantly reproached him with the wrong he was about to inflict on a young, and innocent, and helpless being.

On the night before his departure, he summoned resolution to visit her, intending to impart to her his designs, and to soothe her with such promises and arguments as he could marshal to his aid. He found her alone in the little parlour which had been kindly assigned to her. She started at his entrance, and was hurrying a sheet of paper on which she was writing, into the desk at which she sat. "Treason, treason," said he, detaining the paper, and at the same time kissing her pale cheek. "Then it is treason against my own heart," she replied; for that is but too faithful to you." Redwood was conscience-stricken, and to shelter his embarrassment, he affected to read the letter he had seized: it was blotted with his wife's tears. "No, do not read it," said she, laying her hand on it, "It is only a little scolding; you know I have so few of the privileges of a wife, that I cannot but use those that are not denied me." Redwood's eyes were still fixed on the letter, of which, however, he had not read a single word. She continued, "I am so lonely, that I get low-spirited, and sometimes I think you do not love me."

"Not love you, Mary?" exclaimed Redwood, in whose breast there was not at this moment any feeling so strong as his tenderness for the lovely being before him.

---

16. *'taken at the flood lead on to fortune'*: From IV, iii of Shakespeare's *Julius Caesar.*

"Yes, Henry," she replied, with more courage than she had ever before shown, "and have I not much reason to think so? I am sure I could not make anyone suffer as you make me; I could not live and let such a curse rest upon your blessings."

"A curse. Mary, what do you mean?" replied her husband.

"Oh, is it not a curse," said she, "to feel the misery of guilt and the punishment of folly; to be suspected of crime; to feel the blood freezing in my veins, from the fear of detection; to see, or fancy that I see, the smiles of derision and contempt on the faces of the very slaves of the plantation, as I pass by them; and to blush and feel humbled, when, at the mention of your name, my eye meets the stolen glances of the children? Oh, Henry, I am a woman, and I cannot bear such suspicions; I am a wife, and I ought not to bear them."

Redwood was affected by his wife's appeal; but there was in it an assertion of rights that mortified his pride, and surprised him; surprised him, because Mary had always showed herself a timid being, with unquestioning dependence on his will, and submissive conformity, to his wishes. He defended himself as well as he was able: he pleaded his dependence on his father—his dread to excite his tyrannical passions; he reminded her that she had consented to their clandestine marriage and intercourse.

"But," she replied, "I was young and inexperienced, and quite alone; and I thought, Henry, you could not ask me to do anything it was not right to do; and you promised, before God, to love and cherish me, and I was quite sure I never should suffer any evil that you could shield me from."

"And you shall not, Mary," he replied; "only have a little patience."

"Ah, Henry, patience is the resource of the miserable; and I," she added, turning on him a look full of the confiding spirit of affection, "I ought not to be miserable."

"But what can I do?" said he impatiently.

"Withhold no longer the name to which you have given me a right; save me from cruel suspicions and remarks, and I will endure silently and patiently any other evil; I will live separate from you, if your father requires it, or you wish it; I will never see you again; anything will be better than to endure the torment of shame, for from this torment the consciousness of innocence has not preserved me."

Redwood felt the justice of his wife's cause, and he might have yielded to the best impulses of his nature, but he thought he had gone too far with Alsop to recede; he mentally resolved to shorten his absence as much as possible, and to return to make his wife happy. Having appeased his conscience by this compromise, he appealed to her compassion; he represented with tenfold aggravation, the embarrassments in which he was involved, and he soothed her with professions of tenderness. Gentle and affectionate, she soon relapsed into trustful acquiescence; and with a self-devotion not singular in a woman, she resolved and promised to abide his pleasure. Before they parted, there was an allusion made to a flirtation Redwood had had with his cousin, Maria Manning, and to some tender letters she had written to him since his marriage, to win him back from what she supposed to be his indifference. These letters had frequently been the subject of raillery between the lovers. Mary had never seen them; and Redwood, in no humour now to deny anything which he could grant without too great a sacrifice, promised he would send her the letter the next morning. He then parted from her, but not without betraying real anguish, which his tender-hearted wife blamed herself for having inflicted on him.

The next morning a packet was brought to her. It contained a brief farewell from her husband, the most plausible apology he could frame for his departure, and a sum of money larger than he could well afford to spare from the allowance he had received from his father, but by which, as he said, he meant to enable her to withdraw (if she should prefer to do so during his absence) from the situation she then held. In the hurry of his departure, Redwood had sent, instead of the promised packet, his correspondence with Alsop. What a revelation it contained for this deserted wife! She had reposed in him the unqualified and unsuspecting confidence of youth; she had believed him to be just what he seemed—the natural conclusion of inexperience. How terrible are the reverses of opinion, when those most tenderly loved are the subjects of them! It seemed to Mary Redwood, that she had fallen into an abyss of hopeless misery. She read over and over again these fatal letters, till her head turned, and her heart sunk with the strange confusion of horrible ideas which they communicated. The language of the world, of philosophy (falsely so called), of infidelity, was an unknown tongue to her; a strange jargon, which introduced into her mind but one definite idea, and that a deep conviction that her husband was corrupt, more corrupt in principle than in conduct; and his conduct the natural and necessary result of his principles. Ignorant as she was of the world, and all its intolerance and artificial distinctions, she had never dreamed that her lowly fortune and rank opposed a barrier to her acknowledgment.

The love of women is sometimes ranked with incurable diseases. Mary Redwood's, at least, was not so; perhaps her husband seemed to her to lose his identity from the moment that she discovered his real sentiments; however that may be, the discovery cut the cord that bound her to him; and the repose and happiness of trustful affection, and feminine dependence, and the confidence of youthful expectation, gave place to deep despondency, and to all the apathy of complete alienation. It was impossible for her to conceal a change so suddenly wrought in her feelings, and the good people with whom she was living believed young Redwood's departure for Europe to be the cause of it.

They had for a long time been apprised of his secret visits, and suspicious of his designs; but the purity and gentleness of Mary's manners rebuked suspicion, and they hesitated to communicate their observations to her: besides, they were engaged with their own concerns, and the transient love affair (as they deemed it) of an obscure young girl, seemed to them of no great moment. They felt some regret, when, after the lapse of a few days, she announced her wish to relinquish the care of their children, assigning as a reason the evident decline of her health, and she did not leave them without generous tokens of their gratitude for her fidelity. At the time of her departure, her friend, Mrs. Westall, was absent on a visit to a distant plantation; this she esteemed fortunate, for she wished to escape any observation that would have been stimulated by affection.

She resolved never to reveal the secret of her marriage; and thanking God that her parents were removed from this world, and that none remained to be deeply affected with her misfortunes, she determined to seek out some retreat where she might be sheltered from notice. As the carriage drove away that conveyed her from the door of Mr. Emlyn, Mrs. Emlyn turned from the window where she had stood gazing after her, and said to her husband, "Is it not strange that Mary should not have felt more at parting with the children? She did not seem to notice their caresses, and poor things, they cried as if their little hearts would break; she is kind-hearted too." "And did not you mind, mother," asked one of the little girls, "that when I offered that pretty shell box Mr. Redwood gave me for a keepsake, she shivered as if she had the ague,[17] and dropped it on the floor?"

"Ah," said Mr. Emlyn, looking significantly at his wife, "it is easy enough to see where the shoe pinches. I tell you, my dear, that fellow has nearly broken the girl's heart. It is just so with all your tribe; 'all for love, or the world well lost.'[18] But she will come to her senses. 'Sur les ailes du temps la tristesse s'envole.'"[19]

---

17. *ague*: An acute or high fever that would cause chills.
18. *'all for love, or the world well lost'*: A reference to the play *All for Love or, The World Well Lost* (1677) by John Dryden (1631–1700).
19. *'Sur les ailes du temps la tristesse s'envole'*: From 'La Jeune Veuve' by French author Jean de La Fontaine (1621–95), this can be translated as 'sadness flies away on the wings of time'. 'La Jeune Veuve', or 'The Young Widow', was published in the *premier recueil*, or first collection, of La Fontaine's *Fables* (1668).

CHAPTER IV.

"Si un homme honnête avoit fait un mal irreparable à un être innocent, comment, sans le secours de l'expiation religeuse, s'en consolerait-il jamais."
Madame de Stael.[1]

REDWOOD joined his friend, and they embarked together for Europe, furnished with every facility for an introduction to good society which Americans could then procure. They visited Paris, and gained admission to its highest literary circles: to society the most dangerous, and the most captivating, men and women, who, from having been born thralls to the despotic dogmas and pompous ritual of the Romish church, had identified the corruptions of Christianity with its truth, and rejecting the galling yoke, had loosened all necessary and salutary restraints. There was in them much to be admired by a virtuous person, much to excite the sympathy of the representative of a young republic, for they had an unaffected zeal for the happiness of their species, and a genuine hatred of every mode of tyranny. They had, too, an amenity and exquisite refinement of manners, which they had owed to the vital spirit that Christianity had infused into civilized life, and which remained after the spirit had departed; as the body, from which the soul has fled, retains, while life is still recent, its fair proportions, and beautiful expression; or, as the plant which the passing gale has uprooted, is still decorated with the flowers that owed their birth to the parent earth. In these circles, Redwood's devotion to intellectual power (the ruling passion of his youth) revived, and he resigned himself to the charms of society, to those pleasures which one who was their victim, has, with a few vivid touches, described "la parole n'y est pas seulement comme ailleurs un moyen de se communiquer ses idées, ses sentiments, et ses affaires mais c'est un instrument dont on aime à jouer et qui réanime les esprits, comme la musique chez quelque peuples, et les liqueurs fortes chez

---

1. *'Si un homme honnête . . .'*: Madame de Staël (1766–1817) was a French–Swiss woman of letters, considered the embodiment of the European zeitgeist in the early nineteenth century. This quotation appears in *De l'Allemagne* (1810, *Of Germany*) and can be translated as 'If an honest man had committed an irreparable evil to an innocent person, where else would he ever find comfort if not in the forgiveness of sins?'

CHAPTER IV. 45

quelques autres."*² And in these circles, Redwood felt that Paris "était le lieu du monde où l'on pouvoit le mieux se passer de bonheur."**³

While he remained in the French capital, there was no suspension of excitement, not an hour for reflection, scarcely a solitary moment for the impertinent whispering of conscience. His wife, the young and innocent creature who had surrendered to him the whole treasure of her affections, abandoned, solitary, sick, and heart-broken, was scarcely remembered, or if remembered, was associated with the dark cloud with which she had shaded his future fortunes. But after he had left Paris, in the further prosecution of his travels, there were times when she was remembered; the powers of conscience, spell-bound by the noise and glare of society, were awakened by the voice of the Divinity issuing from the eloquent places of nature. The pure streams, the placid lakes, the green hills, and the "fixed mountains looking tranquillity,"⁴ seemed to reproach him with his desertion of nature's fairer work; for all the works of nature are linked together by an invisible, an "electric chain."⁵ Redwood hurried from place to place; he tried the power of novelty, of activity; he gazed on those objects that have been the marvel, and the delight of the world; and when the first excitement was over, he felt that he could not resist the great moral law which has indissolubly joined virtue and happiness.

On his arrival at Rome he found letters awaiting him there. To avoid the hazard of discovery, he had determined that all intercourse between himself and his wife should be suspended during his absence, and had purposely omitted to furnish her with his address—his anxiety to receive some intelligence from her had, however, become so strong, that he would now have willingly incurred any risk for that gratification. On turning over his letters, he noticed one in a handwriting which he recognized to be that of the clergyman who had married him to Mary Erwine; he hastily tore it open. There was within it a letter from his wife, and a few lines from the clergyman stated that he had received that letter enclosed in another, and post-marked Philadelphia: he was requested to forward it by the first conveyance, and

---

* Conversation is not there, as elsewhere, simply a medium for the communication of ideas and sentiments, and the transaction of business; but it is an instrument on which they delight to play, and which excites their spirits, like music among some nations, and strong liquors among others.

** Paris was that place in the whole world where one might best dispense with happiness.

2. *'la parole n'y est pas seulement . . .'*: From de Staël's *De l'Allemagne.*
3. *'était le lieu du monde . . .'*: From *De l'Allemagne.*
4. *'fixed mountains looking tranquillity'*: A shortened quotation from the narrative poem *Childe Harold's Pilgrimage* (1812) by Lord Byron (1788–1824). The poem's main character is the first example of what became known as the Byronic hero.
5. *'electric chain'*: From Lord Byron's narrative poem *Childe Harold's Pilgrimage* (1812–18).

to inform him to whom it was addressed, that the writer had died two days after closing the letter.

Alsop entered Redwood's apartment a moment after he had read the letter, and while he was yet nearly stunned by the sudden blow: Alsop looked at the unsealed letter which had fallen on the floor, and then took the open one from the unresisting hand of his friend, who, while he hid his convulsed face in his hands, exclaimed, "Oh, I have killed her, Alsop—I have killed her!"

"No, no," replied Alsop, comprehending at a glance the import of the intelligence, "nature sentenced her; you may have hastened the execution—but that's all. What do you mean by this drivelling, Redwood? Is it thus you receive one of fate's happiest strokes? By my soul, man, I have been a sworn knight to my lady Fortune for these twenty years, following her through good and evil report, and for all my devoted services, I have never obtained one such favour."

There was an audacity in this levity, which quickened to keen resentment the awakened feelings of Redwood. He spurned Alsop from him, and resigned himself to the tide of misery that overwhelmed his fortitude. As soon as he could command sufficient courage, he opened his wife's letter—it was cold and brief, without a request or reproach; and simply informed him that after his departure she had sought a retirement where she might prepare herself for that better world, towards which her heavenly Father in his tender mercy was evidently leading her: she had found one; and had received under the humble roof where she should soon close her eyes forever, every kindness that humanity could render. Should any regrets induce Redwood to make any inquiries about her, she informed him they would be vain and useless—vain, for she had taken every precaution to keep the place of her retreat secret—and useless, for she should then be where no human being could confer happiness, or inflict misery on her. Some portions of the letter betrayed strong emotions, but apparently it did not result from the relations which had subsisted between herself and him to whom she wrote. It was an elevated state of feeling with which no personal considerations seemed to mingle, in which she regarded what had passed, not as offences against herself, but as portending misery to Redwood. The letter concluded thus—"you will not," she said, "need the assurance of my forgiveness; believe me I have no sterner feeling than pity for you. I have sought, and till my heart is stilled in death, I shall seek for you his mercy who came to heal the sick, to seek the lost, and to restore the wanderer. Farewell, Redwood, God grant the prayer of your dying wife."

'And is this all,' thought Redwood, 'that remains to me of the tenderness of youthful love; of that innocent, generous affection, that questioned not, suspected not? Oh, I have most foully betrayed her trust! We are severed forever—yes, forever—for surely, if there is a heaven, she has entered it; and I—I have no place—no hope there. I could have borne reproaches, invectives, anything I could have borne better than this calm tone which pronounces the sentence of death—eternal death to our union.'

There is, perhaps, no keener suffering to a generous mind, than the consciousness of having inflicted a wrong which cannot be repaired. Redwood's first hasty resolution was to make the poor amends in his power, to return to his country, proclaim his marriage with Mary Erwine, and endure the infamy his desertion deserved. No sacrifice appeared to him too great to appease the clamors of his conscience, no self-mortification too severe, if he might thereby pay a tribute to her memory, whose life he had embittered, and cut off in its early prime.

But after the first access of grief and contrition gave place to calm and natural considerations, he saw, that however just might be this conduct, still it must be quite useless to the injured being whom he could no longer serve nor harm. She was an orphan, without any near connections to inquire after, or to be afflicted by her destiny: why then should he publish his own infamy, which could never be mitigated in the eye of the world by the knowledge of the virtuous intention and severe remorse, which, as Redwood hoped, in some measure softened its deepest colouring? These were certainly natural considerations; and though everyone must wish that Redwood had followed the simple dictate of right, no one who knows how very cogent arguments appear on that side to which the inclinations lean, will be surprised that his virtuous resolutions should have died away, and his good emotions have subsided; but they did not subside without permanent effects. The wave retreated, but its ravages remained; and Henry Redwood carried through life a fast-rooted misery, a sense of injustice recklessly committed; a feeling of degradation that led him to turn from all that is fair and good, as a sick eye shuts out the light of heaven.

Redwood avoided the poisonous society of Alsop. He left Rome after wandering for a little time about its magnificent ruins; the melancholy tone of his mind suiting well with their gloomy grandeur. From Italy he repaired to England, and after rambling over our parent land, and admiring without enjoying its beauties, he returned to his native country.

Quite indifferent to his own domestic fate, he yielded a ready compliance to the importunate wishes of his father and mother, and solicited and easily obtained the hand of his cousin, Maria Manning, a spoiled child and flattered beauty. Her girlish preference of her handsome cousin had been stimulated by the difficulty of achieving the conquest of his affections; and if her vanity had been piqued by his long apparent indifference and protracted absence, it was quite soothed by the professedly unqualified admiration of one who had gazed on foreign beauties, and had been received with favour in the circles of rank and fashion in countries more polished than our own. The ceremony of Redwood's marriage was celebrated with all due pomp and circumstance. A troop of gratified friends attended him to the altar, whither he led his beautiful bride, the idol of fashion and the favourite of fortune: one person alone in all the assembly rightly interpreted his faltering voice, restless movements, and changing colour, and the fixed gaze that proved his thoughts intent on the visions of his imagination. It was the same church to which at twilight and in secrecy he had led the trustful girl, whose artless tenderness, simple and spiritual beauty, and unsuspecting confidence, haunted him at this moment. The same clergyman officiated who had then recorded his plighted faith. Neither the dogmas of a selfish philosophy, nor the training of the world, had indurated Redwood's heart. At the moment the service concluded, he staggered from the side of his bride, and caught hold of the railing around the altar. The clergyman whispered, "you betray yourself, Mr. Redwood." His father, bustling up to him, called him, in the same breath, "a lucky dog and an odd fish;" and his young friends, crowding around him, mingled with their congratulations well-timed raillery of his timidity. Recovering his self-possession, he parried their attacks skilfully, and apologized to his wife with the adroit courtesy of a well-bred man; and she, with the happy facility of habitual vanity, not knowing what his emotion meant, believed it meant something flattering to herself.

Redwood now entered on the career of politics. His wife was the bright cynosure of the fashionable world; and both were the envy of those who form their childish judgments by externals, forgetting that the most brilliant hues are reflected by empty vapours. Mrs. Redwood survived her marriage but a few years, and left at her death one child, Caroline, whom she consigned to her mother. The child was accordingly transferred to the care of Mrs. Manning, and conveyed to Charleston, South Carolina, the residence of that lady, who evinced her grief for the death of her daughter, by lavishing on the child a twofold measure of the indulgencies and flatteries that had spoiled the mother.

Mrs. Manning's notions of education were not peculiar. In her view, the few accomplishments quite indispensable to a young lady, were dancing, music, and French. To attain them, she used all the arts of persuasion and bribery: she procured a French governess, who was a monument of patience; she employed a succession of teachers, that much enduring order, who bore with all long-suffering the young lady's indolence, caprices, and tyranny. At the age of seven, the grandmother's vanity no longer brooking delay, the child was produced at balls and routes, where her singular beauty attracted every eye, and her dexterous, graceful management of her little person, already disciplined to the rules of Vestris,[6] called forth loud applauses. The child and grandmother were alike bewildered with the incense that was offered to the infant belle, and future heiress; and alike unconscious of the sidelong looks of contempt and whispered sneers which their pride and folly provoked. At fourteen, Miss Redwood, according to the universal phrase to express the debut of a young lady, was "brought out," that is, entered the lists as a candidate for the admiration of fashion, and the pretensions of lovers. At eighteen, the period which has been selected to introduce her to our readers, she was the idol of the fashionable world, and as completely *au fait*[7] in all its arts and mysteries, as a veteran belle of five and twenty.

Mr. Redwood had received the noblest gifts of his Creator: a mind that naturally aspired to heaven, and sensibilities that inclined him to all that was pure, and good, and lovely. The worldly advantages he possessed would have been the means of happiness to a vulgar, or even an ordinary character; but they had no control over a spirit that could not endure to be limited to the objects of selfish gratification, to bound its desires and pursuits within the earthly prison-house. After a few years, he wearied of the toil and strife of political life, resigned its honours, and embarked for Europe, from whence, after having worn out two or three years in a vain effort to escape from the demons of restlessness and ennui, he returned to his own country to seek happiness, where none but the good find it, at home. He was surprised with the ripened beauty of his daughter, but most severely mortified to find her just what he ought to have expected from the influences to which he had abandoned her. He never felt so strong an affection for the child as would seem to have been natural. His indifference to her mother, the circumstances that preceded his marriage, and perhaps the child's resemblance to the parent, accounted in part for this want of affection; and the carelessness that was the result of it was to be expected from one governed more by casual impulses than principle.

Mr. Redwood hoped it was not too late to repair his fault. He perceived that his daughter possessed spirit and talents not quite extinguished by her mode of education and life; and for the purpose of breaking off all unfavourable associations, and removing her from the influence of her doting grandmother, he resolved on a tour through the northern states.

---

6. *rules of Vestris*: Refers either to Gaétan Vestris (1729–1808) or his son, Auguste Vestris (1760–1842), who were both famous French ballet dancers and teachers. The Vestris family popularised the French ballet technique. In her article 'The Ballet: An American Lady's Opinion of the Opera', published in *The New Yorker* in 1841 (not the same publication as today's *New Yorker*), Sedgwick expresses intense dislike of the ballet, citing the artform as both immoral and unwomanly.
7. *au fait*: Skilled.

Mr. Redwood hoped, too, that this jaunt might lead to the accomplishment of a project which he had long secretly cherished; a union between his daughter and Charles Westall, the son of his earliest friend. He had transferred to the son the strong affection he bore to his father; and though he had not seen him since his childhood, he had from report, and from an occasional correspondence, conceived the highest opinion of his character. Time and philosophy had failed to subdue Mr. Redwood's ardent temperament: he still pressed on with eagerness to the accomplishment of his wishes, flattering himself all the while that he had ceased to be the dupe of the promises which the future makes to the inexperienced and the hopeful.

Mr. Redwood and his daughter had made the fashionable tour, that is to say, had visited the lakes, Niagara, and the Canadas,[8] and had turned their course towards Boston, when the unfortunate accident which has been mentioned put a stop to their progress, and deposited them for a while at the house of a respectable New England farmer.

---

8. From 1791 to 1841, the territory that is now the province of Quebec in Canada consisted of two separate British colonies, Upper Canada and Lower Canada.

CHAPTER V.

"She came—she is gone—we have met—
And meet, perhaps, never again."

Cowper.[1]

As the day closed, on which Mr. Redwood's journey had been so suddenly suspended, the full-orbed moon rose above the summit of the highest hills that border the eastern shore of Champlain. Not a vestige of the storm remained, not a cloud stained the clear vault of heaven, and the scene looked the more beautiful as contrasted with its recent turbulence. The vapour was condensed on the low grounds, and instead of impeding the rays of the "bright queen of heaven,"[2] looked as if she had sheltered some favourite spots with a silvery mantle; and the broad lake, glad to be relieved from the stern shadows that shrouded it, smiled and dimpled in the rich flood of light that fell on its bosom, and reflected in its clear mirror the pasture hills, covered with social herds, that descended to its margin; and the water-loving willow, the chestnut with its horizontal branches and pendent blossoms, and the little trig-birch that shadowed its brim. The location of the farmhouses planted here and there on the surrounding hills was marked by the tall Lombardy poplar, which through our country towns is everywhere the sign of a habitation. The moonbeams played on the white dwelling of Mr. Lenox, which had an air of prosperity and refinement above any of its neighbours, from the ample, well-fenced fields around it, a colony of barns behind it, and a neat little courtyard containing peach and cherry trees, and rose-bushes, and vines skilfully guided around the windows, and all enclosed by a curiously wrought fence, on which the village architect had exhausted all the cunning of his art. Mr. Lenox's family had retired to their several apartments, excepting those who were appointed to keep their vigils with the sick stranger. He had complained

---

1. *'She came—she is gone . . .'*: From William Cowper's poem 'Catharina' (composed 1789, published 1795).
2. *'bright queen of heaven'*: In 'The Knot' (1655) by English poet Henry Vaughan (1622–95), this phrase refers to the Virgin Mary, as it also does in a traditional Catholic hymn. However, in this context, the phrase figuratively refers to the sun.

of the closeness of the air, and Deborah had opened doors that communicated by a narrow passage with another apartment. She had then stationed herself near the door, where, after a few moments, her loud breathing announced that she was in a profound sleep. Mr. Redwood observed a female sitting in the passage and obscured by its shadows, who seemed to be stationed there to act as a prompter to Deborah, for whenever he was restless, she awoke the sleeper. In the opposite room he perceived the body of the young man he had heard spoken of; the head was placed directly under a window, through which the full-moon shone so brightly that every object was almost as distinctly seen as by the light of day. At another time, or in health, Mr. Redwood would have been quite unmoved by such a spectacle, for death has no heart-stirring associations to him who deems that the "spirit shall vanish into soft air, and we shall be hereafter as though we had never been,"[3] but there are few minds that are independent of the condition of the animal; and Mr. Redwood, weakened by his sufferings, and his imagination stimulated by a large dose of laudanum that had excited instead of composing him, felt himself yielding to the power of busy and bitter fancies. The light, graceful figure of the young female, as she gently moved to awaken the amazon, seemed to touch some secret spring of his imagination, and once, as he fell into a dreamy state, the wife of his youth was near him, but cold and silent as the dead form he had just closed his eyes upon; and when he started and awoke and saw the young female standing like a statue in the doorway, he identified her with his vision, and exclaimed, "for God's sake, speak to me." Deborah was awakened by the sound, and her coarse voice inquiring what he wanted, restored him at once to realities. She gave him at his request a composing draught, and again resumed her station, and saying she believed she had been almost asleep, she resumed instantly her harsh nasal sounds; the only sounds that broke the stillness of the night, save the falling of the swollen drops of water as they rolled from leaf to leaf on the branches of the trees about the window.

By degrees Mr. Redwood became composed, and was just yielding himself to nature's best medicine, when his attention was aroused by the sound of light footsteps approaching the house. He heard the latch of an outer door gently raised, (for here fastenings were considered a superfluity,) and a young girl glided into the opposite room. Mr. Redwood saw that she passed, observed, but not molested, by his attendant. His attention was now thoroughly excited. She lingered for a moment, apparently from irresolution or timidity, and then throwing aside a shawl in which

---

3. *'spirit shall vanish into soft air, and we shall hereafter be as though we had never been'*: From the Wisdom of Solomon 2: 2 (a biblical book considered apocryphal by some denominations).

CHAPTER V.

she had muffled herself, she knelt beside the body of the young man, and removing the covering from his face, she gazed intently upon it: the light fell on her own, still beautiful, though distorted and almost convulsed with the tumult of her feelings. After remaining for a few moments motionless, she laid her burning forehead on the cold breast of the young man, and sobbed passionately. The young lady who had been a passive spectator of the poor girl's involuntary grief, now advanced to shut the door, apparently with the purpose of sheltering her from the observation of the stranger, but he, perceiving her intention, and unable to repress his curiosity, called to entreat her to permit it to remain open. The loud sobs of the girl awakened the grandmother of the deceased, who, reluctant to separate herself for a moment from the body of her grandson, had insisted on performing herself the customary duty of watching with the dead; but overcome with her grief and infirmities, she had fallen asleep. She recognized immediately in the afflicted girl, the object of her child's youthful and constant affections; whose girlish coquetries and caprices had been the first cause of that "inward disease," which Deborah had pronounced the occasion of his death. She advanced to her with trembling steps, and laying her hand on the girl's head, and stroking back her beautiful hair, "poor, silly child," she said, in a pitiful tone, "you have come too late: once his heart would have leaped at a word from you, but he does not hear you now. He loved you, Annie, and for that I cannot help loving you;" and she stooped and kissed the girl, who was awed into silence by her unexpected appearance, and her calm tone. "A grief have you been to him, Anne; but the Lord changed his mourning into joy; for when friend and lover forsook him, then he turned to the sure friend. Oh," she continued, "he was my last earthly hope, the staff of my age; he was good, always good, but—" and the tears poured down her pale, wrinkled face, "but it was his adversities that made him wise unto salvation. Sorrow upon sorrow, cloud upon cloud, and he from the first such a feeling creature." Mrs. Allen's lamentation was interrupted by the hysterical sobbings of the penitent girl. "My poor child," she said, in a compassionate tone, "do not break your heart; sore mourning is it indeed for a wrong done to the dead, but it was not you, Annie, that killed him; no, that was just the beginning of it; then came his parents' losses, his father's death, and his mother's; but all these were dust on the balance, time to eternity, compared with the backsliding of Emily; his root withered when this branch was lopped off. Oh, my dear boy, how often have I heard you say you would die for her if thereby you could bring her back from her idolatry." Here the aged mourner was again interrupted, and all were startled by the rumbling of an approaching wagon; the young lady, quick as thought, flew to the window. "They are here," she exclaimed, and then turning to the old woman, "I entreat you, dear, dear Mrs. Allen," she said, "to leave the room; indeed you are not able to see them tonight."

"Oh, Ellen, I care not for myself, say not a word; this may be the Lord's set time to call home the wanderer; I will not shrink from the trial; if it was my last breath, I would spend it in setting her sin before her."

"But not now, Mrs. Allen, surely not now; this is not the time to harrow up the poor girl's feelings; consider for one moment she has yet to learn Edward's death; she is exhausted with her journey; spare her, spare yourself tonight."

"Ellen, you know not what you ask," replied the old woman, who seemed to gather strength and energy to obey what she regarded as a call of duty. "Are we not," she asked, "to pluck out the right eye, to pluck off the right arm, if thereby we may save the soul? Ellen, I will speak to her; and if she is not dead to natural affection, that pale, still face will send my words home to her heart."[4]

In vain Ellen argued and entreated. Mrs. Allen seemed persuaded, or as she expressed herself, she felt that now, if ever, was the set time for the deliverance of the child from captivity.

Debby roused at the near approach of the wagon, and again said, "she did not know but she had been dozing;" and listening to the bustle in the opposite apartment, "what does all this mean?" said she; "I thought Ellen was fit to be trusted; is there no discretion in a young head?"

Mr. Redwood assured her, that the young lady had not failed in her duty in the least; that the door had been continued open at his request. "Oh, well, well, it is all very well: it is a good rule never to cross the sick in their notions." While making this sage observation, she advanced to the window.

"For the land's sake," she exclaimed, "what has tempted Susan Allen to come with Emily! It will go nigh to break the old woman's heart to see her. Ah, there will be no good come of it, for there is that old grim master-devil, brother Reuben."

"In the name of heaven," exclaimed Mr. Redwood, "who is Emily? and who is Susan? am I dreaming, or what does it all mean?"

"No, man, you are not dreaming, but I guess in your right mind. Emily Allen is a young girl, twin-sister to Eddy there in the other room; she has been befooled by the shaking Quakers, at least by her Aunt Susan, that has been one these thirty years; and Susan is a half crazy woman

---

4. *Are we not . . . to pluck out the right eye . . . save the soul?*: Mrs. Allen here paraphrases the teaching of Jesus in the Sermon on the Mount that it is better to resist temptation by casting off part of one's body than to succumb to temptation and lose one's soul to damnation (Matthew 5: 28–30).

and half a saint; and there is the old woman that is mother to Susan and grandmother to Emily, that is taking on about them as if they were sold to the evil one. But, sir, we are disobeying Doctor Bristol's orders, and that an't honouring the physician with the honour that is due to him;" and thus concluding, she proceeded to close the door that led through the passage. Mr. Redwood had been beguiled of the tedious, sleepless hours, by the curious spectacle of natural feeling, undisguised by any of the artificial modes of society, and he was now determined to see the new characters that were entering on the scene. He entreated Deborah to permit the door to remain open, and she, after examining his pulse, and looking at his eye to detect any incipient wildness, decided that it would not be indiscreet to gratify him.

To convey to our readers a clear idea of this scene, we shall describe it as it really occurred, and not as it appeared to Mr. Redwood, who by the dim light, and at the distance he was laid from the parties, was compelled to be satisfied with a very imperfect observation.

Ellen opened the outer door for the two females, who entered dressed in the Shaker uniform, only remarkable for its severe simplicity and elaborate neatness. Both wore striped blue and white cotton gowns, with square muslin handkerchiefs pinned formally over the bosom, their hair combed back, and covered with muslin caps with straight borders, and white as the driven snow. Susan, the elder, was between forty and fifty years of age; she was tall and erect; and though rather slender in proportion to her height, well formed. There was an expression of command in all her movements that seemed natural to her, and sat gracefully upon her. Her face had the same character of habitual independence and native dignity: the hues of youth had faded, but a connoisseur would have pronounced her at a single glance to have been handsome. Her features were large, and all finely formed; her eye, there, where "the spirit has its throne of light,"[5] beamed with intelligence and tenderness. It was softened by a rich dark eyelash, and of that equivocal hue, between gray and hazel, which seems best adapted to show every change of feeling; but vain is this description of colour and shape. It was the expression of strong and rebuked passions, of tender and repressed affections, of disciplined serenity, and a soft melancholy, that seemed like the shadow of past sufferings, which altogether constituted the power and interest of her remarkable face.

The younger female was short and slightly formed. Her features were small; her blue eyes, light hair, and fair complexion, would have rendered her face insipid, but that it was rescued by an expression of purity and

---

5. *'spirit has its throne of light'*: A variation on a line from the poet Byron's *The Corsair* (1814).

innocence, and a certain appealing tender look, that suited well her quiet and amiable character.

As they entered, Ellen threw her arms around the younger sister, exclaiming in a tone of the tenderest concern, "Dear Emily, why did you not come sooner?" Emily trembled like an aspen leaf, and her heart beat as if it would have leapt from her bosom, but she made no reply. The elder sister grasped Ellen's hand, "Is it even so?" she said; she rightly interpreted Ellen's silence and sadness: "I foresaw," she continued, "that our coming would be worse than in vain:" then turning to her young companion, she said, "put thy hand on thy mouth and be still, my child. The Mighty One hath done it; strive not against Him, for he giveth not account of any of his matters."

A loud groan was heard in the apartment of the dead. Susan Allen started, and exclaimed, "Is my mother here? Then, mother Anne be with me!"[6] She paused for a moment, and added in a calm tone, "fear not, Emily, my child, in your weakness strength shall be made perfect; we shall not be left without the testimony."[7] Her words were quick, and her voice raised, as if she felt that she was contending against rebellious nature. She entered the room with a slow and firm step. Emily followed her, but it seemed not without faltering, for Ellen had passed her arm around her, and appeared to sustain half her weight. Her face was as pale as marble, and as still.

"Pray speak to them, Mrs. Allen," whispered Ellen. "Yes, speak to them," said Debby, in a voice of authority; "what signifies it! they are your own children, and there is no denying it."

"They were my children, but they have gone out from me, and are not of me," replied the old woman, in a voice scarcely audible. "I am alone; they are uprooted; I am as an old oak, whose leaf has withered; judgment has come out against me."

"She is going clean distracted," whispered Debby to Ellen, "you can do anything with her; make her hear to reason while she has any left, and get her to go out of the room with you."

"No, no," said the old woman, who had overheard Debby's whisper, "have no fear for me; my spirits are a little fluttered, and my soul is in travail for these wanderers, to get them back to my rest, and under my wing; but the Lord's own peace is in my heart, and none can trouble that. Oh," she continued, bursting into tears, as she turned her eyes from Emily to fix them on Susan, "was it not enough that you were led captive by Satan,

---

6. *mother Anne*: A reference to 'Mother' Anne Seton, the founder of the Shaker sect. See the introduction for more discussion of the Shakers.
7. *in your weakness strength shall be made perfect*: A reference to 2 Corinthians 12: 9 in the Bible.

enough for you to put on his livery, but you must tempt this child to follow you in your idolatries?" Strong sensibility is perhaps never extinguished; but Susan's was so subdued, that, obedient to the motion of her will, it had soon returned to flow in its customary channels. She replied to her mother's appeal in her usual deliberate manner. "The child is not my captive, mother, she has obeyed the gospel," and, added she, looking at Emily with affectionate complacency, "she has already travelled very far out of an evil nature, and the believers are looking to see her stand in the foremost light, so clear is the testimony of her life against all sin." Susan had an habitual influence over Emily; she felt that she commanded the springs that governed the mind of her timid disciple. Emily felt it too, and was glad to be saved from the efforts of self-dependence. She approached Susan, who had seated herself by the bedside, when her grandmother took her by the hand, and drawing her towards her, she said, in a voice scarcely audible, for sorrow, infirmity, and despair almost deprived her of utterance. "Oh, Emily, my child, my only child, has she bewitched you?" She drew the unresisting girl towards the body of her brother,—"there, look on him, Emily, though dead, he yet speaketh to you, and if nature is not quite dead in you, you will hear him; he calls to you to break to pieces your idols, and to come out from the abominations of the land whither ye have been carried away captive." Emily sighed heavily and wept, but said nothing. Susan moved to the other side of her, and seeming to lose the spirit of controversy in some gentle remembrance, she said, "Edward was a good youth, and lived up to the light he had. There is one point where all roads meet; one thing certain, mother," she added, an intelligent smile brightening her fine face, "we shall all be judged according to the light we have: some have a small, and some a great privilege."

"She has hit the nail on the head for once," whispered Debby to Ellen: "and now, Ellen, before they get into another snarl, do separate them."

Ellen's heart was full; she felt for all the parties a very tender, and an almost equal interest; and though she would have rejoiced in Emily's renunciation of her errors, she did not probably regard the sincere adoption of them with the terror and despair which the grandmother felt.

"My dear friends," she said, gently taking the hands of the mother and daughter, and joining them, "there is that in the face of your good Edward that bears an admonition to all our hearts, and teaches us all to remember how often we are commanded to love one another, and to be at peace one with another. It was the beloved apostle who said, 'He that doeth good is of God:'[8] may not then those who try to do his will, leave the rest to his mercy?" There was the eagerness and the authority of truth and goodness

---

8. *'He that doeth good is of God'*: From 3 John 1: 11 (KJV).

in Ellen's voice, and manner, and words; the spirit of love and of reconciliation; and the troubled waters would have been laid at rest, for the raised eye of the old lady showed that true devotion was working at her heart; and Susan looked on her acquiescingly and approvingly; and Emily's face shone with an expression of gratitude that her lips could not utter: but at this moment the outer door again opened, and Reuben Harrington, that one of "the brethren" whom Debby had characterized as the "master-devil," entered.

He seemed to have arrived at that age, which the poet has characterized as the period of self-indulgence; and, certainly, he bore no marks of having disobeyed the instincts of nature by any mortifications of the flesh. He was of a middling stature, inclining to corpulency; with a sanguine complexion, a low forehead deeply shaded with bushy black hair, that absolutely refused to conform to the sleekness of his order; a keen gray eye, which had a peculiarly cunning expression from a trick he had early acquired, and of which he could never rid himself, of tipping a knowing wink; a short thick nose turning upward; a wide mouth, with the corners sanctimoniously drawn down, and a prominent, fat chin, following the direction of his nose. In short, he presented a combination and a form to awaken the suspicions of the most credulous, and to confirm the strongest prejudices against a fraternity that would advance such a brother to its highest honours—or, to use their own phrase, to the 'lead.' Reuben advanced to the bedside quite unceremoniously, and seemed to survey the dead and the living with as much indifference as if he did not belong to their species. No one spoke to him, nor did he speak, till his attention was arrested by poor Annie, who had shrunk away from the side of the bed, and sat on a low chair at its foot enveloped in her shawl, and sobbing aloud, apparently unconscious that anyone saw or heard her. "Who is that young woman," inquired Harrington of Debby, "that is making such an unseemly ado; is she kin to the youth?"

"No!" uttered in her harshest voice, was all the reply Debby vouchsafed.

"Some tie of a carnal nature, ha?" pursued Harrington. "No such thing," said Debby, "Eddy was her sweetheart."

"Yea, yea, that is just what I meant, woman. Well," he continued, with a long-drawn guttural groan, "the children of this world must bake as they have brewed; they are in the transgression, and they must drink the bitter draught their own folly has mixed." After this consolatory harangue, he turned from the bedside and began, not humming, but shouting with the utmost power of his voice, a Shaker tune, at all times sufficiently dissonant, and that now, in this apartment of death and sorrow, sounded like the howl of an infernal: to this music he shuffled and whirled in the manner which his sect call dancing and 'labour worship.'

CHAPTER V.

"Stop your dumb pow-wow!" cried Debby, seizing him by the arm with a force that might have made a stouter heart than Reuben's rejoice in the protection of the convenient principle of non-resistance.

"Nay, ye world's woman, let me alone," said he, extricating himself from her grasp, and composing his neckcloth, which Deborah's rough handling had somewhat ruffled; "know me for a peaceable man, that wars not with earthly powers."

"True," replied Debby, "your war is with heavenly powers; but while the Lord is pleased to spare the strength of my right arm, I'll keep you peaceable. Peaceable, indeed! One would have thought all Bedlam had been let loose on us—peaceable! your yells almost scared the old lady's soul out of her body."

Poor Mrs. Allen, to whom Reuben's singing had sounded like a shout of victory from the infernal host, now really seemed in danger of such a catastrophe. She could scarcely raise her heavy eyelids, and the low moaning sounds that escaped her betrayed the infirmity of age, and the grief that words cannot express. Ellen renewed her entreaties that she would retire to her own room. No longer capable of resistance, she silently acquiesced, and Ellen conducted her to her bed, and watched over her, till she perceived that her wearied nature had sunk to repose. She then left her, and was softly closing the door, when she met Debby in the passage. "Now, child," said Deborah, "it is time that for once you should think a little of yourself; go to bed and take a good nap; there is no occasion for your going back to that room; it is quiet enough there now; poor little Annie stole away when nobody saw her, and I got the old man out, and gave him some victuals, and he is making a hearty meal."

"Where are Susan and Emily?" inquired Ellen, "they must need rest more than I do."

"Yes, poor souls, they need it enough, but they will not take it; they are only waiting for Reuben to go away again."

"Away—before the funeral?"

"Yes, and I think Susan has the right of it: she says, 'the dead need them not, and they are no comfort to the living.' And, to tell you the truth," she added, in a lower tone, "I suspect she is afraid to trust Emily here any longer. You know she and our James always had a notion for each other, and I guess Susan has found it out too; for though she is not much used to the world, she is a cute woman by natur',[9] and sees as far into a millstone as a'most anybody. I marked her looking at Emily when James came into the room, for you must know he came in just after you went out, and Emily's

---

9. *a cute woman by natur'*: Sedgwick uses 'cute' as a shortened form of 'acute', meaning smart or perceptive.

face that was as white as curds before, turned red to the very roots of her hair; and when James offered her his hand, she did not take it to be sure, for that is quite contrary to all Shaker rules and regulations; but she did not look the least affronted."

"I cannot think," said Ellen, shaking her head doubtfully, "that Emily has any attachment to James. If she had, why did she join the Shakers?" "Why! ah, that's more than I can tell. It passes the skill of a rational creature to give the whys and the wherefores of the motions of you young girls. I would as soon undertake to give a reason for the shiftings of the wind. But I am as sure that Emily Allen would rather stay with James, than to go back to the Shakers, as that I know a southerly breeze from a northwester." "But, Miss Deborah," asked Ellen, apparently still incredulous, "was there anything said that would warrant your conclusion?"

"Yes, a good deal was said, but very low, and I scarcely heard anything. But I did, however, hear James say, 'Oh, Emily, how can you bear to think of all poor Edward felt for you, and of your old grandmother, for it will certainly kill her, and go back again to those people?' Mind you, he did not say a word about himself, but he looked enough, and I am sure Emily understood him, for girls are quick enough at taking such ideas, and I saw the tears gush from her eyes, and she said, 'It is a great cross, James, but I must bear it.' Susan saw as much as I did, for she seemed as uneasy as a bird when a boy is robbing her nest. And she got up and told Emily, in her calm way, to go with her to the kitchen fire. And Emily followed her, and she will follow her home, though with a heavy heart in her bosom."

"But," said Ellen, "Emily shall not go against her inclination."

"Ah, there is the rub," replied Debby; "Susan has that in her that she can make people of a mind to do what they would hate to do for anybody else. I don't know what it is; she is not a stern woman, but it is a kind of nat'ral Authority, as if she was a born-queen."

"She is very good, certainly," said Ellen, as if trying to discover the secret of Susan's power.

"There it is," replied Debby, "there is no getting such a grapple upon young folks' hearts, without goodness. But come, Ellen, there is no use in our standing here paraphrasing the matter, do you go to bed, and I'll wait till this old vulture has done eating, and see them off, and then go back to the traveller's room; the laudanum has put him to sleep at last, and that is the best thing for him."

Ellen assured Deborah that she would comply with her wishes, after having made one effort to detain Emily. Deborah commended her zeal, but was quite hopeless of success. Ellen said, that if she could not persuade her to remain with them now, she might suggest some considerations that might weigh with her afterwards. Debby thought "that looked rational; but there was no calculating with certainty upon such a feeble piece; if Emily's head had been as strong as her heart, she would never have been led away by such fooleries."

Sanguine hope is the privilege of the young; and Ellen began her expostulations with her ardour unimpaired by Debby's suggestions. She appealed to Emily's reason, and to her feelings, for a long time, without producing any sensible effect. Both Susan and Emily sat in a fixed posture, with their eyes riveted on the floor. At last, the poor girl, unable any longer to smother the voice of nature, sobbed out, "What shall I do? What ought I to do?"

"Resist to the death," exclaimed Susan, in a voice of authority. "It is a strong temptation, child, but there is a way of escape. Come, Reuben," she added, turning to Harrington, "we cannot tarry here in safety any longer."

"I am ready to depart," he replied, "for my decaying nature is greatly refreshed by this carnal food. I feared before I took it, that, as the angel said to the prophet Elijah, my journey had been too great for me."[10]

"That is a small matter," said Susan; and then added in a lower tone, "Reuben, the child's soul is at stake:" and she followed him to the door, apparently to hasten his preparations. Ellen availed herself of this moment to ask Emily, at the same time placing her hand on the latch of the door that led into the apartment of the deceased, "if she would not once more look upon her brother."

"Oh, yes," said she, and for the first time instinctively obeying the impulse of her feelings, she darted through the door: Ellen closed it after her without following; believing that at this moment it was best to leave her to the unassisted workings of her natural affections. But Susan, as soon as she returned from laying her injunctions on Reuben, dreading what Ellen most wished, went to the door, and said, as calmly as she was able, for her fears were increased by seeing James Lenox standing beside Emily, and eagerly addressing her, "Come, my child, we wait for you; be not like a silly dove without heart; take up your cross again, a full cross though it may be, and turn your back upon the world." Emily, after a short struggle obeyed, but with evident reluctance. It was manifest that the cords which bound her were relaxed though not broken. Young Lenox followed her to the door, and unobserved even by Susan's watchful eye, he thrust a paper into her hand, which, without examining or offering to return it, she slipped into her bosom. A person of ordinary sagacity might have predicted, that from this moment the charm of the elder sister's power was dissolved, and that though accident and habit, and the natural submission of weakness, intellectual or physical, to power, might detain the youthful disciple in thralldom, it would no longer be the service of a willing heart. Emily

10. *my journey had been too great for me*: An allusion to 1 Kings 19:7.

took an affectionate leave of Ellen; and Susan, after having simply said, "Farewell," turned and added, "You meant well, Ellen—I know you meant well; but you have the voice of a charmer, and how should I be justified if I suffered this young child to be seduced from her obedience to the gospel?"

"Promise me, at least," said Ellen, "that you will not constrain Emily to remain among you; promise me that you will suffer her to see and hear from her friends."

"Ellen," replied Susan, in a tone of solemnity bordering on displeasure, "we have neither dungeons, bolts, nor chains. We care not for the poor service of the perishing body; but we would bring all into the obedience of the spirit; and," she concluded, looking at Emily with tearful eyes, "we would keep them there, if watching and praying can keep them: we have no other means."

"You promise then, what I ask?"

"I tell you, Ellen," she replied, "I need not promise. Emily is as free as I am—as you are."

"God grant that she may be," said Ellen, in a suppressed voice; and perceiving that she could gain nothing farther from the impracticable enthusiast, she relinquished her hand, which in her eagerness she had taken, and once more bidding farewell, they parted. The wagon drove away, and Ellen went to her own apartment, of which she would have been glad now to have been the sole tenant. She had been too much disturbed by the suffering of those she loved, to be able to compose herself to sleep; and she sat down by an eastern window, to ponder on the various feelings of the heterogeneous group of mourners that Edward's death had brought together.

'Oh,' thought she, as she gazed at the far stars in their "quiet and orderly courses,"[11] and then at the clear, still lake, in whose depths their beautiful images seemed to sleep: 'why is it, that all nature above us, and around is harmony, while we are left to such conflicts? The material world is performing the will of its Creator: the glorious sun is ever on its way, shining on the just and the unjust; the obedient planets roll on, in their appointed paths; the clouds distil their nourishing waters, and the winds are His messengers, as they pass, stirring the leaves and waving the ripening harvest.' Ellen's reflections might have led her to a solution of the mystery, satisfactory to herself at least, but their chain was broken by an exclamation from Miss Redwood, who, waking suddenly, exclaimed, "Good heavens, Miss what's your name, are you up already? Do be good enough to go to bed

---

11. *'quiet and orderly courses'*: From 'Observations on the Roman History' by George, Lord Lyttelton (1709–73), which was published posthumously in *The Works of George Lord Lyttelton* (1774).

again—I can never sleep when anyone is hazing about my room; and close the blind if you please, the light disturbs me."

Ellen smiled, but not thinking it important to explain the cause of her being up at an hour that Miss Redwood deemed so unseasonable, she let fall a neatly woven rush curtain, which but imperfectly excluded the impertinent intrusion of the approaching day; and, laying herself on her bed, she was soon in a sleep that Miss Redwood might have envied.

CHAPTER VI.

"Thus Aristippus mourned his noble race.
Annihilated by a double blow,
Nor son could hope, nor daughter more t'embrace.
And all Cyrene saddened at his woe."

Cowper.[1]

DOCTOR Bristol called on his patient the succeeding day; he found him feverish, and petulant in spite of his habitual politeness; he complained that the opiate had not been powerful enough. He anticipated a long delay; he was used to disappointment, and for himself could bear it; but he dreaded to encounter his daughter's impatience. Doctor Bristol understood too well the arts of his vocation, he was too sagacious a practitioner, not to have observed that a skilful application to the mind is often a surer remedy than any favourite or fashionable drug. He accounted satisfactorily to Mr. Redwood for the increase of fever; he detected and brought to light many favourable symptoms; he spoke of a ball which was to be given in the village, and intimated that some of the most respectable inhabitants would wait on Miss Redwood, and deem themselves honoured by her presence. He produced some late newspapers which he had procured at the post-office; the last foreign reviews; and succeeded in producing as sudden a change of symptoms as an empiric would have promised.

Mr. Redwood described the extraordinary scene he had witnessed during the night; asked many questions, and with particular interest in relation to the young lady whose face and demeanor had impressed him as belonging to an elevated sphere. Doctor Bristol assured him, that his sagacity was not at fault, for Miss Bruce (the young lady in question) was not a member of the Lenox family, but a stranger at Eton, and a friend of the Allens. Mr. Redwood said that the various modes of religious superstition always interested him; he was amused with seeing how willing

---

1. *'Thus Aristippus mourned his noble race . . .'*: From Cowper's translation of Greek verse, 'By Callimacus'.

man was to be the dupe of his own inventions; and intimating, that in the eye of experience and enlightened observation, all the forms of religious faith were equally absurd; shackles which men imposed, or wore, from tyranny or imbecility, he concluded by insinuating a compliment upon the free-thinking which was so common among the enlightened of the doctor's profession. Doctor Bristol, without assuming the attitude of combat, or seeming entirely to comprehend the drift of Mr. Redwood's remarks, observed, that there were, in his fraternity, some distinguished exceptions to the charge which had been laid against them. Everyone acknowledged the authority of Boerhaave's name,[2] "and our own Rush," he said, (speaking with honourable pride of his master,) "is among the most humane and enlightened of philosophers, and the most humble of Christians." Mr. Redwood perceived that he had not proceeded with his usual tact; that he had presumed too far upon what he considered the necessary result of Doctor Bristol's general intelligence. He avoided any farther remarks which might have a tendency to disclose his own sentiments, and confined himself to comments on the persons he had observed the preceding night. He said he hardly knew whether the opinions of those people seemed to him most ridiculous or shocking. "Truly, he knew not which most to pity; the poor old woman, who fancied a silly girl must lose all chance of salvation, because, forsooth, she had forsaken the world, and in good faith, joined a gloomy and self-denying order; or her child, the shaking Quaker who had immolated every right and natural affection to an imaginary duty; who had forsaken all that made life a blessing, to follow an ignorant fanatic, or an impudent impostor." The doctor acknowledged that such mistakes were lamentable; the result of limited knowledge, or accidental prejudices. Still, he thought, that while we lamented the errors to which we were liable, we might rejoice that the light we enjoyed, was light from heaven, though its clearness must depend somewhat on the purity of the atmosphere into which it was introduced; the mists of ignorance might dim, but did not extinguish its pure ray. If an immortal hope led these people to some unnecessary sacrifices, it stimulated them to those that were necessary; for he believed there was no variety of the Christian faith, however distorted from the perfection of the original model, which did not insist on a pure morality.

The doctor invited Mr. Redwood to observe the state of things about him; the wise and excellent institutions which had sprung from the religion of the pilgrims; the intelligence and morality that pervaded the mass of the people, which might be said to emanate from the principle of equality,

---

2. *Boerhaave's name*: Herman Boerhaave (1668–1738) was a Dutch physician credited with founding the bedside method of medical teaching.

derived from the Christian code. He spoke of the religious zeal and the active benevolence which pervades our society, which, not neglecting the means of moral regeneration at home, sends its missionaries to the fearful climate of the east; to the barbarians of the south, and to the savages of our own dangerous wilderness. These noble efforts were not, as in older countries, supported by the pious zeal of a few of the bountiful, or the gifts of the penitent rich, who by a kind of spiritual commutation, expected to purchase, by their brilliant charities, the remission of their sins; but, for the most part, they were the fruit of the virtuous self-denials and exertions of the laborious classes of the community.

Mr. Redwood listened with more patience than could have been expected from one who had philosophic prejudices; more inveterate, perhaps, than those which spring from the conceit of ignorance because they are fortified by the pride of knowledge, and assume the form of independent opinions, which is so flattering to our self-love. There was something, too, in Doctor Bristol's manner that recommended every sentiment he uttered; it was so calm, so dispassionate, there was so much of the serenity of truth in it. There were no extravagant statements; he did not insist that another should believe, because he felt the truth of such and such propositions; he did not enter into a formal argument, but intimated the grounds on which his own opinions had been formed, and permitted Mr. Redwood to draw his own conclusions, hoping they would be such, as seemed to him natural and inevitable.

Mr. Redwood made minute inquiries in relation to the Lenox family. He expressed his surprise and regret that they had not thought proper to interfere and detain by force, if necessary, the foolish little girl, who he predicted would soon be sick of her folly. He was pleased to hear that the doctor, as well as himself, regarded Deborah as an amusing original; and he again intimated some curiosity in relation to Miss Bruce, which the doctor either could not or did not choose to gratify. He did not allow the doctor to leave him till he had requested him to make his visits as long and as frequent as possible, nor till he had expressed, in the most flattering terms, his entire confidence in the doctor's professional ability.

Miss Redwood entered her father's room as Doctor Bristol left it, to make her dutiful inquiries, which were, perhaps, nearly as much a matter of form as the professional visit of the physician. After she had gone through the customary routine of, "how he had slept? how he felt himself," etc., she said, "if you have no objections, papa, I will take a drive this afternoon to the village while this funeral is going on here. Ralph tells me the injury done to the carriage yesterday was very slight, and that he can have it in order by one o'clock, the hour appointed for the funeral."

CHAPTER VI.

"If that is the case, my dear," replied Mr. Redwood, "you will gratify me if you will forego your ride, and offer the carriage for the use of the poor old woman and her young friend: they have not probably as convenient a mode of riding, and I am told it is customary in New England for the female relatives to follow the body to the grave."

"How barbarous!" exclaimed Miss Redwood; "but thank fortune, there is no occasion, for Lilly tells me, the old woman is too sick to go out, and is just to sit up and hear the sermon, and all that; and so, papa, if you have no objections I will take the carriage, and get out of the way: funerals are so disagreeable; I don't see the use of them."

The poet's doctrine, that "sweet are the uses of adversity,"[3] was nearly as foreign from the father's as the daughter's experience: but he perceived that the good will of the Lenox family would be of very material use to them; and thinking that it might be conciliated by the deference to their feelings which would be evinced by Miss Redwood's presence at the funeral solemnity, he requested her to gratify him by deferring her own inclinations. The request had too much authority in it to be denied; and though Miss Redwood thought it great folly to take the trouble to win favour which might be purchased, she did not in the end regret that she had complied with her father's request, so much was she amused with the number and aspect of the crowd which the occasion assembled.

The observances of a funeral in a country town in New England are quite primitive; but their simplicity is more touching than the most pompous ceremonial, for it speaks the language of nature to natural and universal feeling; and even to those who are not of that soft mould that is easily impressed by human sympathies, and who have only witnessed this last scene in the drama of life in a city, the spectacle of a country funeral must always be curious. In town, a funeral procession scarcely attracts the eye of the boy, who is carelessly trundling his hoop, or flying his kite, and the busy and the gay bustle past, as if they cared for none of these things, and had neither part nor lot in them. But in the country, where life is not so plentiful; where each knows his neighbour, the events of his life, and the hope he may have had in death; the full import and significance of this event is felt. Some will attend a funeral, because they remember a kind word or deed of the departed, or, it may be, a kind look that inspired a personal interest; some, from respect for the living; some, because it is good to go to the house of mourning: the old would not shrink from the admonition they hear there, and the old take the young because they ought not to shrink from it: some like to

---

3. *'sweet are the uses of adversity'*: From II, i of Shakespeare's *As You Like It.*

watch the tears of the mourners, and some to note there are no tears. The motives that draw any crowd together are almost as various as the persons that compose it. On this occasion there was an universal sentiment of compassion for the solitary aged mourner, and of respect for the memory of the departed. Miss Redwood took her station at one extremity of the apartment in which the assembly met. She was arrayed with studied elegance; Lilly stood on one side of her chair, and a footman in livery on the other: the body of the deceased was on the opposite side of the room: next to it sat Mrs. Allen, and beside her, and supporting her, Ellen, who, in a simple white dress, her face beaming with tender sympathy, looked like the embodied spirit of religion. Perhaps beauty is never more touching than when, exclusively occupied with the sufferings of others, it is lit up with that divine expression of tender compassion, which, to a religious imagination, is the peculiar attribute of an angel's face. Next Ellen sat Mr. and Mrs. Lenox and their numerous family, all clad in mourning; their sad looks suiting well with their badges of grief. The two youngest children were placed on a bench at their parents' feet, and whenever they could withdraw their eyes from the various objects that attracted them, they would peep into their parents' faces, and catching the expressive language of sorrow, fall to crying, till some new object diverted their attention. Miss Deborah, having no part of her own to perform, acted as mistress of ceremonies. She spoke, perhaps, oftener and louder than was necessary, but on the whole, she conducted her affairs with less official bustle than is common on such occasions. After having made a clear space for the clergyman in the centre of the room, and assigned to others their places, allotting the arrangement of the procession to a gigantic militia Major, who usually filled that office, she seated herself at the foot of the coffin, permitted a large gray cat, that came purring through the crowd, to take its usual station in her lap, composed her muscles to a rigid attention, and motioned to the clergyman to begin his duty. He made an affecting exhortation, founded on the fifteenth chapter of the Epistle to the Corinthians. A funeral hymn was sung, and he then proceeded to close the services with a prayer, not however until Deborah had whispered to him, "The old lady is just spent, be short, sir: pray but a breath or two." The aged mourner had listened without once raising her eyes, without a sigh or a movement. It seemed as if time or grief had dried the fountain of her tears, for not one was seen on her furrowed cheek. The services over, the Major ordered the crowd to fall back to the right and left, while the coffin was carried out. His order was obeyed, (though with somewhat less of military precision than it was given,) and the coffin was placed in the courtyard under the wide-spreading branches of an elm tree. He then returned to the door, and in the tone of military command, desired the mourners to advance and look at the corpse, and added a notice to the assembly to come forward immediately after the mourners had retired, it being necessary that all should take their last looks now, as the lid of the coffin was to be screwed down before the procession moved: a burst of grief from the group of mourners evinced that these commands, given out as the mere forms of preparation, were to them the dreadful signal of a final separation. Mrs. Allen rose from her chair, but even with Ellen's aid was unable to move forward till Doctor Bristol, advancing from the crowd, gave her the support of his stronger arm. She then approached the coffin, and bent for the last time over the body of her child; her tears, which had been checked till this moment, now flowed freely; and as she raised her head, she perceived they had fallen on Edward's face; she said nothing, but carefully wiped them away. "She is right," whispered Doctor Bristol to Ellen. "Edward has nothing more to do with tears: they are all wiped away." "Oh, my son," exclaimed Mrs. Allen, in a low broken voice, "Would to God Emily laid beside you; then would I thankfully lay down my weary body with you." "But," she added, after a moment's pause, in which her piety struggled with her nature, "God's will be done."

"Glad am I to hear those words," said Debby, who stood near enough to catch the feeble sounds: "the poor old lady's cup has been brimful of trouble so long, that it would not be strange if she did think herself something crowded on."

"Crowded on—what can the woman mean?" asked a young man of his companion; but before the inquirer could obtain a reply, he was jostled out of his place by others pressing eagerly forward to gaze for the last time on the face of the deceased. All, as they turned away, looked on Mrs. Allen, and some, perhaps, wondered that the leafless, scathed trunk should have been passed by, and the young sapling cut down in its prime and beauty. Mrs. Allen was led back to the house, attended by Ellen and Doctor Bristol; they passed through the apartment where Miss Redwood still maintained her station, and where she continued to gaze on all that passed before her, with the indifference with which she would have regarded the shifting scenes of a wearisome play: the Major approached her, and with awkward, but well-meant civility, told her she would have a good chance now to look at the corpse, and, being she was a stranger, he would see her through the crowd himself.

"Oh, thank you," she replied, disdainfully, "I have no fancy for looking at dead people, and certainly I shall not look at one dead, that I never saw living." The Major, thus rebuffed, turned away, and meeting Debby, he said in a low tone, "I rather think that young stranger girl has got to find out yet that she is mortal. Why bless my soul! a body would think her road did not lay grave-ward; but young, and handsome, and topping as she is, she must come to it at last. "She is a pretty creature though, to look at," he added, paying her the tribute of another full stare, "she is almost as handsome as the wax-work Rhode Island beauty."[4]

"Pooh, pooh," replied Debby, "handsome is that handsome does," and she glanced her eyes towards Ellen Bruce; "that is my rule, it is an old one, but it will never wear out."

"Miss Debby is right," whispered a pert girl, with the insolence of youth; "quite right to stick to everything that is old."

"Yes, yes," replied Debby, who unluckily overheard her, "quite right, till there is more reason to hope that the rising generation will make good the places of those who have gone before them."

"Miss Debby is right," whispered a pert girl, with the insolence of youth; "quite right to stick to everything that is old." "Yes, yes," replied Debby, who unluckily overheard her, "quite right, till there is more reason to hope that the rising generation will make good the places of those who have gone before them."

A call was now given to form the procession. Mrs. Allen was conducted by her kind attendants, to her own apartment. The rooms were cleared, the procession moved away, and the house was restored to its usual quiet and order.

---

4. *the wax-work Rhode-Island beauty:* Though the precise reference is unknown, travelling exhibitions of wax-work statues were popular in early nineteenth-century New England. While most of the statues were of very famous people, such as the early US presidents or favourite characters from history and literature, it was customary to display statues of living women under titles such as 'The New York Beauty' or, in this case, 'The Rhode Island Beauty' (see chapter 'Waxwork Museums' in Peter Benes, *For a Short Time Only: Itinerants and the Resurgence of Popular Culture in Early America*, University of Massachusetts Press, 2016).

CHAPTER VII.

"What folly I commit I dedicate to you."[1]
Two Gentlemen of Verona.

THE week that followed the funeral would have been passed by Miss Redwood in perfect listlessness, had not Miss Bruce excited her curiosity, and her curiosity been stimulated by the difficulty of its gratification. The following petulant production of her pen, a letter achieved to her grandmother after repeated and painful efforts, will afford a fair view of her feelings. It certainly is not a favourable specimen of her talents, for she had originally a strongly marked character; and abandoned from her infancy to the guidance of a doting and silly grandmother, and early initiated into fashionable and frivolous society, with uncommon intellectual capacities, and strong passions, she was permitted to devote herself to everything that was trifling, and in short, condemned to a perpetual childhood. But no farther remarks shall be intruded on the just inferences which the good sense of our readers will enable them, to deduce from the document itself.

"My dear grandmama,—I can fancy your vexation when you receive this letter; for you, and you alone, can form an adequate notion of my disappointments and present misery. As to papa, you know he never feels, nor thinks as you and I do.

"No doubt in your imagination I am figuring in the drawing-rooms of Boston, displaying those beautiful dresses you imported for this ill-starred journey; leading captive my thousands and my tens of thousands; living in an atmosphere of lovers' sighs, and on the eve of breaking a hundred hearts by my departure for the Springs, where we expected that a second harvest of conquest and glory awaited me. 'Now look on that picture, and on this.'[2] Here I am at a vulgar farmer's, on the outskirts of a town called Eton; and so changed am I, or rather everything about me is so changed, that I can

---

1. *'What folly I commit I dedicate to you.'*: From III, ii of Shakespeare's *Two Gentlemen of Verona.*
2. *'Now look on that picture, and on this'*: Variation on a line in III, iv of Shakespeare's *Hamlet.*

scarcely believe that not much more than one little month has elapsed since I was parading Broadway with Captain Fenwick—(by the way, Broadway is a sublime place for a real show-off,)—and he said to me, as admirer after admirer poured into my train, "You see, Miss Redwood, that you are the centre of the system,—the sun; and we, your satellites, humbly revolve around you." What would he think, what could he say, if he were to see me now; not a creature dazzled by my brightness, though there is not a rival star in the heavens? But a truce to lamentations, I will proceed to facts; and then, dear grandmama, you will perceive how much I deserve and need your pity. I must begin my relation at St. John's, where the only pleasant incident occurred which this letter will contain. You will remember that I wrote you from Montreal the particulars of my first interview with Captain Fitzgerald, *et cetera, et cetera, et cetera*: how many delightful gallantries and flattering speeches are included in these et ceteras! Speaking of Fitzgerald carries me back to Montreal; and I must say, en passant,[3] I was shockingly disappointed in the size and appearance of the city, which I expected to find as large as New York: and still more with the military band, for you know, grandmama, you always told me that since the revolution we had never had any military music fit to be heard. But, to return to our journey. The first person I beheld on arriving at St. John's was Fitzgerald; he had come there, as he whispered to me, to see me once more. Papa was very cold—almost rude to him; but I took care that my pleasure should be sufficiently apparent to compensate him for papa's incivility. It is so strange of papa, when he knows that Fitzgerald is the son of an earl, and brother to a lord; and if he is a little gay, as papa says he is, dissipation is universal among military men, and no fault of theirs of course. I don't see what good it does papa not to be religious, if he will make such a fuss about trifles. My dear grandmama, you would admire Fitzgerald; and you may have an opportunity; for he assured me, that if he could get up a cough that would furnish a pretext to ask leave of absence, he would pass the next winter at Charleston. He hinted at the possibility of meeting me at the Springs. I am ready to die with vexation when I think of what I may lose by our detention in this wretched place. It is but little more than a week, though it seems to me an age, since we met with the shocking accident which has caused our delay. Immediately on getting into our own carriage, (the sight of which was the first thing that revived me after parting with Fitzgerald.) we were overtaken by a tremendous thunder-storm, which, of course, almost deprived me of my senses; the lightning struck a number of trees, and the prodigious blaze that ensued, so terrified the horses, that they leaped over a precipice forty or fifty feet high. Fortunately, the carriage was

---

3. *en passant*: French phrase meaning 'in passing'.

not turned over, owing, I believe, though I never understood clearly how it was, to its being caught among the branches of the trees. I was wild with fright, and poor Lilly as white as my handkerchief. As soon as we were extricated from our perilous situation, we took refuge in the nearest farmhouse, glad, at the moment, of any shelter from the storm. We should have proceeded the same evening to the village, but papa had his arm horribly broken in jumping from the carriage, and here we were obliged to remain; and here we have a prospect of passing the remainder of papa's life; for strange to tell, he has put himself into the hands of a country doctor; and what is worse, though he never believed in anything before, he has taken a freak to place implicit confidence in this man, whose interest it is, you know, to detain him here as long as possible. This, papa does not seem to suspect, clairvoyant as he prides himself on being, and aided too, by the light of my hints, which, you may be sure, I have not spared. What is most extraordinary and provoking of all, is, that papa, who was never contented before in his life, appears as satisfied as if he had entered elysium; and never before patient, has suddenly become as patient as Job.

"There is one solution of the mystery which I hardly dare to commit to paper, lest some bird of the air should carry it to papa.

"You must know, grandmama, there is a young woman here, lady I suppose I must call her, for to confess the truth, she has every appearance of being one, that has inspired papa with the most surprising admiration, from the first moment that he saw her. I dare not say he is in love with her: I will not think it. I should go mad if I believed it; but he has the most unaccountable interest in her. Yesterday I said to him, with as much apparent carelessness as I could assume, 'Lilly tells me that this Miss Bruce is shortly to be married.'

"'Ah,' said he, starting from one of his fits of absence, 'to whom? Where did Lilly pick up this intelligence?' From some of the family; the happy man is a son of our host, a young parson.' 'Impossible!' exclaimed papa. 'Impossible, sir,' I echoed, 'why so?' The dear old gentleman was a little flustered for a moment, and then said, 'Miss Bruce is so superior to this Lenox family, so intelligent and cultivated.' 'But, papa, you are always crying up these Lenoxes for such knowing people.' 'They deserve our respect, Miss Redwood: they are excessively well-informed, and clever: but, Caroline, you must see the disparity between them and Miss Bruce; it is quite apparent: the gracefulness of her demeanor, the uncommon delicacy of her manners, and the very tones of her voice, mark her as a being of the highest order.' It is a gone case, thought I; but, hiding my thoughts in the depths of my heart, I replied, 'She has undoubtedly a more genteel air than these Lenox girls; but why should she be on intimate terms with the family, if she has such superior pretensions?' 'I know not,' he replied, pettishly; 'there is some tie to the Allens, I believe; but of course it is a subject which we cannot with any propriety investigate.' He then told me he was fatigued, and would like to be left alone; and as I came out of the room, he requested me to send Lilly to him. His reluctance to investigation was suddenly vanquished, for, as I afterwards learned from Lilly, he questioned, and cross-questioned her as to the source and amount of her intelligence.—Heaven grant it may be true!

"I cannot imagine how papa can feel any interest in this Lenox family; they are common, working, vulgar farmers. There is one oddity among them, whom they call an 'old girl;' a hideous monster—a giantess: I suspect a descendant of the New England witches; and I verily believe, if the truth was known, she has spell-bound papa. The wretch is really quite fond of him; for him she wrings the necks of her fattest fowls, and I hear her at this moment bawling to one of the boys, to kill the black-eared pig—for him no doubt. Notwithstanding her devotion to papa, she does not pay me the least respect, but lavishes all her favour on Ellen Bruce. I overheard her this morning saying to Mrs. Lenox, that Ellen was as much of a lady as that Caroliny gal, with all her flaunting ruffles and folderols. Ellen, she said, had been brought up to business; but as to that useless piece, she could neither act nor transact. She says, too, that, rather than have a fellow-*creter* tag round after her, as Lilly does after me, she would turn wild Indian.

"Only think, dear grandmama, of my being obliged to hear such rude things said without notice or resentment, for papa is very angry if I betray in the slightest degree my contempt and detestation of these people and their ways: even if I ridicule them, he quotes to me a wise old saw of Caesar's, or somebody's, that, 'He that condemns rusticity is himself a rustic.'[4] In heaven's name, of what use is rank or fortune, if it does not make you independent of such animals!

"In every respect this place is disagreeable to me. It fatigues me to death to see the family labour: labour, as you often say, grandmama, was made for slaves, and slaves for labour, but here, they toil on as if it were a pleasure. They have an immense farm, as they call their plantation, and but two servants, (one a negro,) or as they call them, helps; and well are they thus named, for they do no more work than the rest of the family; and what provokes me more than all, is, that these servants read and write, and are taught arithmetic, and the Lord knows what all; and Lilly and Ralph have this dreadful example before them. But the most ridiculous thing, is, the fuss these people make about learning, as they call all sorts of knowledge; one would think it was the philosopher's stone, by the pains they take to get

---

4. *'He that condemns rusticity is himself a rustic'*: From Julius Caesar's *Commentaries on the Gallic and Civil Wars* (52–51 BC).

it. After the girls 'have done up their work, and put everything to rights,' (this is their jargon,) they walk twice in a week, a mile and a half to the village to hear a man lecture on botany. I am sure you would expire with laughter, to see their boors of brothers come from their work in the fields, laden with flowers for their sisters to analyze, or preserve in their herbariums. There is a village library, and as much eagerness for the dull histories and travels it contains, as you and I ever felt to get a new novel into our possession. As to novels, there is no such thing as obtaining one, unless it be some of Miss Edgeworth's,[5] which scarcely deserve the name of novels. If I could but sleep as we used to in the country, and the country, as far as I can see, was made for nothing else, I could contrive to get rid of more of my time; but the air on the lake shore is so bracing, that for my life I cannot sleep more than nine or ten hours. These people are excessively civil to papa; but they seem to think they have a right to place themselves on an equality with me, and the more haughty my manners, the less attention they pay to me. Papa reads me long lectures about availing myself of this opportunity of studying human nature, and observing the different conditions of human life. Is it not unreasonable to expect me to care about such things? and if I did, I should as soon think of taking Robinson Crusoe's desert island for a study as this place. All of human life that I ever wish to see is limited to the drawing-room, ballroom, and other haunts of the beau monde. I should certainly die of ennui, if it were not that this Ellen Bruce excites my curiosity to such a degree: who can she be? I suspect that she is a natural child of somebody's, for whenever I have asked any questions about her connections, she is evidently troubled, and the people of the house affect to be quite ignorant of her parentage, and in reply to my inquiries, simply say, that she came from a distant part of the country: she is here with an old woman by the name of Allen, to whom she is devoted: she is an intimate friend of Mrs. Lenox, and not a relation of either; and to confess the truth, she is, as papa says, of an order quite superior to them. She is an orphan, and without fortune: so much the Lenoxes have condescended to tell me; without fortune, and yet her dress is of the finest materials; not exactly fashionable, as I said to papa: he replied, with some truth I must allow, 'but a model for fashion, Caroline.'

"One circumstance has excited my curiosity particularly: she rises every morning at the dawn of day, and sallies out, and does not return till the old woman is ready to rise, which is our breakfast hour, (papa's and mine;) and then papa, from great consideration for the trouble of the Lenoxes, begs Miss Bruce will do us the favour to sit at our table. On these occasions she

---

5. *Miss Edgeworth's*: Maria Edgeworth (1768–1849), an Anglo-Irish novelist to whom Sedgwick was frequently compared in her time. See the introduction for further discussion.

departs from her customary pensive style, her complexion, usually of the pale order, is quite brilliant, and her manner and conversation animated. Papa, very innocently, imputes all this to the benefit of morning exercise, and I as innocently, on one occasion, proposed to be her companion, an honour she politely declined without assigning any reason, though she has repeatedly offered to show me the pleasant walks in the neighbourhood.

"She expresses the greatest impatience to have Mrs. Allen well enough to return to her own residence; but this, I think, is mere affectation: and in this guessing, calculating, concluding, country, I have come to the conclusion, that if heaven does not speed the old woman's recovery, or the Lenox match, or some other insuperable obstacle, she and papa will get up a sentimental affair of it. A sentimental affair! papa fifty, and Miss Bruce nineteen or twenty: stranger things have happened—you remember my two old fools of lovers, who were well nigh fifty; they, it is true, were neither sick nor dull, like papa; but then Miss Bruce has neither fortune nor beauty; at least, I am sure you would not call her beautiful—who can she be, grandmama? Papa says she has received a first-rate education; but that is according to his queer, old-fashioned notions. She plays upon no instrument, and is not fond of dancing; of course you know she cannot dance well. As to French, she does not speak it at all, though papa says she is quite familiar with French and Italian authors, and she and papa talk over Racine and Ariosto,[6] and the Lord knows what all, at our interesting déjeuners,[7] which I am resolved to break up as soon as I have ascertained the object of the long morning walks that precede them. Write to me, dear grandmama, and direct to this place, and do not fail to let me know whether papa has the control of my fortune, so that if I should marry contrary to his wishes, he could deprive me of it: and pray ask Le Moine, whether the blue trimming was intended for the white or the brown dress; Lilly has forgotten, and I am quite at a loss about it. By the way, if poor Sarah should die, as you expect, before I return, don't mention it in your letters, for I want a good excuse for not putting on black—which would be horrible; as Maria Crayton says there is not a mantuamaker[8] in New England that can make a dress fit for a Christian to wear, and besides, you know one can have no variety in black. I cannot imagine where Miss Bruce has her dresses made; they are plain

---

6. *talk over Racine and Ariosto:* Jean Baptiste Racine (d. 1699) was a French playwright and, later, historian to Louis XIV. Ludovico Ariosto (1474–1533) was Italian poet of the Renaissance, famous for his epic poem *Orlando Furioso* (1516) and for his vernacular comedies modelled after the Latin style.
7. *déjeuners*: Plural form of the French word that can refer to breakfast or lunch.
8. *mantuamaker*: A mantua was a type of loose dress fashionable in the seventeenth and eighteenth centuries.

enough, but they sit exquisitely. Farewell, dear grandmama, I shall give you the earliest notice of any discoveries I may make.

"Postscript.—Thank heaven! papa has just given me leave to write to Mrs. Westall to come to Eton with Charles, so that I have a prospect of seeing two civilized beings, who will probably think me quite equal to this prodigy, Ellen Bruce: and I do not despair of finding a tolerable beau, *pro tem*,[9] in Charles Westall; though I think he will scarcely drive Fitzgerald out of my head or heart."

As curiosity is in its nature infectious, our readers may possibly have caught Miss Redwood's desire to know something more of Ellen Bruce's history than has yet been disclosed to them, and to gratify this inclination they may be willing to attend to a sketch of some other persons, with whose history hers is inextricably interwoven.

Justyn Allen, the father of Emily and Edward, was born in Connecticut, whence while a minor he emigrated with his father's family to the state of New York. There he and all the rest of the family, with the exception of his mother, were, for a short time, under the dominion of Anne Lee, the founder of the Shaker society: by the charitable deemed an enthusiast—by those of severer judgment, an imposter. At her first appearance in this country, she made many converts from among the respectable class of farmers. Her dominion however over the Allen family was of short duration, and after a few weeks of wild fanatacism, the father and children returned to the half-distracted mother, to lament or deride their delusion. Susan Allen, the youngest child, alone remained constant to her new faith, which she had been the last to adopt, and which had been endeared to her by difficult sacrifices. Justyn Allen as he was preparing, according to the uniform custom of our unportioned young farmers, to seek his fortunes in the west, received the intelligence of the death of a bachelor uncle, who had resided within forty miles of Boston, in a beautiful village, which we shall take the liberty of calling Lansdown. This uncle had bequeathed to Allen a valuable farm and all the appurtenances[10] thereunto belonging. He hastened to take possession of it; and to complete his happiness he married a well-educated and exemplary young woman from his native state. Five years after their marriage, Mrs. Allen returned from a short visit to Connecticut, bringing with her an infant girl, the child, as she said, of a young friend of hers, who had died within the first year of her marriage, and had bequeathed the child to her. There was no improbability in the story; and as no one in Lansdown knew Mrs. Allen's early connections, the busy, questioning spirit of village curiosity was not excited to inquiry or suspicion. Mrs. Allen was a woman who walked straight forward in the direct

---

9. *pro tem*: Latin phrase meaning 'for the time being' or 'temporary'.
10. *appurtenances*: Minor properties or accessories.

line of duty—simple in her manners, and ingenuous in her conduct; there was nothing about her to invite curiosity. It was observed that she loved the child tenderly; but that was natural, for besides that she was a most lovely little creature, she came to Mrs. Allen before she had children of her own to occupy her maternal affections. From the time the child, who had received the name of Ellen, could comprehend anything, Mrs. Allen had been in the habit of talking to her of her mother. But in spite of her efforts it was always in a sad tone; and once the child interrupted her to ask, "was not my mother good?" "Yes, my love, perfectly good." "Well, then, is she not glad to be in such a place as heaven?" "Yes, I believe so." "You need not look so sorry, then, when you are talking about her."

Mrs. Allen felt the propriety of the child's rebuke; but besides that it is always grievous to see a bud so early torn from its parent stock, there were bitter recollections associated with the memory of Ellen's mother, and especially with her death, that clouded Mrs. Allen's brow whenever she spoke of her. She did, however, in compliance with the last injunction of the unfortunate mother, faithfully endeavor to inspire the child with a love for her—to make hope take the place of memory; and by constantly cherishing the expectation of a reunion to her mother, she preserved in its strength the filial bond. It is only when our human affections are consecrated by a belief in their perpetuity, that they can have their perfect influence on the character. Ellen experienced the holy ministration of which they are capable from her earliest years. Before she reasoned, she felt a relation to heaven; her affections were set on things above. This shielded her innocence, and gave a tenderness and elevation to her character, as if the terrestrial had already put on the celestial. The natural gayety of childhood, though sometimes intermitted, was not impaired. Her eyes, it is true, were tearful while she sat on her little bench at Mrs. Allen's feet, and listened to stories of her mother; but the next moment she was playing with her kitten, or bounding away in pursuit of a butterfly—so natural is it for the opening flower to shrink from a chilling influence, and turn to the sunbeams.

Ellen had been told by Mrs. Allen that she had no father; and whenever the child's interest was excited about him, (which was not often, as Mrs. Allen studiously avoided all mention of him,) the answers to her inquiries were discreetly framed to lull her curiosity, without communicating the least information. The impression she received was that he had died at nearly the same time with her mother.

Her childhood glided on to her fifth year, bright as a cloudless morning, when an event occurred, that produced a great sensation in Lansdown, and materially affected the character and destiny of our heroine.

There was an estate adjoining Allen's, which from time immemorial (a period that in our young country may mean half a century) had belonged to the Harrisons, a family residing in Boston. It had the usual fate of the property of absentees— the house was out of repair, the fences in a ruinous condition, and the land from year to year depreciating from unfaithful husbandry.

Allen had gone on in the usual way, buying more cattle to graze his land, and more land to feed his cattle, till smitten with a desire to enlarge his territory, (the ruling passion of our farmers, each one of whom is said to covet all the land adjoining his own,) he cast his longing eyes on the Harrison farm, and easily persuaded himself there were good reasons in the nature of things why it should be united to his own. Both farms lay at the distance of half a mile from the village. Allen's was on an eminence, and divided from the Harrison estate by a small stream, whose annual overflowing enriched the low lands of his neighbour, without reaching to the elevation of his; with every rain the cream of his soil trickled down to his neighbour's, and the droughts that seared his fields left his neighbour's smiling in their verdant prosperity. Still the hand of the diligent, busy on Allen's farm, amply compensated for this natural disparity: and when he realized the profits of his labour and thriftiness, his hankering after the facilities of the adjoining property increased to such a degree, that he sent to the proprietor a proposition for the purchase of it, by one of his townsmen, a member of the State Legislature. Mr. Robert Harrison, the representative of his family, received the proposition with indignation, and failed not to express his surprise that anyone should presume to think he would part with a family estate. The honourable member, who was one of the numerous Cincinnatuses[11] of our country, called from the plough to patriotic duties, felt his new-made honours touched by this reflection on one of his constituents, and he replied, as to 'family estate, that was an old joke; that one family was as good as another nowadays, and that for his part, he must say, it was his humble opinion, that no family could be any honour to an estate, and no estate to a family, when it was left in such a condition as the Harrison farm at Lansdown.' The member's humble opinion stung the family pride of Mr. Robert Harrison; and from that moment he meditated a removal to the neglected farm, which, in the pride of his heart, he loved to call the family estate. Many circumstances strengthened his resolution. At the breaking out of the revolutionary war, Robert Harrison had just attained

---

11. *Cincinnatuses*: According to tradition, Lucius Quinctius Cincinnatus (c.519 BC to c.430 BC) was called upon to defend Rome from the Aequi, but, following a victory, Cincinnatus refused military honours and returned to his farm. George Washington was compared to Cincinnatus when he refused to assume political control of the US after successfully leading the American Revolution and simply returned to his estate until he was elected president.

his majority, and entered into the possession of a large fortune, with the expectation of succeeding to the honours of the provincial government, which his father had always enjoyed. Robert Harrison was allied to some noble families in the mother country, an important circumstance in the estimation of the untitled gentry of the colony. Possessing fortune, the favours of the government, and the distinctions of rank, and priding himself on the unstained loyalty of his ancestors, young Harrison naturally sided with the Tory party. He had everything to lose, and nothing to gain for himself from a change of government; and as to the rights of the people, which were the subject of contest, he held them in too great contempt to acknowledge they had any rights. Harrison, however blind he might be to the principle of natural justice, was soon obliged to feel that "might makes right," and he, with many other stanch friends of the government, in danger of being swept away by the tide of republicanism, sought a shelter in the mother country. There he soon after married a young lady, a Bostonian by birth, who had been sent home, according to the fashion of the most wealthy gentry in the colony, for her education. Similarity of opinion and of fortunes had united Robert Harrison to her father's family, and governed more by the accidents of their condition, than by any congeniality of character, she married him. Mrs. Harrison, from the age of thirteen to nineteen, immured in a boarding-school, came forth from it as ignorant of the motley mass called the world, as if she had been bred in a convent. Happily, her education had been conducted by a superior woman, who, proud of her pupil's extraordinary powers, had added to the common routine of boarding-school accomplishments judicious intellectual cultivation: so that even at this period, when a well-informed woman is neither a monster nor a prodigy, Mrs. Harrison would have been distinguished for her mental attainments. The exact habits of her school had given a preciseness to her manners, that veiled the warmth of her feelings, but never was there a more generous and tender spirit than she possessed.

Robert Harrison had a fine appearance and engaging manners; he was the object of her parents' partiality, and the first suitor for her favour: and, viewing him through the prismatic medium of romantic expectation and youthful fancy, it was not strange that she loved, or believed she loved him. Perhaps she was not herself conscious of the capacity of her affections, till the energies of maternal love were awakened by the birth of a child. This child, a girl, lived but five years; and when she died, her mother resigned her, as she would have done her own soul if it had been demanded, with unquestioning faith in the wisdom of the dispensation. But she never recovered her former spirits, though her mind, too active to remain the passive prey of grief, still pressed forward in the pursuit of some new attainment. She seemed to love knowledge for its own sake; her husband took no part nor interest in her pursuits, and as to the gratification of vanity in display, for that she had neither opportunity nor inclination.

The family remained in England till the peace in 1783, when they returned to this country, with their English affections and prejudices strengthened by habit, and endeared by the privations they had suffered on account of their loyalty. Mr. Harrison claimed his patrimonial estate, and found, to his bitter disappointment, that those persons who had been designated by name in the act of confiscation were excepted in the repeal of that act, and it was not his least mortification in finding himself one of this unfortunate number, that his property had gone to the support of a cause which he detested. The estate at Lansdown,—his household furniture and plate, and some personal property, he saved from the wreck of his fortune. This was a small portion of his rich inheritance; but skilfully managed by the domestic talents of Mrs. Harrison, it was sufficient for the limited expenses of a small establishment. The meanness of his fallen fortunes did not at all degrade his rank in his native town, for if some portions of our country must sustain the reproach of paying undue deference to the vulgar aristocracy of wealth, that part of it has always been exempt from this common fault of a commercial country. Neither did his English feelings render him less acceptable in the society of Boston; the first to prove a rebel child, she never lost in her resistance of authority, her love for the parent land.

But Mr. Harrison had not magnanimity of mind to enjoy the advantages that remained to him. He was perpetually harassed by seeing those who had been distinguished in their country's service, or diligent in the avenues of business which had been recently opened, arriving at wealth and honours which he looked upon as the exclusive right—the birthright of the higher orders. The higher orders had sunk to the uniform level of republicanism, to what Mr. Harrison was fond of calling, a church-yard equality; there even, he was hardly willing the high and the low, the rich and the poor, should meet together. Not all the courtesies and kindness of a cultivated and virtuous society could compensate Mr. Harrison for the mortification of seeing the mansion-house of his family in the possession of one of the mushroom gentry—an appellation he freely bestowed on every name not noted under the provincial government, and entitled to no more credit or honour in his eyes, than a parchment deed without the crown stamp.

The years rolled heavily on; Mrs. Harrison's parents had been gathered to their fathers, and independent in her pursuits, and active in her habits, her life passed without discontent or ennui. When her husband proposed their removal to Lansdown, she acquiesced willingly, in the hope that he would become interested in the little concerns of his farm, and forget the trifling vexations that in Boston disturbed his peace. Confirmed in his wishes by his wife, who exercised a discreet, and therefore an insensible influence over him, Mr. Harrison vested his property in an annuity in the British funds, and removed to Lansdown. This new arrangement of his pecuniary affairs afforded him a larger income than he had enjoyed for a long time, and enabled him to restore the place at Lansdown to its primitive order and dignity. The house was newly painted, the fences rebuilt, and the garden restocked with fruit trees and plants.

Mrs. Harrison gently remonstrated against the removal of the antique and ponderous furniture, and even hazarded the profane suggestion that it would be wise to dispose of it at auction, and to procure that which would be more adapted to their present fortune, and in better keeping with the simplicity of country life, and which would neither expose them to the sneers nor envy of their neighbours.

"Neighbours!" replied the irritated husband, "I wish you to understand once for all, Mrs. Harrison, that I mean to have no neighbours. The people of Lansdown remember the habits of the family too well to presume to associate with us. As to the furniture, I have made up my mind about that, and you know my mind, once made up, is not given to change; therefore, Mrs. Harrison, you will be so good as to order every article of our furniture, large and small, packed up with the greatest possible care." Mrs. Harrison reserved all her opposition to her husband for matters that she deemed important; the furniture was packed; and arranged at Lansdown with her best skill: and there Mr. Harrison surveyed, with infinite complacency, the Turkey carpets, damask curtains and sofas, the cumbrous mahogany chairs, and family plate studiously arranged in an old-fashioned buffet with glass doors, and the loyal garnishing of the walls decorated with approved likenesses of their majesties and their hopeful offspring, and with proof prints of the royal parks and palaces. Mrs. Harrison, though she could but smile at this parade of the relics of their departed wealth and grandeur, took a benevolent pleasure in ministering to the gratification of her husband; and when she left him in the parlour still gazing on the memorials of patrimonial splendour, and retired to arrange in a small apartment adjoining her bedroom (in which were her books and drawing materials) some choice or favourite plants: 'we must both,' she thought, 'have our playthings. If you had lived, my sweet Mary,' she said, turning her eye on a beautiful picture of her child, that hung at the foot of her bed, 'we might have had occupation that would have saved us from thus prolonging our childhood.' Her attention was attracted by the sound of a light footstep, and a beautiful little girl entered her apartment with a basket of fine early peaches, which she timidly offered to Mrs. Harrison, with Mrs. Allen's respects. Mrs. Harrison's mind was at this moment filled with the image of her child, and she saw, or fancied she saw, a striking resemblance between the portrait and the little stranger. She looked from one to the other; the eyes were of the same deep blue, there was the same peculiar, and as she thought, heavenly grace of the mouth; the hair, too, a light and bright brown, fell in the same natural curls over her neck and shoulders. "Oh, my own, dear Mary," she exclaimed, as she placed the child on her lap, and gazed on her, "I can almost fancy you are again in my arms; and yet," she added, as the tears gushed from her eyes, "she has not quite that look my Mary had." Ellen Bruce, (for it was she,) after looking in silent amazement for a few moments at Mrs. Harrison, said, "I wish I was your Mary, and then you would not be so sorry."

"Sweet child," exclaimed Mrs. Harrison, wiping away her tears, and smiling on her, "and who are you—who is your mother?"

"Oh, I don't live with my mother, she lives in heaven, Mrs. Allen says."

"Who then do you live with, my love?"

"I live with our little Emily's mother."

"And who is she?"

"Why, Mrs. Allen; did not you know that she had little twin babies?"

"No, my dear child; but if you will show me the way to Mrs. Allen's, I will go with you and see her:" so saying, she threw on her hat and shawl, and was descending the stairs with the little girl, when she met her husband in quest of her. "My dear," said he, snapping his fingers, and speaking in an unusually animated tone, "here is an English paper—and glorious news! The English have gained a complete victory: thank God! that cowardly rascal Bonaparte is beaten at last."[12]

"I am glad of it," replied Mrs. Harrison, turning from him to pursue her first intention.

"Glad of it! Pshaw, is that all—what is the matter—where are you going? here are all the particulars; the number engaged, the names of the officers, a list of the killed, wounded and prisoners: everything most satisfactory; none of your lying French bulletins, but English—fair John Bull[13] style; every word true—true as the gospel."

"I am very glad of it," repeated Mrs. Harrison, "I will read it the moment I return from leading this little girl home; she has brought us some delicious peaches from one of our neighbours."

"Send one of the servants with her; I am impatient to hear you read these accounts; there are many private letters from the officers that were in the action, and besides," he added, lowering his voice, "the people about us are quite too much inclined to familiarity already. I do not wish you to encourage them. Here Betsey," he vociferated to the servant girl, "lead this child home." Mrs. Harrison led Ellen to the door, and kissing and begging

---

12. Mr. Harrison probably refers here to the British victory over the French army in Alexandria, Egypt, in 1801, which led to the short-lived Peace of Amiens from 1802–3. The Napoleonic Wars between France and Britain resumed in 1803, however, and Napoleon was not decisively defeated until 1815.
13. *John Bull*: Similar to Uncle Sam in the US, John Bull is a fictional figure in England who represents English patriotism and was often featured in political cartoons during the Napoleonic Wars.

her to come again to see her, she transferred her to the care of the servant, and returned to soothe her husband with all the interest she could command in the details of the victory.

Ellen Bruce had received such various and confused impressions during her short visit to the mansion-house that she was unable to give a clear report of it to Mrs. Allen, and, as the child brought no word of acknowledgment for the peaches, Mrs. Allen naturally concluded that her first neighbourly overtures were unkindly taken; her husband completed her mortification by asking her, "how she could make such a mistake as to suppose that the duke (a title already bestowed on Mr. Harrison by his republican neighbours) could eat fruit that did not grow on the 'family estate?'"

Mrs. Allen, with all her good sense, was not quite free from the jealous pride that pervades her class in New England: she resolved not to waste her courtesies upon those who disdained them; and when Ellen, calling to mind Mrs. Harrison's invitation to her, begged leave to carry her some more peaches, Mrs. Allen said, "No! if the peaches were worth sending, they were worth thanking for." Ellen rather felt than understood the reply, and she answered, "but I am sure the lady spoke very kind to me."

"Ah, yes, my dear, that is an easy matter, everybody speaks kind to you; it is not necessary to force you upon anyone's notice; when Mrs. Harrison sends for you, it will be time enough for you to go to her." Ellen had no purpose of disobedience, but surprised at the unwonted strictness of Mrs. Allen, she determined to lay aside all the peaches that were given to her for the lady, whose kind manner to her had made a deep impression.

In the meantime, Mrs. Harrison possessed herself of all that was known in the village of Ellen Bruce's brief history; and the whole amount of it was that she was the orphan child of a friend of Mrs. Allen's, and had been adopted in her infancy by that excellent woman, and treated with maternal kindness. 'Oh, had Providence destined her to my protection, what a solace, what a delight she would have been to me,' thought Mrs. Harrison: 'and even now, could I persuade my husband to indulge me in going to the Allens, I might obtain this little creature to lighten some of my heavy hours.' She determined to watch for some propitious moment before she ventured to explain her wishes: a happy accident might throw the child again in her way, and such an accident she thought had occurred, when, a few days after the first interview, as she was walking with her husband past Mrs. Allen's, she saw the child come bounding towards her with her apron full of peaches.

"Oh, how glad I am," said she, on coming up to Mrs. Harrison, her eyes sparkling, and her cheeks glowing; "here, take them all, they are mine, and I saved them all for you." "For me," replied Mrs. Harrison, kissing her, "and for this gentleman?"

"For the duke! Oh no," replied little Ellen, with fatal simplicity; "Mr. Allen says the duke will not eat our peaches."

"What," exclaimed Mr. Harrison, "does the little impudent baggage mean by calling me the duke?"

"Everybody calls him that name," said Ellen, lowering her voice, and drawing closer to Mrs. Harrison.

"Nevermind, my love," whispered Mrs. Harrison, while she kissed her, "run home, and do come very soon to see me." Then turning to her husband, she said, "I declare our neighbours are half right; you have quite a look of nobility, my dear husband; you might pass in more knowing eyes than theirs for a peer of the realm: to say nothing of a certain dignity that belongs to the born gentleman, your gold-headed cane, your powdered head, and antique buckles give you an air that must be quite provoking to our republican neighbours." "Ah, indeed, I believe it, Mrs. Harrison: but our neighbours, as you call them, mean no compliment; this is a mere mockery on their lips." "Oh yes," replied Mrs. Harrison, "I suppose so: that is to say, it is a jocular title they have given you, to console themselves for your superiority."

"Very likely, very likely," replied the husband, and then added, "I think, Mrs. Harrison, my dear, that you must be convinced by this time that the less you have to do with these people the better." Mrs. Harrison made no reply; she usually conformed to the spirit of the promise contained in the Dutch marriage service,[14] maintaining silence in the presence of her husband; it was the least difficult expression of acquiescence, and long habit had given her a facility in this extraordinary virtue.

The weeks passed on, autumn succeeded to summer, and Mrs. Harrison seemed farther than ever from procuring an intercourse with little Ellen. During the warm weather she had occasionally seen her bounding over the field with the elastic step of joyous childhood, but now her careful guardian kept her cautiously within doors. It was a cold night, the last of November; Mrs. Harrison's household was all in bed except herself, and she, insensible to the blasts that howled about her dwelling, was poring over an interesting book, when she was reminded of the lateness of the hour by the candle sinking into the socket. At this moment a bright light flashed through the window and shone on the opposite wall; she hastened to the window to ascertain the cause, and screamed, "Oh heavens! Allen's house is on fire." Her shriek aroused her husband, who exclaimed, "Lord

---

14. *promise contained in the Dutch marriage service:* The narrator here refers to the marriage service of the Dutch Reformed Church, which at an earlier time had included not only the well-known bridal vow to 'love, honour, and obey' the husband, but to defer or submit to the husband in all matters and to keep any disagreements to herself.

bless me, is it possible! Call the servants, my dear, and send them to help the poor folks."

Mrs. Harrison, without awaiting this direction, had hastened to awaken the servants; and then rushed out of the house herself, and proceeded with all possible speed to the Allens, full of the horrible apprehension that the family would be consumed by the flames. The bright light clearly defined every object; the naked branches of the trees, every twig, every withered leaf she saw plainly, but heard no human voice, nor saw a moving form. Avoiding the public road, which was circuitous, she proceeded in a straight line across the fields, surmounted the fences almost unconsciously, and passed through the shallow stream that divided the farms. She was within a few yards of the house, the fowls roused from their roost were crowing, and the pigeons startled from their nestling-place were fluttering over the flames: still none of the family appeared. She screamed with all the power of her voice, while she hastened onward, despairing of the lives of the unfortunate family. The back part of the house, which she had approached, was enveloped in flames; she passed around to the front, and at that moment the door opened, and Allen and his wife with her twin infants in her arms, rushed, as it appeared, from the midst of the fire. Mrs. Harrison caught her arm as she was passing her; "where," she exclaimed, "is your child?"

"My child!" she replied, amazed with terror. "Oh God! Ellen—she is there;" and hugging her children closer to her breast, she pointed to the flames. Mrs. Harrison looked around for assistance, there was no one near: Allen, stupefied with fright, had gone with a single pail to a well at some distance from the house; other members of the family, who had escaped by different windows, were so bewildered with terror as to be incapable of rendering the slightest aid. Mrs. Harrison's resolution was instantly taken; "Tell me where she sleeps," she cried, "it may be possible to reach her through a window."

"Oh! There is no window, she is in the dark room next mine; and this—this is mine," she added, pointing to a front apartment which the flames had not yet reached. Mrs. Harrison darted forward and entered the house; the flames were above her, before her, around her. The passage was so darkened with smoke that she could not perceive the door she sought, but inspired with preternatural courage, menaced with death on every side, already scorching with the heat, and nearly suffocated with the smoke, she pressed forward till she reached a passage-way that crossed the entrance at right angles. The flames now burst through the wall at the extremity opposite the door she had entered, and the air rushing in, rolled away a volume of smoke, and discovered Ellen standing at her door, with her hand still on the latch, a dog was crouching at her feet, yelping, pulling her night dress with his teeth, and urging her forward with the most expressive supplications: still, the little creature shrunk from the terrors before her, unconscious of the fatal risk of delay. Mrs. Harrison snatched her in her arms, rushed through the door, and in an instant was at Mrs. Allen's side. Both instinctively sunk on their knees—no sound escaped from them, but the rapture of gratitude was in their hearts, and its incense rose to Him who had rescued them from impending death.

The fire had been communicated from a back building, which was joined to the front (recently erected by Allen) by a narrow covered passage. Fortunately the wind, though blowing violently, was in a direction to retard the progress of the flames: to extinguish them was impossible, for the house was of wood, and the only fire-engine in the town was at too great a distance to render any assistance. But had the family been self-collected after they were awakened by Mrs. Harrison's screams, they might have saved all the house contained of value. No one, however, seemed capable of a well-directed effort, till Roger, Mrs. Harrison's English servant, arriving on the field of action, called to Allen to follow him, and forcing his way through the window of Mrs. Allen's apartment, he succeeded in clearing it of the furniture, and placing it at a safe distance from the destructive element. The family, and the few persons who had come to their aid, gathered around the relics; little Ellen stood with one hand in Mrs. Harrison's, one arm lovingly encircled the neck of the faithful animal that first broke her slumbers; the whole group remained impotent and silent spectators, till the house sunk a ruin under the still crackling flames.

Mrs. Harrison first broke silence; "I am sure, my good friends," said she, "you are thinking more of what is left than what is taken."

"Indeed you have guessed right, ma'am," replied Allen, venting his agitated spirits in loud sobs. "The Lord that has spared my wife and little ones and Ellen, is welcome to all the rest. If I could but have saved my Bible that my mother gave me, and my wife's silver tankard, I would just care no more than if it was a bonfire." The mention of the excepted articles seemed to recall to Mrs. Allen's mind something of importance. She exclaimed, "Poor Ellen," and looked anxiously around her, till her eye falling on a trunk, she hastily opened it and took from it a small box; then turning to her husband, "God be praised," she said, "everything of value is saved." The first strong emotions of gratitude having been directed to the Supreme Preserver, they now began, with one voice, to pour out their thanks to Mrs. Harrison, whose generous agency they felt deeply. She begged them to defer all such expressions, and urging the necessity of a shelter for their little ones, she insisted on their going home with her. The good farmer and his wife forgot their scruples in their gratitude and necessities; and in a short time they were comfortably housed at the Harrison mansion. After Mrs. Harrison had made every provision for the refreshment and repose of her guests, and after she had stowed away little Ellen in a room adjoining her own, and extended her hospitalities even to the dog, her faithful coadjutor in the preservation of the child, she retired to her own room, nerved by gratitude and joy, to the task of reconciling her husband to the liberties she had taken with the family mansion. So strikingly did she delineate the dangers and escape of the family, the risk she herself had run, the rescue of the child, and finally, the exertions of Roger, his truly English coolness and intrepidity, that Mr. Harrison himself anticipated the conclusion of the story, by exclaiming, "Lord bless me, my dear! I hope you brought the unfortunate people home with you?" "Certainly, my dear," she replied. "You did right—perfectly right. There is no other establishment in Lansdown equal to giving them all a shelter. But Martha, my dear," he continued, "you ran a great risk—quite an unwarrantable risk, considering the relative importance of your life to that of the child's."

"Oh! Thank you for thinking my life so important. I only acted like a dutiful wife, and emulated your example. You have forgotten at what hazard you saved Charles Lindsay's life." "Forgotten! No, my dear; but then you know a man has always more self-possession than a woman, more mind for emergencies, and besides, Charles was the sole heir of an honourable family—some compensation for the risk. However, all is well that ends well. You have shown a spirit worthy of a noble name, Martha, my dear; and I shall take particular pleasure in writing an account of the whole affair to Sir Harry by the next ship that sails for London."

Mrs. Harrison, having thus succeeded beyond her utmost hopes in making a favourable impression on the mind of her husband, retired to rest; her bosom filled with those sweet emotions that are the peculiar property and rich reward of the virtuous. If Mrs. Harrison felt any anxiety the succeeding day about the intercourse of the host and his guests, it was removed when she saw that the sense of protection and condescending kindness on the one part, and of gratitude on the other, produced a happy state of feeling between the respective parties.

CHAPTER VIII.

"Oh, 'tis the curse of love and still approved,
When women cannot love, when they're beloved."[1]
Two Gentlemen of Verona.

IN the week following the destruction of his own house, Mr. Allen succeeded in obtaining another for the accommodation of his family till the following summer. The rigors of the stern season then approaching, rendering it necessary to defer the rebuilding of his own, Mrs. Harrison proposed to Mrs. Allen to leave Ellen Bruce at the mansion-house till she should again be re-established in her own home. There were such obvious advantages in this arrangement for the child, Mrs. Harrison pressed her request so earnestly, and Mrs. Allen felt that it would be so ungrateful to refuse, that she yielded her own inclination, and left Ellen with her devoted friend. The presence of this sweet child operated on Mrs. Harrison's affections as the first breaking out of the sun after a long series of cloudy weather upon the physical constitution. She had been resigned in afflictions, patient under all those often recurring vexations and petty disappointments that are by general consent pronounced more trying to human virtue than great calamities; she had endured for twenty years the exacting consequential peevish selfishness of a husband, in all respects dissimilar to herself, in most inferior; and she had become neither nervous, petulant, nor selfish. Indeed so successful were her dutiful efforts, that all her acquaintance deemed her quite blind to her husband's faults; and that she was not, never appeared except when, to attain some good purpose, her cautious and adroit approaches to his mind betrayed that she knew where his prejudices were stationed, and where his passions ruled. If the hasty affections of her youth had been alienated by her husband's faults, their place had been supplied by the resolution of virtue, and by the tolerance of a tender nature that felt more pity than aversion for human frailty; and finally, perhaps she loved him; for neither her words nor actions ever expressed that she did not: if the

---

1. *'Oh, 'tis the curse of love and still approved . . .'*: From V, iv of Shakespeare's *Two Gentlemen of Verona.*

maidenly reserve that "never tells a love,"² is the poet's eloquent theme, the matronly virtue that conceals the want of it, is certainly far more deserving of the moralist's praise.

Little Ellen opened the fountain of Mrs. Harrison's affections: and such was the renovating influence produced on her, that her husband, who never dreamed whence it proceeded, remarked how prodigiously the country winter improved her health and spirits; and congratulated himself upon his wise decision to remove from the chilling airs of the coast to the family estate, always noted for its salubrious situation.

Every moment of leisure Mrs. Harrison devoted to her little favourite. She taught her everything she was capable of receiving at the age of five years, in the way of formal instruction. She was the ingenious mistress, and the partaker of her innocent revels. She insinuated moral, and it may be added, religious principles into her mind, in the winning form of stories She warred against the natural selfishness of childhood in all its specious forms, and she completely subdued an impetuosity of temper, that had been suffered, if not nurtured by Mrs. Allen's indulgence: in short, she seemed constantly to realize that she had the training of an immortal creature; and to feel that so sweet a form as Ellen's should "envelope and contain" nought but "celestial spirits."³

Allen began with the return of summer the rebuilding of his house; and assisted by the voluntary contributions of his townsmen, he soon completed it. The prompt benevolence of our country people on such occasions has been justly celebrated by a foreigner, an observer (perhaps a partial one) of our manners.

> "Ici tous sont égaux: l'abondance est commune,
> On ignore les nonas de crime et d'infortune,
> Si le feu, si l'orage a fait un indigent
> La bienfaisance accourt; c'est l'effet d'un moment."⁴

The time at length arrived for Mrs. Allen to reclaim Ellen. Mrs. Harrison urged delay after delay, and was so earnestly seconded by her husband, (who had been beguiled of his uncomfortable stateliness by the playful

---

2. *'never tells a love'*: A variation on 'she never told her love' from II, iv of Shakespeare's *Twelfth Night*.
3. *'envelope and contain'... 'celestial spirits'*: From I, i of Shakespeare's *Henry V*.
4. *'Ici tous sont égaux...'*: The source has not been identified, but the quoted French passage means:
   All are equal here: abundance is shared
   Crime and misfortune are unheard of
   If poverty is brought about by fire or storm
   Charity abounds instantly.

little creature,) that Mrs. Allen finally consented to surrender her own inclinations, and to make a permanent arrangement with Mrs. Harrison, which should allow Ellen to pass half her time at the mansion-house. In this arrangement there was a system of checks and balances, that produced that singular and felicitous union of diversity of qualities which constituted the rare perfection of Ellen's character. Mrs. Harrison communicated her taste and skill in drawing, her knowledge of French and Italian, and all those arts of female handicraft that were the fashion of her day. Her pupil was taught curiously to explore the records of history, and to delight in the creations of poetry. When she might have been in danger of an exclusive taste for the elegant occupations of those who have the privilege of independence and of leisure, she returned to Mrs. Allen to take her lessons in practical life, to share and lighten the domestic cares of her good friend, and to acquire those household arts that it might be the duty of her station to perform, and which it is the duty of every station to understand. Ellen might have caught the pensiveness of Mrs. Harrison's manner, with its grace and polish: she might have forgotten the active duties of life in listening with her to the melody of nature—the music of the passing stream, the rustling of the leaves, or the song of the birds, or in watching the changeful forms of the summer clouds, as their shadows dropped on the mountain's side, or danced in frolic humours over the grassy fields and thick standing corn. But for all this, the danger of secluded life to those who possess sensibility and taste, there was an antidote in the occupations of Mrs. Allen's household—the spell of imagination was dispelled by the actual services of life.

Had Ellen been less grateful or affectionate in her nature, she might have loved one of her guardians to the exclusion of the other; but she felt their gratuitous kindness with the sensibility of a truly generous mind; she saw in them the parents that Providence had provided for her orphanage, and without any of the pride or restlessness of dependence, her devotion to them both evinced her eager desire that they should realize the highest rewards of benevolence.

Had her friends been less excellent than they were, some mischief might have resulted to our heroine from the diversity of their religious opinions. Both were Christians in faith and experience, but Mrs. Harrison was educated in the Episcopal church, and was exact in all its observances: and Mrs. Allen, a lineal descendant of the pilgrims, was as rigid in her faith as was compatible with the mildness of her character. The 'natural enmity' that bigots might have found, or made, between their respective faiths, was destroyed by the spirit of Christianity, as it must be, where that spirit bears rule, and the only strife between these noble-minded women seemed to be, which should most sedulously cultivate the religious principles in their young friend. Mr. Harrison, certainly not remarkable for his Christian graces, was scrupulous in maintaining all the appointments of the established church. He never countenanced by his august presence the worship of the village meeting. It was one of his favourite observations, and he uttered it with the pomp of an oracle, that Puritanism was the mother of rebellion. He was gratified with Ellen's respectful attendance on his reading of the church service; and he noticed more than once how remarkably well her voice sounded in the responses. He blamed his wife for not making an effort to prevent Ellen's going to the village meeting with the Allens during her residence with them, which he said she might easily do, as the girl certainly had sense enough to discern the difference between worship and talking. Allen, too, dissatisfied with what he deemed his wife's lukewarmness, reproved her for not interposing her authority to prevent Ellen from 'wasting the Sabbath in hearing a form of words read over by a man that had no more religion than the Pope, and who all the while flattered himself that none but an Episcopal Tory could go to heaven.' Happily for the peace of our heroine, neither of the ladies deemed it her duty to interfere with the wishes of the other; and she grew up, nurtured in the spirit of our blessed religion, without bigotry to any of the forms with which accident, pride, or prejudice has invested it.

Time rolled on, and every year found Ellen improved in loveliness: the gay and reckless spirit of childhood gave place to the vivacity and sensitiveness of fifteen. Mrs. Allen deemed it inexpedient to delay longer to communicate to her such particulars of her mother's history as she was at liberty to impart. It was impossible any longer to evade her natural and just curiosity on the subject, and as she could not forever be kept in ignorance, Mrs. Allen thought it necessary that she should begin to fortify her mind for the evils that might await her. Ellen received the communication with a gentle submission to the trials of her lot that astonished both her friends,— for Mrs. Harrison had long been in Mrs. Allen's confidence—she saw that dark clouds enveloped her; still—for hope is the element of youth—except in some moments of fearful apprehension, she believed that she should yet enjoy a clear heaven and a bright day.

The progress of time had wrought some changes in the Allen family. Edward, the only son, had been sent to Vermont, to reside in the family of Mr. Lenox his uncle, and George Lenox his cousin, a student in Harvard University, passed his vacations at Lansdown. The mother of Justyn Allen had become a widow, and had been induced by her children to fix her residence with them; and Mr. Allen had been persuaded by one of his neighbours to relinquish the toils of his farm for the easy acquisitions of trade, and to embark all the capital his credit could command in a mercantile enterprise.

CHAPTER VIII.

Mr. Harrison's infirmities had grown with his years. He passed his time in deprecating the encroaching spirit of Jacobinism,[5] and in predicting the certain dissolution of the federal government. His prejudices operated like a distemper, and gave to every object a distorted form and threatening aspect. He saw nothing in our thriving institutions—in the diffusion of intelligence, virtue, and prosperity through the mass of society—but menaces of degradation and elements of disorder. It is reported of our chief magistrate, that during his late visit to our northern metropolis, he exclaimed, on beholding the concourse of well-dressed, well-behaved people, assembled to greet him, "Where are your common people?" This exclamation, so flattering to a just republican pride, would have conveyed to the loyal ears of Robert Harrison a sense of hopeless degradation; for in his view, every elevation of the commonalty depressed the level of the gentleman. Fortunately for him, the respect inspired by the good sense and benevolence of his wife shielded him from the insults which his folly provoked; and his connection with Ellen Bruce was a link between him and his neighbours, which protected him from their open scorn.

Ellen, as her mind matured, became every day more dear and necessary to Mrs. Harrison, with whom, from fifteen to eighteen, her time was passed almost exclusively. Even Mr. Harrison condescended to say that he could not live without her, and his wife, availing herself of this favourable expression, ventured to suggest to him to make some provision for her favourite in case of the misfortune of his death. "He had nothing," he said, "to dispose of, but the family estate, and that he thought could with no propriety be diverted from flowing in its natural channel to the heir at law," a distant relation residing in England. Mrs. Harrison suggested, that, as this gentleman had a noble revenue from his own estates, such an accession as their little property would be but as a drop to the ocean; and she urged that it would be in the spirit of the known generosity of his family to confer his bounty on an orphan: she intimated that Ellen was quite dependent on him, for, except a few hundred dollars inherited from her parents, she had nothing, and could have no rational reliance on the Allens; for it had been for some time whispered in Lansdown that Allen, in his mercantile enterprise, had met with the fate of all those who, since the time of Aesop's fish,[6] have aspired to some other element than that for which Providence had

---

5. *Jacobinism*: The practice of ultra-democratic principles, often derided as a form of anarchy by those of more moderate political leanings. The term originally referred to the anti-royalist ideas of the Jacobin Club, a French political movement that supported the French Revolution.
6. *Aesop's fish*: A reference to Aesop's fable 'The Fisherman and the Fish', in which the fish begs to be released back into the river after he is caught by the fisherman.

destined them. All these arguments she stated so cogently that her husband was persuaded to comply with her wishes, and he promised, that during a visit to Boston, whither he was going the next week to celebrate the king's birthday, he would have his will duly drawn and executed, and devise the "family estate" to Ellen Bruce. This good resolution shared the fate of so many others left at the mercy of the casualties of life. Mr. Harrison went to Boston, and on the birthday, dined at the British Consul's with a select band of loyalists. The illustrious occasion and the good cheer of his host tempted him to the excessive demonstrations of enthusiasm common on such occasions, and the consequence was that he died the succeeding night of an apoplexy.

A few months subsequent to Mr. Harrison's death, Justyn Allen also paid the debt of nature, and in consequence of the unfortunate issue of his mercantile enterprise, left his wife, his old mother, and his children, without any provision. The loss of her husband and the ruin of their affairs aggravated a mortal disease under which Mrs. Allen had been for some time suffering; and as if the family was destined to illustrate the common remark, that troubles never come singly, Emily became so sickly that a physician pronounced change of air necessary to her. At this time Susan Allen (whom our readers may remember as the sister of Justyn Allen, who remained finally attached to the Shaker society) arrived at Lansdown on her way to visit a society of her own people at Harvard. Mrs. Allen, anxious to remove Emily from the distressing scenes that she was conscious awaited her at home, thankfully accepted a proposition which her aunt made, to take her upon this excursion, for the benefit of the ride and change of place. Unforeseen circumstances detained her for a long time within the sphere of her aunt's influence; and her mind weakened, and her spirits dejected, she adopted, as has been seen, the strange faith of her enthusiastic relative. In the meantime, Ellen, devoted to the care of Mrs. Allen, allowed herself no relaxation but passing a few hours occasionally with Mrs. Harrison.

It was during one of these visits that Mrs. Harrison inquired if Allen's affairs were so fatally involved as to render it necessary to surrender the house to his creditors. Ellen believed not. "George Lenox," she said, "had advanced two hundred dollars to redeem a portion of the property."

"George Lenox!" exclaimed Mrs. Harrison, "how, dear Ellen, has he the ability to do so generous an act?"

"He draws on talent and industry," replied Ellen, "and I do not believe his drafts will ever be dishonoured."

"I know, my love," rejoined Mrs. Harrison, "that youth forms vast expectations from those resources, but I likewise know that they are not always answered by ready money."

CHAPTER VIII.

Ellen explained to Mrs. Harrison that young Lenox, after defraying his expenses at the university, had that amount of money remaining—the fruit of his industry and economy.

"Such a gift," said Mrs. Harrison, "his all, was indeed most generous, and deserves the bright reward that is glowing on your cheek at this moment; but still, I do not quite comprehend how your young wits have contrived to satisfy the demand on the portion of the property redeemed with two hundred dollars." The glow that had suffused Ellen's cheek deepened as she replied, "Dearest Mrs. Harrison, forgive me if I have not dealt frankly with you; I wished to avoid exciting your tender, but, believe me, unnecessary solicitude about me. I have made the best use of my little inheritance in appropriating it to the relief of my friends: the sum, as you know, was originally four hundred dollars. It has been more than doubled by Mr. Allen, more prudent in the management of my affairs than his own; and yesterday I had the happiness of giving it into George Lenox's hands, and of seeing the joy of Mrs. Allen, when it was announced to her by her principal creditor that a valuable portion of her property had been redeemed by an unknown friend; and had you seen the expression that lit up her sick face, when she exclaimed, 'Thank God, my old mother will not have to go forth from her son's house to seek a shelter in her old age, and my children, my dear children, may come home, to live again under their father's roof.' Oh, Mrs. Harrison, you might have envied me the pleasure of that moment, had it cost me ten thousand times the paltry sum I sacrificed for it."

"Then she is ignorant of her benefactor?"

"Yes—but do not give me that name—benefactor! Dear Mrs. Harrison, it can only be because I owe to you an equal debt, that you forget my obligations to Mrs. Allen: did not she save my helpless infancy from neglect, and without a mother's instincts or rights, has she not nurtured me with a mother's tenderness?"

"You are right—you are right, my noble-minded Ellen," replied Mrs. Harrison, as Ellen paused in her appeal: "my fear of the possible evils you may encounter (should I be removed from you) from want and dependence, afflicts me with undue anxiety. I hope I should have courage enough not to shrink from any evils that menaced myself, but when I think of your being exposed to a cold, selfish world, I feel a mother's timidity; you, with your strange, mysterious history, Ellen, your inexperience, your generous, confiding temper, with all that refinement that I have foolishly, perhaps sinfully, delighted to watch stealing over your character, with all the graces that fit you for—"

"Oh, stop, dear Mrs. Harrison, this is strange language for you to hold, and me to hear; my highest ambition is to do well my duty in whatever station Providence assigns me. This is an ambition, as you have taught me, that cannot be disappointed; here the race is to the swift, and the battle to the strong. I will not," she added, playfully, "any longer expose my humility to temptation;" and she put on her hat, and stooped to her friend for a farewell kiss, when Mrs. Harrison said, "not yet, Ellen, you must not go till you have explained to me this benevolent sympathy of yours and young Lenox's; this generous union of your fortunes is doubtless received by him as a good omen?"

"The event of our friend's happiness has already interpreted the omen, and explained all its significance," replied Ellen, rising and walking away from Mrs. Harrison.

"Now, come back to me, Ellen," said she, "and seat yourself here on my footstool, and if your tongue will not speak the truth, I must read it in your truth-telling eyes and cheeks."

Ellen turned towards her friend for the first time in her life reluctantly; and reseating herself, she said with an embarrassed air, "I scarcely can conjecture what you expect from me."

"I will not tax your sagacity to conjecture, but come directly to the point—do you love George Lenox?"

"Most certainly I do; I should be the most ungrateful—"

"Pshaw, my dear Ellen, it is not the love that springs from any such dutiful source as gratitude which is in question at this moment; but that mysterious sentiment, inexplicable, uncontrollable, which does not require, and seldom (I fear) admits a reason for its existence."

"I should be sorry, indeed, to confess or to feel such a sentiment for anyone."

"Evading, again! Ah, dear Ellen, the nature of the animal is known by its doublings. You are so deep in the science as to demand the use of technics—tell me, then, are you *in love* with George Lenox?"

"Indeed I am not—you know I am not, Mrs. Harrison."

"I fancied I knew that you were not, but nothing less than a gift of second sight is infallible on such occasions; we must go a little farther, Ellen, even at the risk of deepening the crimson on your cheeks—you surely are not unconscious that Lenox is in love with you?"

"He has never told me so," replied Ellen.

"That may be—young Edwin 'never talked of love'[7]—but without much experience, you know there are expressions that speak this passion more emphatically than language: and, exempt as you are from vanity, I think you cannot have misunderstood this amiable young man's devotion to you—his eagerness for your society, his anxiety to gratify all your wishes, his eye fixed on you as if he were spell-bound—"

---

7. *Edwin 'never talked of love'*: From the English novel *The Vicar of Wakefield* (1766) by Oliver Goldsmith (1730–74).

"O, say no more," exclaimed Ellen, hiding her face on her friend's lap, "I have understood George, but I hoped—"

"To be able to make an appropriate return. Have I made out your meaning?"

"Far from it—I hoped that our approaching separation—that new pursuits, new objects, would efface the accidental preference which has arisen from our early and confidential intercourse."

"In short, you trusted to those accidents over which you have no control to heal the wound that your kindness, your unreserved manner to this poor young man has been for years deepening."

"Oh, dear Mrs. Harrison, of what do you suspect me—of the baseness of coquetry?"

"No, Ellen, no, you are incapable of trifling with the happiness of anyone; your error has arisen from inexperience. I should have cautioned you, but I am not fit to be your guide and counsellor in affairs of this nature; for though I have lived more than half a century, my secluded, childless life has offered few opportunities of observation, and fewer still where my sagacity has been stimulated by interest. I forgive your surprise and your indignation, my love, at what you imagined my suspicion of coquetry, for I know nothing more selfish, heartless, base, and degrading, than for a woman to encourage, nay permit the growth of an affection which she has no intention of returning."

"I should detest such a miserable triumph of vanity," exclaimed Ellen; "I should hate myself were I capable of it, and George, kind, generous as he is, the sufferer. What ought I to do—can I do anything now?" she asked with the impatience of a generous mind to repair the evil it has inflicted."

"No, my love," replied Mrs. Harrison, "it is only by leaving undone, that mischief can be avoided in affairs of this kind. George goes tomorrow; avoid seeing him again, if you can without apparent design, for farewell words and looks furnish food for the sweet and bitter fancies of a brain-sick lover during any interval of absence."

"The severe suffering," she continued, as she marked the deep melancholy that had succeeded Ellen's usually animated expression, "you feel at this moment from having been the involuntary cause of disappointment to your friend, will teach you in future jealously to guard the happiness that may be exposed to the influence of your attraction. You are in no danger of the silly vanity of fancying that civility means love, and of giving importance to every trifling gallantry; but modest—humble in your self-estimate, you are in danger of wounding deeply the bosom that is bared to your involuntary shafts."

"There is no need of caution for the future," replied Ellen, "no one else will ever care for me so much as George does."

"That may be, dear Ellen, but as you are scarce eighteen, it is possible that you have not finished your experience in love affairs; if you preserve that woe-begone visage, indeed, any other safeguard against the effect of your charms will be quite superfluous; come, my love, cheer up, and let me hear your sweet voice at my dinner table, as sweet to me as minstrelsy to an old chieftain."

Ellen made a vain effort to recover her spirits, and then hurried away that she might indulge her ingenuous sorrow without giving pain to her friend. She was careful to follow Mrs. Harrison's prudent counsel, and when George Lenox came to pass his last evening with her, he received a friendly farewell message, with the information that her duty to Mrs. Allen precluded her seeing him again. Before the morning dawned George was in a stagecoach on his way to the south. He passed the boundary of Lansdown with almost as heavy a heart as our first parent bore through the gates of Paradise: feeling, like all true lovers, "that the world is divided into two parts; that where *she* is, and that where *she* is not."[8]

It would be difficult to say whether Mrs. Harrison was most gratified or disappointed by the result of her investigation into the state of Ellen's affections. While she lived, her annuity was ample for the support of Ellen and herself; but nothing could be more precarious than such a dependence, and Ellen might be left to encounter alone the wants of life. Young Lenox had promising talents, and those "getting along" faculties, that are a warrant for success: his devoted attachment was merit in the eyes of Mrs. Harrison; still he wanted those refined habits, that delicacy of taste, the result of cultivation, and those graces of manner, to all which Mrs. Harrison, from her early habits and associations, gave (it may be) an undue importance. There is such a taste for learning (we use the word in its provincial sense) pervading all ranks in New England—if indeed ranks can be predicated of a society where none dare to define the dividing lines, and few can perceive them— that we often see those advanced to the most conspicuous stations in society, whose boyish years have been spent in ploughing the narrow fields of the patrimonial farm. There are some disagreeable results from this state of things, on the whole so honourable; and Mrs. Harrison felt that in implanting in Ellen the tastes that belong to the highest grades of society, and in cultivating the habits of the "born lady," she had conferred a superiority of doubtful value: and she was almost led to regret the fastidiousness which had been her own work, when she felt herself compelled to trace to it Ellen's

---

8. *'that the world is divided into two parts; that she where she is, and that where she is not'*: From *Eloisa, or, A Series of Original Letters* (1796) by Jean-Jacques Rousseau (1712–78).

rejection of the affection of one who was her equal in all important respects, and whose excellent character and flattering prospects would have rendered a connection with him highly advantageous. We said Mrs. Harrison *almost* regretted the state of Ellen's heart, we fear she did not *quite*, for in common with the best individuals, she sometimes sacrificed general and immutable principles to the indulgence of her favourite peculiarities.

Mrs. Allen's life closed at the end of a few painful weeks, and Ellen, after having performed every service for her with the strictest fidelity, wept over her with filial sorrow. Old Mrs. Allen soon after joined her grandson at Eton, and Ellen, thus unfettered by duty, returned to Mrs. Harrison's, where her life passed happily in pursuits congenial to her taste, till she was summoned to Vermont by intelligence of the threatening illness of Edward Allen.

CHAPTER IX.

"See what a ready tongue suspicion hath."[1]

Henry IV.

OUR readers no doubt will think it is quite time that we should return from our long digression to the family at Eton. There nothing occurred worthy their notice, till one evening Mrs. Lenox, entering Miss Bruce's apartment, said, "Ellen, are you here, and quite alone?" "Quite alone," replied Ellen; "Miss Redwood has not left her father's room since they took their tea."

"I am glad of it—glad the girl has the grace to stay with him even for half an hour, though her society seems to be of little use or consolation; and particularly glad, dear Ellen, to find you alone. I must interrupt your starlight meditations, or rather give you an interesting subject for them: but we shall want a light, for I have brought you a letter to read."

"A letter!"—

"Yes, my dear, a letter, and to me the most delightful I ever received." She was about to proceed to divulge its contents, when both she and Ellen were startled by a sound about Miss Redwood's bed. Mrs. Lenox advanced to the bed and laid her hand on it. "There is no one here," she said, "I fancied I heard a sound." "I fancied so too," said Ellen.

"Happily we were both mistaken, my dear, for I should be very sorry to tell my story to any ears but yours. Ellen, I am the proudest and happiest of mothers; I have just received a letter from George, which proves that he is worthy of his prosperity."

"I am very glad of it."

"And do you not yet, Ellen, suspect the reason you have to be glad—do you not know that George loves you?"

"Oh, I hope not!" exclaimed Ellen involuntarily.

"Hope not, my dear Ellen! I am sure there is not another in the world so worthy of his love—not another who would be such an ornament to the station in which George will place his wife—not another that I should be

---

1. *'See what a ready tongue suspicion hath'*: From I, i of Shakespeare's *Henry IV Part II.*

so happy to call my child." She paused for a moment for a reply, but Ellen said nothing.

"Do not," Mrs. Lenox continued, "repress your feelings. George, like a dutiful son, has made me his confidante, and why should not you? George himself can hardly love you better than I do."

"Thank you—thank you, Mrs. Lenox."

"No, my dear, you must not thank me, you are worthy your good fortune, and your own merit has secured it. I have used no influence, though I would have done anything to have brought about the connection; but this is George's unbiassed decision, he confesses to me he has loved you ever since he was a boy. Is not such a good and constant heart worth having, Ellen, not to mention being the wife of a celebrated young clergyman?"

Here the happy mother again paused, and again wondered she received no reply.

"Not a word, Ellen? well, you shall have your own way; it is in vain to expect common sense, or a common way of showing it, from girls in love: so I will just bring you a candle, and leave you to read the letter by yourself: only remember that the southern mail goes out tomorrow, and that lovers like to have their declarations come back to them as quick as echoes."

Thus saying, Mrs. Lenox rose to leave the room, when Ellen caught her by the arm, and exclaimed, "stop one moment, Mrs. Lenox, and hear me."

"Hear you, dear Ellen; George himself could scarcely be more delighted to hear you." Ellen's tongue seemed to be again paralyzing, but making a strong effort, she said, "you know, Mrs. Lenox, what reasons I have for wishing to defer for the present all thoughts of marriage; you know that I ought not to involve anyone in my unhappy destiny; you know—George does not—that possible disgrace awaits me."

"But, my dearest Ellen, what is all this to the purpose? Have you so poor an opinion of my son's attachment to you, as to fancy that the worst issue of your uncertainties which you can apprehend would be a straw in his way? No! he loves you for yourself alone—truly—devotedly loves you."

Ellen was quite overcome with the generous, affectionate zeal of the mother, and bursting into tears, she clasped Mrs. Lenox's hand in hers, and said, "I do not deserve this, my dear, kind friend; I have not been frank with you. I do not," she added, faltering, "I do not love George."

"Not love him!" exclaimed Mrs. Lenox, drawing back from Ellen, "not love him, Ellen! it can't be, child—it is impossible." Poor Ellen at this moment wished it were impossible; she sunk back in her chair, and dark as the room was, instinctively covered her face with her handkerchief, while her friend, in great agitation, walked up and down the room, talking half to herself and half to Ellen. "Not love him! I cannot believe it; you have always known him. You know there is not a blemish on his character. A pious minister—a man of education and talents—very good talents—quite uncommon talents—and a better tempered boy never lived; and as to his appearance, there may be handsomer men than George, but there never was a pleasanter look—a good faithful son he has been, and brother, and that is a sure sign he will be a good husband: and he loves you, Ellen;" she concluded, pausing, and placing her hand on Ellen's shoulder, "and you can't be in your right mind if you do not love him."

Ellen felt that it would be in vain to attempt to convince the fond mother that that could be a right mind which did not, as she would think, justly appreciate George's merits: and she was too delicate, too gentle to attempt to vindicate herself. She was grateful for the mother's and the son's generous preference of an isolated being; and approaching alone the crisis of her fate, she was reluctant to refuse the kind protecting arm that was stretched out to succor and protect her.

She faltered for a moment in the resolution she had instinctively taken: she could not bear to afflict, perhaps to alienate her partial friends—she might be able to command her affections. But, alas! the spirit would not come when she did call it; for when Mrs. Lenox, suspecting some infirmity of purpose from Ellen's continued silence, said, in a softened tone, "It was but a girlish, silly feeling after all—was it, dear Ellen? you will not be such a child as to throw away the prize you have drawn." She replied with a dignified decision that blasted Mrs. Lenox's reviving hopes: "I have nothing to give for that prize, and it cannot be mine. George must seek someone who can return his affections, and thus deserve them—I cannot."

"Well, this is most extraordinary," replied Mrs. Lenox; "why what do you wish for? what do you expect, Ellen?"

"Nothing, nothing in the world, Mrs. Lenox, but your and your son's forgiveness for what must seem to you ingratitude, insensibility; for myself," she added, "my path is a solitary one; but there is light on it from heaven; and, if I can preserve the kindness of my friends, I shall have courage and patience for the rest." There was so much purity and truth and feeling in Ellen's words, that Mrs. Lenox could not retain the resentment that, in spite of her better feelings, had arisen in her bosom. "Our forgiveness!" she replied, kindly, "Oh, Ellen, you need not ask our forgiveness. George, poor fellow, thinks you can do no wrong, and I always did think so: and even now I do not feel so much for my son as to see you so blind to your own happiness."

How long this conference, so unsatisfactory to the mother and embarrassing to Ellen, might have continued, it is impossible to say, had it not been interrupted by the entrance of Miss Redwood.

"Ah!" she exclaimed, "a tête a tête, confidential, no doubt; I am sorry to interrupt it," she continued, looking at both the ladies, and observing the signs of emotion that were too evident to escape notice; "it seems to have been interesting. Come, Lilly, you lazy wretch," she added, turning to the servant, who was lying stretched out on the floor at the foot of the bed, "get up and undress me; I have been dying with sleep this half hour, while papa was prosing away at me."

Lilly's appearance on the floor at the entrance of the light explained to the ladies the noise they had heard; they exchanged looks of mutual intelligence, but both concluding she had been asleep, they gave themselves no farther concern about her. Mrs. Lenox bade the young ladies good night, and repaired to her husband with a heavy heart to acquaint him with the result of George's suit. He, good, easy man, after expressing some surprise, concluded with the truisms, that girls were apt to be notional; that to be sure Ellen was a likely young woman, but there were plenty of fish in the sea, and good ones too, that would spring at a poorer bait than George could throw out; and besides, he added, by way of consolation, there was something of a mist about Ellen, and though he should not have made that an objection, seeing that she was a good girl, and George had an idea about her, yet, as matters had turned out as they had, he believed it was all for the best. Mrs. Lenox thought her husband had very inadequate notions of Ellen Bruce's merits, but she was wise enough to refrain from disturbing his philosophy on this trying occasion.

Soon after Mrs. Lenox left the young ladies' apartment, Miss Bruce took her hat and shawl and stole softly downstairs. Miss Redwood listened to her footsteps till she heard the house door close after her. "In the name of Heaven, Lilly," she demanded of her servant, "what can she have gone out for at this time in the evening?"

"I am not the witch that can tell that, Miss Caroline; but one thing I can tell; I heard her say to Doctor Bristol, as I passed them standing together in the entry just before he went away today, 'I shall not fail to be there.'"

Nothing could be more indefinite than Lilly's information; however, it was more satisfactory than none, and after pondering on it for a moment, her mistress said, "your ears are worth having, girl—tell me, did you hear what Miss Bruce and Mrs. Lenox were talking about in the dark here?" "That did I, Miss Caroline; trust me for using my ears. I waked when Mrs. Lenox came into the room, and was just starting up, when, thinks I to myself, they'll be saying something about Miss Cary, and I'll just lie snug and hear it—it will be nuts for her."

"Did they talk about me? What said they? Tell me quick."

"Why, Miss Cary, they said just nothing at all about you; no more than if you was'ent nobody."

"What in the name of wonder then did they talk about—what could they have to say?" asked Miss Redwood, wondering internally that there should be any field of vision in which she was not the most conspicuous object.

"Oh, Miss Cary," replied Lilly," their talk was all about themselves; that is to say, about Miss Bruce and George Lenox, that I told you was going to marry her; but it appears she is all off the notion of it now, though his mother begged as hard as a body might beg for your striped gown that you don't wear anymore, Miss Cary."

"My striped gown—you may have it, Lilly, but tell me what Mrs. Lenox said, and what Miss Bruce, and all about it." Lilly proceeded to the details, and by her skilful use of the powers of memory and invention, she made out a much longer conversation than we have reported to our readers; from which conversation Caroline deduced the natural inference, that Miss Bruce would not sacrifice the opportunity of an advantageous connection without a good and sufficient reason. What could be that reason? The attempt to solve this mystery led her into a labyrinth of conjectures, from which there was no clue for extrication but the apparent and mutual interest that subsisted between her father and Miss Bruce. It was possible that Ellen indulged hopes of a more splendid alliance than that with George Lenox. Caroline really had too much sense to allow much force to this extraordinary conclusion; still she continued alternately to dwell on that, and on the reason of Miss Bruce's absence, till Lilly spoke of the expected arrival of the Westalls. This opened a new channel for her thoughts—the debut of a new beau, a possible admirer, could rival any other interest, and before she sunk to sleep, Ellen's affairs subsided to the insignificance which they really bore in relation to Miss Redwood.

Caroline found other influences as unfriendly to sleep as the 'bracing air of the lake.' She awoke with the first beam of day, and instinctively raised her head from the pillow to ascertain whether Ellen Bruce's bed was unoccupied; it was, but her ear caught the sound of a footstep in the entry, and immediately after Ellen entered with as little noise as possible. "You need not be so quiet, Miss Bruce," said Caroline, "I am wide awake."

"I am happy if I do not disturb you," replied Ellen, "still I must be quiet on account of the family." 'Ah,' thought Caroline, 'the family then know nothing of this manoeuvre.' "You look excessively pale and wearied, Miss Bruce."

"I am wearied," replied Ellen, without gratifying or even noticing Miss Redwood's curiosity, "but," she added, as she threw herself on the bed, "I shall have time before breakfast to refresh myself."

Caroline, with the transmuting power of jealousy, had converted Ellen's simplest actions into aliments for her suspicions, and now that a circumstance had occurred which did not readily admit of an explanation, she exulted in the expectation of a triumph over her father, who had treated her curiosity in relation to Ellen as quite childish and groundless. "Your favourite, papa," she said, seizing a favourable opportunity when she was sitting alone with her father after dinner, "has a singular taste for walking."

"It may appear singular to you, Caroline, with your southern habits; but I imagine you will not find it uncommon at the north."

"O, north or south, papa, I fancy it is not common for lady pedestrians to pass the whole night in promenades."

"The whole night—what do you mean, my child?" Caroline explained. Her father listened to her detail with undisguised interest, and after a few moments' pause, he said, "It would have been natural and quite proper, as you are Miss Bruce's roommate, that you should have asked of her the reason of her absence last night—did you so?"

"Oh, thank you, papa, no; I have not yet taken lessons enough of these question-asking Yankees, to inquire into that which this lady of mysteries evidently chooses to keep secret, even from her dear friends the Lenoxes."

"Well, my dear, since you will not or cannot gratify your curiosity, I advise you to suspend it, and to do yourself and Miss Bruce the justice to remember the remark of a sagacious observer, that the 'simplest characters sometimes baffle all the art of decipherers.'[2] You look displeased, Caroline—let us talk on some subject on which we shall agree better. I think we may look for the Westalls today."

"Thank Heaven!—any change will be agreeable."

"Agreeable as a change, no doubt—but the society of the Westalls will, I hope, have some more enduring charm than novelty; the mother, I am certain, will be quite to your taste—and to the son, if report speaks truly, no young lady can be indifferent."

"How, papa; is he handsome, clever, rich, accomplished?"

"Handsome—if I had seen Charles Westall within the last half-hour, I should hardly presume to decide on so delicate a point: he was but four years old when I parted from him, of course I only recollect him as a child. I have been told however by some Virginians who have visited the north, that he is the image of his father; if so, he has an appearance that ladies usually honour with their favour—manly, intelligent, and expressive of every benevolent affection."

"No tone of your soft-amiable gentle-zephyr youths, I hope, papa?—they are my aversion."

"Not precisely; but if his face resembles his father's, it rather indicates a natural taste for domestic life than for the 'shrill fife and spirit-stirring drum'[3]—for the peace than the war establishment; but I shall leave you to decide on his beauty, Caroline," continued Mr. Redwood, as he noticed a

---

2. *'simplest characters sometimes baffle all the art of decipherers'*: A variation on a passage from *Leonora* (1806) by Maria Edgeworth.
3. *'shrill fife and spirit-stirring drum'*: A variation on a line from III, iii of Shakespeare's *Othello*.

slight blush on his daughter's cheek at what she considered an allusion to her military preference. "'Is he clever?' is, I think, the second question in the order of your interrogatories; to this point I have the most satisfactory testimonials; he has received the first honours of the first university in our country—has finished the study of the law with one of the most eminent men at the north, and has received the proposal of a most advantageous partnership with his instructor, which he has just accepted."

"Then if he is going into the drudgery of business, he is not rich of course, papa?"

"No, Caroline, he is not rich,"—Mr. Redwood was on the point of adding, "and of what consequence is that to us?" but he remembered in time, that it was his policy to conceal from his wayward daughter his own views; and he said, after a momentary pause, "his father's rash generosity impoverished his estate. The father was an enthusiast, Caroline; he thought as we all do of the curse of slavery."

"The curse of slavery? Lord, papa, what do you mean? There is no living without slaves."

"I fear, my child, that we shall find there is no living with them; but besides the universal feeling in relation to the evil of slavery, Westall's father had some peculiar notions.—During his life he gave to many of his slaves their freedom."

"Oh, shameful!" exclaimed Caroline, "when everybody allows, that all our danger is from the freed slaves."

"Westall endeavored as far as possible to obviate that danger. He reserved the noble gift for those who were qualified for it by some useful art, or power of independent industry. At his death he bequeathed their liberty to all who remained on the plantation. This it appears he deemed not generous but just; as he stated in his will, that in resigning his property in them he merely restored to them a natural right which they had received from their Creator, and which he had only withheld in the hope of fitting them to enjoy it, but which he would not leave in the power of anyone to detain from them."

"What nonsense, papa! And so by the indulgence of these whims he beggared poor Charles?"

"It cannot be denied that young Westall's inheritance was impaired by his father's singular, or it may be fanatical, notions of justice; for the value of a southern plantation is graduated by the number of its slaves, and without them it is much in the condition of a cart without a horse. There was no hypocrisy in my friend's professed dislike of slavery; it was deep-rooted and unconquerable, and to it he sacrificed every pecuniary advantage. According to the absolute provision of his will his plantation was sold, and his widow and son removed to the north. Charles's fortune, though reduced, has been adequate to the expenses of a first-rate education; he has inherited the disinterestedness of his father's spirit, for I find that since coming of age he has vested nearly all that remained of his property in an annuity for his mother; he has a few thousand dollars left to start with, and as the 'winds and waves are always favourable to the ablest navigators,'[4] I do not doubt that his talents and industry will insure him success. As to his 'accomplishments,' Caroline, you and I affix probably different meanings to the term, and therefore I will leave you to satisfy your interrogatory on that head after you shall have seen him."

"Different meanings, papa! Everybody knows what accomplished means—does he speak French?—does he dance well?—Is he genteel and elegant, and all that?"

"Oh perfectly genteel, my dear," replied the father with a bitter smile, "he was born and bred a gentleman, and has the mind and spirit of a gentleman; he is, I am told, approved by wise fathers, courted by discreet mothers, and what you will probably consider much more unequivocal testimony—the favourite of fair daughters. But, Caroline," continued Mr. Redwood, checking himself from the fear that his daughter would perceive his solicitude to secure her favourable opinion of Westall, "your long confinement to the house has robbed you of your bloom. The rumour of your beauty has doubtless reached the ears of my young friend, and I should be sorry that your first appearance should not answer his expectations—ah, there goes Miss Bruce on one of her walking expeditions. Miss Bruce," he added, speaking to Ellen through the window, "you are an absolute devotee to nature—will you permit my daughter to be the companion of your walk, and show her some of the shrines at which you worship?"

"I am only an admirer, not an idolater," replied Ellen, smiling; "and I am certain, that if Miss Redwood will do me the favour to go with me, she will answer for me that my homage is reasonable." Miss Redwood readily acquiesced in the arrangement—the wish to restore her bloom was a controlling motive; and the animating expectation of the arrival of the Westalls had for the moment made her forget her dislike to Ellen: Lilly was summoned with her hat and gloves, and the young ladies proceeded arm in arm towards the lake.

"What a delightful compensation we have," said Ellen, "for the suffering from our long sultry summer days in the reviving influence of the approaching evening; its sweet cool breath refreshes all nature, and restores elasticity and vigor to mind and body."

---

4. *'the winds and waves are always favourable to the ablest navigators'*: From *The Decline and Fall of the Roman Empire* (published between 1776 and 1788) by Edward Gibbon (1737–94).

"You have, no doubt, an advantage in your cool evenings," replied Caroline, "the only one, as far as I see, of the north over the south."

Ellen suppressed her opinion—perhaps partial—that her companion did not see very far. "I am not such a bigot," said she, "as to believe that your country does not possess, in many respects, the advantage over ours; but I confess I have prejudices so strong in favour of our lofty mountains, deep valleys, and broad lakes, that I do not believe I should ever admire the tame level of Carolina; but it is hardly necessary for me to be boastful while this scene is itself so eloquently pleading its claims to your admiration: look, Miss Redwood," she continued, "where the lake reflects the bright tints of the evening sky, and there where the long shadows of the trees seem to sleep on its bosom—is there, can there be in the wide world a lovelier spot than this?"

"It may be," replied Caroline, "it is, no doubt, exceedingly pretty; but to own the truth to you, Miss Bruce, I can never forget that this lake shore was the scene of our disaster. After that horrible storm and fright it is natural it should have no beauty in my eyes; besides, you know, one that is not used to the country gets so tired of it, that it is quite impossible to admire it; but see," she added, changing her languid tone to one nearly as animated as Ellen's had been: "See, Miss Bruce, those wild flowers that are growing there close to the water's edge; I should so like to get them to dress my hair against the Westalls arrive: they would form a beautiful contrast. I had a bunch of snow-drops last winter that all the world said were particularly becoming to me; these flowers are as white and beautiful, and being natural, they would have quite a rural pretty effect."

"A beautiful effect no doubt, Miss Redwood, but alas! they are 'not to be come at by the willing hand;'[5] if we had the imagination of some poets, who are fond of infusing their own sensations into flowers, we might fancy these were enjoying their security, and laughing at the vanity of your wishes."

"But," said Caroline, "it surely is not impossible to get at them;" and espying a fisherman's canoe which was fastened to a tree against which they were standing, she proposed to Ellen, who, she said, she was sure knew how to guide it, to procure the flowers for her.

"Indeed, Miss Redwood," replied Ellen, "I am no water nymph, and these canoes require as much skill to guide them as the egg-shells in which witches traverse the waters."

"But, the water is not deep," insisted Caroline, "and if the worst happens you will but get your clothes wet, and you have nothing on that can be injured."

---

5. *'not to be come at by the willing hand'*: This quotation appears in *The Grave* (1743) by Robert Blair (1699–1746), a poem which is credited with inspiring the graveyard school of poetry.

The inexorable Ellen resisted this argument, though Miss Redwood enforced it by a rapid glance of comparison from Ellen's simple muslin frock to her own richly trimmed silk dress.

There was an inlet of water where the ladies stood, around which the margin curved to the point where the flowers grew at the base of a rock, and so near the water's edge (for the earth had been worn away by the surge) that it could hardly be said from which element they sprung, earth or water. A small birch-tree had grown out of a cleft in the rock, and was completely overgrown by a grapevine, which, after embowering it, dropped its rich drapery over the perpendicular side of the rock, and hung there, in festoons so light and graceful, that one might fancy they had sportively peeped over the rock to look at their beautiful image in the pure mirror below. After Caroline's last argument had failed, she jumped into the canoe herself, and unhooking it from the tree to which it was attached, she exultingly exclaimed, "nothing venture, nothing have" and gayly pushed off towards the object of her wishes.

The water was shallow, and apparently there was not the least danger. Caroline, however, had given too powerful an impetus to the frail bark she was guiding, and it struck against the rock with so much force as to recoil with a fluttering motion. Caroline was frightened, and increased by her agitation the irregular motion of the canoe; Ellen perceived the dangerous operation of her terrors, but before she could make her comprehend that all that was necessary was that she should sit down quietly, Caroline had grasped the pendant vine, which was strong and tenacious, and the canoe had passed from under her. It drifted a few yards, and then remained stationary at the base of the rock. The rock was perpendicular, and too high for Miss Redwood to reach its summit. Ellen perceived the dilemma in which Caroline's fears had involved her, and adopted the only mode of extricating her from her awkward situation. She ran around the curve of the shore, ascended the rock where the ascent was gradual, and letting herself down as gently as possible into the canoe, she rowed immediately to the relief of the distressed damsel, whose arms already trembled with the weight which they sustained. "Oh, I am dead with fright!" she exclaimed, as soon as a certainty of recovered safety restored to her the use of her tongue: "for heaven's sake tell me, Ellen, how you got to me; I thought you dropped from the skies." Ellen explained that she had reached her by natural and easy means. "Well," said Caroline, "it was very good—very kind of you—and I never, never shall forget it; but pray get me back to the shore—for all the flowers in Paradise I would not endure such another fright."

"But we will not," said Ellen, "return to the shore without a trophy for your daring to venture to the only place where even fear could create peril.

These flowers," she added, plucking them, "were the cause of all the mischief, and they shall die for it."

She then rowed back to the shore, and was tastefully arranging the flowers in Caroline's hair, saying, at the same time, that "if she had made herself a water-nymph, they would still have been a fit coronal for her," when the attention of both the ladies was attracted by the rapid approach of a gentleman, whom they perceived to be a stranger. A frock-coat and madras cravat[6] announced a traveller; and a brief glance of Caroline's practised eye satisfied her who it must be that so gracefully wore this costume—and as he came up to them she exclaimed, "Mr. Westall!" It was Charles Westall, conducted by little Lucy Lenox. He courteously thanked Miss Redwood for saving him from the awkward necessity of introducing himself. He had, as he said, just arrived at Mr. Lenox's with his mother, and had been sent by her with his little guide in quest of Miss Redwood; that while descending the hill he had been a witness of Miss Redwood's danger, and had hastened on in the hope of being so fortunate as to assist at her rescue; but fate had been unkind to him, for the pleasure of playing the hero on this occasion was not only wrested from him, but he was forced to witness and admire the celerity with which the rescue had been effected without his aid. Miss Redwood turned to introduce Ellen, but she had walked forward with Lucy, who, with childish eagerness, was telling her how frightened she was when she saw her slide from the rock, and that for a million Miss Redwoods she would not have had Ellen run the risk of being drowned.

Never was there a happier moment for the power of Miss Redwood's beauty. The joy of recovered safety, and the pleasure of surprise had deepened her colour; her gratitude to Ellen had given a touch of unwonted softness to her expression, and the simple decoration of the white flowers mingling with her jet glossy curls, was far more beautiful than their usually elaborate arrangement.

When the ceremony of introduction to Mrs. Westall was over, and Caroline with extraordinary animation had expressed her pleasure at the interview, Mrs. Westall, impatient to ascertain the first impression on her son, whispered, "Charles, is she as beautiful as you expected?"

"As beautiful, mother! you do too much honour to my imagination; she is more beautiful than any vision of my dull brain."

For a few days after the arrival of the Westalls the "sands of time" were "diamond sparks" to the visitors at Eton.[7] Charles Westall and Caroline Redwood seemed verging towards that point of happy agreement so much

---

6. *madras cravat*: A tie made of fabric associated with Madras, India.
7. *the 'sands of time' were 'diamond sparks'*: A variation on a line from 'Too Late I Stayed' (1811) by William Robert Spencer (1770–1834).

desired by both their parents—desired by Mr. Redwood, because his experience had taught him that virtue is the only basis of confidence or happiness, and with an inconsistency not uncommon or surprising, he preferred that virtue should be fortified by religious principle. He had preserved an affectionate recollection of Westall's father, and he fancied that he was paying him a tribute in giving to his son the noble fortune of his own child, and when his conscience whispered that the fortune was a poor compensation for the incumbrance that went with it, he found some consolation in attributing Caroline's faults to the bad influence of her grandmother, and in the hope that, young as she was, her character might be remoulded. All that he had heard of Westall from the reports of others, or had gathered from occasional correspondence with him, had inspired regard for him; that regard was now becoming affection. Charles Westall's resemblance to his father recalled to him the early and happiest period of his life, that period when his heart was light and fearless, and his mind unclouded by the dark shadows that a vain and false philosophy had since cast upon it.

Mr. Redwood's apprehensions that Captain Fitzgerald had taken such possession of his daughter's imagination as to endanger the success of a rival vanished when he perceived that she devoted herself with characteristic childishness to the present object. Of the happy result of her efforts to captivate Charles Westall he had no doubt; and common experience would perhaps justify his conclusion that no young man could resist the apparent preference of a spirited young beauty with fortune enough to outweigh a thousand faults. A superficial observation satisfied him that he was secure of Mrs. Westall's influence for his daughter; he perceived that the progress of time had not diminished the worldliness of disposition which his sagacity had detected even when it was sheltered by the charms of youth.

Mrs. Westall was one of those ladies who are universal favourites: her face was pleasing, her person graceful, and her manners courteous; with these medium charms, she attracted attention without provoking envy: she had no strong-holds in her mind for prejudice or austere principle. She was one of that large class who take their form and pressure from the society in which they happen to be cast;—a thorough conformist. In our eastern country, she was, if not strict, quite exact in her religious observances. She would have preferred the lenient bosom of episcopacy, because of its agreeable medium between the latitudinarians and the puritans, and perhaps too on account of its superior gentility.[8] But as her location in a

---

8. *She would have preferred the lenient bosom of episcopacy, because of its agreeable medium between the latitudinarians and the puritans*: Puritans represent the extreme of conservative Christianity and the latitudinarians represent the opposite liberal extreme. Episcopacy appeals to Mrs. Westall because it is a median position between conservative and liberal Christianity.

country town precluded the privilege of choice, she offered an edifying example, by quietly waiting on the services of a congregational meeting every Sunday, and occasionally attending a 'lecture' or a 'conference' during the week. She contributed to the utmost limit of her ability to the good and religious objects that engage the zeal and affections of our community. This virtuous conduct was more the effect of imitation than of independent opinion; for Mrs. Westall, with the resources of fortune and in fashionable life, had remonstrated with some energy (she was not capable of much) against the strictness and enthusiasm of her husband. If again restored to the world, she would without an effort have conformed to its usages, and *endured* the excesses of genteel dissipation. In one of our cities she might have held Sunday evening levees,[9] or in Paris have strolled out the day of "holy rest" in the public gardens, or forgotten it at the opera, or a fashionable card party.

How such a woman could interest Edmund Westall, those only ought to inquire who have never observed how much early attachments are controlled by local and (as it seems) purely accidental circumstances! Westall, during his college life, resided in the family of his wife's parents. He was captivated by the sweetness of her temper and the grace of her manners, he trusted for the rest with the facility of youthful love, that hopes, believes, and expects all things.[10] He did not live long enough to awake from the lover's dream, though he occasionally saw a trait of worldliness, which he imputed to the humble circumstances in which his wife had been bred, thinking that they (as they too often do) had led her to an undue estimation of the advantages of wealth, rank, and fashion. Westall was deemed an enthusiast, and perhaps he was so, for his interest in the happiness of others often led him to a singular forgetfulness of himself, and his means were sometimes inadequate to effect his benevolent and philanthropic plans. Like other enthusiasts, he was apt to forget that the materials he had to work with were sordid and earthly, and, like them, he was compelled to endure the ridicule of those base spirits that were making idols of their silver and their gold, while he was on the mount in the service of the living God. Charles Westall was four years old when he lost this parent: the recollections he preserved of him were like the "glimpse a saint has of heaven in his dreams."[11] He remembered being led by him to the cabins of his infirm or sick slaves, and some particulars of his humane attentions to

---

9. *levees:* Receptions of visitors.
10. *hopes, believes, and expects all things:* A variation on 1 Corinthians 13: 7 (KJV), in which love 'believeth all things, hopeth all things, and endureth all things'.
11. *'glimpse a saint has of heaven in his dreams':* From *Lalla-Rookh, an Oriental Romance* (1817) by Thomas Moore (1779–1852).

them. He recollected the melting tenderness of his eye and the tone of his voice when he had commended him for a kind action. But his most vivid impression was of the last moment of his father's life, when he had laid his hand upon his child's head, and in the act of resigning him, had fervently prayed that he might be kept "unspotted from the world."[12] Charles could not then comprehend the full import of the words; but afterwards, amidst the temptations of life, he felt their efficacy. At an early period his mother had given into his possession his father's private papers. Through them he came to an intimate knowledge of his father's character—of his many virtuous efforts and sacrifices—of his hopes and fears in relation to himself—of his deepest and holiest feelings: thus the son was admitted into the sanctuary of the father's heart, and held, as it were, a spiritual communion with him. From these precious documents Charles Westall realized all that has been hoped from the ministry of a guardian spirit; they became a kind of external conscience to him: saving him from many an error into which the buoyant careless spirit of youth might otherwise have betrayed him. Few living parents exert such an influence over the character of a child.

12. *'unspotted from the world'*: From James 1: 27 (KJV).

CHAPTER X.

"They're here that ken and here that disna ken,
The wimpled meaning o' your unco tale,
Whilk soon will make a noise o'er muir and dale.'[1]
Ramsay's Gentle Shepherd.

THOSE only who have observed the magical effect produced upon a young lady by the presence of a candidate for her favour, whom she deems it worth her efforts to obtain or retain, can have an adequate notion of the change wrought on Caroline Redwood since the arrival of the Westalls. Instead of the listless, sullen girl, who yawned away her days in discontent or apathy, she became spirited, active, and good-humoured. Even her interest in the concerns of Ellen Bruce, and her suspicions of that artless girl's designs, were suspended in the ardour of her present pursuit, and she seemed to think of nothing and to care for nothing but how she should secure the triumph of her vanity. Everyone noticed the change, (excepting Ellen, who had of late almost wholly withdrawn from the family circle,) indeed it was so manifest that Miss Deborah, who had taken a decided dislike to Caroline, and who was rather remarkable for the inveteracy of her opinions, was heard to say, that "since the girl's sweetheart had come, she was as bright as a September day after the fog was lifted; but for her part she liked to see people have sunshine within them like Ellen." This declaration was made by Miss Debby in an imprudently loud tone of voice, as she stood at a window gazing on Mr. Redwood's carriage that had been ordered for an afternoon's drive. Mr. Redwood, Caroline, and Mrs. Westall were already in the carriage, and Charles Westall had returned to the parlour in quest of some article Mr. Redwood had forgotten; while he was looking for it Deborah's comment fell on his ear, and probably gave a new direction to his thoughts, for during the ride Caroline rallied him on his extraordinary pensiveness; and finally perceiving that his gravity resisted all her efforts to dissipate it,

---

1. *'They're here that ken and here that disna ken . . .'*: From III, ii of *The Gentle Shepherd* (1725) by Allan Ramsay (1686–1758).

she proposed that if he had not lost the use of his limbs as well as of his tongue, he should alight from the carriage with her and walk to a cottage to which they perceived a direct path through a field, while the carriage approached by the high road which ran along the lake shore and was circuitous. Westall assented rather with politeness than eagerness; but when he was alone with Caroline, when she roused all her powers to charm him, he yielded to the influence of her beauty and her vivacity. Never had she appeared so engaging—never so beautiful—the afternoon was delicious—their path ran along the skirts of an enchanting wood—its soft shadows fell over them, the birds poured forth their melody; and in short, all nature conspired to stimulate the lover's imagination and to quicken his sensibility. Charles forgot the sage resolutions he had made to withhold his declaration till he had satisfied certain doubts that had sometimes obtruded on him, that all in Caroline was not as fair and lovely as it seemed; he forgot Miss Deborah's hint—forgot everything but the power and the presence of his beautiful companion, and only hesitated for language to express what his eyes had already told her. At this moment both his and Miss Redwood's attention was withdrawn from themselves to a little girl who appeared at the door of the cottage, from which they were now not many yards distant. On perceiving them she bounded over the door-step, then stopped, put up her hand to shade her eyes from the sun, and gazed fixedly on them for a moment, then again sprang forward, again stopped, covered her eyes with both her hands, threw herself at full length on the grass, laid her ear to the ground and seemed for a moment to listen intently; she then rose, put her apron to her eyes, and appeared to be weeping, while she retraced her way languidly to the cottage. Caroline and Westall, moved by the same impulse, quickened their pace, and in a few moments reached the cottage door, to which a woman had been attracted by the sobs of the child, and was expostulating with her in an earnest tone. "God help us, Peggy, you'll just ruin all if you go on in this way;" she paused on perceiving that the child had attracted the attention of the strangers; and in reply to Westall's asking what ailed the little girl, she said, "It's just her simplicity, sir; but if you and the lady will condescend to walk into my poor place here, I will tell you all about it, or Peggy shall tell it herself, for when she gets upon it her tongue runs faster than mine: but bless us, here comes a grand coach—look up, Peggy, you never saw a real coach in your life. Peggy now let fall the apron with which she had covered her face—a face if not beautiful, full of feeling and intelligence. She seemed instantly to forget her affliction, whatever it was, in the pleasure of gazing on the spectacle of a real coach. "Ah, Aunt Betty," she exclaimed, "it is the grand sick gentleman that is staying at Mr. Lenox's." The carriage drew up to the door, and Mrs. Westall and Mr. Redwood, attracted by the uncommonly neat appearance of the cottage, alighted and followed Caroline and Charles, who had already entered it. The good woman, middle-aged, and of a cheerful countenance, was delighted with the honour conferred on her, bustled around to furnish seats for her guests—shook up the cushion of a rocking-chair for Mr. Redwood, and made a thousand apologies for the confusion and dirt of her house, which had the usual if not the intended effect of calling forth abundance of compliments on its perfect order and neatness. "And now, Peggy," she said, as soon as they were all quietly seated, "take the pitcher and bring some cold water from the spring, that's what the poor have, thank God, as good as the rich, and it is all we have to offer." The little girl obeyed, and as soon as she was out of hearing, the woman turned to Westall. "It was your wish, sir, to know what ailed the child; the poor thing has just got the use of her eye-sight, and she has been expecting someone that she loves better than all the world; and when she saw this young lady with you, she thought it was her friend—though to be sure she is shorter than this lady; but then Peggy, poor thing, does not see quite right yet, and then when she is puzzled, she just lies down to the ground as you saw her, for that was her way to listen, and she knows Miss Ellen's step, for as light as it is, when my poor ear can't hear a sound."

"How did she become blind, my good woman, and how did she recover her sight?" asked Westall.

"It is a long story, sir: when she was one year old, she laid in the measles, and her mother dying at the same time, and I sick of a fever, and the child, God forgive me, was neglected, and there came a blind over her eyes, and shut them up in darkness." "Not all darkness," said the little heroine of the story, who re-entered with the water, "you know, Aunt Betty, I could see a glimmer of sunshine." "Yes, and that it was that gave the doctor hopes of her." "No, no," interrupted the child, "it was Miss Ellen that gave the doctor hopes."

"Lord bless her," continued the woman, smiling, "Peggy thinks there's nothing good done in the world, but Miss Ellen does it, and, to be sure, she has been an angel to Peggy."

"And how," asked Mr. Redwood, whose interest in Peggy's history seemed much augmented since the mention of Miss Ellen—"how came Miss Bruce to know your child?"

"God brought them together, sir; it was his own work; but the child is not mine, her poor mother lies in the graveyard there in the village, far from all her own people, for we are from Old England, sir. My sister, poor Fanny, was a wild thing, the youngest of ten of us, and I the oldest. My mother died, and left her a baby in my arms; and she was like my own, and we all, and father more than all, petted her, and when she was sixteen, she

CHAPTER X.

had just her own way, and married a young soldier lad of our village, and my father turned her from his door, and would not hear to forgiving her: but I, Lord help me! I had no right not to forgive her; and so I came over to Canada with her when her husband's regiment was ordered there. I had a little money of my own, and we paid our own way, but when that was gone our distresses and hardships threw her in the consumption. Her husband got into bad company, deserted, and came off to the States; we followed—she with the baby—Peggy that is—in her arms. We persuaded her husband to take this bit of a place, but he soon left us, and, as I told you before, Fanny died, and left me alone in the world, as you may say, with Peggy—and she blind; but, sir, I have always been of a contented disposition, and I meant to be resigned to whatever it pleased the Lord to send upon me; but I must own, when I found Peggy was blind, and the doctors told me nothing could be done for her, I had my match.—It was the bitterest sorrow I ever felt when life was spared, but I thought to myself, what can't be cured must be endured; so I went to work. The Lord has blessed us, and Peggy and I have lived these six years as comfortable and as contented, maybe, as those that are richer, and seem to be happier."

"No doubt, no doubt, my good woman," said Mr. Redwood, struck with admiration of the simple creature's practical philosophy; "but you have told us so much of your story that you must give us the rest."

"Yes, yes," said little Peggy, "do, Aunt Betty, tell them about Miss Ellen, they'll like to hear that best of all: now don't go away," said she, turning to Caroline, who had risen from her chair, and was walking towards the door.

"I am not going away, child," she answered, pettishly, "I prefer standing at the door."

"It is five weeks tomorrow," continued the narrator, "since I first saw Miss Ellen; it was the very morning after young Mr. Allen's funeral. I saw her that morning and the next, sitting on that rock, by the elm-tree yonder, ladies; she had a pencil in her hand, and a big book on her lap, and a paper on it; and the second morning Peggy heard her humming some songs to herself, and she crept close to her: the silly thing would any time leave her breakfast for an end of a song. I saw the young lady noticed Peggy, and then I made bold to walk up to her; and will you believe me, ladies! she had been picturing on her paper this little hut and the half withered tree, and that old bench with my wash-tub turned up on it, and my old cow as she stands eating her morning mess, and Peggy stroking her! and I could not but ask her why she did not choose to draw out some of the nice houses in the village with two chimneys, and a square roof to them, and a pretty fence to the door-yard, and the straight, tall poplars; but she smiled, and said, 'this suited her fancy better;' and then she began talking to me of Peggy, and when she found she was quite blind, she just laid down her pencil and her book and all, and took the child in her lap, and said, 'something must be done for her;' and when she said so, the tears stood in her blue eyes; and God knows, I never saw tears so becoming; and from that time, ladies, she came every morning and sat here three or four hours, teaching Peggy to sew, and learning her hymns and songs."

"Caroline, Caroline, do you hear that?" asked Mr. Redwood, impetuously.

"Lord, papa, I am not deaf—certainly I hear."

"Go on, good woman," said Mr. Redwood.

"The child's quickness, sir," continued the aunt, "seemed a miracle to me, for, God forgive me, I had never thought of her learning anything. Peggy, get those bags you made, that Miss Ellen said you might sell."

The child instantly produced the bags, which were made of bits of calico very neatly sewn together. Caroline interrupted the story while she bargained with the little girl for the bags, for which she paid her munificently.

The aunt seemed more sensible of the extent of Miss Redwood's generosity than the child, for she was voluble in her thanks; and then proceeded to say that Miss Ellen, not satisfied with doing so much, brought Doctor Bristol to look at Peggy's eyes. "Doctor Bristol," she said, "had come to live in Eton since she had given up Peggy's eyes as quite gone, and therefore she had never shown the child to him. But Doctor Bristol had learned some new-fashioned ways that other doctors in the country knew nothing about, and as soon as he looked at the child, he said one of the eyes might be restored. Then poor Peggy was so frightened with the thought of an operation, and I could do nothing with her, for I had always let her have her own way; for who, ladies, could have the heart to cross a blind child? But Miss Ellen, God bless her, could always make her mind without crossing her, for she loves Miss Ellen better than anything on earth, or in heaven either, I fear me; and she would liken her to strawberries and roses, and everything that was most pleasant to the senses the poor thing had left: and she would say that her voice was sweeter than the music of birds, or the sound of the waters breaking on the shore, when a gentle breeze came over the lake of a still evening, for that was the sound she loved best of all, and would listen to it sometimes for an hour together without speaking or moving."

It seemed that Miss Redwood's patience could no longer brook the minute and excursive style of the narrator, as she proposed to Mrs. Westall in a whisper, that they should cut the woman's never-ending story short, and pursue their ride. Mrs. Westall acquiesced, with a 'just as you please, my dear;' but Mr. Redwood, guessing the purport of his daughter's whisper, interposed with a request in a low voice, that she would not prolong their delay by interrupting the good woman's story, as the pain in his arm warned him that it was time for him to return; then turning to the aunt, he asked her "how she brought the girl finally to consent to the operation?"

"Oh, it was Miss Ellen that made her consent, and she would only do it by promising that she would stay by her and hold her head. God knows, I could not have done it, well as I love her, to have saved her eyes; for I was all in a shiver when I saw the doctor fix her by that window, and Miss Ellen stood behind her, and Peggy leaned her head back on to Miss Ellen's breast, and one of Miss Ellen's hands was on the child's forehead, and the other under her chin, and she looked, God bless her, as white as marble and as beautiful as an angel. I had but a glance at them, for when the doctor took out his long needle I covered my eyes, till I heard them say it was all over, and Peggy had not made a movement or a groan. Miss Ellen bade me not to speak yet, and the bandage was put over the child's eyes, and she was laid there on the bed, and Miss Ellen motioned me to go out with her, and as I stepped from the door, she sunk like a dying person into my arms; but still it seemed she could only think of Peggy, for she put up her hand for a sign to me to be quiet, and then the breath seemed quite gone out of her. I laid her on the turf and fetched some cold water, and she soon came to herself, and bade me say nothing of it to the doctor, and she came in again and told the doctor she should come back in the evening and sit the night with Peggy, for she would trust no one else for the first night, for the doctor said all depended on keeping her quiet; and the last word she said, was to beg he would not tell any of the family at Mr. Lenox's that she was coming here, for they, she said, fancied she was not well, and would not permit it." At this simple explanation of the absence which Caroline had placed in a suspicious light, her father turned on her a look full of meaning; she blushed deeply, but neither spoke, and the aunt proceeded.

"All went on well to the third day, and then Miss Ellen came with leave to take off the bandage, and she asked Peggy what she wished most in the world to see. "Oh, you, you, Miss Ellen," she said; and then the dear young lady stood before her, and took off the bandage; and then, bless you, ladies, her piercing scream of joy when the light touched her eye—oh!—I heard my father curse poor Fanny—I saw her die in a strange land; but never anything went so deep into my heart as that scream. I fell on my knees, and heard nothing and saw nothing, till I felt Peggy's arms round my neck, and heard her say, 'Oh, aunt, I see her—I see you.'"

Many more eloquent tales have produced less sensation than the simple story of this good aunt. Mrs. Westall wiped the tears from her eyes; Caroline put her handkerchief to hers; Mr. Redwood's speaking face showed that other and deeper feelings than compassion and sympathy had been awakened; and Charles, who had drawn the little girl close to him, asked a hundred questions in relation to Miss Bruce, and expressed by his caresses his pleasure in her simple expressions of gratitude and love.

The party now took a very kind leave of Peggy and her aunt, and returned home—all in rather a contemplative frame of mind. Mr. Redwood once turned abruptly to his daughter, and asked her if she remembered the quotation he had made to her, that the "simplest characters sometimes baffle all the art of decipherers?"[2]

"She remembered it," she said, "but she thought simple characters were not worth deciphering." After they reached home, the ceremony of tea came in aid of Caroline's efforts, and changed the train of association, and seconded by Mrs. Westall, she succeeded in exciting a more lively tone of spirits in the party; but fate seemed determined not to suspend its persecutions, for after tea, when she seemed quite to have forgotten the incidents of the ride, and her gayety had arrived to its usual pitch, it was suddenly checked by Miss Deborah, who came into the parlour and informed Mr. Redwood "that Billy Raymond, the lame boy that supported his old mother by fishing, had called to see if the stranger gentleman would have the generosity to pay him the damages for his fishing-tackle, that Miss Redwood had lost at the time of her frolic in his canoe?" This was the first time Mr. Redwood had heard any hint of the canoe adventure, and he inquired into the particulars. Caroline carelessly detailed them, and Mr. Redwood, ascertaining from Deborah the amount of the boy's loss, gave her a sum for the applicant which she deemed a most liberal compensation, for shaking the silver in her hand, while her eye glistened with an honest joy at the good fortune of her protegé—

"Thank'e, thank'e, squire," said she, "this is profit, and no loss to Bill—the lad is a worthy lad, and thank the Lord, his bread has not been cast on the waters without coming to him again. It is well, young folks," she continued, turning her eyes on Miss Redwood and Westall—"it is well when the heart and the purse of a gentleman fall in company—here," and she opened her hand and surveyed the glittering coins, "here is what will make a young heart leap with joy—and an old one too, and that is not so easy a matter—and after all, squire, it is but a drop from your full bucket. Oh, you rich ones might be god-like on the earth if ye would."

"And how, Miss Debby?" inquired Mr. Redwood, pleased with her earnestness; "if you will furnish me an easy rule I may possibly adopt it."

"Make the cause of the poor thine own: the rule is not overly easy, squire, as maybe you have found. It is a hard tug to keep up with them scripter rules, they are all ahead of us."

---

2. See note 2 on page 105.

"Miss Deborah's sagacity or experience," observed Westall to Mr. Redwood, "has led her to one of the most satisfactory proofs of the divine origin of our religion." Mr. Redwood averted his eyes, and adjusted the sling of his arm, while Caroline, putting up her fan to shelter herself from her father's observation, whispered: "Lord, Mr. Westall, do you not know that papa is an infidel?"

"Your father?"

"Oh yes—it is indeed quite shocking"—how far the sudden gravity of Westall's face would have prompted her to proceed in her lamentations, is uncertain, for her attention was called by her father, who, willing to divert the conversation from the channel into which it had fallen, asked her why she had never mentioned the affair of the canoe to him?

"Oh, I quite forgot it, sir," she replied, "in my pleasure at seeing Mrs. Westall"—and her son, her eyes added, as she sent a sparkling glance to Charles. Her reply did not appear entirely to satisfy Westall, even with the flattering appendage to it which her kind look had supplied; after musing a moment he said, "I hope Miss Redwood has not forgotten her friend's presence of mind on that occasion?"

"Miss Bruce's?—certainly not—though it deprived me of the romance of being rescued by you, Mr. Westall, which you know would have been quite an incident for a novel."

"I don't know about incidents," said Debby, who was arrested as she was leaving the room by the allusion to Ellen, "but I think if anybody had saved me from the accident of being drowned or ducked, I should not have left it to other folks to tell of it."

There was one unsuspected and most unwilling auditor of this conversation—Ellen Bruce. She had been indulging herself with the refreshment of a short walk, and was just re-entering the door, and lingering to gaze on the dewy landscape glittering in the moonbeams, when her ear caught Charles Westall's inquiry in relation to herself she was awkwardly situated, for she could not advance without being observed, nor remain without being an involuntary listener to a conversation that seemed now to have turned upon herself. While she was hesitating, Mr. Redwood inquired of Debby "why Miss Bruce latterly confined herself so much to Mrs. Allen's room?"

"Why," said Deborah, "the fact is, that the old lady is broke to pieces with her troubles, and the moment Ellen is out of her sight she moans for her like a child fretting for its mother: we all try to spell her, but none of us can do anything right but Ellen: it is past all belief what she does for the old lady—it is enough to wear out the strength of Sampson. I talk to Mrs. Allen, but she is quite past hearing to reason, though there was never a nicer reasonabler woman than she has been in her day."

"It is quite surprising," observed Caroline, languidly, to Mrs. Westall, "what labours these New England women perform."

"Surprising, indeed," echoed Mrs. Westall, "but it's all in habit, my dear."

"New England women—habit!" exclaimed Deborah. "I'll tell you what—it is not being born here or there, it is not habit; it is not strength of limb, but here," and she struck her hand against her heart—"here is what gives Ellen Bruce strength and patience."

There was energy if not eloquence in Deborah's manner, and Charles Westall, who had listened to the conversation from the beginning, with an interest that had manifestly nettled Caroline, inquired "what relation Mrs. Allen bore to Miss Bruce?" "None," replied Deborah, and then seeming suddenly to recollect that the fisherman was awaiting her, she left the room.

"This is an uncommon devotion on the part of Miss Bruce," said Westall; "but after what we have heard this afternoon it cannot surprise us—there is something singularly lovely in her whole expression and manner, in perfect unison with her disinterested conduct."

"She is indeed quite a genteel young woman," observed Mrs. Westall. "Pray, Miss Redwood, how is she connected with the Lenoxes?"

"Not at all, as far as I can ascertain," replied Caroline. "She seems to be quite as mysterious a personage as the man in the iron mask. I have tried in vain to find out whether she has, or ever had, father or mother, brethren or sisters—and I have finally come to the conclusion that she is, as you know, papa, old Colonel Linston used to call such people, of the Melchisedeck family."[3]

There was a harshness, a levity bordering on impiety in Miss Redwood's reply; it sent a sudden light in upon Charles Westall's mind. He had been amusing himself with drawing and undrawing the strings of Caroline's reticule—he threw it aside, not with that love-like manner that resembles so much the profound reverence with which the priest handles the consecrated vessels, but very carelessly—and left the room. In the passage he met Ellen, who, on his approach, had darted forward in the hope of avoiding him. It was impossible—and it was apparent that she had overheard the conversation—her face was flushed and her manner troubled—her eye met Westall's: a single glance intimated the suffering of the one and the indignant feeling of the other—their fine spirits had been kindled by the same spark—it was one of those moments when the soul sends its bright illuminations to the face, and does not need the intervention of language. Ellen's

---

3. *of the Melchisedeck family*: The Canaanite priest–king Melchisedeck first appears in Genesis 14 after Melchisedeck blesses Abraham and, in return, Abraham pays a tithe to him; he then appears in some subsequent biblical passages, including Hebrew 7: 3, which describes him as 'without father, without mother, without descent'. Thus, being 'of the Melchisedeck family' implies illegitimate parentage.

first impulse had been to pass to her own apartment, but Westall's look had changed the current of her feelings—such is the power of sympathy. "Stay one moment, Mr. Westall," said she, hastily entering Mr. Redwood's apartment, while Westall paused at the door.

Her appearance was electrifying—Caroline rose from her seat, Mr. Redwood exclaimed, "good heavens!" and Mrs. Westall sighed out, "what a pity!"

"Miss Redwood," said Ellen, "I have not come to excuse my listening, that was involuntary, but as far as I am able, to shield the memory of my mother from your reckless insinuations." The word "mother," seemed to choke her; a sudden faintness came over her, and she clung for support to the side of the easy chair on which Mr. Redwood was sitting: after a moment's struggle with her feelings, the blood that had retreated to her heart flowed again to her cheeks, and she went on:

"Miss Redwood, it is true I am solitary in this world, but I have not sought to wrap myself in mystery; I hoped the obscurity of my condition would shelter me from observation and curiosity—it has not—there may be mystery in my brief story, but there is no disgrace. My mother died while I was still an infant. I only know that my father survived her—and that he was—her husband." Here Ellen's voice quite failed her, but after a moment's pause she proceeded with tolerable composure. "This was her last solemn declaration. The proofs of her marriage and other private documents are in my hands, in a locked casket. It was my mother's dying injunction that it should not be opened till a period arrived, which she named. I have guarded it," she added, clasping her hands and raising her fine eyes, "as the Israelites guarded the ark of the living God. The time is now not far distant when I am at liberty to examine its contents—to explore my own history."

"But, my God!" interrupted Mr. Redwood, "Miss Bruce—Ellen—my poor child—have you quietly complied with so strange, so arbitrary a request?"

"I never heard anything so unaccountable, so ridiculous," exclaimed Caroline. "Nor I," said Mrs. Westall; "it is indeed inexplicable."

Westall said nothing: his eyes were riveted with intense eagerness on Ellen, who replied, "Can it be inexplicable to you, Mrs. Westall, who have a devoted son; to you, Miss Redwood, who can render a daily service to your parent, that I should hold sacred and dear the only act of filial duty that remains to me?"

"You are too scrupulous, Miss Bruce," said Mr. Redwood. "It cannot be your duty to comply with so irrational a restriction: you may have a parent living, to whom your filial piety might be of some avail while you are rendering this fanciful homage to her who is insensible and unknowing as the clods of the valley."

"I do not believe it, sir!" replied Ellen with impetuosity; "My mother seems always near to me; I hear her voice, I feel her influence in every event of my life—why she imposed this restriction on me I know not, but that it had a sufficient cause I may trust to the tenderness of a dying mother's heart."

Charles Westall had listened with breathless interest; he now advanced involuntarily, and seizing Ellen's hand, "Admirable being!" he exclaimed, "Your enthusiasm cannot be taken from you—persevere—and," he added, in a softened and tremulous voice, "God shield you from the shafts of the careless, the cruel, or the envious."

Ellen certainly felt a glow of gratitude and delight that there was one who perfectly understood her: such sympathies are well compared to the perfect accords of fine instruments. She had hardly uttered a fervent "thank you, Mr. Westall," before a sudden feeling of the awkwardness of her conspicuous situation came over her;—her natural timidity had been controlled by stronger feelings, but now yielding to it, she trembled, became pale, and abruptly left the room to seek the shelter of her own apartment.

Westall's last words to Ellen were still ringing in Caroline's ears. "I trust, sir," said she, addressing herself to him, "that you did not mean to do me the honour to class me among the 'careless, cruel, or envious?'"

"Oh no, my sweet Caroline," exclaimed Mrs. Westall, "how can you ask such a question: he did not indeed—you did not, my son—of course you could not?"

Westall did not second his mother's earnest defence; he merely said coldly, "that he hoped Miss Redwood was not conscious of deserving to be so classed."

"Lord bless me!—no;" replied Caroline, "I had not thought of hurting the girl's feelings; who could have dreamed that she was listening at the door? But you know the old proverb, Mrs. Westall, 'listeners never hear any good of themselves.'"[4]

"That is too often true, my love," replied Mrs. Westall.

"Mother!"—exclaimed Charles Westall, in a tone that savoured of reproach, but had still more of grief than resentment in it; and then unable to endure any longer his mother's sycophancy, and perhaps unwilling to expose his own emotion, he left the room.

"Shame on you, Caroline!" said her father.

"Now really," interposed Mrs. Westall, "I do not see that Caroline is at all in fault: how could she divine that Miss Bruce was within hearing?—indeed, my dear sir, it was mere pleasantry on her part. It is a pity Miss

---

4. *'listeners never hear any good of themselves'*: A proverbial saying of the seventeenth century.

Bruce, who appears so amiable, should tell such an incredible story; no one can believe it, you know, unless it be Charles. It is just like him to be taken with such romance; it was my dear husband's greatest fault; but I own, Caroline, I am shocked at Charles's inadvertence; I am sure it was unintentional."

"It is quite indifferent to me, whether it was or not," replied Caroline, pouting, and evidently far enough from the stoical feeling she professed. Mrs. Westall perceived that this was not a propitious moment, and whispering to Caroline that Charles should do penance by going home at an hour so much earlier than usual, she took her leave, and returned to the village with her son. This was the first time that their return had not been animated by a conversation about Miss Redwood. This evening her name was not mentioned—neither spoke of the scene at the cottage, nor of Ellen's extraordinary disclosure. They mutually understood that their feelings did not harmonize, and both maintained silence. When they parted for the night, Charles kissed his mother, as was his custom, tenderly; and as he closed the door, she heard him sigh deeply.—She regretted that she had pained him, but she thought it a pity that he had such *peculiar feelings*.

CHAPTER XI.

"I'll be so bold to break the seal for once."[1]
Two Gentlemen of Verona.

As soon as the Westalls were gone, Caroline rose to leave her father's room. "Stop for one moment, my child," said he. "I hope that the experience of this day and evening has taught you, if not to be more generous in your judgments, to be more careful in the expression of them. I think you cannot fail to learn this lesson from the story of the blind child, which has furnished the solution to those mysterious morning walks, and that more mysterious night's absence which perplexed you so much, while you had nothing else to employ your thoughts upon."

"Yes, sir, that riddle is read; but Miss Bruce has been so good as to give out another, which even you may be puzzled to solve."

"I shall not make the effort, Caroline. I entreat you to atone by your attentions to Miss Bruce for your unjust suspicions, and for your rudeness this evening; common justice requires that you should do so; and besides, I can assure you, it will not be an easy matter to efface the impression that your unfortunate remarks in relation to her have made on Westall's mind."

"I care not, sir, whether they are effaced or not," replied Caroline, sullenly.

"Pursue your own way then, Miss Redwood, I shall not attempt to guide you."

"Thank you, sir," replied the daughter in a cool sarcastic tone which she could sometimes assume; and then wishing her father a good night, she retired to her own apartment in a state of mind resembling that of a petted child deprived of its playthings.

She was surprised to find that Ellen, who had of late been constantly with Mrs. Allen, was already in her room. Ellen, believing that Caroline was still occupied with her guests, had taken her precious casket from one of her drawers, had placed it on the window-ledge, and was sitting in a

---

1. *'I'll be so bold to break the seal for once'*: From III, i of Shakespeare's *Two Gentlemen of Verona*.

deep reverie with her cheek leaning on it, when Caroline's entrance startled and somewhat disconcerted her.

We ought not perhaps to draw aside the veil and disclose her secret meditations. It is better to appeal to the experience of other young ladies to determine whether it is not probable that the thoughts of Westall, and of the animated interest he had expressed for her, had not some part in her reverie, and whether the pleasure he had awakened did not more than counterbalance the pain Caroline had inflicted. There was a newly fallen tear on the box, which would not perhaps justify such a conclusion, but then her face was so bright and peaceful, that a malignant spirit might have shrunk in despair from the attempt to cast a shadow over it. She rose at Caroline's entrance, to replace the box in the drawer. "Ah," said Caroline, "that is your precious casket—is it, Miss Bruce? Pray allow me to look at it." She took it from Ellen's hand, and carelessly shaking it, said, "It is quite light, there is something rattles though—should it be a miniature? Lord! I would open it, perhaps the painting will be spoiled—I should like of all things to know whether it is a hoax—now do not look so like a tragedy-queen—all I mean is that it may have been a way your mother adopted to save your feelings— after all, perhaps it is nothing, it is not larger than one of my jewel cases."

"It contains all my jewels, Miss Redwood; permit me to take it," replied Ellen, with some emotion; for she could no longer endure to see that handled and discussed with so much levity, which she had never touched but with a sentiment resembling religious awe.

While Ellen replaced the box in the drawer, Caroline watched her, saying at the same time, (for she was displeased at Ellen's manner of resuming it,) "I cannot have the slightest curiosity about the contents of your box, of course, Miss Bruce—but if they were as important to me as they are to you, I should not hesitate: it is quite silly to suppose there would be any harm in just taking a peep."

"My mind is entirely at rest on the subject," replied Ellen. "There are feelings, Miss Redwood, that can control curiosity—even the most natural and reasonable curiosity. I am sorry that my poor concerns have been obtruded on your notice, but since they have been, the greatest favour you can do me now is to forget them;" then bidding Caroline good night, she returned to Mrs. Allen.

'Forget them,' Caroline could not—the demon of curiosity had taken possession of her mind. She had suffered injurious thoughts of Ellen till she had come to consider her as an enemy of whom it was right to take any advantage. Her self-importance had been mortified by the deference paid to Ellen by the Lenoxes—her self-love offended by her father's excessive admiration. Caroline had the passions of a strong character, and the habits of a weak one. In her idleness her thoughts had brooded over Ellen's conduct, till she had magnified the most trivial circumstances into a ground of alarm or anxiety, but since the arrival of Charles Westall she had almost forgotten her, and quite forgotten her silly fancy of the danger of what she called a "sentimental affair" between Ellen and her father. The events of the day and evening had thrown a strong light on her rival, and cast her quite into the shade: this was enough to relume the fires of envy in Caroline's bosom, if they were not already kindled by the interest Westall had manifested in Ellen.

A most convenient opportunity now offered to gratify her curiosity, perhaps to confirm her malicious conjectures. It was possible that the key to one of her trinket cases might open Ellen's box; there could be no harm in trying just to see if one would suit. She drew out the drawer in which she had seen Ellen replace her casket, and then paused for a moment—but, "c'est le premier pas qui coute;"[2] the first wrong step taken, or resolved on, the next is easy and almost certain. She carried the box to the light, found a key that exactly fitted, and then the gratification could not be resisted.

She opened the box—a miniature laid on the top of it. Caroline started at the first glance as if she had seen a spectre—she took it out and examined it—a name legibly written on the reverse of the picture confirmed her first impressions. She replaced it in the box—she would have given worlds that she had never seen it—but the bold, bad deed was done; and, "past who can recall, or done undo?"[3] After pacing the room for a few moments in agitation of mind bordering on distraction, she returned to the examination of the box: there was in it a letter directed "To my child."—it was unsealed, unless a tress of beautiful hair which was bound around it might be called a seal. There was also a certificate of the marriage of Ellen's mother to the original of the picture. Caroline's first impulse was to destroy the records: she went to the window, threw up the sash, and prepared to give Ellen's treasure to the disposition of the winds; but, as she unbound the lock of hair that she might reduce the letter to fragments, it curled around her hand, and awakened a feeling of awe and superstition. She paused, she was familiar with folly, but not with crime; she had not virtue enough to restore Ellen's right, nor hardihood enough to annihilate the proof of it: a feeble purpose of future restitution dawned in her mind—the

2. *'c'est le premier pas qui coûte'*: French for 'The first step is the most difficult,' this version is a variation on a quotation from Madame du Deffand (1697–1780), originally written in a 1767 letter to Horace Walpole (1717–97). This quotation was subsequently referenced in Gibbon's *The Decline and Fall of the Roman Empire*.
3. *'past who can recall or done undo?'*: From Book IX of *Paradise Lost* (1667) by John Milton (1608–74).

CHAPTER XI.   129

articles might be safely retained in her own keeping—future circumstances should decide their destiny—her grandmother ought to see them. This last consideration fixed her wavering mind, and she proceeded to make her arrangements with the caution that conscious guilt already inspired. She let fall the window-curtains, secured herself from interruption by placing her scissors over the latch of the door, and then refolded the letter, and carefully removed the miniature from its setting, tore the name from the back of it, and placed it with the hair, the letter, and the certificate, in a box of her own, which she securely deposited at the bottom of one of her trunks. In order to avoid a suspicion that might arise in Ellen's mind should she miss the sound of the miniature, Caroline prudently restored the setting to the box, and then locked and replaced it in the drawer.

For a moment she felt a glow of triumph that the result of her investigation had made her the mistress of Ellen's destiny; but this was quickly succeeded by a deep feeling of mortification, a consciousness of injustice and degradation, and a fearful apprehension of the future; even at this moment, who would not rather have been the innocent Ellen, spoiled of the object of years, of patient waiting and intense expectation, than the selfish—ruthless Caroline! Who would not rather have been the injured than the injurer!

Caroline endeavored to compose herself before she summoned her servant, for she already shrunk from the eye of an obsequious menial—so surely do fear and shame follow guilt. When Lilly came in obedience to her call, and entering, exclaimed, "The Lord pity us! Miss Cary, you are as pale as a ghost, and all in a tremble,—do let me speak to Mistress Lenox." Caroline replied, "No, no, Lilly, I am only shivering with the horrid air from the lake: mind your own affairs and undress me, and do not leave my bedside till you see I am quite fast asleep. These terrible cold, damp evenings at the north, make one so wakeful and restless!"

The succeeding morning Charles Westall came as usual with his mother to Mr. Lenox's. On their way Mrs. Westall, assiduous to gratify her favourite, had lingered to gather some wild honeysuckles for her, saying at the same time to her son, that those beautiful and fragrant flowers were emblematical of Caroline. Charles made no reply, but he thought that though the beauty of the flowers might be emblematical of Caroline, their fragrance was a truer emblem of that virtue which sends sweet incense to heaven, and is to beauty what the perfume is to the flower. As he proceeded forward, at a sudden turn of the road he caught a glimpse of Miss Redwood, just issuing from Mr. Lenox's courtyard. He felt an invincible disinclination to meet her alone, and seeing that he was not perceived by her, he placed his hand on the garden-fence and sprang over it, and turning around some shrubbery, he was no longer within the range of Miss Redwood's observation. The spell of her beauty was broken; the power of the enchantress over him forever lost by the revelation which she had made of her character in the conversation of the preceding day. "Thank heaven," exclaimed Westall, audibly, "I have awoke before it is too late."

"And what is that you thank heaven for, young man?" inquired Debby, who was sitting under the shade of an apple-tree, shelling some beans.

"Why, Miss Deborah," replied Westall, smiling at his own abstraction, "is there not always enough of good received or danger escaped to be thankful for?"

"A plenty, young man—a plenty, especially with you young folks, who have not the clearest light to walk by, and are too full of conceit to see by the candle of older people's experience. Pride and conceit are your ruin: I don't mean yours in particular, Mr. Westall," Deborah continued, casting a side and approving glance at his fine modest and benignant countenance, "but the rising generation in general—it is pride and conceit that keep up such a will-worship, as the great Bunyan would call it.[4] There is that Car'liny girl, all natur could not convince her that all God's creaturs wern't made for her sarvice and convenience.—The girl is no fool neither, nat'rally she is rather bright; the fault is in her bringing up; that I own is a master-puzzle to me, how such a reasonable smart man as Squire Redwood—a very pretty behaved man too, especially when you consider that he has lived in a slave country—how he could have good materials worked up into such poor manufactur. It is quite a pleasure," continued Deborah, stimulated to proceed as others might have been by so patient a listener,—"It is quite a pleasure to meet such a man as the Squire, who has travelled in the old countries and taken note of what he has seen; for he a'nt like those travellers I have heard a man liken to Jonah in the whale's belly, who go a great ways and see nothing. But, after all," she continued, giving the tin pan into which she was shelling her beans an energetic shake—"after all, I don't know what good such stores of knowledge do people, if they don't make them of some sarvice in their conduct and happiness. To my mind, Mr. Westall, it is as if men were to gather all the nourishing rains into great cisterns, and there keep them, instead of letting them fall upon the earth to bring forth good entertainment for man and horse, as the tavern signs say.[5] Now there is my sister Lenox: she has not what are called shining talents;

---

4. *keep up such a will-worship, as the great Bunyan would call it*: The concept of 'will-worship' refers to worship that originates from the self rather than from the Divine. John Bunyan (1628–88) refers to this concept as a source of division in the Church in *An Exhortation to Peace and Unity*.
5. *to bring forth good entertainment for man and horse, as the tavern signs say*: Tavern signs in nineteenth-century America often advertised their hospitality with the words 'entertainment for man and horse'.

but, Mr. Westall, she has used all she has, in the true scriptur way. Just cast your eye about this garden;—I don't mean to praise myself, though I take all the care of it, 'bating the help I get from the boys, but poor tools at such work—look round at the long saace, the short saace, and the green saace;* they are all of my planting, and as you may observe, there is not a spot in the garden as big as your hat crown that has not some good and useful thing tucked into it, except it may be the pinies and pinks and roses—and them are good for sore eyes and other kinds of ailments, besides being pretty notions for the children;—well, this garden is a parfect pictur of Miss Lenox's management of her family.' Eleven children has she brought up, that is, the most of them are "brought up and the rest in a thriving way—and an honour and a credit will they be to her, and a blessing to the world, when she has played her part out above ground; and that time must come to her, as to all," continued Debby, passing the back of her hand across her eyes, "and it is a time she need not shrink from,—for such a life is what you may call a continual making ready for it. In my view, though it has never fallen to my lot to be married and have children—but that is neither here nor there—in my view there can't be so praiseful a monument to the memory of a parent as a real good child. I never mind this rhodomontade upon tombstones any more than so much novel writing; some of it may be true—the poor creatures that's mouldering away below, has lived and died, so much we know is sartin; but for the most part it's like one of the stories of that Gulliver revived, that's so divarting to the boys. Yes, a real virtuous child is a crown of glory to the parent; and as I said before, all the tomb-stones in the world, even them peramids and obelisks, and things cut out of brass, and made in a kind of marble mason-work that Squire Redwood tells about in the old countries, they a'nt to be mentioned with it."

"It surprises me," said Westall, who was evidently greatly interested by the honest and affectionate zeal with which Deborah lauded her sister—"it surprises me, Miss Deborah, that with such very correct views of the happiness and duties of parents, you should have chosen a single life."

Deborah's smile showed she was not insensible to the compliment implied in the word *chosen*; for like other maidens, she preferred it should be understood that she did not walk in the solitary path of celibacy by compulsion. "Oh, it was a whim of my own," she replied, "and there is no danger of such whims being catching—sooner or later everybody slides off into the beaten road of matrimony."

---

* Sauce, pronounced saace or sarse, is in the most secluded parts of New England the vulgar name for culinary vegetables:—e. g. long saace—for beets, carrots, etc.; short saace—for potatoes and turnips.

"But it is a pity, Miss Deborah, that you should have been governed by such a whim."

"Why I don't know, Mr. Westall—I don't know. In the first place, there is no danger in the example, for there's few that will follow it of their own good-will. I don't wish to speak my own epitaph, 'logium, or whatever you call it, but to my mind, a lone woman that no one notices, no one praises, that is not coaxed into goodness, that envies no one, minds her own affairs, is contented and happy—such a woman is a sight to behold!"

"And to admire—certainly. I agree with you entirely, Miss Debby," replied Westall.

Deborah turned her eye upon Westall, pleased with his cordial concurrence in her own opinion; but his had been attracted by a group that seemed to have just taken their stations at the entrance door, which we have before had occasion to notice, on the north side of Mr. Lenox's house. "Oh, I see how it is, young man," she said, good-naturedly, "old women have no chance at ears or eyes when young ones come in sight, especially those so comely as she is."

"I do not see Miss Redwood," replied Westall, his eyes still riveted to the spot.

"Bless your dear heart, no, but you see one that is worth as many of her as can stand 'twixt here and Car'liny."

"But it was beauty you spoke of, Miss Debby; and with all your partiality, I presume you do not pretend that Miss Bruce has as much beauty as Miss Redwood?"

"Do not—but indeed I do though, and I could prove it too, to the satisfaction of any reasonable person."

"Ah," replied Westall, "that is a matter of taste, that has not much to do with proof or reason; but let me see, Miss Debby, how you make out your case. I will be the champion of Miss Redwood's beauty, and sure no knight ever had surer ground to stand upon. What do you say to that incomparable hair, black and glossy as a raven's plumage, turning into rich curls whenever it escapes from the classic braids that confine it?"

"Oh, you talk too high grammar for me, Mr. Westall. Well, I never before heard there was any beauty in black hair; why, mine was as black as hers before it turned gray, and I never heard a word said about the beauty of it. Now, tell me, Mr. Westall, on your conscience, if you can think that black hair plaited, and twisted, and fussified, to be compared with Ellen's beautiful brown hair? Why man, I don't believe you ever saw it when she was combing it."

"No, I certainly never had that privilege."

"Well," proceeded Debby in her earnestness, not heeding the smile that hovered on Westall's lip, "I can tell you it reaches almost to the tops of her shoes; and then, when she doubles it into them rich folds, and fastens it with her comb, and parts it from the front in a kind of a wave—did you ever see anything that had a cleaner, prettier look? And so bright and polished as if the sun was shining into it."

"I yield the point of the hair, Miss Debby, but what do you say to Miss Redwood's high marble brow?"

"Proud, proud, sir, and as cold as marble. Now Ellen's is just what a woman's should be, modest and meek. I am not gifted at description; but if you ever saw that pictur of the Virgin Mary that our George sent home to his mother, (and between you and I, I always thought it was because it was such a likeness of Ellen that he sent it) you will know what I mean: look at the forehead, the temple, the mouth, the eyes—yes, most especially the eyes, and you will say, 'this is an immortal creatur'—you need not smile, Mr. Westall: what I mean is, that that face has been lit up by a spark from heaven, as the hymn-book says, 'a vital spark of heavenly flame,'[6] and a spark that will never die. Now I should like to know if you get any such idee from Miss Redwood's flesh and blood?"

"Oh, Miss Debby, I confess myself vanquished: I give up the face, but you will certainly have the candor to allow that Miss Redwood has the finest figure; so tall and graceful—she moves like Juno."[7]

"That I won't deny. She is just like one of them heathen idols: every motion—sitting or rising, walking or standing—seems to say, look at me! worship me! but Ellen, she is behind a cloud just now; but if you had seen her as I have seen her, every step as light and springy as a fawn's; and now, if you take notice, her motions are all as free as a child's, she never seems to think anyone is looking at her. I never read any to speak of, in poetry, and novel books, and such things, so I can't compare Miss Redwood to any of the gentry you find there, but she always brings to my mind the daughters of Zion spoken of by the Prophet Isaiah in his third chapter, 16th verse, and on; while Ellen is like those Christian women the apostle commends, whose adorning is not outwardly, but that of a meek and quiet spirit: there is just the difference between the two girls that there is between the pomp and show and to-do of the old Jewish worship, and of that of our times, which is (that is, ought to be) in spirit and in truth."

"Oh, you are blind, Miss Debby," replied Westall, laughing, "there is no use in contesting the point with you, but I will go and see if I can discover any of these surprising charms;" so saying, he walked towards the house, while Deborah, following him with her eyes, could not help wondering that

---

6. *'a vital spark of heavenly flame'*: From the poem 'The Dying Christian to His Soul' (1712) by Pope, which was later converted into a hymn.
7. *she moves like Juno*: The Roman goddess of women and marriage, and the wife of Jupiter.

a young man, who seemed to her not to want sense or discernment, should not, after all, know darkness from light.

There had been showers during the night, which had changed the air from extreme sultriness to a delicious purity and coolness. Even old Mrs. Allen's frame seemed newly braced by the sweet freshening breezes that came over the lake. Ellen had persuaded her to have her easy chair drawn to the door, in the hope that she would be cheered by the bright scene before her. After adjusting her pillows, placing a footstool at her feet, and putting her snuffbox and handkerchief into her lap, "Oh," said she, "Mrs. Allen, is it not a glorious morning? Look at the mountains beyond the lake, how bright and distinct they look."

"My eyes are dim, child—I cannot see them."

"Now," said Ellen, placing the old lady's spectacles over her eyes, "now you can see: oh, only look where the mist still rests between the mountains, and looks like a flood of melted silver; and there where it is rising up the side of the mountain—so bright, one might fancy it enrobed spirits of the air—and above, what a silvery curtain it hangs over that highest point—and there it has risen, and is melting away on the pure blue of the sky: the lake too is alive with the spirit of the morning, and the merry waves as they come dancing on before the breeze, seem to laugh as they break on the shore." Ellen was an enthusiast in her susceptibility to the influence of natural beauty; the bright scene before her had kindled a rapturous sensation which might excuse one moment of forgetfulness that her old friend's senses were dull and cold; that the chords were broken, over which the glad voice of nature might breathe, discoursing sweet music. "Here, Ellen," said she, languidly, "put away these spectacles—the days have come that I have no pleasure in them: there is a heavy weight on my heart, child, and it will not bound at such sights."

"But, dear Mrs. Allen, throw aside the weight for a little while," said Ellen, while she playfully held the spectacles over the old lady's eyes, "You must enjoy this morning—all nature rejoices—the birds fill the sweet air with their music; and see those insects, what myriads of them are whirling in a giddy circle."

"And look, aunt Allen," said little Lucy Lenox, who had just joined them, "look at the hay-makers, how busy and happy they are!"

"But, Eddy is not among them," replied the old lady, giving way to a childish burst of tears; "where shall I look for my children, Ellen?"

"Oh, Mrs. Allen, all this beauty is but a shadow of that brighter sphere to which Edward is gone."

"But, my little Emily, that lost one!"

"The lost one may be yet found, dear Mrs. Allen; it is not right for you to despair."

"Your ministry is a kind one, my young friend," said Mr. Redwood, advancing from his room where he had been listening to Ellen; "but vain, I am afraid. The sick cannot swallow the food of the healthy, Mrs. Allen; I have travelled so far on this wearisome journey of life, that I have exhausted the resources of youth."

Mrs. Allen either did not hear or heed Mr. Redwood. "Lucy," she said, "get your Testament and read me a few chapters; that is all the comfort left to me."

"There are then," said Ellen, looking timidly at Mr. Redwood, "some resources that cannot be exhausted."

"Happy are those who think so," replied Mr. Redwood, with an equivocal smile, which indicated that his respect for Ellen alone prevented him from saying, 'that such a nostrum might do for an old woman, but had no efficacy for more enlightened subjects.'

Lucy brought her Testament, and seating herself on Mrs. Allen's footstool, began her reading.

"Lucy," said Ellen to Mr. Redwood, "is quite a rustic, like the rest of us,—unlearned in the forms of courtesy."

"I should be sorry, Miss Bruce, that you should deem me such a bigot to the usages of the world, as to require that an essential kindness should be deferred to the forms of politeness. No, so far from it, that if Miss Lucy will permit me, I will be one of her auditors." So saying, he seated himself, and Ellen, having brought her portfolio from an adjoining room, placed herself on a bench under the elm-tree which grew a few yards from the doorstep. She was just finishing a sketch of the view from Mr. Lenox's house, which she had promised to George Lenox. Lucy proceeded with her reading, and Mr. Redwood listened with apparent interest, which might be accounted for by the novelty of the book to him; for, 'en philosophe,'[8] he had judged and condemned without examining the only record that pretends to any credible authority to teach us our duties and our destiny.

The lecture would have been long, and might have been profitable, but it was interrupted by the approach of Mrs. Westall and Miss Redwood; they had been joined by Mr. Lenox, and Charles Westall, who was just issuing from the garden gate as the ladies entered the yard. "I did not know that this was an accomplishment of yours, Miss Bruce," said Westall, advancing to her, and casting his eye over her drawing, which was too faithful a copy of the scene before them to be mistaken.

"My knowledge of the art does not merit so dignified a name, Mr. Westall; slight as it is, however, it is a great gratification when it gives me the opportunity of gratifying an absent friend."

---

8. *'en philosophe'*: Like a philosopher.

"And do you limit your benevolence to the absent, or will you permit me to examine the contents of your portfolio?"

"Certainly," said Ellen, "although it will hardly reward you for the trouble." Ellen was unostentatious, and at the same time free from that false modesty which has its source in pride. She would have shrunk from anything approaching to an exhibition of any of her talents, but she did not, either from vanity or false humility, imagine that there was in the efforts of her skill in drawing anything either to do her honour or discredit.

Westall seemed in a most provokingly admiring humour. Not a graceful line, a happy light, or fortunate shadow escaped his observation. He called his mother and Miss Redwood, to point out to them a thousand beauties. Caroline's colour, brilliant from exercise, was certainly heightened as she approached Ellen. She looked over the drawings languidly, and said, "they were pretty sketches for anyone who fancied landscapes." Her mind was evidently intent on something beside the drawings, for her eye wandered from her father to Ellen for a few moments, when she seated herself with an expression of sullenness and abstraction that recalled the transactions of the preceding evening to all that had witnessed them: an awkwardness came over the whole party. Ellen busied herself with arranging and replacing her drawings; the operation did not seem to be accelerated by Westall's efforts to aid her.

Mr. Redwood gazed on the two girls with feelings sufficiently mortifying to his paternal pride; he had abused the noblest feelings of his nature, but not extinguished them; his aspirations went beyond the mean gratification of his vanity, which might have been derived from the rare beauty of his daughter. The classic elegance of her figure, the brilliancy of her complexion, (the more striking for its singularity in our southern country,) the symmetry of her features, and that perfect control of her graceful movements which pride and fashionable success had given to her, invested her with a right to the infallible decision of the beau-monde,[9] which had already pronounced her an unrivalled beauty. 'Ah,' thought her father, as he explored her face in vain for some expression that might consecrate so fair a temple, and sighed at the pride, discontent, and scorn which he met there, 'ah, my child, you look like a fit idol for a pagan worship; men would deify you, but you are all earthly. This Ellen Bruce,' thought he, as he turned his eye towards her, 'has such a look of spirituality, so bright, and so tranquil too, that if there is a heaven she is surely destined to it.' Ellen had in truth a face of the beatitudes.[10] *'My* child,' thought Mr. Redwood, as

---

9. *beau-monde*: Fashionable society.
10. *a face of the beatitudes*: A face of special blessedness.

he pursued his melancholy reflections, 'has no right to such an expression. Ellen's is "full of notable morality which it doth delightfully teach,"[11] and might almost inspire.'

Mr. Redwood was roused from his reverie by Lenox, who observing that his guest looked unusually grave, said, "Why how now, Squire Redwood, can't all these women folks keep you in heart—or maybe you are heart-whole, but it is the arm pains you?"

"No," replied Mr. Redwood, "the arm is doing well enough, and will I hope soon be at the service of any of the ladies; but it is not their province, sir, to keep the heart whole."

"I don't know as to that," replied Lenox: "It is true, my wife gave mine something of a jerk when I was young; but I am one of the contented sort, sir, and contentment, as likely you may have observed, is an article that is not to be bought."

"I believe not, friend Lenox, for if all men were of my mind, they would be all buyers and no sellers."

"Well, that is honest, Squire, I like that. If it was to be bought, I'm thinking you could make the purchase, if anybody, for I judge you to be something of a nabob.[12] What may be your yearly income, Squire?"

Mr. Redwood was not prepared for so direct an investigation of his pecuniary affairs: he replied, "Indeed, sir, I do not know."

"Don't know!" exclaimed Lenox, quite unsuspicious of the impropriety of his inquiry—"That's surprising—I took the Squire for one of those smart people that understands all about their own affairs. It must take," he continued, surveying Caroline, "a pretty considerable handsome sum to furnish your daughter with all the fine clothes I see her wear. I dare say that her gewgaws (no offence, Miss Caroline, I only mean the flourishes) and your coach, and such kind of knickknacks, cost you as much as it does a plain man like me to support my whole family, and bring them up in what may be called an honourable manner."

"It is very possible," replied Mr. Redwood.

"Well," pursued the indefatigable man, "this is a free country, and every man has a right to do what he will with his own; if you are a mind to dress Miss Caroline in diamonds and gold beads, it is none of my affair. You never had any other child I believe, sir?"

"No, sir."

---

11. *'full of notable morality which it doth delightfully teach'*: From *The Defence of Poesie* (written in 1582, published in 1595), also known as *An Apology for Poetry,* by Sir Philip Sidney (1554–86).
12. *nabob*: Here, a person of wealth or high status in general. The term originates from the Indian word *nawab*, meaning a viceroy under the Mughal empire, and later came to refer to one who had made a fortune in India.

"That is a pity—such a fortune as you have to give makes a girl a sort of prey to all the hungry hunters after money; but maybe you calculate to divide some of your property with your other relations?"

"I have made no calculations on the subject, sir."

"I wonder you have never married again, Mr. Redwood; I conclude you was never married but once?"

"You have a right to your own conclusions, sir," replied Mr. Redwood so sternly, that Ellen involuntarily looked towards him. His eye met hers, and he was mortified that he should have betrayed his vexation, and he became still more disconcerted when Ellen said playfully, "Oh, Mr. Lenox, do not expect Mr. Redwood to tell all the secrets of his life before the 'women folks.'"

"Secrets of my life!" echoed Mr. Redwood, but in a smothered voice, while Caroline, who had been listening intently to the close of the conversation, sprang on her feet, and grasping Ellen's arm, exclaimed, looking on her as if she would have pierced her soul with the inquiry, "Ellen Bruce! What do you mean?"

The movement had been involuntary. Caroline, unused to control her slightest emotions, could not resist the mastery of a strong passion. Ellen turned on her a look of such surprise and innocence, that she sunk back alarmed at her own precipitancy: every eye was now fixed on her, as if to demand an explanation, while Mr. Redwood, whose mottled cheek and contracted brow betrayed strong emotion, was the first to recover his self-possession; and when Caroline, hiding her face with her handkerchief, said, "Excuse me, Miss Bruce, I am not well this morning," her father said, sternly, "your extraordinary conduct needs that apology, Caroline—oblige me with a few minutes in my room."

The request had too much the tone of a command to be disregarded, and Caroline (glad too to escape observation) followed her father. Mr. Redwood before entering his room turned to Mr. Lenox, and with the air of courtesy that always distinguished him, said, "My good friend Lenox, you must forgive my rudeness. We southern people are a little shy, and do not understand this game of question and answer as well as you frank northerners."

"Oh, no offence, sir, none in the world," said the good-natured Lenox, "it is a free country, sir, that we live in, and every man has a right to his own notions—be they ever so notional—that is my doctrine."

"And a very liberal one, sir," replied Mr. Redwood, slightly bowing, and smiling as he closed the door after him.

"Well, well," said Lenox, "women are strange cattle. Why, what ailed the girl, Ellen: is she hystericky? Or maybe," he added, lowering his voice, and chuckling with the pride of a discoverer—"maybe she is afraid you'll get away her sweetheart, Ellen, ha? Have I guessed it?" It was now poor Ellen's

CHAPTER XI.   139

turn to blush: she recollected suddenly that Mrs. Allen had been sitting in the air too long, and begged Mr. Lenox to assist her to her room; whither she followed, leaving Mrs. Westall and her son to their own musings.

Charles Westall returned to the examination of the drawings, which Ellen in the haste of her attention to Mrs. Allen had forgotten.

Little Lucy stood by his side: "There," said he, to the child, "do you know that Miss Bruce has put you into the picture, just as you sat reading to your aunt?"

"Oh, has she! George will be glad to see me there."

"George! Who is George?" inquired Charles Westall.

"My brother? don't you know George?"

"No, I do not. Is the picture for him, Lucy?"

"Oh, yes, Mr. Westall; and pray why should not it be for him?" asked the simple child, giving a very natural interpretation to the shade that flitted over Westall's face. "I am sure," she continued, "George has sent a great many beautiful books to Ellen, and George loves her."

"Does he?" exclaimed Westall.

"Yes, indeed he does; don't you, Mr. Westall? I thought everybody loved Ellen."

Lenox at this moment rejoined them. "Like father, like child," exclaimed he, with a hearty laugh; "come along, Lucy, you and I ask plaguy unlucky questions this morning. Young man," he added, turning to Charles, "I take a fancy to you—and if you do get any whims into your head, all the harm I wish you is, that you may have better luck than poor George."

We will not pretend to say whether it was the information insinuated in the kind-hearted Lenox's wish, or the expression of his favour, but one or the other, or both, certainly kindled a bright expression of pleasure in Westall's face: his mother noticed it, and after Mr. Lenox had walked away, she said to her son, "I am surprised, Charles, that you do not repress that man's familiarity; he is really becoming intolerable."

"Oh, not at all so to me, my dear mother."

"But, Charles, did you ever hear anything so impertinent as his questions to Mr. Redwood?"

"They scarcely deserve to be so stigmatized. Mr. Lenox lives in a simple state of society, where each man knows every particular of his neighbour's affairs, and he never suspected that his guest would not be as free to tell as he to ask. It is very easy to see all the imperfections of unpolished surfaces; but, perhaps, dear mother, as your eye seems somewhat dazzled by Miss Redwood's charms, you did not notice her strange start of passion."

"I noticed it, Charles, but I did not think it strange. Caroline has been out of spirits all the morning—quite dejected. You wounded her feelings last night, my son, too severely; it was that which made her so sensitive this morning. She was vexed, as she ought to have been, with the idle questions of this man Lenox; and perhaps she thought (for I thought so myself) that there was something too familiar in Miss Bruce's manner and observation."

"I confess, mother, that a young lady who gives such energetic demonstrations of her vexation at an offence so trifling, is rather formidable; and I think, with you, that it would be prudent to avoid her resentment."

"But, Charles, I am in earnest—you are trifling with your own interest; and I am sorry to say, my son, that you seem to have forgotten the deep obligations we are under to Mr. Redwood—his friendship for your father—for you. Caroline's only offence seems to be a predilection (perhaps too obvious) for you, and the kindest, most generous affection for me." Mrs. Westall paused—she thought Charles's silence indicated conviction, and she ventured to proceed a step farther: "As to this Miss Bruce, her story is quite an incredible one. Do not look at me thus, my son. I do not mean that it is an intentional imposture of hers—I dare say she is—that is, she may be, quite innocent about it; but as Caroline says, and Caroline has uncommon penetration—in that she resembles her father—Caroline says that it must be an invention of Ellen's mother to screen the disgrace of her birth; of course you know a woman of the sort that her mother must have been would not scruple a contrivance of that kind, which might induce some credulous fellow, as Caroline says, to marry her daughter. No considerate man, certainly, would think of marrying a woman whose history is so involved in mystery—as Caroline says, no man in his senses should forget the old proverb, 'like mother, like daughter.'"

"For heaven's sake, my dear mother," exclaimed Westall, unable any longer to maintain his dutiful patience, "speak from your own heart, and do not retail to me any more of Miss Redwood's sayings; forgive me—I cannot endure to see her play on your kind dispositions. I appeal, my dear mother, to your own heart. Is there not something touching—sacred—in Ellen Bruce's faith in her mother's truth—in her scrupulous and patient fidelity? I declare to you, if Miss Redwood is right in her worst conjectures, I think the parent's fault is redeemed by the daughter's virtue."

Mrs. Westall knew that her son was unmanageable in any matter in which his feelings were earnestly engaged, though habitually yielding in trifles; she saw the impossibility of stemming the present current that had set against her. Although dazzled by the brilliant prospects that she had imagined were opening to her son, she was not quite insensible to the virtuous feelings that governed him, and when she concluded the conversation by saying, "Charles, you are a singular being," there was a mixture of satisfaction and disappointment in the confession.

CHAPTER XI.

The purely accidental inquiries of honest Lenox had operated like the apple of discord[13] on the group assembled at the good man's door. It is too well known to require remark, that this busy spirit of investigation pervades the mass of society in New England—'leaveneth the whole lump.'[14] It appears among the illiterate, in what the polite call 'idle and impertinent questions,' and among the educated, in a very free and sometimes inconvenient spirit of inquiry into what the prudent or austere would deem unquestionable. Whether this passion is blamable or praiseworthy, we leave to those whom it may concern to determine; but certain we are that it is incurable: since it has been our chance to see an old lady, perfectly blind and deaf, who, by taking the hand of a friend, and understanding from a strong or feeble pressure an affirmative or negative, contrived so ingeniously and indefatigably to vary and multiply her questions, as to ascertain all the details of all the affairs of all her acquaintance.

There had been so many agreeable circumstances in Mr. Redwood's situation, that he had for the most part endured this inevitable evil with good-nature; but sometimes his wincing would show that he was galled, and once or twice he thought that the case of the poor Dutchman, who is said to have been questioned to death by a relentless Yankee,[15] would not have been a singular instance of the fatal effects of this curious mode of persecution.

---

13. *like the apple of discord*: Referencing the Greek myth that Eris, the goddess of discord, threw a golden apple inscribed with 'For the fairest' into the midst of the wedding feast of Peleus and Thetis, leading to conflict among Hera, Athene and Aphrodite.
14. *'leaventh the whole lump'*: From Galatians 5: 9 (KJV).
15. *the case of the poor dutchman, who is said to have been questioned to death by a relentless Yankee*: Possibly an allusion to Washington Irving's *Knickerbocker's History of New York, Sketchbook:* 'Many enormities were committed on the highways, where several unoffending burghers were brought to a stand, and tortured with questions and guesses, which outrages occasioned as much vexation and heart-burning as does the modern right of search on the high seas.'

CHAPTER XII.

"But I have seen since past the Tweed,
What much has changed my skeptic creed."[1]

Marmion.

Mr. Redwood, as has been said, retreated to his room; and Caroline, with the appearance at least of passive obedience, followed him. A few moments reflection restored to her her self-confidence. She now for the first time in her life felt the operation of powerful motives, and the strength of her own passions. She was destitute of natural sensitiveness, and emboldened by the hardy resolution that had never experienced trial nor defeat. Determined to repair the faults of her sudden gust of passion by a wariness that should baffle her father's penetration, she folded her arms and seated herself very composedly, as if awaiting her father's pleasure—while he walked the room in extreme, and as his varying colour indicated, uncontrollable agitation. He complained of his arm—it was excessively painful. "Then, sir," said his daughter, with the most perfect nonchalance, "the attendance of the physician would be more appropriate than mine."

"No!" replied Mr. Redwood, in a thrilling tone; "no— there is no physician that can heal my wounds. Oh Caroline!" he continued, suddenly taking her hand, "you are my child, my only child"—he was choked by his emotion, and unable to proceed; he again turned from her, while she, with a coolness which bordered on insult, replied, "Yes, sir, so I flattered myself; but you announce it as if it were a discovery."

Mr. Redwood sunk into a chair; his face betrayed the strong mental conflict he was suffering. The emotion his daughter had manifested at the question and remarks, to which, as he thought, his conscience could alone give significance, had led him to suppose that she had in some way possessed herself of his early history, and he had suddenly resolved to obtain from her all she knew, and to disclose to her all of which she was ignorant. Her manner had checked—congealed the current of his feelings; his habitual reserve, which in this moment of excitement, a kind

---

1. *'But I have seen since past the Tweed . . .'*: From Scott's *Marmion* (1808).

tone, a single expression of gentleness, of affectionate sympathy, would have dissipated forever, resumed its power over him. He sat silent and abstracted until Caroline said, "As you seem to have no farther occasion for me, sir, I will go to my own apartment."

"No, stay, Caroline—you must first explain to me your singular conduct to Miss Bruce."

Miss Redwood said there was nothing to explain—she meant nothing—she thought it very extraordinary that she must give a reason for every movement—her manner might have been a little hurried—she was not very well, she was fatigued with her walk—teased to death with old Lenox's impertinence, and disgusted with Miss Bruce.

"But why disgusted, Caroline? It seems to me nothing could be more proper than the gentle check Miss Bruce gave to Lenox; nothing more innocent and unmeaning than what she said."

"You certainly, sir, are the most competent judge of her meaning—if you were not offended, it was quite unnecessary that I should be provoked."

"Caroline! what would you say—what would you insinuate?"

"Nothing in the world, sir," she answered, and added with a bitter smile, "nothing but what you may choose to understand. I am not accustomed," she continued, undisturbedly enduring her father's piercing gaze, "I am not accustomed to have so much importance attached to my expressions. Miss Bruce may walk in mystery, and talk enigmas with impunity, while my poor simple phrases are received like the dark sayings of a sybil."[2]

Mr. Redwood's suspicions were again averted by his daughter's skill and daring in parrying his question. After a few moments' consideration, he wondered they had been excited, and believed that she had accidentally touched the secret spring which he alone commanded. He said something of the excitability of his feelings in his present weak state, and did not permit Caroline to leave him without exhorting her to be more careful and conciliating in her manners for the little time they should remain at Eton. He again departed from the strict reserve he had imposed upon himself, and hinted how much he should be pained by Caroline's losing the esteem of Westall, and even how much he should be gratified by her securing and returning the young man's affections. She replied, 'that to secure Mr. Westall's affections she had no reason to believe would be a difficult enterprise—as to her own, she was in no haste to dispose of them.'

Her father commended her reserve, said he had no wish to control her choice of a husband, and perhaps no right to expect her confidence.

---

2. *a sybil*: A prophetess or a fortune-teller.

"Our intercourse, sir," she said, rising to leave the room, "has not been particularly confidential."

"Strange girl!" exclaimed her father, as she closed the door after her; "what has so suddenly invested you with the power to torture me?"

Mr. Redwood began now to talk of recommencing his journey, which Dr. Bristol assured him he might do after a few days without any hazard. As the time approached for his departure, he felt a growing reluctance to leave the rustic friends from whom he had received such genuine kindness, and whose simple and tranquil pleasures had in some degree restored a healthful tone to his mind. From day to day he delayed fixing the time of their departure, for which both Mrs. Westall and Caroline had become excessively impatient. The blessing, whatever it may be, of 'those that wait,' seemed to have descended upon Charles Westall. He was, as he insisted it became him to be, since he was in attendance on his superior, a monument of patience. It is possible that his virtue was in part owing to his being indulged almost constantly with Miss Bruce's society. Mrs. Allen, as Deborah had suggested, had become quite childish; and of late she had taken a whim to sit constantly in the parlour, where the company was in the habit of assembling. She took no part in the conversation, which she probably did not understand, but (as we have sometimes remarked of persons at her stage of existence) the variety of tones and objects appeared to afford her a kind of excitement and relief.

Caroline was evidently annoyed by this new arrangement, but she had tact enough to conceal how hard it was for her to submit to it, and to deport herself with such decent decorum and medium civility, as in general to avert observation, and most effectually to conceal her secret sentiments. Mrs. Westall, who was really amiable when not perverted by a bad influence, was sometimes won by the sweetness of Ellen's manners to forget the superior attractions of Miss Redwood; and Ellen, happy in her own integrity, and unconscious of design, was frank, natural, and often spirited: so much so, that Westall thought that if she had not all the pensive and serious beauty which Deborah had attributed to her, she possessed a variety and animation that were more in harmony with the spring-time of life. For himself, with the *inconsequence* of a feeling and generous nature, he abandoned himself without a calculation for the future to present influences. If the ladies walked, and the mother flattered herself that by her skilful disposition she had secured Charles's attendance to Caroline, he was sure to revert to Ellen's side in some direct way, that distanced manoeuvring—if he read aloud, at every fine passage his eye appealed to Ellen—in every conversation they expressed almost simultaneously the same sentiment.

On one occasion their sympathy was elicited in a way that excited some apprehension in the observers as to its dangerous tendency. Caroline had arranged a Turkish turban on Mrs. Westall's head, which she pronounced to be surprisingly becoming.

"See, papa," she said, "does not Mrs. Westall look twenty years younger for this turban?"

"The turban does you infinite credit certainly, Caroline," replied her father, "but I cannot pay it a compliment which would imply that any disposition of her dress could make Mrs. Westall look twenty years younger."

"Ah, my dear Caroline," interposed Mrs. Westall, "you know not how far you tax your father's sincerity; he knew me twenty years ago—and he perceives that (as Miss Debby insists, you know) 'every year has made its mark.' Time makes sad havoc in twenty years," she continued, addressing herself to Mr. Redwood; "I think it is little more than that since my beautiful friend, Mary Erwine, was staying with me, and you were almost constantly at our house—bless me, Caroline, you have run that pin halfway into my head."

Caroline 'begged pardon—said she had put the last pin in the turban, and would go and meet Mr. Westall, who she saw coming up from the lake, and bespeak his suffrage for her taste.'

The mention of Mary Erwine appeared to have revived the past in Mrs. Westall's memory. "Pray, Mr. Redwood," she asked, "did you ever see Mary after she went to live with the Emlyns?"

"Yes—repeatedly."

There was something startling in the tone of Mr. Redwood's voice, for Ellen, who was sitting beside Mrs. Allen at one extremity of the room, let fall a book which she was intently perusing, and looked involuntarily at him: and Mrs. Westall said, with a smile, "you remind me of one of my dear Edmund's sentimental fancies—he thought you were in love with Mary." Mr. Redwood made no reply, and she continued—"I knew you would not think of her of course; poor Mary—she was a sweet creature—such simplicity and tenderness—and such perfect beauty. She left Virginia, I think, soon after you embarked for Europe: indeed it was not long after that she died. I never could endure to think of her melancholy fate—so beautiful and so young—not seventeen when she died."

"Miss Bruce," interrupted Mr. Redwood, "may I trouble you for a glass of water?" Ellen brought one from an adjoining room.

"Upon my word," said Mrs. Westall, "it never struck me before, but I really fancy Miss Bruce resembles Mary—did it ever occur to you?"

"Yes, madam—I perceived it—I was struck with it the first time I saw Miss Bruce."

Mr. Redwood spoke quick and with a tremulous voice—he knew that he had betrayed emotion, and anxious to put a stop to the conversation, he turned suddenly to Ellen, and asked her what book she was reading.

"*The Absentee.*"[3]

"*The Absentee*—a tale of Miss Edgeworth's, I believe—will you do me the favour to read aloud?"

"Certainly—but I am near the conclusion of the book."

"That is of no consequence; the story is in my view always a subordinate part—and the sense and spirit of Miss Edgeworth's dialogue—open her books where you will—is sure to instruct and entertain you."

"Well, sir, then I will begin where I am—just at the adjustment of an account with a Mr. Solo, 'no vulgar tradesman.'"

Ellen read aloud, but she had not read far when Caroline entered with Charles Westall; and she laid aside her book while the turban was discussed. Westall pronounced it to be beautiful, declared it could not have been in better taste if his mother had had the Graces for her coiffeurs.[4]

"But, Miss Bruce," he said, addressing Ellen, "I entreat that we may not interrupt your reading."

"No, Miss Ellen," said Mr. Redwood, "they must not—I as an invalid have a right to be humoured—I beg you will proceed."

Ellen resumed the book, and read with feeling and expression the ever memorable scene of Colambre's declaration to Grace Nugent,[5] till she came to the passage where Colambre says, there is an "invincible obstacle" to their union. Her voice faltered, but she would have had enough self-command to proceed, had not Mr. Redwood inquired, "What obstacle could be invincible where a creature, so frank, so charming, was in question?"

"A sufficient obstacle, papa," interposed Caroline; "Lord Colambre believed that Miss Nugent's mother was not '*sans reproche.*'"[6]

"That may be a sufficient obstruction in a work of fiction," replied Mr. Redwood, "but in real life, with a man of sense and feeling, a man deeply in love too, I fancy it would not be a very serious objection. What say you, Charles, you are a young man of the class I have named?"

Mr. Redwood looked to Westall for a reply; he perceived his question had disconcerted him—he looked at Ellen, her face was crimson—the application that had been made of the fictitious incident instantly flashed across his mind. "I perceive," he added, with his usual adroitness, "that I

---

3. *The Absentee*: A novel by Maria Edgeworth, published in 1812.
4. *the Graces for her coiffeurs*: Charles is alluding to the three Greek goddesses often associated with Aphrodite, whom the poet Hesiod identifies as Aglaia, Euphrosyne and Thalia. Often considered the personifications of beauty, charm and grace, the three Graces would be ideal 'Coiffeurs', or hairdressers.
5. *Colambre's declaration to Grace Nugent*: Refers to characters in Edgeworth's *The Absentee*.
6. '*sans reproche*': Without reproach.

have proposed a nice question in ethics. I am no casuist,[7] and was not aware that it admitted a doubt."

"Nor does it," said Westall, recovering himself completely. "I know not how it may be in conventional ethics, but it seems to me to be the decision of natural justice, that the fault of one person cannot be transferred to another—that it cannot be right to make an innocent child suffer for the guilt of its parent."

Ellen took a long breath, and oppressed with the consciousness of feelings which she feared to expose, she experienced the greatest relief from an opportunity that was afforded her to escape from the apartment without attracting observation to herself, by Deborah's appearance at the door with a letter in her hand, and a summons to Mrs. Lenox.

Mrs. Westall and Caroline fell into a conversation which, though conducted in a whisper, appeared to be very interesting to themselves. Westall took up the book Ellen had laid down, his eyes seemed spell-bound to the page she had been reading, for Mr. Redwood (whose vigilance was now thoroughly awakened), observed that he did not turn the leaf; and Mr. Redwood had himself an ample fund for meditation in the possibility that had now for the first time occurred to him that Ellen, the undesigning artless Ellen, might frustrate his long cherished project.

In the evening, after Mrs. Westall and her son had returned to the village, and Miss Redwood had retired to her apartment, Mr. Redwood was still sitting in the parlour, reading some newspapers which had been received by the day's mail; when Ellen entered, and after apologizing for interrupting him, said, "that she had just determined on leaving Eton in the morning, and she was not willing to go without expressing her gratitude to Mr. Redwood for the kind attentions he had bestowed on her."

Mr. Redwood, after expressing his surprise and regret, inquired the cause of this sudden arrangement, and Ellen stated to him that Mrs. Allen had just received a letter from Emily, in which, without expressly allowing that she was unhappy, she betrayed discontent. It professed to be written merely to inform her grandmother that 'she was well, and that she hoped she was enjoying the same blessing'; she said 'it was a big cross she had taken up; that all that called themselves Shakers, were not Shakers indeed; that wherever there were true disciples, there was also a Judas; that she had many thoughts of her grandmother, and sometimes it was so much in her heart to go home to her, that she believed she had a call to leave "the people;" but that her elder sister, who was gifted to interpret, told her such thoughts were temptation.' The conclusion of the letter, Ellen said, was evidently drenched

---

7. *casuist*: A person who raises and resolves doubtful questions of ethics or duty.

with the poor girl's tears. She had written one sentence repeatedly, and as often crossed it out; they had been able, after many vain attempts, to decipher it; it ran thus:—"I send my kind remembrance, as in duty bound, to James Lenox for all his goodness to my natural brother, and to me in times past: tell James also, that if he knew what trouble some people have, he would not blame them, but rather pity them from his heart."

"This, sir," continued Ellen, "is to you an unmeaning jargon, but we, from our knowledge of poor Emily, infer from it that she is tired of her unnatural seclusion; that her early attachment to James has revived in spite of her dutiful efforts to extinguish it; and we have fears that she is suffering persecution in some way which she dare not communicate. The letter must have been written and conveyed away secretly, as it was post-marked 'Albany;' and the elders would never have permitted such a document to issue from their retreat."

"And why," asked Mr. Redwood, "should this letter occasion your departure?"

"It has been determined in a family conference," replied Ellen, "that an effort shall be made to rescue Emily. James, who in truth has long loved her, is most earnest in her cause. He frankly avows his attachment, but is afraid of appearing in the enterprise, lest Emily should be persuaded by her spiritual guides that he is an emissary from the arch enemy. Deborah, who looks upon herself as a natural protector of the weak and oppressed, has volunteered a crusade to the Shakers, provided I will accompany her. She has an extraordinary confidence in my influence with Emily—and with Susan too, the 'elder sister.'"

Mr. Redwood inquired 'if it were possible that she would undertake such an enterprise with no protector but Deborah?'

Ellen assured him 'that nothing was more common or safe, than for females to travel from one extremity of New England to the other without any other safeguard than the good morals and civility of the inhabitants; that where there was no danger there was no need of protection, and that for her own part, she should esteem her good friend Deborah's right arm as sufficient a defence for these modern times, as a gallant knight or baron bold would have been in the days of danger and of chivalry.'

Mr. Redwood ventured to hint, that although Miss Debby might be a sturdy protector, she certainly was a ludicrous chaperone for a young lady.

Ellen frankly confessed that she felt a little squeamishness on that account: "but, sir," said she, "I never could forgive myself, if I permitted a foolish scruple of that kind to prevent me from rendering an essential service to the Allens. I owe them a vast debt, and I have small means to pay it."

Mr. Redwood commended her motive, and half an hour after was, perhaps, glad that it controlled her, but at this moment his reluctance to part with her overcame his apprehension that she might possibly interfere with the accomplishment of his favourite project—he earnestly urged delay; but Ellen said there were domestic reasons for their going at once which she could not oppose.

"Then, my dear Miss Bruce, if I must part with you, allow me to say, that I feel an interest almost paternal in the issue of your hopes—not the generous hopes you are indulging for this little Shaker girl, but those which relate to the development of your own history. Oh, Ellen!" he continued with emotion, and fixing his melancholy eye steadfastly upon her, "you little dream of the supernatural power your face possesses over my feelings—my memory: there are thoughts that quite unman me;" he clasped his hands and was silent, while Ellen awaited in amazement and trembling expectation what he should next say: but after a moment's pause, he resumed his composure, and proceeded in his ordinary tone. "Your society, Ellen, has been a cordial to my weary spirit. I have worn out the world; but here, in this still place—amid these quiet scenes —where the sweet spirit of contentment dwells, here," he added, taking Ellen's hand, "where I have seen that it is possible to forego the display of talent and the gratification of taste, to practise "the obscure virtues which are the peculiar boast of your religion—the virtues silent and secret, that neither ask nor expect earthly notice or reward—here I have felt a new influence—I have seemed to breathe a purer, a heavenly air—and I have sometimes hoped"—

"What, sir, what?" exclaimed Ellen, eagerly.

"That you would make a convert of me, my sweet friend."

"Would to heaven!" said Ellen.

"Nay," replied Mr. Redwood, mournfully shaking his head, "I believe it is too late. It is a beautiful illusion; but I have outlived all illusions, Ellen: the man cannot return to the leading-strings of infancy—he cannot unlearn his philosophy—he cannot forget his experience."

"But he can examine if his philosophy be the true one—Oh Mr. Redwood"—Ellen blushed and faltered, her heart was overflowing—but the natural timidity of a woman in the presence of a man, her elder and superior, restrained her: she was frightened at her own daring—and while she hesitated, Mr. Redwood said, "Spare yourself any farther trouble about me, Ellen—I am too rigid to bend to a new yoke. It would be as impossible for me to adopt your faith as for you to assume the manacles of your friend Susan Allen. But I am not cruel enough to wish to weaken your hopes—we will waive this subject—do you go without seeing the Westalls?"

"Yes, sir, we go early."

"I am sorry for it; they will regret it—they both esteem you, Miss Bruce. We must all support your departure as well as we can—when you are gone, much as I like the Lenoxes, I shall no longer find it impossible to tear myself away. The Westalls will, I hope, accompany us to New York and Philadelphia—perhaps to Virginia. Westall shall never leave us if we can detain him. Ellen, you are worthy of all confidence, and I will venture to tell you, what indeed you may have already discerned, that I am extremely desirous to ally my daughter with Charles Westall. You look grave—you do not think Caroline worthy so happy a destiny?"

Mr. Redwood perceived that Ellen was embarrassed, and he proceeded: "I will not tax your sincerity, Miss Bruce; my daughter has faults, great faults—still she has splendid attractions: her beauty might gratify the pride of any man—her fortune is immense—and if she has faults, why, I know no one so likely to cure them as Charles Westall. I have not, I confess, as yet observed any indications of a particular interest in her; but she has insinuated in a conversation that we have had together, that she has it in her power to receive or reject him."

Ellen walked to the window and threw up the sash. "You look pale, Miss Bruce, are you not well?" continued Mr. Redwood.

"Perfectly well," she replied, "but the evening is oppressively warm."

"I was not aware of that," said Mr. Redwood, shivering as the chill air blew on him from the window.

"I believe it is not very warm," replied Ellen, closing the window. "I am fatigued with the preparations for our journey," she added, reseating herself with her face averted from Mr. Redwood.

"I will detain you but one moment longer, Miss Bruce; should you from your own observations conclude that Westall was interested in my daughter?"

"I cannot say, sir—I know nothing of the manners of the world."

"It is not necessary you should: women have an instinct on this subject that surpasses the sagacity of experience—tell me then frankly the result of your observations."

Ellen, after making a vain effort to reply with composure, stammered out, that "Miss Redwood certainly must know, and Miss Redwood had said—" Here she hesitated again, and Mr. Redwood compassionating her embarrassment, said, "You are right, Ellen—you are too prudent to flatter my wishes."

Ellen, anxious to avail herself of this moment, rose, and giving Mr. Redwood her hand, bade him farewell—he reiterated his expression of interest and kindness, and they parted. 'Poor girl!' thought Mr. Redwood, as she closed the door; it is as I suspected: the most virtuous seem always the most persecuted by destiny. Why should another thorn be planted in her innocent bosom? Mr. Redwood felt a consciousness that he might avert the destiny he deprecated—he had virtue for good emotions, but not for the difficult sacrifice of a favourite object. Believing as he had, that the best owe most of their virtue to the applause of society, or to the flattery of their little world; the unostentatious goodness of Ellen (dignified as he deemed her by talents and cultivation) had made a deep and ineffaceable impression on him. He sat for a long time meditating on her character and singular history; he thought that if there were ever two beings formed to make a joyous path over this wilderness world, they were Ellen and Westall. He reproached himself with wishing to interpose his plans to frustrate such possible happiness. He thought he never came in contact with the good and lovely without inflicting suffering on them.

It had been Mr. Redwood's destiny through life to feel right and to act wrong—to see and to feel, deeply feel, the beauty of virtue, but to resign himself to the convenience or expediency of wrong. His impulses were good—but what is impulse without principle? What is it to resist the eternal solicitations of selfishness, the sweeping tempests of passion?

Mr. Redwood had an unconquerable wish to bestow some benefit on Ellen. He had none in his power but of a pecuniary nature, and that it was difficult to offer without offending her delicacy. He determined, however, to do it, and he enclosed bank notes to the amount of five hundred dollars in the following note:

"My dear Miss Bruce must not punish my temerity in offering her the enclosed, by refusing to accept it. Being a parent, I understand the wants of a young lady—allow me then to act as the representative of your father. By permitting me now and in future to supply those vulgar wants, from which none of us are exempt, you will make me a convert to the common opinion, that a rich man is enviable."

After sealing the packet, he gave it to Deborah, with a request that she would not deliver it until after she and her companion had left Eton.

Ellen retired to her room to occupy herself with the preparations for her journey. Her wardrobe was simple, but neat, and not inelegant. It had been amply furnished, not only with necessaries, but with the little luxuries of a lady's equipage by Mrs. Harrison, from the abundant stores of her youthful and prosperous days. The costume in which a lady of fortune had figured twenty years gone by, would have been quite too antique, but, happily, Ellen's taste and ingenuity enabled her gracefully to adapt it to her own person and the fashion of the day. The journey she was about to undertake was a long one, and, in obedience to the wise caution of Mrs. Lenox, she prepared for any delay that might occur; a prudence enforced by Deborah, who said that, as she had not journeyed for twenty years, she should not hurry home. After packing her trunk, she made a safe corner in it for her casket, little dreaming that the spirit was not there. She had never been separated from it since it was first transferred to her possession. She locked

her trunk, arranged her dressing-case, and took up her Bible to place in it—a beautiful little Bible with gold clasps, the gift too of Mrs. Harrison. Her recent conversation with Mr. Redwood made her feel its value, particularly at this moment. Her eye glistened while she kissed it with an emotion of gratitude at the thought of the solace it had been, and would be to her. Such emotions prove that religious sufferers have a compensation for their trials. A wish suddenly arose in Ellen's mind that she could impart the truths and consolations of that book to Mr. Redwood. The thought seemed like inspiration. If she was enthusiastic, who can blame an enthusiasm so benevolent? She wrapped the book with this short note in an envelope:—
"My dear Mr. Redwood, accept and value this treasure for the sake of your friend Ellen Bruce—may I not say for your own sake—God bless you."

She left the packet with Mrs. Lenox to be delivered after her departure. As she was returning to her own room she heard Westall's voice in the parlour: he had come back with some message from his mother for Miss Redwood. Ellen obeyed the first impulse of her feeling, and moved towards the parlour door: she felt her heart beating violently, and surprised and alarmed at her own agitation, she retreated reluctantly to her apartment. 'Perhaps,' she thought, 'Mr. Redwood will tell him that I am going away, and he will ask to see me.' But soon after she heard him shut the parlour door—heard him go out of the house—and at the last sound of his retiring footsteps she burst into tears. Shocked at the discovery of her own feelings, she hastily undressed, and threw herself on the bed in the hope that sleep would dispel the images that crowded her mind—but sleep she could not. In the multitude of her thoughts; her anxiety for Emily, her concern at leaving Mrs. Allen, her regret at parting with Mr. Redwood, there was still one that predominated over every other. Was it possible that Westall, pure, excellent, elevated as he was, could love Caroline Redwood? or worse—not loving, could he marry her? It must be so—if it were not, all womanly feeling would have forbidden the communication Caroline had made to her father. Ellen tried to persuade herself that she had no other interest in it than that benevolent one which it was natural and right to feel in Westall's happiness: but alas! The melancholy result of her 'maiden meditation,' was that she was not 'fancy free;'[8] and, involuntarily, she covered her face with her hands as if she would have hidden from her own consciousness the tears and blushes which the discovery cost her.

At this moment she was startled by a loud shriek from Caroline. She sprang to her bedside, and Caroline grasping her arm, stared wildly at her, as if the phantom that had scared her sleep had not yet vanished.

---

8. *'maiden mediation'. . . 'fancy free'*: From II, i of Shakespeare's *Midsummer Night's Dream*.

CHAPTER XII.

"You were dreaming, Miss Redwood."

"Dreaming! Was I dreaming?" said Caroline, still continuing her fixed gaze on Ellen, "Bring the light nearer, Ellen. —Yes, thank God! I was dreaming."

"What dream, Miss Redwood, could thus terrify you?"

"Oh, Ellen, I thought I saw you and Westall standing together on the summit of that rock on the lake-shore; and there was a soft silvery cloud floating just over you—it parted, and I saw a beautiful spiritual creature bending from it—her garments of light floated on the bright cloud—she had a chaplet of white flowers in her hand like those you plucked for me: while I was gazing to see if she would place it on your head the earth trembled where I stood, a frightful chasm yawned before me, and my father was hurling me into it, when I awoke."

"It was a strange dream," said Ellen, with a melancholy smile.

"How strange, Miss Bruce? Can you read dreams? Have you faith in them?"

"Not the least; and it is well for me that I have not, for in this case, as dreams are interpreted by contraries, you would be on the rock and I in the chasm."

"That is true," replied Caroline; "but it was, as you say, a strange dream; even now I see his eye bent on you."

"Whose eye?" inquired Ellen, who began to think Caroline had really lost her senses.

"Westall's," she replied, her brow again contracting.

"Your dream then is already working by rule, for his eye will never be bent on me again."

"Never! What do you mean, Miss Bruce?"

Ellen explained to Caroline that she was to leave Eton in the morning, and should not return for some weeks.

"Thank God!" exclaimed Caroline, springing from the bed, entirely unable to control the relief she felt from Ellen's information.

Ellen rose also: she said nothing, but her face expressed so plainly—"In what have I offended?" that after a moment's pause, Caroline proceeded to say, "It is in vain, Ellen Bruce—it is useless longer to conceal my feelings towards you—sleeping or waking they are always the same; from the first moment that we met, you have in every way injured me—crossed my purposes—baffled my hopes--and all under cover of such artlessness, such simplicity. Above all things I hate hypocrisy, and I will have the satisfaction of telling you before you go, that I at least have seen through your disguises, and neither set you down for an innocent nor a saint."

Ellen was confounded with this sudden burst of passion. "I know not, Miss Redwood," she said, calmly, "what you mean by your insinuations. I know not how I have interfered with you: but one thing I know, that your opinion, determined as you are to misunderstand and misrepresent me, ought not—cannot affect my happiness."

"Lord bless me, how heroic! But there is one whose opinion *may* possibly affect your happiness. Mrs. Westall sees through you as plainly as I do, and if she can help it, I assure you you will not succeed in wheedling her son out of his affections and senses, with all your pretty romantic devices."

"My devices! Oh, Miss Redwood, you are cruel—what are my devices?"

"Really, Miss Ellen Bruce, you flatter yourself they have all passed current with us simple ones—the trumpery story about the box—a fine Arabian night's entertainment, truly; your dragging that old woman day after day into the parlour to practise your benevolence upon, as the milliners display their fashions on the blocks; the pretty tale of the blind girl, admirably got up to be sure, with a hundred other inferior instances of your mode of practice upon the romantic unsuspecting Westall."

Ellen could have borne unmoved Caroline's malice, but the thought of the odious light in which she should be presented to Westall quite overcame her fortitude. "I could not have believed Mrs. Westall so ungenerous—so unjust," said she, bursting into tears.

'Ah,' thought Caroline, 'I have touched the vulnerable spot;' and she would have proceeded with savage barbarity in the application of her tortures, but she was interrupted. Mrs. Lenox tapped at the door to say that Deborah was in readiness, and to beg Ellen to despatch her preparations.

Mrs. Lenox's voice operated as a sedative upon Caroline: she sat down and fixed her eyes on Ellen, while she, with trembling hands proceeded to array herself for her departure. When everything was in readiness, she approached Caroline, and said, with a faltering voice, "Miss Redwood, I forgive you; may God forgive your unkind, unnatural treatment of one who never injured you in thought, word, or deed. I would ask you to spare me when I am gone, but I have no reason to hope for that. To God," she continued, with a solemnity that appalled Caroline, "to God, my father and my friend, I commit my cause—I have no earthly protector, and I need none. We part forever; this forever compasses the limit of our earthly career, and brings us to that presence where we must next meet, where all injustice will be exposed—all wrong repaired."

Caroline had covered her eyes as if to shut out the vision of innocence and loveliness. Ellen's words touched her with a feeling of remorse, and awakened appalling fears: her passions were turbulent, but not yet hardened into the resolution of one inured to the practice of evil. As Ellen turned from her, she started from the bed and exclaimed, "Stay, Ellen Bruce, stay—give me one moment's time." Ellen paused and looked at her with mute amazement, while she walked the room in an agony of indecision. Among other valuable branches of education, Caroline had been taught to believe in dreams and all their train of signs, omens, and premonitions; her fancy had been excited by the airy nothings of the night's vision. Ellen's last words struck upon her ear like the voice of prophecy. She imagined that her innocent victim was wrested from her, and that she beheld the visible interposition of heaven in her behalf—that chasm, that dark, deep, frightful chasm, yawned before her, and the thought that she could in no way close it up, but by the restoration of the rifled treasure, came to her like an impulse from a good spirit: obedient to it she had risen from the bed, but she faltered in the execution of her good purpose: she shrunk from the train of evils that her busy thoughts suggested: the certain loss of Westall—Ellen's advancement to fortune, rank, and fashion equal to her own—the exposure of her own baseness,—that she could not brook; and 'I cannot humble myself to her,' was the mental conclusion of her deliberations. 'When she is gone, I can, if I choose, restore the articles as secretly as I took them; the discovery will then be delayed—Westall secured.'

This feeble intention to render imperfect justice quieted her conscience: while she was deliberating what gloss she should put on her mysterious conduct Deborah opened the door. "Heyday," said she, "are you up, Miss Caroline? well, I am glad of it, you will have a chance to see the sun rise once in your life; and when he comes a sailing over those hills, and pours a shower of light on Champlain, you'll own there is not such a sight in all the Car'linas: good luck, and a husband to you, girl. Come Ellen, come, what signifies losing any more lost time?"

Ellen assured Deborah she was quite ready; and Deborah, who would not on compulsion have performed a menial service for a queen, took Ellen's trunk in her arms, and commanding her to follow 'with the knickknacks,' she left the apartment.

Ellen looked inquiringly at Caroline: "I have nothing farther to say, Miss Bruce."

"Then, farewell," said Ellen. Caroline bowed, and they parted.

END OF VOLUME I.

REDWOOD. VOLUME II

CHAPTER XIII.

"Lassie, say thou lo'est me,
Or if thou wilt na be my ain,
Say na thou'lt refuse me."[1]

Burns.

THE breakfast was soon despatched, and our travellers, after receiving many wise cautions from Mrs. Lenox, and earnest injunctions from James, mounted into an old-fashioned chaise, and commenced their journey.

We hope our romantic readers will not regret that our heroine could not be accommodated with a more poetical or dignified vehicle. They ought rather to rejoice that she did not fall upon these evil times, when, beyond a doubt, she would have been compelled to perform the journey in a one-horse wagon—a 'kill-devil'—or, to give it its original and appropriate designation—a Dearborn; so called from the illustrious author of the invention;[2] a vehicle that commends itself so strongly to the social temper of the Yankees, that it has in the interior of New England nearly superseded the use of every other carriage, drawn by one horse.

Our travellers had proceeded a few miles when Deborah thought she might give Ellen the packet with which she had been entrusted, without violating the letter of Mr. Redwood's direction. Her surprise surpassed Ellen's when she beheld its contents. She begged her to read the letter aloud. Ellen read it with a trembling voice. "The Lord bless his dear heart!" exclaimed Deborah.

"Oh Ellen, I wish he had you for his child, instead of that; nevermind, I'll overlook her for the sake of her father—count the money, girl, count it—you can't!" she added, looking at Ellen, whose eyes were overflowing, "Give it to me; my sight is rather dull too," and she dashed off the tears that

---

1. '*Lassie, say thou lo'est me . . .*': From the song 'Wilt Thou Be My Dearie?' (1794) by Robert Burns (1759–96).
2. *dearborn; so called from the illustrious author of the invention*: A dearborn was a popular four-wheeled carriage named after either Major General Henry Dearborn (1751–1829) or his son, Henry A. S. Dearborn (1783–1851).

clouded her vision. "Five hundred is it? You are rich; you are an heiress, Ellen!"

"I am indeed," replied Ellen, "rich in kind friends; but this money, Miss Deborah, must be returned."

"Returned!" echoed Debby; "Why, you would not be such a born fool, girl? A thirsty man might as well throw away a draught from an eternal fountain. No, no, Ellen, when the rich give, let the poor receive and be thankful; that is always encouragement to them to go on. Returned indeed! It would be a slighting o' Providence to return it, Ellen—quite out of all reason and natur. Just like one of Mrs. Harrison's superstitious, high-flown notions."

It was impossible for Ellen to communicate all the motives that led her to decline a pecuniary favour from Miss Redwood's father; but she suggested reasons which she thought would appeal to her companion's characteristic independence. The veteran maiden opposed them all—she had advanced into the cold climate of worldly prudence, but Ellen was at that age when sentiment controls interest. In vain Debby continued her remonstrances. Ellen, heedless of them all, wrote with a pencil an affecting expression of her gratitude on the envelope of the packet, and reversing it, she directed it to Mr. Redwood, intending to procure at the next village a trusty person to re-convey it to Eton.

The travellers had just reached a small brook which intercepted the road: there was a bridge over it, and a road by the side of the bridge by which passengers descended to the brook for the purpose of watering their horses. Deborah thought it was time to perform that kind office for her steed; she alighted to arrange the bridle, and desiring Ellen to drive through the stream, said she would herself walk up the hill on the other side. The passage to the brook was shaded and hidden by thick clumps of willow trees. As Ellen reined her horse into the narrow way she encountered Westall, who had gone out for a morning ride.

"Miss Bruce, is it possible?" he exclaimed, with a tone and expression of delight that changed instantly on noticing her riding-dress and other indications of travelling. "Where," he continued, "are you going? What can be the reason of your sudden departure?"

Ellen communicated, as briefly as possible, the object of her journey, and the place of her destination. In the meantime the poor beast, quite at a loss to account for the restraint put upon his movements, and not a whit inclined to play Tantalus[3] in full view of the pure tempting rivulet, threw

---

3. *Tantalus*: In Greek mythology, Tantalus's punishment for offending the gods was submersion in water up to his chin which only receded when he tried to quench his thirst. Fruit was dangled above his head, but it also moved further away as he tried to satisfy his hunger. The verb 'to tantalise' is derived from the story of Tantalus.

up his head, pawed the dust, and showed all the signs of impatience common on such occasions. Ellen, usually sufficiently accomplished in the art of driving, now, from some cause or other, seemed as maladroit[4] as most women: she pulled the wrong rein, and was, or Westall thought she was, in imminent danger of an overturn. He dismounted from his horse, and springing into the chaise beside her, took upon himself the conduct of affairs. He then, with laudable discretion, permitted the animal to drink, and drove him to the opposite bank, before the conversation was renewed. As he paused there, Ellen said, with the best voice she could command, "I thank you for your assistance; I must proceed now—Deborah waits for me."

"For heaven's sake!" he replied, "let her wait—I cannot, I will not part with you, till I have laid open my heart to you."

"It is unnecessary, I already have heard from Mr. Redwood what you would say," replied Ellen, confused, and shrinking from the communication, which her conversation with Mr. Redwood the preceding evening led her to anticipate.

"From Mr. Redwood?" exclaimed Westall, "impossible! Has he then read my soul?"

"Not he, but his daughter," answered Ellen.

"His daughter!" reiterated Westall, and was proceeding to entreat Ellen to explain herself, when they were both startled by a hoarse and impatient call from Deborah, who was evidently drawing near to them with rapid strides.

"Ellen!" she screamed, "Ellen Bruce, you'll founder the horse; drive out of the brook, girl, if he has not drank it dry already."

The lovers were too much confounded to make any reply, and Deborah, apprehending some fatal disaster to Ellen, doubled her speed, and darting into the path that led to the watering place, quickly arrived in full view of the objects of her search and alarm. There is, to the best-natured, something irresistibly provoking in the apparent tranquillity of those who have produced within them all the tumult of anxiety. Deborah, at a single glance, ascertained the safety of Ellen, and of the horse, and approaching the latter, she patted him, saying, "I think you have the most sense of the three; if you had not been dumb, poor beast, you would not have let me run the breath out of my body without answering me a word."

Charles Westall, though his mind was on other thoughts intent, could not but smile at the indirect reproach of Debby, which their truly lover-like forgetfulness of her and of everything else so justly merited. "Forgive me, Miss Deborah," he said, springing from the chaise; "your horse was

---

4. *maladroit*: Awkward or clumsy.

restive, and I assumed your seat to aid Miss Bruce, who was quite unequal to managing him."

"You are a great manager, truly," replied Deborah, half smiling and half vexed; "the beast seems as quiet now as you could wish him. Is it your will and pleasure, Miss Ellen, to proceed?"

"Certainly," replied Ellen.

"Well, come, Mr. Westall," continued Deborah, whose heat of body and mind had already subsided, "we won't part in anger—young folks must be young folks. Farewell, and a long and happy life to you."

"Stay one moment, Miss Deborah, I have a favour to beg—I have something to say to Miss Bruce. Miss Bruce," he added, turning to Ellen, "I entreat you to grant me a few moments—it may the last favour I shall ever ask of you—Miss Deborah will drive slowly up the hill—the path is shaded from the morning sun—you will not find the walk unpleasant—"

"You forget, young man," interposed Debby, "which way the sun shines this morning; when I came down the road, it was hot enough to boil all the blood in my veins"—

"Ellen," continued Westall, unheeding in his eagerness Deborah's crosscut, "do not—do not deny me this favour."

"Why, Ellen," said Debby, "what ails you, girl—why should you deny it?"

This was too direct a question to be answered in any way but by compliance. Some gleams of light had flashed athwart Ellen's mind that rendered her less reluctant than she had been at the onset, to listen to a communication from Westall. She suffered him to hand her out of the chaise; and Deborah, assuming the reins, and setting off the horse *'en connoisseur,'*[5] said she had the advantage now, for if they forgot her, she could ride instead of walking back.

The moments were too few and precious to be wasted in circumlocution. Westall, after saying that he was sure there was some misunderstanding—Caroline Redwood was the last person in the world to whom he should confide any sentiment that interested him, proceeded to make a frank declaration of the unqualified affection which Ellen had inspired. When he paused Ellen made no reply; and he proceeded, while he urged his suit, to say, with the consistency usual on such occasions, that he knew he had no right to expect a return—that her abrupt departure alone could, and that must, justify his obtruding on her his feelings and his hopes, after so brief an acquaintance.

Ellen was all simplicity and truth, and in other circumstances she would not—she could not have withheld from Westall the confession that would have been to him heaven to hear. She had not a particle of coquetry, and

---

5. *'en connoisseur'*: Like an expert.

she would not have delayed the confession for a moment for the pleasure of feeling her power. Various feelings struggled for mastery in her bosom—first, and perhaps ruling every other, was the delightful consciousness of possessing Westall's affections; then came the thought of the mystery that hung over her parentage—it had never before inflicted such an exquisite pang as at this moment; and last, and most painful, was the remembrance of Mrs. Westall's unkind suspicions, and of the malicious interpretation Caroline Redwood had given to her actions. While she hesitated in what terms to reply, Westall said, "There is then, Ellen, no feeling in your heart that pleads for my rashness?"

"It is, indeed, rashness, after so brief an acquaintance, to commit your happiness"—

"Oh, Ellen," interrupted Westall, "I meant rather presumption than rashness."

"Whatever it is, let us both forget it," replied Ellen, in a tone of affected calmness, that would have indicated repressed emotion to a cooler observer than Westall: "It is time that we should part, and we must part as we met—strangers."

"Have you not, then, Ellen, a spark of kindness for me, which years of the most devoted affection and service might kindle? Is there not the slightest foundation on which I might rest a hope for the future?"

Ellen, in a broken voice, alluded to the possibility that her name was a dishonoured one—"a possibility," she said, "which ought to set an impassable barrier to her affections."

Westall protested and entreated. "If," he said, "the worst she could apprehend should prove true, it should be the business, the happiness of his life to make her forget it."

Ellen felt that her scruples were yielding to the impetuous feeling of her lover. Who can resist the pleadings of tenderness when they coincide with the secret, the strongest, though the resisted inclinations of the heart? She was silent for some time, and when she did speak, her voice was faltering, and her opposition such as a lover might hope to overcome. Westall's hopes were reanimated, and he pressed his suit more eagerly than ever. "At least," he said, "Ellen, delay this journey one day; do not now make an irrevocable decision; return to Eton; let my mother join her entreaties to mine?"

The thought of Westall's mother reinvigorated Ellen's dying resolution. "Urge me no farther, Mr. Westall," said she, "I have not been so happy as to obtain your mother's esteem; and were every other obstacle removed, I never would obtrude myself on her undesired; no, nor unsolicited."

"My mother, Ellen!"—But the assurance of his mother's favour, which he was about instinctively to pronounce, was checked by the consciousness of the real state of the case—"My mother, Ellen," he continued, in a subdued tone, "has been dazzled by gilded dreams long indulged; but she is kind, affectionate, and will, I am certain, be easily reconciled to any step on which she knows my happiness depends."

"It would not," replied Ellen, "be very consolatory to me if she should become reconciled to an inevitable evil. I have already listened too long," she added, and casting her eye towards Deborah, who had halted under the broad shadow of an elm tree on the summit of the hill, she hurried forward.

"Can you," said Westall, "when you see how you afflict me, thus hasten from me without a regret?"

Ellen could not trust her voice to answer; but when she had reached the chaise, she turned and gave him her hand: her eloquent face (not governed by the law she had imposed on her tongue) expressed anything but insensibility. "God reward you," she said, "for your generous purpose—we must now part."

"And to meet again," replied Westall, while he fervently kissed the hand she had extended to him, "as surely as there is truth in heaven."

Ellen sunk back into her seat and hid her face with her handkerchief; while honest Debby, heartily sympathizing in the evident affliction of the lovers, said in a whining voice, that contrasted ludicrously enough with her customary harsh tone—"Good-by to you, Mr. Westall, good-by to you, sir; it is hard parting, but keep a good heart; we shall all three meet again in the Lord's own time." After having uttered this consolatory expression of her trust in Providence, she gave the whip to her steed, and set off with a speed that promised to make up for lost time. After driving a few yards she stopped again, and calling to Westall, who was standing as if riveted to the spot on which they had left him, she threw out Mr. Redwood's packet, saying, "These with all care and speed to Squire Redwood"—then kindly nodding, she drove on.

Deborah exercised on this occasion that discretion, resulting from good sense and good feeling, which, in all its modifications, still preserves the convenient designation of tact: she left Ellen to the operation of her feelings without molesting her with a remark or inquiry. Ellen resigned herself for a while to emotions the more violent for having been repressed. The same fountain had to her sent forth sweet and bitter waters. If the uncertainty of her fate, and the anguish of parting with Westall, were evils nearly intolerable, there was a heart-cheering consciousness of the treasure she had acquired in his affections—there was the sweetest consolation in the thought that there was one who felt with her and for her; and the recollection of Westall's last words was like the bright gleam along the western horizon, that smiling in triumph at the dark overhanging clouds, speaks a sure promise of a fair coming day.

As for Westall, after the few first moments of absolute despair, he began to think the case not quite desperate—and though Ellen had not spoken a word of encouragement on which he might hang a hope, neither had she said or intimated that there existed in her feelings any obstacle to his wishes—there were certain tones and expressions of the face, which are the universal language of tenderness, that he had noticed, and which he now laid up in his memory and cherished there, as the faithful fix their eyes on the twilight of prophecy.

In the course of the morning Charles Westall joined the circle at Mr. Lenox's, whither his mother had already gone. He perceived that the tone of the ladies' spirits was raised (as was indeed too plain) by Ellen's departure.

Westall delivered to Mr. Redwood the packet with which he had been entrusted. Mr. Redwood received it with evident surprise, and said, "You have then seen Miss Bruce this morning?" All eyes were now fixed on Westall, who, colouring deeply, replied, "that he had met her accidentally during his morning ride."

"Miss Bruce is quite a character," said Caroline: "everything connected with her is involved in an interesting veil of mystery—*par exemple*—your son, Mrs. Westall, cannot speak of meeting her even accidentally, without the most portentous blushes; and there is my dear father—the very soul of frankness—thrusting into his pocket a bundle of private communications received from this same fair one. Upon my word, it is a pity she had not flourished at a court; she would have made a pretty *intriguante*,[6] instead of resembling the man your favourite Moliere describes, papa, when he says,

> "De la moindre vétille il fait une merveille,
> Et jusques au bon jour, il dit tout a l'oreille."*[7]

Mr. Redwood darted an angry look on his daughter, and changing his purpose, he tore off the envelope and threw the bank notes on the table, saying at the same time, "Behold the solution of the mystery that provokes your wit, Caroline. I offered Ellen Bruce a little of that which gives us all our boasted superiority to her, and she declined receiving it"—

"With the advice and consent of counsel, no doubt," answered Caroline, glancing her eye at Charles Westall.

"Wrath is cruel, and anger is outrageous, but who is able to stand before envy?"[8]—rose to Westall's lips; he had the grace, however, to suppress it, and to say in a calm tone, "Miss Bruce is her own best counsellor."

---

* "He swells each trifle to a wonder's height,
  And takes his friend aside to say 'good night.'"
6. *intriguante*: A woman of intrigue.
7. *Moliere describes, papa, when he says, 'De la moindre . . .'*: From *The Misanthrope* (performed in 1666, published in 1667), a drama by French playwright Molière (1622–73).
8. *Wrath is cruel, and anger is outrageous, but who is able to stand before envy?*: From Proverbs 27: 4 (KJV).

"Doubtless," replied Caroline, "Miss Bruce is wondrous wise; but she is not the first divinity who has admitted mortals to her deliberations.—What say you, Mrs. Westall? Does not your son look guilty of aiding and abetting this most dignified refusal of my father's extraordinary patronage?"

"If I look guilty of aught," said Westall, "but the involuntary fault of listening to an implication against Miss Bruce, my face does me great injustice."

"Really, Caroline, my love," said Mrs. Westall, in the hope of averting observation from her son, and perceiving the necessity of turning Miss Redwood from her pursuit, "your raillery is quite too much for Charles this morning: I must interpose my maternal shield. What say you to a truce and a ride?"

"A truce, certainly; for I am too generous to fight with one hors du combat,[9] and a ride with all my heart," answered Caroline, "provided Mr. Westall is not fatigued by his *accidental* morning escort—excursion, I mean."

Mr. Westall, with more gravity than gallantry, and in spite of his mother's entreating looks, said "that he must decline the privilege offered him, to fulfil an engagement in the village"—and on this pretext he left the party to pursue their design, while he gave the rein to his own meditations.

---

9. *one hors du combat*: A person unable to fight.

CHAPTER XIV.

> "Who made the heart, 'tis he alone
>   Decidedly can try us;
> He knows each chord—its various tone,
>   Each spring—its various bias."[1]
>
> *Burns.*

WE must now leave the party at Eton which we hope that our readers will think has lost its chief interest since the departure of our heroine, and we shall exempt them from attending her in her wearisome progress, since it was diversified by no danger, real or imaginary, to recall their attention to the sorrows of the simple, amiable little fanatic, Emily Allen.

She returned to her monastic seclusion with her aunt, or as she called her (according to the fashion of "the Believers," who acknowledge none but primitive titles and relations,) her 'elder sister,' more from a habit of passive obedience, than from any distaste to the world. Our readers may recollect, that at parting with James Lenox she had received from him a slip of paper, and succeeded in hiding it in her bosom. He had written on it a strong expression of his love, and an entreaty that she would abandon her false religion. From the moment she placed it in her bosom, her heart fluttered and struggled as an imprisoned bird when her mate approaches her cage. She regarded it as a temptation, but had no strength, hardly a wish, to resist it. All her solitary moments (they were rare and brief) were devoted to reading this note over and over again. She felt herself immured in a dungeon, and from this, the only gleam of light, she could not for a moment turn her thoughts.

The uniform habits and monotonous occupations of this singular community have a strong tendency to check every irregular feeling, and to intercept every vagrant desire. But in vain did Emily try their sedative influence. She was one of the highest, and even there, where few distinctions obtain, most privileged order, called, par excellence, 'the church.' Susan's

---

1. *'Who made the heart, 'tis he alone. . . .'*: From Burns's 'Address to the Unco Guid, or the Rigidly Righteous' (1786).

gifts had advanced her to the lead, and Emily's graces were looked upon by the fraternity as the herald blossoms of like precious fruit. But since her return from her fatal visit to the "world's people," she had become an object of intense anxiety to Susan, and of solicitude or distrust to the rest of the society. Susan had no suspicion of the real cause of her discontent; she imputed it to the workings of her natural affections, the dying sparks of which, not quite extinguished by grace, had been rekindled by her late visit to her kindred.

Little did this stern enthusiast imagine, as she watched over her young disciple with maternal tenderness, how much there was of natural and original feeling in her own affection for her. She saw the bright colour, the beautiful signal of youth and health, fading day by day from her cheeks, till her face became almost as white as the snowy cap border that fringed it. She saw her take her accustomed place at the formal meal, but she noticed that her food was often untasted, and never relished. She observed her slow step and abstracted look, as she passed over the broad flag-stones to the offices to perform her daily tasks, and that though she went through them with fidelity, her trembling hands and frequent sighs evinced that her heart and strength were gone. She uniformly appeared with the sisters that thronged to the evening worship, and went forth with them to 'labour in the dance,'[2] but her movements were heavy and mechanical; and it was too plain, even to the lenient judgment of Susan, that the spirit was not there.

The kind-hearted old women, who thought she was falling into a weakly way, consulted with Susan as to the nature of her complaints. Susan humoured their conjectures, and allowed them to believe they had detected some latent malady. They prepared their simples, and Susan permitted Emily to swallow them, because she knew them to be innocent, and that they possessed that best recommendation of any drug, viz., that 'if it does no good it can do no harm.'[3]

Some were of opinion that she had an incipient consumption, some that it was only a 'drying of the lungs,' some pronounced it an 'inward rheumatism,' while others sagaciously intimated that it might be a 'palsy of the heart.' In short, the wise sisters discovered many diseases that have not yet a place in the nomenclature of the learned faculty; and poor Emily, without a word of remonstrance or complaint, listened to their skilful suggestions, and tried all their remedies, till their *materia medica*[4] was exhausted,

---

2. *'labour in the dance'*: The Shakers' worship included a unique form of organised dancing, which drew curiosity from spectators from the outside world. Joseph Meacham, a pivotal leader in eighteenth-century Shakerism, introduced this dancing or 'labouring'.
3. *'if it does no good it can do no harm'*: A folk saying.
4. *materia medica*: Medical resources.

without effect. She took bitters fasting and feasting—she swallowed syrups 'nine days,' and 'three days,' and 'every other day'—she took conserves, and 'health waters,' and 'life waters,' and every other water that 'with a blessing always cures'—but still she had the same deadly paleness—the same sunken eye—the same trembling at the heart —and all the symptoms of a mysterious disease, which the most sagacious deemed nothing short of a 'healing gift' could cure.

The elder brethren, ever strict in their watch over the young converts, now became alarmed in their turn. They held frequent and long consultations, at which Reuben Harrington had a gift to preside. Whether these veterans derived their light from the experience of similar conflicts cannot be ascertained; but certain is it that they soon came to the decision that Emily's disease was a moral one; and to Reuben was assigned the task of stilling her natural yearnings after the world, and of bringing back her wandering affections to the fold—to the wolf was committed the guardianship of the lamb.

Reuben was aware that nothing could be effected without the consent and concurrence of Susan; and to obtain that to the mode of operation which he had proposed to himself, he knew was no easy matter, now that her natural sagacity was stimulated by strong affection and deep anxiety.

After the brethren had closed their deliberations, Reuben proposed calling the elder sister to the conference, to advise with her as to the best means of pursuing their righteous end. Susan came at his bidding; but she was cautious and reserved in her communications, till one of the brethren roused her, by saying, (after a prolonged groan,) "It is evident the girl is given over to the sifting of Satan,"—Susan raised her eyes, and fixed them on the speaker—"and," he continued, "according to my light, she should stand before the congregation of the people on the coming Lord's day, and, in the presence of the chosen vessels, receive an open rebuke for sin."

"What sin, Obadiah?" inquired Susan, with a trembling voice.

"Sin of the heart—doth not all sin proceed from the heart, woman?"

"Verily it doth, Obadiah—but who hath seen the sin proceeding from the heart of this afflicted child?—and who hath given you authority to discern the thoughts and intents of the heart?—would you treat the young lambs like the fat calves of the stall?"—

"Nay, sister, this is unprofitable," interposed Reuben. "It is too true that the fine gold has become dim,[5] and we must seek for a gift to restore its brightness. Let us each labour for it in the evening worship, and he or she to whom it may be given shall forthwith undertake the cure of this precious soul."

---

5. *the fine gold has become dim*: A reference to Lamentations 4: 1 (KJV): 'How is the gold become dim! How is the most fine gold changed!'

Susan did not venture to withhold her assent to this proposition, regarded as it evidently was by the brethren as a direct inspiration, but her spirit still hovered over the child of her affection as a bird fluttereth over her nest. "My light has been," she said, "to leave Emily to the work of time and grace—but it may be that seeking, brethren, ye may find a quicker cure—it is a duty to remember that in months past the testimony of the child's life against all sin has been very clear. The enemy has taken advantage of her late visit to her kindred, and has carried her back to the path of natural affection out of which she had travelled far; and seeing nature reviving, and grace sleeping, he hath taken that moment to bind her again with carnal bonds."

"You have ever been gifted, sister," replied Reuben, "with that hidden wisdom that quickly discerneth. It may be you see the true evil; but even now I can comfort you with a prophecy that the young woman will awake as from a sleep, and break these carnal bonds like thread—her conflict is sore, but great will be her victory—for I predict of her as Christian Love, the holy martyr of Cromwell's time,[6] predicted of our mother Anne,[7] that this our young sister shall yet shine out, 'a bright star, whose light and power shall make the heavens to quake and knock under.'"[8]

"Amen!" exclaimed Susan, devoutly clasping her hands; and "Amen!" responded all the veteran counsellors in one voice, animated by that vaunted "spontaneous spirit of union which flows through the whole body"—when governed by a master spirit.

Susan, on issuing from the brethren's apartment, passed through a narrow passage to the common entry from whence all the passages diverge, and in the centre of which is placed a large clock, the work of one of the ingenious brethren. Emily stood at the foot of the staircase, her face so much averted from Susan, that she did not notice her approach,—her footsteps she could not hear, for it is the law of the society, which carries its war with the flesh into the most minute particulars, that everyone shall tread softly, and shall shut the doors with the least possible sound—to these laws such due observance is paid, that a stranger, ignorant of their habits, would imagine their houses were untenanted. Emily had paused at the staircase from extreme weakness; the loud ticking of the clock had arrested her attention; this sound, always the same, seems like the natural voice of this

---

6. *Christian Love, the holy martyr of Cromwell's time*: Christopher Love was a minister who was executed in 1651 as a sympathiser with Charles II.
7. *mother Anne*: See Introduction, p. xxiv.
8. *'A bright star, whose light and power . . .'*: A prediction made by Christopher Love. Benjamin Seth Youngs (1774–1855) records the Shaker belief that Love's prophecy refers to Mother Anne in the tract *The Testimony of Christ's Second Appearing*, one of the first written records of Shaker beliefs (1808).

monotonous solitude. "Oh," said Emily, unconsciously uttering audibly her thoughts, "to what purpose is time measured here? There is no pleasure to come—there is none past that I dare to remember."

"Do you ask to what purpose?" said Susan, in a voice of unwonted austerity that startled Emily, "and are you then so far relapsed into nature!—Oh, have you already forgotten when every stroke of that clock was as a holy monitor to you, arousing you to redeem the time?—have you forgotten, Emily, when you wrestled with vain thoughts, and sinful thoughts, and overcame them?—have you forgotten, or do you tremble to remember, when the stroke of every hour carried with it the record of your innocence?"

"Oh, spare me, spare me!" interrupted the poor girl, grasping the elder sister's arm, and clinging to it, "I am sick—very sick."

Susan's heart melted within her at this appeal, and hearing the brethren approaching, she instinctively drew, or rather carried Emily away from their observation, to her own apartment, the door of which she closed, and turned a button that secured her from intrusion. She seated herself, and would have placed Emily beside her, but she, as if desperate now the veil had fallen, sunk into Susan's lap, and folding her arms around her, sobbed on her bosom.

This was the language of nature; and the elder sister was surprised into what she deemed an amazing sin. She wept too, freely and audibly, but

> "When she had wrestled down
> Feelings her nature strove to own"[9]

and could command her voice, she said, "I thought all these natural affections were rooted out—and they were, Emily, but since you came among us the enemy hath sown tares among the wheat. Poor child! I see where your temptation lies—the world—the world calls you; but be not discouraged, if you overcome the temptation you will be stronger than one that hath never been tempted. This is not the first time that the serpent has entered our garden. Many a time after I joined myself to the people, my soul thirsted after the world, as the hart panteth for the water-courses.[10]

"Emily, I have never told you my trials, for I thought the world was as a strange country to you; now you shall know them all,—and the Lord grant they may prove a beacon to you!"

Susan paused for a few moments, to nerve her mind to the recollection and detail of long past sorrows; and then began in a calm subdued tone, while Emily continued with her face hidden on her bosom, sobbing at intervals like a child that cannot forget its griefs.

9. *'When she had wrestled down . . .'*: A variation on a quotation from Canto II of Scott's *Marmion*.
10. *My soul thirsted after the world, as the hart panteth for the water courses*: An allusion to Psalm 42: 1 (KJV).

"Emily, I was the youngest of your grandmother's seven children. My natural father was a good man, living up to the light he had, till our mother Anne, having had a safe path made for her through the waters, came a swift witness to this new world, which being, as it were, born out of due time, was accounted worthy of her ministry, having been, under Providence, discovered and civilized to become the inheritance of the believers. My father, as you have often heard, was one of the first fruits of the work: he and my natural brothers and sisters were among the first that joined the people, and set out for the Lord. I was left alone with your grandmother, and she in possession of all her husband's property—a handsome farm on the other side of the mountain. Emily, I had wicked thoughts then. I believed my family were led away by a deceiver, and an antichrist. I listened eagerly to the stories of those that reviled our mother's name. Some said that she and her elders were the offscourings of the English jails; others, seeing that her work far transcended natural power, accused her of witchcraft; some insisted that she was a man in woman's apparel; and although she predicted the independence of this favoured land, and could not act against her own testimony, there were some who charged her with treasonable practices, and threw her into jail. I was willing to believe all that the voice of the slanderer uttered; and when my father came to take me to her, in obedience to him I went, but blinded by my prepossessions. It was then that mother and William Lee[11] and our ancients were gathering the believers at Niskeyuna,[12] and there your grandfather carried me.

"We arrived at the close of a November day;—the sun had just set in clouds—the sky was dark and foreboding. I had been chilled and wearied with our long ride and fasting; but when we turned from the high road into a woody path, and my father pointing to a smoke that curled upward from a deep wood, said, 'there dwells the bright star,' I forgot all the weakness and the wants of the flesh. The adversary put forth all his strength to secure his dominion in my weak and troubled mind;—a trembling seized me—it seemed to me that I was hurried on to a precipice, and I had no power to resist the cruel force that pressed me onward. I tried to pray, but my spirit died away within me. The low murmurs of the little stream along which we rode—the wind that sighed through the naked branches of the trees—the rustling of the fallen leaves over which we passed, all seemed to speak a voice of warning to my fearful spirit.

"I was always a feeling and a thoughtful girl, Emily, and it had long been borne in upon my mind that great things awaited me: still I hated the

---

11. *William Lee*: The brother of Mother Anne and leader in the Shaker community.
12. *Niskeyuna*: A town in central New York state.

way that was opened, and joyfully would I have turned my back upon the light that was ready to dawn on me.

"As we approached the house the believers were closing the afternoon worship; I caught the sound of the evening hymn: it was so ordered, that I did not then, nor till long after, witness the going forth in the dance. My faith was not yet strong enough for it, and for a long time, the Lord forgive me! it was a cross to me.

"When we were about to enter the door, my father perceived that my limbs were sinking under me, and he led, or rather dragged me into the room. Oh Emily, I shall never forget that moment.

"The apartment, though in a log house, was a large one, the brethren having in their early gathering removed all the partitions to give space for the labour worship. There was a bright fire on the hearth from some pine knots, but no other light in the room. The brethren, with their broad-brimmed hats slouched, and casting a deep shadow over their faces, were sitting on one side of the room as is their custom—the sisters on the other; their arms were folded, and their eyes all cast down; and exhausted by the evening labour they were pale as spectres. Our mother stood in the centre of the apartment alone—her arms also folded across her breast. I looked fearfully around—I saw my natural brothers and sisters, as the flame burned brightly and shone upon their faces, but none of them regarded me. It seemed to me that I had come into an assembly of the dead. I turned to beg my father to lead me away, but he had quitted my side, and taken his place among the brethren. My head grew giddy, and I thought myself sinking to the earth.

"At this moment, mother Anne advanced to me; 'And is this,' she said, 'the one stray lamb that I have so longed to get into the fold? My bonnet had fallen back—she laid her hand upon my head—her hand and arm were bare, and white and smooth as if they had been rounded out of the purest marble. My hair was dressed after the fashion of the world. 'You must forsake these vanities, Susan,' said she—she did not speak sharply, though she could sometimes sharply rebuke sin:—she made a short pause, and then fixing her clear piercing blue eye steadfastly on me, as if she penetrated to the depths of my soul, she added, in a low solemn tone, 'Susan, I bear a message to you—the Master saith, "forsake all and follow me, and ye shall have in this world an hundred fold, and in the world to come, life everlasting."'[13]

"Emily, there was a celestial melody in mother's voice in the gift of speaking, and a weight in all her words, and though I gave no outward sign, they sunk deeply into my heart. She said no more to me at that time—she was never forward to speak. In her looks there was a boldness and an innocence

---

13. *'forsake all and follow me . . .'*: A variation on Luke 14: 33 (KJV).

that seemed, as it were, like the truth and the gentleness of the gospel she preached, written for a testimony in every line of her face.

"Ah! she had," continued the enthusiast, her eyes kindling and her face brightening, while her imagination magnified the graces of the leader who had captivated her youthful affections.— "Ah, she had all the sweet qualities of woman, and yet, Emily, for a season I turned my back on her. I returned to my natural mother—to the world, to—yes it is fitting you should know all my temptations—to one to whom I was deeply bound in my affections."

Susan paused—and Emily's sobbing, which had continued at intervals till this moment, ceased. She raised her face, now gleaming with faint streaks of red, from Susan's bosom, and fixed her eye on the speaker, who after some effort continued.

"William Harwood was a pleasant lad; we had been mates from our infancy, and had loved one another (loving no one else), with that faith which is the boast of the world's people: little did I think, till the gospel was opened to me, that that love was the fruit of a depraved nature—that, if I would not perish eternally, it must be plucked off and cast from me. William pleaded for it, and my own heart pleaded more stoutly—Oh Emily! you know not how the natural man can talk—and oh, my innocent child, be thankful; you know not how the unregenerate heart goes forth in what the world calls love—how the breath of the body and the life of the soul seem bound up in the life and breath of another; how cheap the sacrifice of earth—yea heaven, to the idol seems"—

"Oh stop, stop," exclaimed Emily, falling on her knees, and clasping her hands in agony, "do not say any more to me, I cannot bear it."

"Nay, my child," replied Susan, recovering her calm tone, and the self-command which had for a moment given way before the rush of natural feeling.—"Nay, be quiet and listen, for grace obtained the victory. The conflict lasted for many months. I saw that I could in no way be justified but by obeying the gospel and setting out with the believers. Your grandmother hated the faith then as she does now. I could answer all she said, but when William told me, with despairing looks, that he should be a ruined man if I forsook him, my heart sunk within me. My flesh consumed on my bones as if there had been a curse upon me, and often, often between the setting and the rising of the sun my eyelids have not met, and in the morning I could wring from my handkerchief the tears that had poured from my eyes like rain in the night. But finally grace triumphed over nature: the strong man was bound, and I joined myself to the people. It is now thirty years since I believed, and," added she, raising her hands and eyes, and speaking with more energy than she had yet spoken, "I say the truth before God, and lie not: I have not repented for a moment—I have been heartily thankful that I have borne my testimony—I have purchased a peace that cannot be taken away, and cheaply purchased it."

CHAPTER XIV.

"Then I am lost," exclaimed Emily.

"Nay, do not mistake me, child—I mean that having put my hand to the plough, I never turned back; but I had many heavy dragging hours, much hungering after forsaken joys. It could not be otherwise, but again I say I never repented. You know already that when tribulation came, many fell away. Our mother was carried to prison. My father, your father, all my natural kindred left her—I alone remained to abide our day of wasteness and desolation."

"And did you ever again see William Harwood?" inquired Emily.

"Yea, yea, child, that was my chiefest sorrow; he never gave me up—he would not believe that I would persevere in a celibious life—and after our family removed hither he came every month, and sometimes every week to see me. He once came into our worshipping assembly, but the moment that I went forth in the dance, he fainted and fell to the floor. After that I saw him but seldom."

Susan paused, and Emily asked "if he never married?"

"Nay," replied Susan.

"And is he dead?" inquired Emily.

"Wait a moment, child, and ye shall hear it all—yea all." She pressed her hands on her forehead—"My head is giddy, and these thoughts have kindled strange fire in my heart." She remained silent for a few moments, and then, resuming her usual deliberate manner, she said, "William was an only, and an indulged child. His parents had never crossed him in anything; and though he had a kind and tender disposition, he could not brook a disappointment. He fell into a weakly way, and then he took to ruinous habits. His poor old parents died, I fear, of a wounded spirit; for they laid his misfortune sadly to heart. After their death his worldly affairs went fast to destruction, and he became a miserable vagrant. He would come here and sit for hours on the door-step; at these times I kept to my room, for I could do nothing for him; and if he chanced to see me in his fits of intoxication, he would either upbraid me bitterly, or cry like a child—both were trying to me.

"It is ten years ago the tenth day of last January—it had stormed for three days, and the roads were blocked with the drifted snows—it had been a cruel cold night—and in the morning, a Sabbath morning too, when we had risen and kindled a fire, one of the brethren opened the outer door, and there was lying a poor wretch across the door-stone—frozen to death—we all gathered round him—and oh, Emily, child, it was"—

"William?"

"Yea—yea—it was William himself."

"Oh misery, misery!" exclaimed Emily, with a burst of sympathy which she could not repress.

"Yea, it was misery. I forgot myself—forgot all that stood about me. I saw not his tattered dirty garments, nor his bloated face, but I saw him as in the days of our youth and our love,—and I fell on his neck and wept—I could not help it—but thanks be rendered," she added, raising her eyes, "it was the last struggle of nature—and it has been forgiven."

"And have you suffered thus?" asked Emily, after a moment's pause.

"Do not so speak, child," replied Susan, "rather be grateful that I have been accounted worthy thus to suffer."

Susan's raised feelings did not permit her to add anything farther. She became silent and abstracted; and Emily, exhausted with her emotions, laid her head in her elder sister's lap, and like a child wept herself to sleep.

Susan's narrative had not precisely the effect on the mind of her disciple that she had designed and anticipated. Emily's excited imagination was deeply impressed by Harwood's death, and the instinctive conclusion of her feelings was, perhaps, as just as if it had been a logical deduction from a process of reasoning. She felt that the faith which exacted such sacrifices, and produced such effects, was stern in its requisitions and cruel in its consequences. Her fidelity to this strange religion hung, as it were, by a hair, its vibration at the mercy of every passing influence: unlike Susan, whose strong feelings being set one way by some powerful impetus, were as little liable, as a tide of the ocean, to fluctuate from human interposition.

CHAPTER XV.

"Le bonheur se compose d'une suite d'actions et de sensations continuellement répétées et renouvelées; simplicité et monotonie voila en général ce qui le forme et le constitue."[1]

Madame de Genlis.

THE Shaker society at Hancock, in Massachusetts, is one of the eldest establishments of this sect, which has extended its limits far beyond the anticipations of the 'unbelieving world,' and now boasts that its outposts have advanced to the frontiers of civilization—to Kentucky—Ohio—and Indiana; and rejoices in the verification of the prophecy, "a little one shall become a thousand, and a small one a strong nation."[2]

The society is distributed into several families of a convenient size,* for domestic arrangements, and the whole body is guided and governed by 'elder brothers' and 'elder sisters,' whose 'gifts' of superior wisdom, knowledge, or cunning, obtain for them these titles, and secure to them their rights and immunities. There are gradations of rank, or, as they choose to designate their distinctions, of 'privilege' among them; but none are exempt from the equitable law of their religious community, which requires each individual to 'labour with his hands according to his strength.'[3]

A village is divided into lots of various dimensions. Each enclosure contains a family, whose members are clothed from one storehouse, fed at

---

* No family, we believe, is permitted to exceed a hundred members. Hear and admire, ye housewives.

1. *'Le bonheur se compose d'une suite . . .'*: From *Contes moraux* (1785) by Madame de Genlis (1746–1830), a French writer known for her writings on education, and can be translated as 'Happiness is made up of a series of continually repeated and renewed actions and feelings; simplicity and monotony are usually what form and build it.'
2. *'a little one shall become a thousand . . .'*: A prophecy from Isaiah 60: 22 (KJV).
3. *'labour with his hands according to his strength'*: This precept from Seth Young's Testimony echoes several passages from the Bible, including the parable of the talents in Matthew 25: 14–30, that generally prescribe that members of the church are to work as much as their strength allows and give generously to the church so that the abundance may be shared with others according to their needs.

the same board, and perform their domestic worship together. In the centre of the enclosure is a large building, which contains their eating-room and kitchen, their sleeping apartments, and two large rooms, connected by folding-doors, where they receive their visitors, and assemble for their evening religious service. All their mechanical and manual labours, distinct from the housewifery (a profane term in this application), are performed in offices at a convenient distance from the main dwelling, and within the enclosure. In these offices may be heard, from the rising to the setting of the sun, the cheerful sounds of voluntary industry—sounds as significant to the moral sense, as the smith's stroke upon his anvil to the musical ear. One edifice is erected over a cold perennial stream, and devoted to the various operations of the dairy—from another proceed the sounds of the heavy loom and the flying shuttle, and the buzz of the swift wheels. In one apartment is a group of sisters, selected chiefly from the old and feeble, but among whom were also some of the young and tasteful, weaving the delicate basket—another is devoted to the dress-makers (a class that obtains even among Shaking Quakers), who are employed in fashioning, after a uniform model, the striped cotton for summer wear, or the sad-coloured winter russet; here is the patient teacher, and there the ingenious manufacturer; and wherever labour is performed, there are many valuable contrivances by which toil is lightened and success ensured.

 The villages of Lebanon* and Hancock have been visited by foreigners and strangers from all parts of our union—all are shocked or disgusted by some of the absurdities of the Shaker faith, but none have withheld their admiration from the results of their industry, ingenuity, order, frugality, and temperance. The perfection of these virtues among them may, perhaps, be traced with propriety to the founder of their sect, who united practical wisdom with the wildest fanaticism, and who proved that she understood the intricate machine of the human mind, when she declared that temporal prosperity was the indication and would be the reward of spiritual fidelity.

 The prosperity of the society's agriculture is a beautiful illustration of the philosophical remark, that "to temperance every day is bright, and every hour propitious to diligence."[4] Their skilful cultivation preserves them from many of the disasters that fall like a curse upon the slovenly husbandry of the farmers in their vicinity. Their gardens always flourish in spite of late frosts and early frosts—blasts and mildew ravage their neighbours' fields without invading their territory—the mischievous daisy, that spreads its starry mantle over the rich meadows of the 'world's people,'

---

* The village at Lebanon is distinguished as the United Societies' centre of Union.

4. *'to temperance every day is bright . . .'*: From an 1758 essay by Samuel Johnson, published in no. 11 of *The Idler.*

does not presume to lift its yellow head in their green fields—and even the Canada thistle, that bristled little warrior, armed at all points, that comes in from the north, extirpating in its march, like the hordes of barbarous invaders, all the fair fruits of civilization, is not permitted to intrude upon their grounds.

It is sufficiently manifest that this felicity is the natural consequence and appropriate reward of their skill, vigilance, and unwearied toil; but they believe it (or affect to believe it) to be a spiritual blessing—an assurance of peculiar favour, like that which exempted the Israelites from the seven Egyptian plagues—an accomplishment of the promise that everyone that "hath forsaken houses, or brethren, or sisters, or father, or mother, or wife, or children, or lands, for my name's sake, shall *receive an hundred fold.*"[5]

The sisters, too, have their peculiar and appropriate blessings and exemptions. They are saved from those scourges of our land of liberty and equality, 'poor help,' and 'no help.' There are no scolding mistresses, nor eye-servants among them.

It might be curious to ascertain by what magical process these felicitous sisters have expelled from their thrifty housewifery that busy, mischievous principle of all evil in the domestic economy of the 'world's people,' known in all its Protean shapes by the name of 'bad luck;' the modern successor of Robin Goodfellow,[6] with all the spite, but without the genius of that frolic-loving little spirit, he who

> "Frights the maidens of the villagery,
> Skims milk, and sometimes labours in the quern,
> And bootless makes the breathless housewife churn,
> And sometimes makes the drink to bear no barm."[7]

How much broken china, spoiled batches of bread, ruined tempers, and other common domestic disasters might be avoided by the discovery of this secret; what tribes of mice, ants, flies, and other household demons, might be driven from their strongholds. We hope that none of those provoking solvers of mysteries, who are so fond of finding out the 'reason of the thing,' that they are daily circumscribing within most barren and inconvenient limits the dominion of the imagination, will pretend to have found the clue to this mystery in the exact order and elaborate neatness of the sisterhood.

---

5. *'hath forsaken houses, or brethren . . .'*: From Mark 10: 29–30 (KJV).
6. *Robin Goodfellow*: Also known as Puck, Robin Goodfellow is a fictional fairy or demon who appears in English folklore and, particularly, in Shakespeare's *Midsummer Night's Dream*.
7. *'Frights the maidens of the villagery . . .'*: From II, i of Shakespeare's *Midsummer Night's Dream*.

The sisters themselves certainly hint at a sublime cause of their success, when in reply to a stranger's involuntary admiration of their stainless walls, polished floors, snow white linen, and all the detail of their precise arrangement and ornamental neatness, they say, with the utmost gravity, 'God is the God of order and not of confusion.'[8]

The most signal triumph of the society is in the discipline of the children. Of these there are many among them: a few are received together with their 'believing' parents; in some instances orphans, and even orphan families are adopted; and many are brought to the society by parents, who, either from the despair of poverty, or the carelessness of vice, choose to commit their offspring to the guardianship of the Shakers. Now that the first fervours of enthusiasm are abated, and conversions have become rare, the adoption of children is a principal cause of the continuance and preservation of the society. These little born rebels, natural enemies to the social compact, lose in their hands their prescriptive right to uproar and misrule, and soon become as silent, as formal, and as orderly as their elders.

We hope we shall not be suspected of speaking the language of panegyric rather than justice, if we add that the hospitalities of these people are never refused to the weary way-worn traveller, nor their alms to the needy; and that their faith (however absurd and indefensible its peculiarities) is tempered by some generous and enlightened principles, which those who had rather learn than scoff would do well to adopt. In short, those who know them well, and judge them equitably, will not withhold from them the praise of moral conduct which they claim, in professing themselves, as a community, a 'harmless, just, and upright people.'[9]

It is time that we should return from our long digression to give some account of the spiritual and physical labours of Reuben Harrington. At nine o'clock in the evening that followed the day of the brethren's sage council, the bell, according to the uniform custom, sounded for the evening worship. The brethren and sisters poured in equal streams into the two large apartments, which were now thrown into one by the opening of the wide folding doors. A few candles were hung around the walls, casting a dim and quivering light upon the strange throng. The men took their stations in one apartment, the women in the other, and arranged themselves opposite to each other in straight lines, extending across the room. The eldest were placed in the front ranks—by this arrangement the young people were saved from the temptation to wandering looks, and their consequence, wandering thoughts—not uncommon in the most orthodox congregations.

---

8. *'God is the God of order and not of confusion'*: An allusion to a concept in 1 Corinthians 14: 33–40.
9. *'harmless, just and upright people'*: From Benjamin Seth Youngs's *The Testimony of Christ's Second Appearing* (1808).

After a few moments, the deep and reverential silence of the assembly was broken by a shout, in which every voice was simultaneously lifted to its highest pitch. The shout was followed by a hymn, but sung so loud, with such discordant and irregular sounds, (for music it could not be called,) that it was impossible to distinguish any words, excepting 'our mother' and 'Mother Anne,' which seemed to form a kind of chorus. The singing was accompanied by an equal and steady motion, an alternating from one foot to the other, which resembles, to a profane eye, the *pas bas*[10] of the world's dancers. This deafening yell and uniform motion continued till their breath was spent, when all the assembly, as if governed by one instinct, relapsed into silence.

They remained as motionless as so many statues till the profound stillness was broken by Harrington—"Brethren and sisters," he said, "we labour this evening for a special gift, and to encourage our hearts, and enliven our faith, it is meet that we should bear upon our minds all those holy men and women of old, who, according to their light have worshipped in the dance. Sisters, bethink yourselves of Miriam—of Miriam, the sister of Aaron, a prophetess—the first in the female line—who, when she sang the glorious triumph of the Lord over the Egyptian host, 'took a timbrel in her hand, and all the women went out after her with timbrels and with dances'[11]—Remember the daughters of Shiloh, who went 'yearly to the feast of the Lord to dance in dances—and King David, who leaped and danced before the Lord, so that Michal, profane Michal, despised him in her heart, even as the world's people in these latter times despise us, and deride our labour-worship.[12]

"Ye believers need not be told that the Psalmist justifies his deeds by his words, and exhorts the faithful again and again 'to praise the Lord with the timbrel and the dance[13]—to praise His name in the dance.'[14] Solomon tells us 'there is a time to dance,'[15] and manifestly he could not mean there was a time for those vain festive rites, wherewith the carnal children of this world worship their god.—Hath not the holy prophet Jeremiah predicted our day in those memorable words— 'then shall the Virgin rejoice in the *dance*, both young men and old together?'[16] When was this prediction verified in the ball-rooms of the world's people?—There the young man goes not forth with the aged brother, but selects the fair and youthful maiden

---

10. *pas bas*: A term for a particular step in classical ballet.
11. '*took a timbrel in her hand . . .*': From Exodus 15: 20 (KJV).
12. '*yearly to the feast of the L[o]rd . . .*': A variation on Judges 21: 19–21 (KJV).
13. '*to praise the Lord with the timbrel and the dance . . .*': From Psalm 150: 4 (KJV).
14. '*to praise His name in the dance*': From Psalm 149: 3 (KJV).
15. '*there is a time to dance . . .*': A variation on Ecclesiastes 3: 4 (KJV).
16. '*then shall the Virgin rejoice . . .*': From Jeremiah 31: 13 (KJV).

for his partner in the dance; and nothing can be more unlike our spiritual labours, than the movements of their bodies, and the exercises of their minds!—Again the same prophet saith, 'O Virgin of Israel, thou shalt again be adorned with thy tabrets, and go forth in the *dances*.'"[17]

Here Reuben paused, either to take breath, or because he had exhausted his authorities; and the assembly, without any visible external direction, but apparently in obedience to a common impulse, broke up their ranks,— arranged in pairs, the elder taking precedence of the younger, and the sisters of the brethren, they made in a dancing procession the circuit of the two apartments. A small knot of brethren and sisters remained in the centre of each room, shouting strange music for the dancers, and slowly turning, so as to keep their faces towards the procession, which moved on with a uniform shuffling step, as if it was composed of so many automatons, their arms rising and falling mechanically; and their monotonous movements, solemn, melancholy, or stupid aspects, contrasting ludicrously with the festive throngs which are usually seen stepping on "light fantastic toe"[18] through the mazy dance.

There was but one in all this assembly that seemed to be governed by natural feeling; this was Emily, who in obedience to the stern requisition of her aunt had come, or rather been dragged into the room; but unable to perform her part of the insane worship, unable in truth to support her own weight, she had sunk on her knees in a recess of the window near which she was standing; her cap had fallen from her head, and laid beside her—her fair hair, thus permitted to escape from its bondage, had fallen over her neck and shoulders; she had covered her face with her hands, and disordered, pale, and trembling, there she remained, till the assembly forming into the procession, exposed her to every eye, looking like a culprit awaiting her sentence.

Susan had missed her from her side, and had hoped that she had stolen away to her own apartment, and that her disappearance would remain unobserved. Vain were the elder sister's efforts to command peace in her own troubled mind, when she beheld the humiliating and sorrowful spectacle. The burning colour that flushed her usually sallow cheek, and her unsteady movements, betrayed her affliction. She would have given the world to have sheltered her fallen favourite from the disgrace of such an exposure, but to move from the ranks was impossible. The elders and the disciplined passed Emily in their rounds without any other notice than a languid and brief glance; but the younger, and especially the children, unable to control their curiosity, gazed on her till their heads were at right angles with their

---

17. *'O Virgin of Israel, thou shalt again be adorned . . .'*: From Jeremiah 31: 4 (KJV).
18. *'light fantastic toe'*: From Milton's poem 'L'Allegro' (1645).

bodies. Suddenly the procession stopped; and Harrington, advancing from the ranks, "laboured alone with great power,"[19] and whirling around like a top, to which his form bore no faint resemblance, he continued his violent exercise for an hour; then approaching Emily, and laying his hand upon her head—"To me, brethren and sisters," he said, "is assigned the task and given the gift to snatch this prey from Satan. The work is to be wrought out in private conference, when words of rebuke, of wisdom, and of conviction will flow from my lips, as the water flowed from the rock at the touch of Moses.—Fear not, young maiden—tremble not—be not thus disheartened—the devil shall release you from his toils, and you shall yet shine out a bright star among the faithful."

The assembly acquiesced silently in the result of Reuben's extraordinary worship. They dispersed to their several apartments; and Susan, without one word of inquiry or reprimand, led Emily to her own room, and spent the silent watches of the night in weeping and praying for her.

On the following day Harrington began, and continued for many successive days, his private conferences with Emily. For some time he confined himself to harangues on the peculiar doctrines of his sect. Emily listened dutifully, but the more she listened, the more her growing aversion to them strengthened. He insisted that the net in which Satan had caught her, could not be broken, unless she would be governed by his wisdom—guided by his inward light. Emily sighed and wept, but never attempted a reply.

After a while he changed his tone; he occasionally softened his rebukes with praise, sometimes mingled flattery with his admonitions, and darkly intimated a purpose that he dared not yet fully disclose. Still Emily listened patiently: she had been always remarkable for singleness of heart, a soft temper, and tender affections, but never for a quick or keen perception. Her mind, too, had been recently weakened by the hard conflict between her natural affections and her mistaken sense of duty: it was not wonderful, therefore, that she did not distrust Harrington's integrity, nor suspect the meaning that glimmered through his mystical language.

He continued gradually preparing her mind for the proposition he had in reserve for her, nothing doubting of its final acceptance; for Reuben, in common with all thorough hypocrites, was quite incredulous as to the existence of goodness, and believed that the seemingly upright only wanted the opportunity and the motive to turn aside from the straight and narrow way. At last, impatient at his own slow and serpentine advances to Emily's understanding, and afraid that in spite of her habitual passiveness, her patience

---

19. *'laboured alone with great power'*: A variation on this quotation – 'laboured in the worship of God with great power' – appears in Seth Youngs's *The Testimony of Christ's Second Coming*.

would be exhausted before he had approached the attainment of his purpose, and hoping too, against hope, that her uniform silence foreboded his final success—he took a bold, straight-forward step. At his accustomed hour he entered the room where Emily was sitting with the elder sister. He detained Susan for a moment to inquire "if she yet perceived any smoking of the flax—any symptom of revival in the child?" She shook her head mournfully, and slowly withdrew, leaving him alone with Emily with evident reluctance.

He then drew his chair close to the poor girl, and taking her hand (a freedom he had never before ventured upon), and not rebuked by the innocent look of surprise and inquiry which she turned on him, he proceeded to say, in the softest voice he could assume, "You are a worthy maiden, Emily—a chosen vessel—a vessel selected for a great ministry—if you have been cast into the furnace, it is that you may come out as gold seven times tried—the honoured instrument must be made bright and keen in the fires of tribulation. Awake, maiden! awake! and survey the path that I am appointed to open to your view—the path we must travel together; for we are not permitted longer to remain here, mere watchmen on the walls of Zion, but are commanded to march boldly forward to the enemy's camp.

"Listen, while I disclose to you the revelation that has been vouchsafed to me. I have obtained a great advance upon the forward wheel—it has been made plain to me that we are together to accomplish a great work—to turn and overturn till we bring to pass the conversion of the world."

A faint light dawned on Emily's mind, and fearfulness mingled with the amazement with which she had hitherto gazed on Harrington. He perceived that she was startled, but he went on undaunted. "The Israelites were commanded to spoil the Egyptians, and we are permitted—nay, ordered, to take of the lucre (which belongeth equally to our brethren and to us) in order to help us forward in our blessed mission, and to reward our labours. A goodly sum in the bank at Albany awaiteth us. All these matters it is duty for a season to hide from our brethren and sisters—they cannot yet receive them. Our departure must be secret—at night—yea, this night."

Astonished, alarmed, and still uncertain, Emily did not utter a word: her eyes were fixed on Reuben, and looked as though they would have started from their sockets.

"Nay, precious maiden," he continued, misinterpreting her silence, "do not tremble thus—ye need not be alarmed. We have a farther dispensation: as we go among the world's people, we are permitted to be united in wedlock by one of the world's priests."—Till this moment Reuben's meaning had but partially appeared to Emily through the fog of cant phrases in which he had artfully involved it; but his last words, and the fond look that

CHAPTER XV.

accompanied them, were like the touch of Ithuriel[20]—her persecutor stood revealed in his true light. She snatched her hand from him, and groaning aloud, she sprang towards the door—the door opened, and Susan entered.

"Oh for mercy's sake, save me—take me away!" cried the poor girl, clinging to her aunt in desperation.

"What means this?" inquired Susan, looking at Harrington; "have you dared to insult the innocent girl?—Be calm, Emily, my child, be calm."

"Smooth your brow, sister," replied Harrington, with perfect coolness, "and I will tell you all that has passed between us."

"Say on," she answered, without in the least relaxing her features, "and bear it in mind that I shall know from this afflicted girl, who never opened her mouth to speak a lie, whether ye speak truly."

"My word," replied Reuben, "will go farther, much farther with the people than that poor far-gone sinner's."

"That may be, Reuben, but not with me; therefore speak quickly and truly."

There is a moral power in virtuous resolution that the most vicious find it difficult to resist. Reuben perceived that he could neither conceal nor deny, and that his best, indeed his only policy was to state the truth, and to varnish it over with the best gloss his ready wit could invent. He said that all his attempts to reclaim Emily had hitherto been fruitless; that as elder sister knew, he had laboured in season, and out of season, and all in vain—all without producing a sign of life in the child.

"That morning," he said, "it had been sent in upon his mind to try her with a temptation, in order to ascertain how far she was under the dominion of Satan; or at least to drive away the dumb devil that possessed her—in that he had succeeded." He then went on to detail what he had said to Emily verbatim, omitting nothing but his design on the funds of the society; a circumstance that he rightly judged his last monstrous proposition had effaced from Emily's mind. "And now, sister," he said, in conclusion, "I think your conscience will tell you that you have judged me with unrighteous judgment; that nature has so far gotten the upper hand of grace with you, that you are blinded, sorely blinded; and henceforth you will feel it to be duty to leave the girl to my appointed ministry."

"Never, never," replied Susan, firmly: "she has been unkindly dealt with already—nature and grace both speak for the child, Reuben—both tell me that she needs 'more gentle usage.'"

"But, woman, I have the gift."

---

20. *touch of Ithuriel*: Ithuriel is an archangel of heaven who appears in Book 4 of Milton's *Paradise Lost*. When Satan approaches the sleeping Eve, Ithuriel effectively disrupts Satan's mischief by lightly touching him with his spear because 'no falsehood can endure Touch of Celestial Temper'.

"I have a gift also, Reuben: and sooner shall you have my heart's blood, than I will trust this girl with you again; ye need not lift your voice in the congregation; ye need not whisper among the brethren. Remember, I am your elder; I fear you not, Reuben; I suspect you."

The determined look with which Susan accompanied her words, quelled Harrington's spirit: he dared not attempt a reply, and smothering an imprecation, he departed to digest as he best could his rage and mortification.

Susan did not think it expedient to make any farther direct disclosure to Emily of her suspicions of Harrington, but she cautiously questioned and cross-questioned her. Emily, confounded by Reuben's subtlety, and feeble and exhausted, could not remember that he had said to her any more or other, than he had repeated to the elder sister.

Notwithstanding the agreement of the simple girl's testimony with Reuben's story, Susan was too sagacious to be deceived by the interpretation the crafty brother had put upon the language he had held to her, and having for a long time felt a growing dislike and distrust of him, she was not convinced that she had been mistaken in her conclusions; and she remained quite satisfied that she had done right in refusing him any further communication with Emily.

Emily's melancholy became every day deeper and more fixed, and Susan began to fear the total annihilation of her mind. She imposed no restraint on her, but permitted her to walk when she chose; to remain secluded from observation in her own room, and sometimes to lie all day on the bed in a state of listlessness and vacuity in which she appeared scarcely conscious of her existence.

CHAPTER XVI.

"Curse on his perjured arts! dissembling, smooth!
Are honour, virtue, conscience, all exil'd?
Is there no pity, no relenting ruth?"[1]

Burns.

EMILY was one day sitting by her window, when she saw a party of travellers from Lebanon Springs stop at their gate. It suddenly occurred to her that she might, through the agency of someone of the party, get a letter conveyed to her friends. The thought that this might be the first step towards leaving the society, flitted across her mind, but without forming any distinct purpose, she hastily penned the letter which was the occasion of Ellen's abrupt departure from Eton. She then stationed herself at a door that opened into one of the passages through which the visitors were to pass; and arresting the attention of a romantic young lady who was in the rear of the throng, she slipped the letter into her hand, unobserved by anyone, and entreating her to convey it safely to a post-office, she disappeared, leaving her confidant quite elated with the trust which had been confided to her by the pale interesting little Shaker, and which she discharged as has been seen, with laudable fidelity.

Activity is as necessary to the health of the mind, as exercise to that of the body. Emily derived more benefit from the effort she had made in writing and despatching her letter than she had felt from the combined skill, moral and medical, of the whole fraternity. For a few days her heart was cheered, and her countenance brightened. She had no settled purpose of leaving the society: she still believed it her duty to remain with them, and the tender sympathy and forbearance of her aunt had strengthened the almost filial love she bore her—the only sentiment that alleviated the misery of her condition. Still her belief of Harrington's hypocrisy, countenanced and confirmed as it was by Susan, had shaken her faith in the monstrous pretensions of the believers: she fancied she saw deceit lurking under many a broad brim, and she felt a secret revulsion from the dancing

---

1. *'Curse on his perjured arts! . . .'*: From Burns's 'The Cotter's Saturday Night' (1785).

worship which she had never joined in, or even witnessed since the memorable night of Harrington's inspiration.

A few days after the despatch of the letter, and just at twilight—the sweet hour consecrated by all young ladies in their teens to sentiment and romantic meditations—Emily, availing herself of the liberty she had recently enjoyed, strolled out without any other purpose than to be alone, and think her own thoughts. She had not walked far when she perceived Reuben approaching her. He did not appear to have observed her, and to escape his notice she turned into a little enclosure she had just then reached, which a few broken stones marked as a place of interment. She paused a moment at the graves, and almost envied their silent tenants.

The Shakers preserve all their austere formality in the disposition of their dead: the brethren and sisters are laid in separate and parallel lines, as if they contemplated the same restrictions in the other world which they impose here: each grave is designated by a rough-hewn stone inscribed (with ostentatious humility) with the initials only of the name borne by the person who reposes beneath it. Emily's thoughts naturally reverted to the village churchyard where her father and her mother slept. That seemed a social place when compared with the Shaker burial-ground. Her imagination pictured the storied monuments—the sacred spot where her parents laid—the beautiful willow that drooped over it, and the neatly carved white stone that stood under its shadow, setting forth in its long inscription their virtues and their sufferings. "Oh, that I was there," was the involuntary breathing of her spirit.

After lingering for a few moments lost in melancholy contemplations, she turned away and pursued her walk through a secluded path to the garden which lay at a short distance from her. As she entered it she passed an old man arranging a bed of violets, which with many other beautiful flowers obtain sufferance among these ascetics on account of some real or fancied medical virtue.

"I am glad to see ye, child," said the good-natured old man, "I think ye are picking up a little, and I am heartily glad to see it: I would not have you a drooping lily all your days. It is a short pilgrimage through this world, and a thorny path it may be, but seeing it leads to the garden of Paradise, it is not worthwhile for a reasonable person to worry with the troubles by the way; they can't last long—that is a comfort," continued the speaker, striking his spade into the earth, and resting upon it. "I have seen mothers wailing for their first-born as if their very souls died with them, and in a few days, or a few years at worst, that passed away like a vapour, they too were cut down and lying quiet beside them. I have seen children withering away like a severed branch at the death of their parents, and a frost has come and nipped them in their flower. I have seen people wearying themselves for riches and honours, and just when they had got them, leave them all for the shroud and the cold earth. I tell you, my young sister, life is a short journey—therefore don't be discouraged if the road is not quite to your liking."

Emily made no reply to this kind exhortation, but she plucked some of the violets, and asked the old man if they were not sometimes called "heart's-ease."

"Yea, I believe some folks call them heart's ease."

"And do they grow nowhere but on the believers' ground?" she asked.

"Yea, yea," replied the man, smiling significantly, as if he understood the import of her inquiry; "they grow all about among the neighbours—everywhere."

He paused and looked at Emily for a moment, and then casting his eyes in every direction, and ascertaining there was no one in hearing, he lowered his voice and said, "I believe you to be a discreet good little body, and that you'll keep the counsel I give you to yourself. You are wearied with this kind of strange, still life, child—your mind is running upon your relations, your home—may be upon some sweetheart—now ye need not look so frightened, it is nat'ral, it is nat'ral—I don't blame you for it. I always feel sorry to see a young and tender plant put into soil it don't love; it never takes root fairly—never thrives. Now my advice is, that you pluck up courage, tell the people the plain truth, go home to your friends, get a good husband, and 'guide the house.'[2] Ye can take scripture warrant with you, for it's God's own word, that 'in *every nation*, he that feareth him and worketh righteousness is accepted of him.'"[3]

Emily with very natural surprise gazed at the old man as if she discredited her senses. "Are you a Shaker?" she asked.

"A Shaker, girl!" he replied, laughing—"yea, and a very good Shaker." His muscles contracted as he added," I have been what is called an unfortunate man in the world. Everything went against me. I lost my wife, my children—lost my property—and I thought I could not do better than to get a shelter in this peaceable place; and as I had a remarkable gift for gardening, the people were glad to have me with them."

"Then you are not a Shaker?" said Emily, bewildered by the contrariety of his motives with those she had always heard professed by the Shakers.

"Yea, but I am—that is to say, in the main a believer. Our people are foolish about some things, but then I never saw any religion, but there were some weeds among it; and to speak truly, I am too near the end of my summer to care much where my leaves drop—but it is a pity you should be growing, nay, growing you are not, but withering in the shade: say nothing, but store

---

2. *'guide the house'*: From 1 Timothy 5: 14 (KJV).
3. *'in every nation, he that feareth him . . .'*: From Acts 10: 35 (KJV).

my counsel in your heart, and let it bring forth its fruit in season:"—thus concluding, the kind-hearted old gardener turned away and left Emily to reflect on his singular communication.

Though not a very skilful reasoner, she came to the just conclusion, that such Shakers as the crafty Harrington and the frank gardener, were not Shakers by divine impulse; that the ties which attached others to the society were not in all cases indissoluble—and the society itself did not exist by prescriptive divine right.

She sought a sequestered part of the garden, and seating herself in the shade of some fruit-trees, and, as she thought, secure from observation, she drew from her bosom the precious little scroll which linked her to the world. All that was there written was more legibly inscribed on her heart, but still she loved to look on it. The sight of it touched her imagination like a conjurer's wand, and brought before her all those images she most loved to dwell upon. She resigned herself to the visions of her fancy, forgot the formal habitations around her, the severe brethren and the pale sisters; and was restored to the Lenox family, joining in their bustling occupations, sharing their pleasures, the object of the kindness of all, and the chosen, loved partner of James. She beheld her old grandmother cheerful and approving—Ellen Bruce smiling on her with sisterly kindness—the merry faces of the children; she heard their unrebuked mirth—Debby's loud laugh,—she saw and she heard all, till awakened from her reverie by an approaching footstep, she looked up and beheld Harrington coming towards her. She instinctively started on her feet, and intending to restore the scroll to its hiding place, she unconsciously dropped it. As she walked hastily past Harrington homeward, he said, "Stop, Emily—stop, my good girl—I have something particular to say to you."

"I cannot hear it now," she replied, redoubling her speed.

"You cannot," muttered Reuben, looking after her, "the time will come when you shall hear me—and hear me patiently and quietly."

Provoked at being defeated in his purpose of speaking to her, he remained where she left him, whetting his resentment and brooding vengeance, when the note she had dropped caught his eye. He took it up and read it. 'Ah now,' thought he, 'I see the reason why my fair offers were received with horror and disdain—the little fool has a younger sweetheart—but she shall find the old fox an overmatch for the young hound.'

Never did a vulture fasten his talons around his victim with more exultation than Harrington thrust poor little Emily's lost talisman into his pocket—he did not see exactly how he should turn it to account; but it gave him power, and power in his hands was the sure means of mischief. It would not be very edifying to thread all the intricate windings of his bad mind—to examine the projects he conceived and dismissed, till, favoured by an unlooked-for chance, he devised one which flattered him with the hope of the certain destruction of his innocent victim, and with the prospect of complete vengeance on the elder sister, who he well knew was vulnerable alone through this object of her natural affection.

Subtle and active, it was not long before his plans were matured. Two days after he had obtained possession of the note, for which Emily had anxiously and vainly sought, he came on some pretext of business into an apartment where she and one of the sisters were sitting. Emily felt as strong an impulse to leave the room as if a venomous reptile had crept into it, but afraid of attracting the notice of a third person, she remained with as much tranquillity as she could command.

After a few moments a traveller chanced to pass in a wagon. Emily's companion was attracted to the window. Harrington followed her, and looking earnestly at the traveller, he said, carelessly, "that young man favours James Lenox—it is possible it may be him"—he paused, and Emily instinctively sprang towards the window. Reuben looked at her, and conscience-smitten, she shrunk back into her chair.

"I am told young Lenox is in these parts," pursued Harrington, "and I judged he might ride over here to see some of his old friends." Again he turned his eyes on Emily, hers met his—her face and neck were crimson. "I wish, Judy," said he, to the young woman, who was still gazing out of the window, "that ye would go to the sewing-room and inquire if my coat is finished?"

Judy went, and Emily rose to follow her. "Stop, Emily," said Harrington, in a low voice, and unobserved by Judy, laying his hand on her arm, and closing the door, "with all your gettings, get discretion, young woman: your ready step, your burning cheeks, would this moment have betrayed your secret to me, if I had not known it before. Nay, now you must hear me—be calm, do not tremble, we have no time to waste—take this note," said he, restoring her treasure, "and be thankful that it fell into friendly hands. The hint I gave you was spoken in earnest: James Lenox is in Lebanon. The silly boy sent a letter to you sealed; it fell into my hands; it was my duty to open it, and my duty as you well know I perform at all risks—here it is." Emily hastily caught it without observing the diabolical sneer on Reuben's face. "Now, mark me, young woman," he continued.—"I see it is a vain struggle you are keeping up—ye cannot abide here; and as you are of the earth earthy, I cannot counsel you to abide—you shall see that I am your friend, and will return good for evil. Lenox urges you to join him at Lebanon: he thinks if he comes here, ye will not be able to resist the open opposition of the people—ye'll read his letter, and ye'll find this is the last day of his stay in these parts; and if ye do not join him before tomorrow, he concludes you are still in bonds to the believers.

"I have had the letter in my possession four days, and you may thank yourself that you have not got it sooner; ye have fled from me as if I had been a tiger, or a rattlesnake. Now, mark me, if you take my counsel you'll go tonight quietly and secretly. Little as you deserve it from me, it is in my mind to help you: if you will come to the supper-table with your cap tied, I'll take it for a signal that you are determined to go, and I will be ready one hour after sunset with a wagon and horses, just at the turning of the road that leads to North-house. I wish to go thus early that I may return before daylight, for it is not needful the brethren should know that I take up for you. They might not view your departure as I do; for after all it is but acting up to your light, which is all we profess to require. Now go, young woman, and the Lord direct all your steps."

He gazed after her as she passed through the passage, and exclaimed, exultingly rubbing his hands, "I have caught her—I have caught her at last. Let the fox but clear the ground, and the old one may bark till doomsday."

It was some time after Emily reached her own apartment before she became sufficiently composed to read the letter: her head swam, and her hands shook violently; but at last, making a great effort, she did read it. It was filled with passionate declarations of love, and earnest and repeated entreaties that she would join the writer at Lebanon, where he said he should await her four days. He alleged many very plausible reasons for not coming to the village. He rested his earnest suit mainly on his ardent, devoted attachment to her; but at the close of the letter he insinuated that if she did not return to Eton with him, her grandmother's death must lie at her door, so much had her desertion of the poor old lady shattered her health and spirits.

Emily perused and re-perused the letter—she felt her cheeks burning while she read it, and she wondered that James should write in a style so impassioned—'surely he ought not,' she thought, and the next moment mentally accused herself of injustice. "Alas," she said, "if my heart beats thus at the bare thought of meeting him, can I blame him if he talks in the fashion of the world's people?—my head is in such strange confusion, that it may be I do not understand him aright."

But every other consideration was swallowed up in the necessity of coming to an immediate decision whether to go or remain. Emily's convictions, as they had been deemed, had gradually subsided as her early attachments revived, and her inclinations for the world strengthened; and now no strong tie remained to be broken but her love for the elder sister, which had produced such habitual dependence on her, that she had become a mere machine, governed by a power which she could neither understand nor resist.

There was now a demand on her for extraordinary energy—she must act independently, promptly, and secretly. Much cause as she had to distrust

Harrington's integrity, she did not on this occasion doubt the sincerity of his kindness. In the confusion and agitation of her mind, she did not look behind. Her mind was engrossed by the great circumstance of her departure, and she scarcely thought of the means by which it was to be effected. Once, indeed, the thought flitted across her mind, that Reuben's compassionate interference in her behalf was very strange, and for the moment she felt an almost invincible repugnance to trust herself with him; but there was no alternative—she had no other means of meeting James. She could, it was true, declare her resolution to leave the society. No one was ever detained by physical force; but to a weak and irresolute mind there are moral barriers that are as impassable as prison-walls, and Emily felt that she had not the courage necessary to persevere against the deliberate opposition of the society—to withstand the counsel, rebuke, or sneer that she must expect from the different characters that composed that strange community—and above all to meet the elder sister's eye. But how could she bear to deceive her, to steal away from her tenderest friend as from an enemy! The thought of making this treacherous return to her maternal kindness quite overcame the poor girl, and Susan entering at this moment, found her wringing her hands and sobbing most piteously.

"What has happened to you Emily, child?" she asked, in her kindest voice: "this distress is something more than common with you."

Emily made no other reply than by throwing her arms around Susan's neck, and hiding her face on her bosom.

"Nay, child," said Susan, folding her arms around her, "ye must not. It is but a tempting of Providence. Ye'll be quite worn out in the struggle, and if ye cannot conquer, why—ye had better yield."

'Now—now, if ever,' thought Emily, 'is the moment;' and she raised her head from Susan's bosom with the full purpose of confessing her weakness and her wishes. But when she lifted her tearful eyes, and saw the calm, fixed resolution marked on the elder sister's face, and met her eye, in which there was the majesty of command, it awed her spirit as that of man is said to awe the inferior animals. Her head fell again on Susan's bosom. "Ye are a strange wayward child," said she: "I am sorry to leave you at this moment," she added—"nay, do not start, I shall return tomorrow."

"Tomorrow!" echoed Emily.

"Yea, tomorrow; and Judy has promised to keep you company tonight. One of the elders at Lebanon draws near his end, and they have sent for me, to consult upon some temporalities to be settled before his departure. Now sit down and compose yourself—it troubles me to leave you thus."

Susan led Emily to a chair, and at this moment one of the sisters gave her notice that the brethren were already in the wagon and waiting for her. While she hastened her preparations, she exhorted Emily to be more tranquil, and above all not to permit anyone to see how far the adversary yet maintained his power over her. Emily, though she groaned aloud as the door closed after the elder sister, suffered her to depart without any farther communication.

She passed the remainder of the day in severe struggles; finally, at the close of it, she came to the supper-table leaning on Judy, with her cap tied; and one hour after, having evaded her companion's observation, she stole, unnoticed by anyone, to the appointed place of rendezvous, where she found Harrington, and took with him the road to Lebanon.

Harrington, for reasons all-important to himself, abandoned the road usually travelled, and turned, at the western extremity of the village, into one which passes in a northerly direction over the mountain to the town of Lebanon. There are on this sequestered road but two or three habitations for a distance of several miles, and though it presents many enchanting views of the uplands and valleys, and ought therefore to attract the lovers of the picturesque, few of that (in our country) small and select class ever heard of it; and business travellers preferring the more levelled and turnpike road, this remains unfrequented and grass-grown.

The necessity that Harrington should reach Albany with all possible expedition, and execute his business there before it was practicable that he should be overtaken, forbade his permitting Emily to remain in ignorance of his purposes, and he had scarcely passed the boundary of the village, before he began to unfold them to her. His language was entirely changed—all the mysterious phrases, and the obscure and technical words, with which he was wont, as he expressed himself, to 'sanctify his discourse,' to guard it with equivocal meanings and veil it in unintelligible terms, were exchanged for the concise language of the man of business. Emily soon comprehended that she was the dupe of his arts—'that the decoy letter was forged by him, after the model of the note, (he, as he boasted, holding the pen of a ready writer)—that James Lenox neither expected nor wished for her—and finally, that her reputation being destroyed by her elopement with Harrington, her only resource was to proceed with him, without any ado, to the nearest justice, who could perform the marriage ceremony, to accept his hand, which he generously proffered, and then pursue her way with him to Albany, where he insultingly concluded he should possess himself of a sum of money that would enable him to make a lady of her for the rest of her life.'

Emily heard him through with dismay; and springing from his side, she would have cleared the wagon in an instant, but he perceiving her design, passed his arm around her, and pulled her back on to the seat, and there detained her in his strong grasp. She screamed for help with reiterated cries, and the only answer she received was, "Be quiet, sweetheart—you spend your breath in vain—there is nothing in these woods to hear you but the bats and owls—no 'elder sister' to snatch you from me."

"Oh!" exclaimed Emily, turning to him with a look of helplessness and appeal that might have awakened compassion in a tiger.—"Oh, do pity me."

"Pity you, indeed!" he replied; "I have none of that article on hand; I used it all up on myself while I staid among those devilish fools. Take wit in your anger, girl—what can't be cured must be endured. I foresaw that I should have trouble with your stubborn nature, and I have provided accordingly. But fair play is a jewel, and the Lord knows, I would like to treat you handsomely if you will hear to reason and let me." They had now nearly attained the summit of the hill, and Harrington stopped his horses. "Now, Emily Allen," said he, "I leave it to your free choice to go with me to the first Justice we can find, and there quietly, and as it were willingly, be made Mrs. Harrington, so that man can't put asunder what God joins together—or abide here, where I have bespoke a cage and a keeper for you till my return, when you will be glad enough to take me on my own terms."

Emily listened in silence to the particulars of the wretch's plot against her: her whole frame trembled, and her lips quivered: she made no other reply than by attempting again to scream for help, but her voice was so faint and incapable of articulation, that it sounded like the smothered cry of a person attempting to scream in the agony of a frightful dream.

"Well," said Reuben, after pausing but a moment, "if you won't hear to reason, you must e'en abide by the consequences." He then turned his horses from the road into a deeply shaded passage through the woods, where, by the imperfect starlight, not a trace of a footstep could be discerned. The way however had been used, during the winter, for the transportation of wood to the neighbouring villages, and was sufficiently cleared from impediments, to allow the cautious Reuben to pass slowly and safely through it. Emily looked around her in utter despair—she cast her eyes up to the heavens as if to appeal for mercy there—their stillness and serene beauty seemed to mock and aggravate her misery: she tried to frame a mental petition to the only Power that could rescue her, but her mind was so shaken by terror that she could not command her thoughts for the effort.

They had proceeded about half a mile, and Harrington again stopped. A bright light streamed through a vista in the woods on their right. Emily looked in the direction whence it proceeded, and saw through the open door of a hovel, a human figure enveloped in a blanket, and extended on the ground before a blazing fire. The light played fitfully on the figure, now almost dying away, and then streaming upward nearly to the aperture in the roof through which the smoke found its way. Happily imagination could not aggravate her terrors; and now fully aware of her own helplessness, she sat as still as if she had been turned to stone, while Harrington vociferated

"Holla! Sooduck—doctor! the devil take the lazy loon, is he asleep, or drunk?" Reuben's repeated calls at length roused a dog, whose head laid on his master's bosom, and his barking awakened the sleeper. He raised his head, shook back the long black locks that shaded his eyes, and looked around as if uncertain whence the sound had proceeded.

"Who's wanting the doctor?" he asked, in a surly tone: "fools—will they never learn not to come to me at the moon's full?"

He then drew his blanket around him, and was about to resume his sleeping posture, when Harrington roused him effectually. "Here, Sooduck," he screamed, "here I am on the spot—have you forgotten, old fellow? Here is the jug well filled, and here is the girl."

"Ah! is it you, friend Reuben? Here I am, true as steel, watching for you."

"A devil of a pretty watch you keep," muttered Harrington. "Come, come along, doctor, I have no time to lose, every minute is worth a golden guinea to me." The old man moved slowly and with difficulty towards the wagon—"Why, how now, Emily, girl," continued Harrington, "it's hard parting, is it? She clings to me, doctor, like a bur."

"What have you brought here?" asked the old man, looking inquiringly at Emily, who, quite spent with terror, had sunk insensible into Harrington's arms. "No, no, friend," he added, turning away, "since the breath is gone, I'll have nothing to do with her: it is bad luck meddling with the dead, and there was no death in the bargain."

"Stop, you old fool," exclaimed Harrington.

"Fool I may be, friend Reuben, but I'll not be fool to a fool—I tell you again, I'll not undertake with the dead."

"Excuse me, doctor," said Reuben, in a moderated, soothing tone, "you have mistaken your case for the first time in your life: the girl is no more dead than you or I—she is as fearful as a fawn, Sooduck, and your old Indian face has frightened her out of her wits—she is faint too, poor little sweetheart, with grief at parting. Here, take the jug first," he added, well knowing that he offered an argument irresistible to Sooduck: there is life of man for you, doctor—it will make your lazy blood race through your old veins again, and warm your cold heart to do a good turn to a friend."

"Ah, Reuben, Reuben," replied the old man, grasping the jug and swallowing a draught from it, "you know what is needful. The stuff," he added, after repeating the application, "has put life into me already—now give me my prisoner and be off."

Reuben, with the little aid that Sooduck was able to afford him, succeeded in lifting Emily from the wagon and conveying her to the hut, where he placed her on some fresh straw that appeared to have been provided for the purpose, and then left her, enjoining it on the old man to watch her narrowly, and treat her kindly. After having once gone to the wagon, he returned to advise

Sooduck to administer a sleeping potion, "it would save trouble," he said, "and make safe work."

"Never you fear, friend Reuben," replied Sooduck; "trust me and my dog to guard this little she-pigeon." Harrington thought there was in truth very little to apprehend, and he departed exulting in the expectation of the final success of his savage scheme.

Emily soon recovered from her fainting fit, but she passed the night in a state of nervous excitement little short of distraction. Before morning, however, she sunk into a quiet sleep, in consequence of a composing draught, which Sooduck half compelled and half persuaded her to swallow—repose had its usual beneficent effect, and she awoke with the first beam of daylight quite tranquillized. She had now for the first time sufficient presence of mind to examine her prison and her jailer. The hut was about ten feet square, and constructed of slender poles well secured in the ground, and bent together at the upper extremity in the form of an arbor—the sides and top were filled in with flexible brush-wood closely matted together. Some brands and ashes, the relics of the evening's fire, laid on and about two flat stones which composed the fireplace. A chair so rough, that one might have fancied it the first barbarous essay towards forming that indispensable domestic article; an iron pot and two skillets, were the only furniture of this tenement, rude as the rudest structures of the primitive inhabitants. The remnant of an Indian cake laid on a scorched board near the firestones; and some trout, that had been caught the preceding day in a mountain stream, were languidly moving in a large wooden bowl nearly filled with water. Sooduck, still stupefied by the copious draughts he had taken from Reuben's jug, was stretched on a mat before the door—his dog laid beside him. The faithful animal ever and anon would start from his sleep, look inquiringly around him, lick his master's face, and fall asleep again on his bosom.

Sooduck, the Indian (for such he was) had all the peculiarities of his race. Though so old that he looked as if 'death had forgotten to strike him'[4]—his gigantic form was still erect and muscular. In vain Emily explored his long face, as the increasing light of day revealed its rigid lines and worn channels, for some trace of humanity, some signal of compassion; but it was a visage to pierce the heart of one who sought for mercy with utter despair— a visage in which brutal sensuality was mingled with a fierceness that neither time nor events could tame. She remembered to have heard this man described, and marvellous medical skill imputed to him. She recognized

---

4. *'death had forgotten to strike him'*: This saying may have been a common maxim to describe extreme old age, rather than a quotation from a specific source. It appears again in quotation marks in the second issue of the Transcendentalist journal *The Dial* in October 1844, where it is prefaced as a 'quaint quotation' but lists no source.

some of the signs of his profession hanging around the interior of his hut; strings of the rattles of rattlesnakes—skins of snakes—snakes salted and dried in the air—bunches of herbs and roots—the plumage of birds—their carcasses and eggs—in short, he seemed to have levied his contributions equally on the elements of earth, air, and water.

There are still in the most civilized parts of our country, some individuals of the aboriginal race, who, like the remnants of their sacrifice-rocks, remain among us monuments of past ages. They seek the most secluded and wildest spots, where the face of nature, yet untouched by man, expresses some sympathy for them—owns an alliance with them. Some of them are pretenders to medical skill, and receive the significant appellation of "root doctors." They no longer affect to possess the charms, and use the spells of the ancient *pow-wows*, but their preparations are made with a studied secrecy which, by its influence over the imaginations of the vulgar, produces magical effects. Without taxing our credulity to believe in all the marvellous cures that are ascribed to them, we see no reason why the simples they extract from the bosom of our kind mother earth should not prove as innocent and quite as efficacious as the drugs of foreign soils.

Everyone has felt the inspiring influence of returning daylight—the most timid are emboldened by it. Emily inhaled the cool and fragrant morning air; she saw through the open door the dewy foliage glittering in the sunbeams, and the cheerful light that checkered the shaded footpath, and the still voice of nature seemed to whisper encouragement to her spirit. She heard the shrill voice of the lark, and the clear note of the robin, and they sounded in her ear like the voices of her familiar friends. Exhausted as she was by long sufferings and recent terrors, hope nerved her to attempt her liberty. The rattling of the straw as she moved from it startled the vigilant dog; she saw him fix his eye upon her, and looking around for some means of diverting his attention, she espied a piece of dried meat hanging over the door; she cautiously took it down, stooped over him and patted him coaxingly, while she offered him the tempting bribe; but he shook off her arm, and with a low growl expressed his disdain of her arts.

Finding the dog impracticable, she trusted that he would not be able to awaken his master from his deep sleep, and stealing timidly around his feet, and having attained the threshold of the door, she ascertained by one fearful glance that he still slept soundly, and rashly bounded over the door step; but she was suddenly arrested by the dog, who having jealously watched her stolen movements, now sprang after her, and caught her garments between his teeth. While she made an effort to extricate herself, the yelping of the animal awoke his master, who growled on her more fiercely than his dog. She turned towards him, and sunk on her knees, and with tears and entreaties, besought him, 'as he hoped for that mercy from

CHAPTER XVI.

Heaven which he would so soon need, that he would have mercy on her.' He heeded her no more than if she had spoken to him in a dead language; and after gazing on her for a few moments silently, and with a mixture of sullen anger and brute indifference, he commended and caressed his dog, and then pulled the helpless despairing girl into the hut. She sunk back on her straw bed, while Sooduck, apparently unconscious of her sobs, and even of her presence, proceeded to make preparations for his breakfast.

He first whetted his appetite by a copious draught of Reuben's liquor, and then kindled a fire, on which, without any fastidious preparation, he threw the still gasping trout. When they were but half roasted, he offered one on a piece of Indian cake to Emily, who, as might be anticipated, rejected his hospitality, though her fast had been a long one. Quite unaffected by the scruples of his guest, Sooduck devoured his savage repast with a voracious appetite. He then left the hut, secured the door as well as he was able with a stout cord, and attaching his dog by his collar to a chain which was fastened in a staple driven into one of the upright posts, he left the trusty animal to guard his prisoner, while he with his pole and line sauntered to a little brook near his dwelling, but hidden by a thick growth of trees which it nourished on its sides.

Emily remained stretched on her rude bed, now giving way to a burst of grief as the recollection of the past, or the gloomy portents of the future overpowered her—and now relapsing into profound silence, rendered more grievous by the sweet music of nature which struck on the poor prisoner's sickening sense. The melody of the birds, as they flew about her prison house, breathed freedom and gladness; and the brook, which she distinctly heard as it gurgled around the roots of the trees that impeded its way, or bounded over the stones that vainly obstructed its free passage, seemed to mock her with the song of liberty.

She was sometimes startled by the shrill whistle of the Indian, who, still pursuing his drowsy pleasure in the shelter of the wood, sent his greeting to his dog, whose hoarse response answered the purpose of the sentinel call of "all is well."

CHAPTER XVII.

"Proud of her parts, but gracious in her pride—
She bore a gay good nature in her face,
And in her air was dignity and grace."[1]

Crabbe.

WHILE the transactions so fatal to the peace of Emily Allen were going on, Deborah and Ellen were quietly pursuing their journey, though not as expeditiously as Ellen could have wished. She had not, as has been seen, left Eton in the most tranquil state of mind, and she was perhaps more impatient at the little accidents that retarded their progress than she would have been at another time, or under other circumstances. Sometimes the old racked chaise needed repair—sometimes the horse, who as Deborah said, "had like herself seen better days, and needed to be favoured," required a day's delay—and sometimes they came into the neighbourhood of an old acquaintance or far-off cousin of Deborah's, and she judged it right to diverge from their direct route to prove to them her friendly remembrance; for she scrupulously maintained the New England custom, (which among the degenerate moderns is becoming a little unfashionable,) of noticing a relative to the remotest degree. Ellen often felt inclined to remonstrate against these repeated delays; but Deborah was so much accustomed to exercise the petty tyranny of having her own way, that Ellen rightly concluded it would be much easier for her to acquiesce than for Deborah to relinquish her habitual control.

Ten days had elapsed, when they stopped at a village inn in the vicinity of the Shaker settlement at Hancock: a hostler[2] advanced to take charge of the horse; Deborah, before she resigned the reins, gave to him the most minute directions as to the refection of her beast; but the man, puffed up with the transient importance which he derived from an unusual concourse

---

1. *'Proud of her parts. . . .'*: A variation on a quotation from 'Edward Shore', a poem by George Crabbe (1754–1832), which appears in *Tales in Verse* (1812). In the original poem, the subject pronouns are male rather than female.
2. *hostler*: A stableman at an inn.

of travellers that had filled the stables and stable-yards of the inn with fine horses and fine equipages, was evidently quite heedless of Miss Debby's directions. She at last had recourse to the usual expedient of travellers, and though she utterly disapproved the use of such appliances, which she thought were little better than bribery and corruption, she reluctantly drew a four-pence half-penny from her pocket, and giving it to the man, with the air of one who offers ample consideration for 'value received,' "Here," said she, "take this and deal kindly with the beast—poor fellow, he has had a tough morning of it, what with the heat and the hills."

The hostler took the bit of money, looked at it and turned it over with mock gravity, balanced it on the end of his finger, as if weighing it, and then tossed it high in air, accompanying this last expression of his contempt with an insolent laugh, in which he was joined by half a dozen of his associates who had gathered around him.

Deborah picked up the money as it fell, and deliberately replacing it in her pocket, said with perfect coolness, "A fool and his money are soon parted—this is a right punishment for my giving in to these new-fangled ways—here, fellow, give me the reins, and call the master of the house to me."

This appeal to his principal reduced the menial to his proper insignificance, and turned the laugh against him, and Deborah remained fairly mistress of the field till the landlord made his appearance. The raised voices of the different parties attracted several persons to the windows and door of the inn, and Ellen felt herself rather awkwardly situated as she stood awaiting the termination of Deborah's arrangements.

"Walk in, Miss—walk in," said the landlord to her, "here, this way, in the parlour; the house is considerable full, but you'll find room enough to spare yet—I'll attend to your mother—walk in."

The attention was now withdrawn from Deborah to Ellen, and each observer probably noticed the disparity between the supposed mother and daughter.

"Impossible," whispered a young man who stood in the doorway to a lady beside him; "that she-grenadier cannot be mother to this pretty, graceful girl."

"Impossible is a rash word for you, Mr. Philosopher," replied the young lady: "look there," she added, pointing to a prickly pear in flower, "there are strange productions—odd relations in nature."

Ellen's ear caught enough of these remarks as she passed along, to inform her that she was the subject of them; and her embarrassment was increased when the landlord opened the parlour door to usher her in, and she perceived that the room was already occupied by a large party of travellers—she shrunk back, and begged her conductor to show her to a private apartment. He said that was impossible, for his rooms were all taken up.

The young lady at the door observed Ellen's embarrassment, and advancing, with a mixture of good-nature and graceful politeness, begged Ellen to enter.

"Our party," she said, "is of such an unconscionable size! We travel *en masse* like the patriarchs—men, women, and children, and much cattle—and when we have gained possession of a territory we are quite terrible; but the parlour of a country inn you know is neutral ground, where all parties have equal rights."

A smile and a bow from Ellen expressed her sense of the proffered courtesy, and she passed in and seated herself at an unoccupied window.

"You are a rash woman, Miss Campbell," said the gentleman in a low voice, whom Ellen had first seen at the door, and who had followed to the parlour. "I see a storm lowering on Mrs. Norton's brow, and I fear she will not permit you the privilege of neutrality."

"I care not, Mr. Howard—the motto of my family arms is, 'dauntless in war, gentle in peace.'"

"My family's boastful motto, also," replied Mr. Howard.

"Indeed!" exclaimed Miss Campbell, "That is singular; but I hope you are not ashamed of it," she added, noticing a little embarrassment in Mr. Howard's manner.

"Oh, certainly not; though one might blush at thinking how little we degenerate sons can do in these peaceful times to verify the pretensions of our fighting forefathers—but see, the storm is ready to burst on your devoted head. Mrs. Norton is beckoning to you—and even that look of invincible good nature which you have assumed will not mollify her." Mr. Howard's eyes followed Miss Campbell with an expression that seemed to say, 'That look is as potent as the beauty that in the olden time disarmed the wild beasts of their ferocity.'

"My dear Miss Campbell," began Mrs. Norton, drawing up her severe features to as stern an expression, as if she was taking up her testimony against the depravity of the age. "My dear Miss Campbell, I really wonder at you."

"Wonder! Can you, Mrs. Norton, condescend to so vulgar an emotion as wonder?"

"But I am serious, Miss Grace."

"So I perceive, ma'am."

"There can be no doubt, I fancy, that you understand me?"

"Indeed I have not that pleasure."

Few things are more mortifying to a person of self-consequence, than to be called on to explain the cause of a personal irritation, which one had imagined quite obvious. After a little fidgeting on her chair, and clearing of her throat, all which Miss Campbell awaited with the most provoking serenity, the lady spoke with the manner of one who in her own little sphere has been looked upon as quite oracular.

"Miss Campbell, it has ever been my opinion, confirmed by all my experience, and I have had more than most people;"—she paused again, probably from the difficulty of giving sufficient dignity to a very small subject, and Miss Campbell slipped in—"Incontrovertibly, ma'am, few people live to be more than three score."

"I did not mean, Miss Grace, the experience of age; everyone who lives to a certain time has that—but the experience of—"

"Wisdom, ma'am—sagacious observation, &c., &c.,—I understand you."

"Oh, cousin Grace, you are such a tease;" said a young lady who sat at Mrs. Norton's right hand, and who perceived she was quite as much provoked by being understood, as by not being understood.

"Your cousin Grace," said Mrs. Norton, "may tease you young ladies, Miss Sarah, but I assure you that I am not a subject for teasing."

"My dear Sarah," said Miss Campbell, with affected gravity, "how could you suspect me of taking such high aim— you know mine are all random shafts, and if they wound, are 'heaven directed';[3] but, Mrs. Norton, pray do not deprive me of that valuable opinion of yours—the result, if I remember, of unparalleled experience."

"I shall not be deterred from expressing it by your ridicule, Miss Campbell; self-respect renders one quite superior to ridicule."

"Self-respect renders one quite superior to ridicule," repeated Miss Campbell with deliberation and emphasis—at the same time taking out her pocket-book, seemingly with the purpose of recording on her tablets Mrs. Norton's saying—"self-respect," she again repeated, as she drew out her pencil, when Mrs. Norton stopped her by exclaiming—"Do you mean to insult me, Miss Campbell?"

"Insult you! My dear Mrs. Norton, Lord bless me! No—really, if I have been so unfortunate as to misunderstand you again, you must not lay all the blame on my poor intellects; for you talk so much in the style of the venerable Greeks, that to such a desultory personage as I am every sentence sounds like an apothegm."[4]

Mrs. Armstead, the aunt of Miss Campbell, thought her niece was carrying matters too far—she perceived that Mrs. Norton felt as awkwardly as a warrior of the olden time, who should be in his heavy coat of mail, assaulted by a light-armed soldier of the present day.

---

3. *'heaven directed'*: Most likely refers to Pope's *Epilogue to the Satires*, in which 'heaven-directed' is taken to mean providential guidance of the divine. Though 'heaven-directed' appears in print prior to Pope's *Epilogue*, Samuel Johnson's *Dictionary of the English Language* uses quotations from Pope's works to explicate its meaning.
4. *apothegm*: A pithy maxim which expresses a truth in few words.

"My dear Grace," she said, "you have not allowed Mrs. Norton time to explain herself. She noticed the companion of the young woman, towards whom you have thought proper to give yourself such an air of patronizing hospitality, in an altercation with the hostler—she says she is an excessively vulgar woman, and she thinks, my dear, that it is a great piece of presumption for this young woman to come into our parlour without an invitation, and rather ill-advised in you to encourage her assurance."

"Thank you, my dear aunt," replied Grace Campbell, bowing her head with affected deference, "for possessing me of Mrs. Norton's views of my conduct: and now, my dear madam," she added, turning to Mrs. Norton, "pray do not withhold from me your own expression of your golden opinion."

Mrs. Norton had strong motives for keeping well with Miss Campbell: she was conscious that the lady's fortune, fashion, and talents placed her in the first class, let her make that class as small as she would. She had been excessively provoked at Miss Campbell's contempt, or, at best, indifference for her, but, having no alternative, she made to herself a great merit of forgiveness; obliged to suppress her wrath against Miss Campbell, she meant to indemnify[5] herself by wreaking her vengeance on the innocent stranger, and when she spoke, she spoke calmly, but loud enough to be heard by Ellen.

"Miss Grace," she said, "there is much excuse for one who is ignorant of the presumption of the common people: you have lived for the most part in town, where you did not come in contact with them."

"Yes—unfortunately, Mrs. Norton, but I have now and then taken a trip to the country, and indemnified myself for the privation. There is nothing in life so tiresome to me as the endless inanities of the genteel gentlemen and ladies one meets forever in town—we flatter one another's prejudices—we adopt one another's opinions and tastes and habits till everything individual and peculiar is gone—we are all formed in the same mould, and all receive the same impression—pure gold and base copper—all must bear the same stamp to be current coin. It is a refreshment to me to see the natural character as it is developed in the strong peculiarities one meets in the country. I love the common people—an unpardonable sin it may be, Mrs. Norton, but I do love them—I love to see the undisciplined movements of natural feeling—I sympathise with their unaffected griefs—I love to witness their hearty pleasures—I had rather receive the expression of their cordial good will, than the compliments of a successful winter's campaign"—

"For heaven's sake tell me, cousin Grace," said a gentleman who was standing near to her, "are you addressing this tirade in favour of rusticity to Mrs. Norton or to Howard?"

---

5. *indemnify*: To compensate for an annoyance or to protect from harm.

CHAPTER XVII.

A deep blush suffused Miss Campbell's cheeks: she was conscious that though she had in the onset addressed herself to Mrs. Norton, she had involuntarily, and in obedience to the impulse of sympathy, directed her eyes to Howard. The blush was followed by a beautiful smile, as she replied to her cousin—"Is it strange, William, that my enthusiasm in behalf of the contemned and neglected should impel my eyes instinctively to a Howard?"

"Beware instinct, Howard—instinct is a great matter," whispered young Armstead, and added aloud, "do not bow so like simple Mr. Slender, as if you believed every word of that rattle-brained cousin of mine. She has drank a draught of sentiment this morning on these romantic hills; but this love of the country and its sweet simplicity is not her first love: she will return to town, and run the course of fashion and folly with the swiftest of her rivals."

"For shame, my son: I will not suffer your insinuations against Grace," said Mrs. Armstead; "I am sure she was never fond of dissipation."

"Oh no, my dear mother; dissipation is a self-denying ordinance with Grace; and the admiration of half the men, and the envy of all the women, are her voluntary mortifications."

"Ah, Will," replied Miss Campbell, "you are a snarler—a predestined old bachelor—but you shall see that I will deny the world and all ungodliness—forswear your company, and live soberly in this present life."

"I am certain Miss Campbell has the ability to verify the prophecy she utters," said Howard.

"I see it is all in vain, my good friends," retorted young Armstead, assuming the gravity of a sage; "you pour in your poisons faster than I can administer my antidotes; so go on, and in a few years you will drive my cousin Grace, in spite of her good sense, into the rank of the infallibles: our dear mother would even now persuade you, Grace, as the worthy Bishop Hoadley said, 'not that you cannot err, but that you do not err.'"[6]

"My good aunt's blindness is not likely to prove fatal to me while I have so clear-sighted a cousin, who, with one keen glance of his eye, can pierce the fog of vanity. But here, William, comes a newer if not fairer subject for your sharpshooting."

All eyes were now directed to the door, and Deborah entered.

The pause occasioned by her entrance gave Mrs. Norton an opportunity to speak, and obliged others to listen to her. She poured forth many wise maxims upon the necessity of jealously guarding the few distinctions of

---

6. *Bishop Hoadley said, 'not that you cannot err, but that you do not err'*: A variation on quotation from the satirical *Dedication to Pope Clement XI* (1715) by Bishop Benjamin Hoadley (1676–1761). Originally, the *Dedication* appeared in *An Account of the Roman Catholic Religion throughout the World* (1715) by Richard Steele (1672–1729).

rank that remain among us, and concluded with the condescending declaration, that she always made it a point to speak to persons she met at an inn, but she took good care they should understand, 'thus far shalt thou come, and no farther.'[7]

Young Armstead ventured to express a fear that the wave of the multitude would be too strong for her supreme command; but for the most part the good lady talked without being heeded. Every eye seemed fixed on Deborah, who on entering had given a good-natured nod to the Armstead party, and had proceeded in her operations with as much nonchalance as if she had been in her own little bedroom at home, and mistress of all she surveyed. She walked up to a small looking-glass—threw aside her bonnet, and began smoothing her refractory locks with a pocket-comb, while she recounted to Ellen, in her homeliest phrase, and with all the exultation of a victor, her success in securing the best hospitalities of the manger for her good steed, and boasted that like a faithful mistress she had insisted on being an eye-witness of his accommodations.

It must be confessed that Ellen felt a little disturbed at the ludicrous figure her companion made in the eyes of the fashionable party who were observing her. She perceived that the mirth of the young people was only kept within decent limits by the gravity of their elders, and that gravity was maintained by a difficult effort. She averted her eyes and looked out of the window, when Deborah, who had finished her toilette, and was surveying some pictures that garnished the walls, again exacted her attention.

"For the land's sake, Ellen," she said, "come and look at these picturs and tell me what this means—here is something that puzzles me;" and she fixed her eyes on an embroidered Hector and Andromache,[8] the fruit of at least three months' labour of one of the young lady artists of the inn.

"That man," she said, pointing to the Trojan hero, "is dressed in the uniform of the Connecticut reg'lars, at least it is as much like that as anything, and I take it to be the likeness of Col. Smith. I remember he had a wife and one child, and he parted from them just before the battle of Garmantown, where he lost his life, and a great many other brave fellows that have never been stitched into a pictur, lost theirs too. It's always your generals and colonels that get all the profit and honour while they live, and the glory when they are gone, while the poor fellows that suffer hunger and cold die, and are never named nor thought of. But what signifies it! For the 'same event happeneth to all,'[9] as Solomon says."

---

7. *'thus far shalt thou come and no farther'*: A variation on Job 38: 11.
8. *Hector and Andromache*: In classical mythology, Prince Hector of Troy was a warrior who died at the hands of Achilles during the Trojan War. Andromache was his wife.
9. *'same event happeneth to all,' as Solomon says*: A variation on Ecclesiastes 2: 14.

CHAPTER XVII.   207

"And it is the honest life that precedes the 'event,' and not the honour which follows it, that makes all the difference," said Miss Campbell, advancing to Deborah, and entering into her feelings with evident pleasure.

"Very true, Miss,—and very well said," replied Debby, heartily. "Maybe, Miss," she added, with an earnest manner, which indicated that a very slight observation of Miss Campbell had inspired a great respect for her powers, "maybe, Miss, you can help Ellen explain these outlandish names that puzzle me. I am sure there was not in all the Connecticut reg'lars such a name as Hector, and as to the other, I can't make anything out of it."

"They are fancy names, I imagine," said Ellen, willing to avoid an explanation.

Deborah passed on to a coarse engraving of Solomon's temple, which she gazed on with at least as honest a rapture as a connoisseur would have felt at the cartoons of Raphael. She commented on its length, breadth, and depth, with critical accuracy, observed the number of porches, pillars, windows, and doors, and concluded with expressing her delight that she had "at last seen a pictur of old King Solomon's temple."

Deborah poured forth her comments without heeding the whispers, the stares, and smiles that her oddity excited; but Ellen saw and heard all; and more pained that her honest friend should be the subject of ridicule, than mortified on her own account, she drew her out of the room into the little piazza in front of the house, and earnestly recommended their proceeding on their journey immediately. Her arguments however had no weight with Deborah; but while she still urged them, their attention was attracted by an alarming outcry. The cause of it was at once obvious. A chaise had been overset in the village street, the horse was running with the broken vehicle at his heels at full speed, while half a score of men were in breathless pursuit; a little child stood in the road before the door, his danger was apparent, and his destruction seemed inevitable: the party in the house joined their cries to those in the street, while a voice of terror and agony loud above all the rest, screamed, "*My* child, *my* child!" The horse received a new impetus from these frightful screams, while the little fellow stood facing the danger quite unappalled, and resolutely threw his hat at the horse.

Deborah and Ellen darted forward at the same instant—Deborah attempted to stop the horse: she failed in that, but the force of her arm turned him aside from his course, while Ellen snatched the child, and turning, placed it in the arms of its mother, who had just reached the door, and trembling, almost fainting, extended them to receive her child. This was all the operation of an instant. The whole party from the parlour now surrounded Deborah and Ellen.

Mrs. Armstead (for she was the mother), as soon as she had tranquillized her feelings sufficiently to speak, overwhelmed the preservers of her child with expressions of gratitude. The brothers and sisters crowded about, and embraced the little boy, who seemed to wonder why he had caused such emotion;—while Miss Campbell advancing to Ellen, and gracefully offering her hand, said that her "little 'scape-death cousin had obtained for her the right to beg the name and acquaintance of her whose kind intervention had saved his life." She proceeded to lavish praises on Ellen for her prompt courage; but Ellen modestly declined them, saying, she had been impelled by instinct to the action, and was quite unconscious of any danger till it was past.

The ice being thus broken, the young ladies, after discussing every particular of the 'hair-breadth 'scape,' proceeded to an animated conversation on various subjects, which elicited the characters of each, and inspired them with mutual admiration. Perhaps they liked each other the better, because, though there was a general agreement between them in tastes and sentiments, there was a striking difference in some particulars. Ellen's manners, without any of the awkwardness or gaucherie of bashfulness or ignorance, were timid, and, with strangers, rather reserved and retiring; while Miss Campbell had the assured air of one who has held a high command in society, and whose right and habit it was to take the lead in the world of fashion. Ellen, with one of the sweetest voices in the world, talked in rather a low tone—the style of her conversation was unambitious and simple, and though it often took a rich colouring from the bright rays of genius and feeling, like those glowing hues which fall on the summer landscape, and which no contrivance of art can produce or imitate, there was nothing said to court attention or excite admiration.

Miss Campbell talked rather loud, and with spirit and fluency; she had the fearless manner of one who has often felt her own power, and the weakness of others: she dashed on like an impetuous mountain stream, disdaining obstruction and careless of opposition. She had evidently been accustomed to occupy the foreground of the picture, to be the primary object of attention. She would have been at a loss to comprehend the feeling that suffused Ellen's face with blushes, and imparted tremulousness to her voice, when she found herself the object of an admiring observation. Miss Campbell had been so accustomed to the homage of society, that the excitement had become as necessary to her as the applause of an audience to a popular actor. In the midst of her most animated and eloquent sallies, her eye would glance rapidly around her circle of auditors, to catch new inspiration from the silent tribute of their enchained attention. With these faults she had such a fund of good sense, such invincible good-humour and unaffected benevolence, that she commanded the love, the respect even of those who were most sensible of her imperfections. Her virtues were her own, the luxuriant growth of a rich soil; her faults the result of accident, the weeds permitted by neglect, or occasioned by improper cultivation. Miss

Campbell was not a regular beauty, but her graceful person and fine expression gave to her the effect of beauty.

Mrs. Armstead, her aunt, resided in Philadelphia, and was on a jaunt to Boston by the way of Lebanon Springs. Mrs. Norton was an old acquaintance and distant relation, whom she had met accidentally. Mr. Howard had been introduced by young Armstead into his mother's family a few weeks before they left home, and recommended to their regard as an old college friend from Boston.

This introduction is necessary to our readers, but even these concise particulars are more than our travellers ascertained of their new friends. The little boy who had been rescued seemed to have been struck by the manly genius of Deborah, and attached himself to her—and the whole party, with the exception of Mrs. Norton, were emulous of showing civility to Deborah, and admiration of Miss Bruce. Mrs. Armstead, anxious to improve her brief opportunity of expressing her gratitude, lavished her attentions on Ellen, placed her next herself at table, and melted away all reserve by the warmth of her kindness.

The dinner being over, preparations were made for the departure of all parties. Deborah's primitive-looking chaise and respectable old horse, were led to the door in the rear of Mrs. Armstead's elegant carriage, which, with the dashing gig and tandem of her son, and the horses of their out riders, effectually 'stopped the way.' While the servants were adjusting some light baggage, dried fruits and cakes for the young people, the late publications for their elders, etc., etc., Miss Campbell said to Ellen, "you must allow me to borrow a New England phrase, to ask whither you are 'journeying?' We cannot part from you without the hope at least of meeting again."

"It is not impossible we may," replied Ellen, "for my companion has just announced to me, that if we are successful in attaining the object of our coming to this vicinity, she intends visiting Lebanon springs for a few days."

"Successful or not successful, Ellen," interrupted Deborah, "I shall go to the pool, for I hear those waters are a master-cure for the rheumatis."

"Oh, I am told quite equal to Bethesda,"[10] said Miss Campbell; "and as you take along with you an angel to trouble them, you may be sure of experiencing their efficacy. But, seriously, Miss Bruce, I hope no consideration will deter you: we are to linger in the adjacent villages for a day or two, and then go to Lebanon, and I am certain that if we are so happy as to meet you there, my aunt will insist on your attaching yourselves to our party."

---

10. *Bethesda*: In John 5, the pool of Bethesda was a place of healing for the infirm. It was thought that the first person to enter the pool when the water was stirred up would be healed of his or her ailment.

"Grace," said Mrs. Armstead, "you anticipate my wishes—you would, indeed, Miss Bruce, do me a great favour by enrolling yourselves in my party." And the young ladies exclaimed, "how glad I shall be—and how pleasant it will be."

Ellen gracefully returned her thanks to each and all, while Deborah, quite ignorant of the tactics of the polite world, comprehended nothing of the offered civility, but that it was meant in kindness, and therefore deserved the hearty thanks with which she replied to it.

"Come, my dear girls," said Mrs. Armstead, "we must despatch this leave-taking; everything, I see, is in readiness."

"Our friends," said Miss Campbell, "must start first. Be good enough, William, to order the servant to lead forward Miss Lenox's horse. I am sure," she added, smiling, "his age and virtues entitle him to precedence."

The two parties now proceeded to make their adieus; and the young ladies each, as they took Ellen's hand, slipped on her finger a ring, which they begged her to take for a keepsake.

The little boy, watchful of everything concerning his new friends, observed this—he drew from his pocket a net purse, through the interstices of which shone a golden guinea, and swelling with manly pride, he offered it to Deborah.

Deborah patted him on the head, called him a young prince, said his life was worth saving, and, as a matter of course, she handed the purse to his mother.

"Oh, no, no, Miss Lenox," said Mrs. Armstead, "you must keep it; indeed, it would quite break my little boy's heart if you despised his gift."

"Despise it, ma'am," rejoined Deborah, surveying it with unfeigned delight. "I was never the owner of a golden guinea in my life, and I thought it would be an imposition to take it—but I shall take good care of it," and she carefully deposited it in her pocket, adding, "Mr. John, your guinea will seldom see daylight while I live."

The last parting words were said—the last kind looks reciprocated, and all parties arranging themselves in their own places, Deborah drove off in one direction, and Mrs. Armstead and her suite in another. As the children stretched their necks out of the carriage to send their last lingering look towards the old chaise and the humble Rosinante[11] that drew it heavily along, Mrs. Armstead remarked, "How little the young and the truly wise estimate that which is essentially good and lovely by external appearances."

---

11. *Rosinante*: A reference to Rocinante, the bony horse of Don Quixote in Miguel de Cervantes's epic novel, *The Ingenious Gentleman Don Quixote of La Mancha* (1605–15).

"As I cannot in conscience, my dear aunt," said Miss Campbell, "take a place in either of those classes, being not very young, and certainly not belonging to the 'select few' of the 'truly wise,' I must investigate the cause of my prompt admiration of our new acquaintance." She shook her head after a moment's deliberation, and added, "I can take no praise to myself, for that charming Miss Bruce is a self-evident lady—and her companion—an exception to all rules—just hit one of my wayward fancies."

"And I rather think, Grace," said young Armstead, (who had taken his sister's place in the carriage,) "you were not sorry to have an opportunity of giving to our cousin Norton a practical instance of your contempt of her aristocracy—and of manifesting to another observer your elevation above the prejudices of society."

Miss Campbell did not notice the last clause of her cousin's sentence except by a slight blush: she pleaded guilty to the desire of mortifying the baseless pride of Mrs. Norton. "There was nothing," she said, "more essentially vulgar than the consequence that betrayed, by its perpetual vigilance and jealousy, a consciousness that there existed no intrinsic superiority—an exclusive bigoted spirit ought not to receive any toleration in our society—it was opposed to the genius and tendencies of everything about us—we were happily exempt from the servitude of oriental castes, and the scarcely less arbitrary classifications of more liberal countries. Superior talents—education—manners—the habits of refined life, were the only distinctions that ought to obtain among us, and they were quite obvious."

"Ah, coz, I see how it is. Like the Duchess of Gordon,[12] who replied to the managers of the city assembly at New York, when they apologized for not being able to offer her the precedence to which her rank entitled her, 'Nevermind, gentlemen, wherever I am, there is the Duchess of Gordon.' Like her Grace, you are satisfied that Miss Campbell's is the first place—that this modern heraldry of merit will always give her precedence."

"Thank you, William, for your generous personal application of my principles—you need not shake your head—I am in no danger of mistaking anything you say to me for a compliment."

"Believe me, Grace," replied her cousin, affectionately taking her hand, "I never was in more imminent danger of joining my voice to the choral song of your flatterers. I sympathise entirely in your desire to dissipate the illusions of our conceited and, thank Heaven, 'far-off' cousin Norton—in your admiration of our new acquaintance and in some other new feelings," he added, lowering his voice to a whisper, "that are getting the mastery in

---

12. *The Duchess of Gordon*: Refers to Jane Maxwell, Duchess of Gordon, Scotland (c.1749–1812), but neither the source nor the accuracy of the anecdote is known.

your heart—and I pray Heaven you may always show yourself as entirely superior to the adventitious distinctions of the world, as with your character you may afford to be."

"A bona fide compliment from William Armstead!—Saul among the prophets!"[13] exclaimed Grace Campbell.

---

13. *Saul among the prophets!*: An allusion to 1 Samuel 10: 11 and 1 Samuel 19: 24.

CHAPTER XVIII.

"Il y a dans l'aspect de la contrée quelque chose de calme et de doux qui prépare l'âme à sortir des agitations de la vie."[1]
Madame de Stael.

IT was a fine afternoon in the month of August when our travellers passed the romantic road which traverses the mountain that forms the eastern boundary of the valley of Hancock. The varied pleasures they had enjoyed during the day, and the excitement of drawing near to the object of their long journey, animated them both with unusual spirits. Deborah's tongue was voluble in praise of the rich farms that spread out on the declivities of the hills, or, embosomed in the protected valleys, called forth, as they deserved, the enthusiastic commendations of our experienced rustic. Ellen listened in silence while she gazed with the eye of an amateur upon this beautiful country, which possesses all the elements of the picturesque. Green hills crowned with flourishing villages—village spires rising just where they should rise; for the scene is nature's temple, and the altar should be there—lakes sparkling like gems in the distant valleys—Saddle Mountain lifting his broad shoulders to the northern sky, and the Catskills defining with their blue and misty outline the western horizon.

A sudden exclamation from Deborah fixed Ellen's attention to one spot in the widespread landscape. "As I live," she said, "there is the very place at last—see, Ellen, the yellow houses they told us of."

Ellen turned her eye to the long line of habitations of a uniform colour and appearance, which, stretching along the plain and sheltered by the surrounding hills, seem sequestered from the world, and present an aspect of peace and comfort, if not of happiness.

Ellen, as others have done, wondered that this strange people, who in their austere judgment would condemn the delight that springs from

---

1. *'Il y a dans l'aspect . . .'*: From Madame de Staël's *De l'Allemagne* and can be translated as 'There is something quiet and gentle about the appearance of the country which makes the soul abandon the agitations of life.'

natural beauty as the gratification of the 'lust of the eye,'[2] should have selected a spot of such peculiar charms.

"Ah," said Debby, as her eye wandered over the stubble fields and the rich crops that were yet unreaped, "these are knowing people—they understand their temporals—they have chosen their land well."

'Then,' thought Ellen, 'it may be that the maxim, the 'useful is the beautiful,'[3] holds good in relation to our mother earth, and that she lavishes her smiles upon those of her loyal children who seek her favours: sure I am, no professed admirers of the beauties of nature—no connoisseur in all the charms of the various combinations of mountain and valley, pasture hills and rich meadows, dashing streams and quiet lakes, could have selected a more beautiful residence than this.'

Her meditations were suddenly cut short by another exclamation from Deborah, who had now turned an angle in the road and entered the village street.

"Well, if this does not beat all! Just look here, Ellen, at this little bright stream," and she pointed to a small rivulet that sparkled like a chain of burnished silver in the sunbeams; "see where it comes racing down the hill yonder, and here, where it crosses the street, it darts underground as if to hide its capers from these solemn people—the thing has sense in it."

Ellen smiled, and asked "if it would not be well to imitate its discretion, and inquire at which house they should find the elder sister Susan?"

Deborah immediately stopped her horse, and waited for the coming up of one of the brethren, who was approaching them from an adjoining field. She spent the few moments of waiting in admiring the large richly-stocked garden, without weeds or waste places, the fine stone-posts to the fences, the neatly sawn wood, piled with mathematical exactness, the clean swept street, and all the neat arrangements of the Shaker economy, so striking to an eye accustomed only to the slipshod ways of our country people.

In the meanwhile Ellen was looking eagerly at the windows of a large house near which they had halted, to discern, if possible, the well-known features of Susan or Emily on any of the sisters who, as they passed the windows like shadows, stole an inquiring glance at the travellers.

When the man had arrived within speaking distance, Deborah asked, 'if she would be so good as to direct her where she could find Susan Allen.'

"Yea," he replied, "she dwells there;" and he pointed to the large house Ellen was surveying.

"Is she at home?" asked Deborah.

"Yea, I believe so."

---

2. *'lust of the eye'*: From 1 John 2: 16 (KJV).
3. *'useful is the beautiful'*: From Plato's (c. 428–348 BCE) dialogue *The Greater Hippias*.

Either Deborah's imagination was busy, or her sagacity detected more meaning in the man's face than was expressed in his brief answers. "Is Susan sick?" she asked, hastily.

"If ye have business with her ye can inquire for her at the house," was all the reply vouchsafed.

"Much thanks for his information," said Debby, who felt too conscious of the liberty of free inquiry at all times and places, to need the permission granted in a manner so surly. They stopped at the house designated, and were admitted by one of the sisters, who, in reply to their inquiry for Susan Allen, said, after a little hesitation, that "she was not right well, and would not be able, she believed, to see strangers."

"Can we, then," asked Ellen, "see Emily Allen?"

"Emily Allen!" exclaimed the sister, put a little off her guard by surprise, and then, after a momentary pause, and without making any explanations, she added, "I will acquaint elder sister that there are strangers here—if she knows who you are she may choose to see ye—be pleased to give me your names." They gave them, and added an earnest request that Susan would see them.

She had scarcely given Deborah and Ellen time to interchange their mutual apprehensions, ere she returned and bade them follow her. She led them upstairs and through a long passage to the elder sister's apartment, only distinguished from the others by being larger and more commodious. Their conductor showed them into the room, and then left them, closing the door after her.

Susan was seated with her back to the door. On hearing it close she rose from her chair with apparent effort, like one enfeebled by disease, and advanced towards Deborah and Ellen. Her face was ghastly pale, but there was no other sign of emotion. She gave a hand to each of her visitors, and said, faintly, "Ye are welcome—sit down, sit down." They obeyed her, and she reseated herself; a dead silence followed—even Deborah, fearless as she was, was awed into the deference of a momentary silence by the imposing solemnity of Susan's deportment. It was but for a moment, for her courage flowing back, "What signifies it?" said she; an expression that, with her, always signified the utter demolition of all barriers that opposed her purpose: "what signifies it—we may as well come to it first as last; what has happened to Emily?"

"Emily is gone," replied Susan, in a deep, low tone, her eyes downcast, and her whole person fixed in statue-like stillness.

"Gone!" echoed Deborah and Ellen in the same breath; "how—what is it you mean—she is not dead, surely?"

"Would to God she had died," replied Susan, clasping her hands and raising her eyes, from which the tears now flowed freely: "Would to God she had died—in the faith." Terrifying and incomprehensible as were Susan's words, neither Deborah nor Ellen ventured another question. There was something so strange and unnatural in her convulsive emotion, that it affected them as if a being that had passed the bounds of human feeling, should wake again to the pangs of mortal suffering.

After some moments of 'strong crying and tears,'[4] she said, "I could have looked on and seen the breath of life leave her body, and yet have said with the Shunammite woman, 'it is well.'[5] I could have laid her away from me in the cold earth, and yet felt that it was well; who might not endure the brief space of time deprived of the dearest and the best?—but," she added, shuddering, "I have lost her for time, and for eternity—this it is that wrings my heart with such grief as I thought never to have felt again."

Ellen was filled with frightful apprehensions for Emily's fate, and yet she knew not how to frame an inquiry about her. Even Deborah could not rally courage to hasten an explanation: she walked to the window desirous to conceal the feeling she could neither control nor express; but the frequent application of her handkerchief to her nose made the honest creature's sympathy quite audible.

It was not long before Susan recovered a degree of composure that enabled her to relieve the impatient anxiety of her visitors, as far as the information she had to communicate could relieve it. She began her relation with the fact of Emily's clandestine departure with Harrington. She had herself first learned it on the succeeding morning, when she returned from Lebanon, whither she had, as our readers may remember, been suddenly summoned. She said she should herself have believed that Emily had not been a party to Harrington's treachery. She should have been sure he had forced her away, but that she remembered the child's emotion when she parted with her, and the mysterious language she then held, which was but too clearly explained by the event. The wiles of Harrington, or rather, she said, the wiles of Satan by his servant Harrington, had been too much for the poor girl; she had been caught in the toils, but she thanked God she had not fallen an easy prey.

Ellen inquired 'if nothing had been heard of the fugitives since their departure?'

"Nothing.—One of the brethren had been despatched to Albany, where, they had reason to believe, Harrington meant to put into execution a plan to defraud the society of a considerable sum of money. It was now the third day

---

4. *'strong crying and tears'*: From Hebrews 5: 7 (KJV).
5. *with the Shunammite woman, 'it is well'*: The Shunammite woman appears in 2 Kings 4: 8–37. After her son dies, the Shunammite woman affirms, 'It is well' and seeks the prophet Elijah, who raises her son from the dead.

since Harrington's departure, and on the next day they expected the return of their agent, and it was more than probable that he would bring some intelligence of the fugitives. But, oh Ellen!" she concluded, "There is nothing to hope for—there is nothing more to fear—the worst has happened."

Ellen would not allow the case to be desperate; not that she could see any rational ground for favourable expectations, but hope is the happy instinct of youth. She showed Susan Emily's letter to her Eton friends, which at least intimated a wish to leave the society; she hinted at the attachment she believed Emily to have cherished for James Lenox, and she finished with expressing the belief that the poor girl had been the innocent dupe of Harrington's artifices, and had availed herself of his departure, as affording her an opportunity of returning to her friends.

At another time this would have sounded like harsh consolation to Susan; but now, in comparison with what she feared, this was innocence and happiness, and she eagerly grasped at Ellen's suggestions. "God grant it may be so! God grant it!" she reiterated. "Oh had I but known, Ellen, that it was in the child's heart to go back to you, I would have given her up as freely as Abraham yielded up Isaac. It would have been but honestly following her light, and though but a dim one, still she would have been saved from this utter ruin;—and now if I could believe that she had fallen innocently, I might weep for her—yea, I *must* weep for her—but not these bitter, hopeless tears."

Ellen entreated her to mitigate her grief, at least till she had more certain knowledge of the motives of Emily's departure. Susan evidently felt humbled to find herself the subject of the compassionate efforts of even the loveliest of the world's people; but she yielded insensibly to Ellen's beneficent influence, and even admitted that there was some consolation in her rational suggestions.

Deborah had tact enough to perceive this was too delicate a case for her handling—quite out of her province, and beyond her skill; and therefore she had remained silent till she perceived that the elder sister was tranquillized, and that Ellen had expended all her consolatory arguments; she then, like a prudent officer, thought it best to retreat before another occasion for action should discover that their strength was exhausted, and she abruptly proposed their departure. Ellen, grieved to think they had no reason for delay, assented; and Susan, who at another time would have insisted on performing the rites of hospitality to friends that she both valued and loved, silently acquiesced, probably deeming it prudent in the present state of her feelings to exclude every exciting cause. This caution would seem incompatible with strong emotion; but it must be remembered that caution was habitual to the elder sister—was virtue in her estimation—and was essential to the preservation of her influence with the society, and had yielded for a short time only to the mastery of those powerful affections over which it had held a long and secure dominion. Such an exhibition of her feelings as that into which she had been surprised by the sudden appearance of Emily's friends would, she well knew, in the view of her brethren and sisters, degrade her to a level far below the frozen summits where they remained secure, regarding with equal contempt the earthly influences that bless and fertilize, or ravage and destroy.

Before parting, she promised to despatch a messenger to Lebanon Springs (whither Deborah informed her that she and Ellen were going, and should remain for a few days,) with any intelligence that she might receive of the fugitives: she then summoned one of the sisters, and having requested her to provide some refreshments for her friends, she bade them farewell with her usual composure, save a little faltering of the voice, and trembling of the lip.

The travellers were then conducted to a small parlour, where a table was quickly spread for their entertainment. It was covered with a cloth of the purest white by one of the sisters, who lingered in adjusting it, smoothing down the folds, pulling it first on one side, and then on the other, till this artifice of her innocent vanity had succeeded, and Deborah's liberal praises were bestowed on the delicate manufacture which had employed the skill and taste of the sisterhood.

All the varieties of the 'staff of life'[6] were now displayed: bread made of the 'finest of the wheat',[7] interspersed with slices produced from the native Indian corn, which, in its prepared state, deserves still to retain the poetical epithet of golden; next to this plate, groaning with its burden, were placed some tempting slices of the sad-coloured rye: these gifts of Ceres[8] were so perfect in their kind, that the delicate goddess herself might have banqueted on them: then came delicious butter, and the purest honey—the fruits in season, and pies, cakes, and sweetmeats, accompanied (it may be thought somewhat incongruously) by cheese, pickles, and cider; and to crown all, the aromatic teapot, diffusing, like the censer at the ancient feasts, its fragrant fumes over all the board. With such incitement, what mortal with mortal senses would have condemned the fare?

If the truth must be told, the spirituelle Ellen Bruce, after her long abstinence, did not regard this repast with the indifference of a true heroine; and Deborah played her part as well as one of Homer's heroes might have done, had he had the good fortune to sit at a Shaking Quaker tea-table.

---

6. *'staff of life'*: Meaning bread. A variation on this phrase, 'staff of bread', appears in Psalm 105: 16 (KJV).
7. *'finest of the wheat'*: From Psalms 81: 16 (KJV).
8. *Ceres*: The Roman goddess of agriculture, particularly of cereal grains.

She was yielding to the hospitable solicitations of the sister in attendance, and taking her fifth cup of tea, when Ellen reminded her a second time that the sun was fast declining, and that, without despatch, they should be overtaken by the night before they reached Lebanon. Deborah's appetite submitted to the necessity of the case, and our travellers, after thanking their kind entertainer, took leave of her, and left the village, as many other travellers have done; with a grateful sense of the hospitality of its simple inhabitants.

CHAPTER XIX.

> "Say from whence you owe this strange intelligence,
> Or why you stop our way with such prophetic greetings?"[1]
>
> *Macbeth.*

ELLEN's mind had been so filled with commiseration for Susan, she was so much more in the habit of attending to others' feelings than her own, that until she had turned her back upon the Shaker village, she did not feel the full weight of her own disappointment in regard to Emily. The thought of old Mrs. Allen's grief, and the most gloomy apprehensions in relation to the poor girl's destiny, engrossed her attention, and prevented her heeding Deborah's profound remarks on the "pattern people," as she termed them. We would not insinuate that Deborah herself was unmoved by Emily's sorrowful case: she would have gone to the ends of the earth to have served her, or any other fellow-creature in distress, but it was an inviolable principle with her 'never to cry for spilt milk.' After expressing some conjectures as to the uncertain fate of the poor girl,—bewailing alternately her folly and her misfortunes, and anticipating with compassion the effect of this last, severest stroke upon the old grandmother—she subsided into silence, and permitted Ellen to pursue her sad meditations undisturbed. She was at length awakened from them by the deepening of the twilight, and after a slight observation of the road, she asked Deborah "if she was quite sure she had not mistaken the way?"

Deborah was certain she had taken the road that had been pointed out to her as the shortest cut to the springs, but she began to think they should have been wiser to have remained at the village, or to have taken the more travelled and more thickly-settled road. "However," she said, "it can be, Ellen, but four or five miles to the pool, and if the daylight does not last, we have a moon tonight, and thanks to fortune, neither you nor I are afraid of anything."

"Oh, afraid—no, I trust not," said Ellen, assuming a courage she did not feel, for her dejected mind had coloured with a melancholy hue the face of

---

1. *'Say from whence you owe this strange intelligence . . .'*: From I, iii of Shakespeare's *Macbeth*.

nature; and the hoarse sounds of the brawling brook on her right, and the deep, unbroken wood on the left, affected her imagination with an undefined impression of some possible evil. They proceeded at a very slow rate, the ground was ascending, and the jaded old horse lagged along as if he felt the folly of turning his back upon the hospitalities of the village.

They had pursued their way for some time in profound silence. Meanwhile the last traces of daylight had faded from the sky, and the stars began to shed their scanty light upon the grass-grown road. Deborah's patience was at last quite exhausted. "Ellen," she said, "this is the most tedious, lonesome way ever I travelled; it will never do to creep on this fashion, our horse, poor fellow, is coming to a dead stand—let us walk up the rest of the hill; you always go like a bird, and a walk will limber my old joints, and serve to warm me this chilly night."

Ellen acquiesced—and as they walked on together, Deborah said, she "had been thinking of all she had heard Squire Redwood say of the dangers of the old countries, and she was thinking it would be a pretty risky business for two defenceless women to be travelling alone at night in any land but our own."

"Yes, indeed," replied Ellen; "but here, thank heaven, there can be no danger;" and as she spoke she drew nearer to Deborah, for she fancied she heard a rustling in the woods on her left. Deborah heard it too, for she stopped the horse, saying, "Hark—what can that be?" She had hardly uttered the words when a large dog sprang upon them; both were startled, and looked anxiously in the direction from which the dog had come, but there was neither motion nor sound there.

"Off, off, you brute!" said Deborah; and the dog, thus harshly repulsed, turned as if to appeal to Ellen, crouched at her feet, ran from her, and then returned yelping—raised himself quite erect, fawned again on Ellen, wagged his tail, and expressed over and over again his mute and painful entreaties.

"Words can't speak no plainer," said Debby. "The poor creatur would have us go with him; but we must drive him away, this is no place nor time to be hindered."

"Certainly not—but,"—

"But what, Ellen? speak out, girl."

"Why I cannot bear to turn away from the poor thing, it seems wicked to deny him." As she spoke she patted and caressed the dog: "There may be, I think there must be, some person in distress in these woods—someone hunting may have been wounded, such accidents are common." The dog seemed to understand her words or her caresses—he sprang again towards the wood, again returned, repeated all his modes of entreaty, pressing his suit with redoubled vigor, and Ellen replied to him by turning to Deborah, and saying, with determination, "I *must* follow him."

"Are you clean out of your wits, child, to think of patrolling these woods after this dog—and in case there should be anybody here, for the Lord's sake, what could you or I do? Come, come along, it grows late." But Ellen still hesitated, and Deborah added, "We cannot be far from a house, and we will alarm some men and send them here, which will be much the properest way."

Ellen, from her childhood, and ever since the memorable night when a dog had aided in her preservation from the fire, had felt a strong attachment to the whole race, had studied their instincts and history; and while she stood looking at the petitioning animal, a thousand stories of similar significant actions glanced through her mind, and confirmed her resolution.

"I *must* follow him, Deborah," she repeated; "Wait for me here a few moments, I will not go beyond call;" and she turned quickly away to avoid Debby's remonstrance.

"Stop, Ellen—stop, girl—do you think I will let you go alone after this jack-o'-lantern?[2] If you won't hear to reason, why there's an end on't—I must go with you."

Ellen waited while Deborah secured the horse, and they then plunged into the wood after the dog, who trotted along the narrow footpath, turning round often as if to assure himself they still followed him. "Well," said Deborah, "I don't speak from any fear—I never was afraid in my life, for I never saw danger; if I had, I might have been as scared as other people; but I think for two rational women, we are in an odd place, and following a strange leader."

"And that is as it should be," replied Ellen, in an encouraging tone; "two errant damsels as we are, in quest of adventures—danger there is not, cannot be here, and we will not go much farther."

"No, that we will not; there is reason in all things—and as old Gilpin says,

> "'Twas for your pleasure you came here,
> You shall go back for mine."[3]

"Certainly," replied Ellen, smiling; "only go a little way farther, the moon is rising, there is a cleared place before us, and if we see nothing there, I will consent to return."

Ellen's benevolent purpose had conquered her womanish timidity: her tender and youthful spirit was susceptible to romantic influences that her

---

2. *jack-o'-lantern*: Another name for ignis fatuus, but, more specifically, something that lures one into danger.
3. *as old Gilpin says, 'Twas for your pleasure you came here . . .'*: From Cowper's poem 'The Diverting History of John Gilpin' (1782).

companion could neither feel nor comprehend, and she pressed eagerly on, even in advance of Deborah, till on issuing from the wood, the dog bounded before her, and with one desperate howl threw himself beside a lifeless body. "Good heavens!" exclaimed Ellen, involuntarily shrinking back and seizing Deborah's arm, and pointing to the figure, which by the dusky light she could only discern to be that of a man, whether dead or living she knew not.

Deborah, without speaking, without faltering or hesitating in the least, walked rapidly forward to the body, and stooping down, eagerly gazed on it for a moment, and then raising both her hands in token of astonishment to Ellen, who was timidly approaching, she exclaimed, "A dead Indian—as sure as I am a living woman, a dead Indian."

"Is he certainly dead?" asked Ellen, compassionately bending over him.

"Dead, child! Look at his fallen jaw, his stark stiff limbs—poor soul! He is as dead as Christopher Columbus."

Ellen sat down on a prostrate trunk of a tree beside which the body lay, while Deborah examined it for the purpose of ascertaining the cause of the poor wretch's death. There was a wound on the temple from which the blood had flowed freely, and which Deborah thought might have been occasioned by his fall, as there was a stone lying near his head which it had probably first struck. Fragments of an earthen jug were lying about the body, and Deborah pointing to them, said, "He has died Indian fashion, Ellen, his dog and his jug by him; after all, for aught we know, he may have died of old age, for he looks as old as Methusalem."[4]

"Poor creature!" said Ellen; "and to die at last without a being to care for him."

"Oh as to that, that is nothing," said Debby, "and if it were, just look at that dog"—the dog was licking his master's face and breast—"There's many a one, Ellen, that dies on a feather-bed, and them too that have houses and lands, without so true a friend and mourner as that poor brute. But come, Ellen, we can do no good here sermonizing the matter; we had best make our way back, and give notice of the man's death, that somebody may come and put him under ground, which is fitting should be done, seeing he is a human being, though an old Indian."

They rose to depart, and looking around, they both perceived at the same moment the hut of Sooduck, (our readers no doubt have anticipated that this Indian was none other,) which till now had been hidden from them by the deep shadows of the wood. "His wigwam, I declare!" exclaimed Deborah: "We'll get the poor carr'on[5] into it; for I should be loath, for his

---

4. *as old as Methusalem*: Methusalem (or Methuselah) is the oldest man in the Bible, who is said to have died at the age of 969.
5. *carr'on*: Carrion, or a corpse.

dog's sake, that anything should happen to it till we can get it honourable burial. Do you, Ellen, open the door of the hut, and I will manage to drag the old carcass in."

Deborah made this division of labour to save Ellen the painful necessity of touching the dead body, and Ellen hastened to execute her appointed task. The door was fastened with a rope, and she found so much difficulty in extricating the knots, that Deborah came up with the body before she had effected it. Suddenly she stopped, and whispering to Debby, "Hark," she said, "do you not hear a sound—a low moaning?"

"Pooh, child, you are vapoury—it is nothing but a kitten," replied Deborah: and laying down the body, she drew from her pocket a knife, with which she cut the cord that had fallen from Ellen's trembling hands—the door flew open; and a loud shriek from within startled even Deborah. She however stepped boldly forward, and saw before her, in the farthest corner of the hut, a terrified girl, who had sunk upon her knees, and covered her face with her hands, in apparent expectation of some dreadful evil.

"Merciful heaven! save me, save me!" she cried, as Deborah approached her.

"What in the world is the matter with you, child?" said Deborah, "There is no one here that will hurt a hair of your head."

"We are friends—look at us, come to the light," said Ellen.

At the sound of Ellen's kind and gentle voice the spirit of fear departed from the half-frantic girl: she rose, and looked with trembling hope at her deliverers: they all advanced to the door, the light fell on their faces, and an instant recognition followed.

"Ellen!"—"Emily!"—"Deborah!"—"Is it possible?"—"It cannot be!"—they exclaimed in one breath.

The joyful sense of hope, of protection, of safety, was almost too much for Emily. She threw her arms around Ellen's neck, and nearly fainted on her bosom. Her friends drew her to a little distance from the hut, and far enough to avoid her observation of the Indian: there Deborah left her to the soothing efforts of Ellen, while she returned to finish the arrangements for Sooduck's body.

'An evil creature he was, no doubt,' thought Deborah, (for the discovery of Emily had thrown a strong light on Sooduck's character,) an evil creature, but it is all passed to his own account now, poor wretch!'

These and similar reflections of a compassionate nature filled Deborah's mind while she dragged in the body, composed it decently on the straw, and covered it with a blanket. The faithful dog took his station beside it, and there Deborah left him to keep guard, until she could send some persons to perform the last offices for his master.

CHAPTER XIX.

These arrangements occupied but a few moments, but they gave Emily time to recover a sufficient degree of strength and calmness to accompany her friends back to the chaise. The tide of joy that comes from a sense of deliverance from great danger is prompt and powerful in its operations. The timid despairing girl, released from her captivity, and in the presence of her friends, felt as if she had been translated to another world, and before they reached the chaise she relieved their worst apprehensions by giving them a sufficiently clear account of Reuben's treachery.

From them she first learned Sooduck's death, and could afford no clue to its cause. He had left her as usual in the morning, and she had heard nothing since but the terrible uproar made by the dog, when (as she now conjectured) on seeing his fallen master, he had struggled, and at last successfully, to release himself from his confinement.

It seemed probable that Sooduck, tempted by the superior quality of the liquor furnished by Harrington, or by its abundance, had indulged his appetite to such excess as to extinguish his feeble spark of life; or, as Deborah concluded, his fall had occasioned his death. After quite as much consideration as the miserable subject merited, the verdict of our fair jury was 'accidental death.' Emily accounted for her terrors on the appearance of her friends by saying, that her fear of Harrington had converted every sound into a notice of his return. It seemed utterly impossible for the poor girl to express her joy that she had been rescued from him, and her gratitude to her deliverers. She had not once mentioned the elder sister's name in her brief relation of her flight, but Ellen, ever considerate of others, proposed as they reached the chaise, that they should return to the village and relieve Susan at once from her painful apprehensions. Emily said nothing, for she hesitated between her wish to see and to relieve her kind friend, and her reluctance to venture within her prison bounds.

Deborah cut the deliberation short by saying, "No, no, Ellen, you have had your way once, and a good way it proved, and I shall think to my dying day that the Lord led you up through them woods—but now I must have mine. There is no knowing," she whispered to Ellen, "what might happen if we went back; 'a bird in the hand,' you know—Come, jump in, Ellen—jump in, Emily, my little godsend, and we'll on as fast as possible."

Ellen acquiesced, secretly resolving with the morning dawn to despatch a messenger with the good news to Susan: a resolution she exactly performed. The travellers then proceeded at good speed to Lebanon Springs, and arrived there before midnight without any other interruption than that occasioned by Deborah's 'keeping good faith with the dog,' as she termed it, by stopping at the first house on their way to give information of Sooduck's death.

As Emily Allen's connection ceased from this time forever with the Shaker society, it may be best to inform our readers now, without troubling them again to recur to the subject, with the result of Harrington's expedition to Albany. Harrington had received from Freeborn, the ruling elder of the society at Hancock, a check for five thousand dollars, which was the principal part of a sum lodged to the credit of the society in a bank in Albany, where they were in the habit of depositing the surplus money which they received from the sale of their productions of agriculture and manufactures. This money had been at various times received in the market of Albany, and deposited in the bank for safe keeping; and these five thousand dollars were now wanted to pay the purchase-money of an adjoining farm, which the elders had determined to add to their possessions. It was however designed by Harrington for a very different application. Eager to secure the money, he went to the bank immediately upon its being opened in the morning, and presented the check for payment.

The clerk who received it observed that the check was payable not to bearer, but to order, and that it must be endorsed before it could be paid. Harrington said that he would endorse it, which he immediately did, and presented it again for payment. This delay and conversation attracted the notice of the cashier, who took up and examined the draft as the clerk was counting out the money to Harrington.

"Stop," said he, "the check is payable to the order of Reuben Harrington and John Jacobs, and must be endorsed by them both. Elder Freeborn is a very exact man about worldly matters, and as he has made his check payable to the order of two people, we must have the order of both of them."

Harrington could not restrain the expression of a little more impatience than became his garb and assumed character: he however received back the check, and said that he would step to friend Jacobs, who lived in the next street, and procure his endorsement. He then called on Jacobs and requested him to endorse the check. This Jacobs was a sober, staid citizen, who had often had dealings with the Shaker society, and had contracted some acquaintance with the elders, and particularly elder Freeborn.

When Harrington had explained the business, Jacobs, after a little reflection, said that he saw no harm which could come to him from endorsing the check, which he accordingly did. "Friend Freeborn," said he, "is a careful man, and likes to have his business done right. I will step and get the money for you myself." He went out, and returned after a few minutes with bank notes to the amount of the check. He then entered into some general conversation with Harrington, who restrained his impatience for the actual possession of the prize as much as possible: at last, however, he observed that he must be going, as he had business to do in the city that day before he returned home. Jacobs took no notice of this hint, but continued

CHAPTER XIX.

the conversation upon the subject of some Shaker ploughs which he had for sale on commission. At last Harrington asked him directly for the money.

"You shall have it," replied Jacobs, "as soon as you give me elder Freeborn's order for it." Harrington said that he had no such order, and that none was necessary; that the check was in his favour as well as that of Jacobs', and that he was an elder as well as Freeborn.

"Elder Freeborn," said Jacobs, "has the care of the prudentials. At any rate, I have received this money upon his check, and I must have his order before I pay it away to anybody."

Harrington entreated and remonstrated, but the man of business seemed inclined to adhere to his punctilio.[6] Harrington had before entertained some apprehension that his fraudulent designs were not wholly unsuspected by the shrewd and cautious Freeborn, and it now occurred to him that the embarrassment in which he was placed might not be wholly accidental. His threats and flatteries only served to confirm the cool and wary Jacobs in his suspicion of Harrington's dishonest intentions—at last, quite discouraged, Harrington left the impracticable trader, cursing the superior cunning that had baffled his well-concerted project.

His next concern was in regard to Emily. It appeared easiest, and would certainly be safest, to abandon the wreck—to give up the ship; but he had so long flattered himself with the possession of this young creature, he so thirsted for revenge against Susan, and his pride was so much interested in at least a partial success, that after some anxious deliberation with himself, he determined to return to Emily, not doubting that she would accept her liberty on any terms he should vouchsafe to offer. Accordingly he left Albany late in the afternoon, and having travelled all night, he arrived at Sooduck's hut just at the break of day on the morning after Emily's escape. It is not necessary, and certainly would be difficult to paint his consternation at the sight that there greeted him. But there was no time for inquiry or delay. It was important to him that he should not be recognized in that neighbourhood. He was not, however, destined to escape without farther mortification. On re-entering the public road he was met by some men, who had collected in consequence of Deborah's notice, to dispose of Sooduck's body. They had heard the story of his villainy, which was already in general circulation. They knew him well, and moved by an intuitive love of justice, as well as by a friendly feeling to the society, they stopped his horses, bound him hand and foot, and drove him in triumph back to his Shaker brethren.

The messenger despatched by Ellen arrived about the same time; and Susan, thus relieved from her anxiety, and rejoicing in the innocence and safety of Emily, was able to assist at the council that was called to deliberate

---

6. *punctilio*: A ceremony or scruple.

on the proper measures to be taken in regard to the culprit. The result of a short conference was equivalent to the sentence of the Quaker against his dog. 'I will not myself kill thee,' he said, 'but I'll turn thee on the world and give thee a bad name.'[7] Reuben Harrington was dispossessed of everything he held belonging to the society, but the clothes that covered him, and sent out to wander upon the earth, despised and avoided, enduring all the misery of unsuccessful and unrepented guilt.

7. *'I will not myself kill thee . . .'*: This story seems to have been a common illustration of the concept of honouring the letter but not the spirit of the law that many authors used in the nineteenth century. As Quakers are pacifist and cannot use violence, this proverbial Quaker commits no violence directly on the dog, but rather brands his dog 'mad', an epithet which turns the town against the dog. In this way, the town may punish the dog in ways that would be against the Quaker's religious beliefs; thus the Quaker has upheld the letter of his law while breaking it in spirit.

CHAPTER XX.

"The billows on the ocean,
The breezes idly roaming,
The clouds' uncertain motion,
They are but types of woman."[1]

Burns.

It is probably well known to most of our readers, that Lebanon is a favourite resort during the hot months. It lies on a post-road from Boston to Albany—is of easy access from New York—and from the beauty of its scenery, the salubrity of its air, and its proximity to Saratoga Springs, attracts, for a short time at least, the throng of visitors to those celebrated waters. The mineral spring that is nominally the chief attraction of the place, should not be forgotten; if not as efficacious as its neighbours would fain believe, it is at least innocent—no one can forget it who has seen the bright waters forever bubbling up from the bosom of the earth, and admired the sycamore tree that stands beside the sparkling fountain, like its guardian genius, and drops its protecting branches over it.

Our travellers were fortunate in the time of their arrival: large parties had left the place the preceding day, and they were able to obtain two apartments in Mr. Hull's well-known house;[2] one was assigned to Ellen, and the other Emily shared with her relative and true friend Deborah.

Ellen, wearied as she was, did not retire to bed until she had written a note to the 'elder sister,' containing all the particulars of Emily's distressful experiences and providential rescue; nor till she had obtained a promise from her landlord that he would despatch it with the first ray of light. The commission was faithfully executed, as might have been expected from his obliging character.

Even after Ellen had performed this duty, it was long ere she could compose her mind to sleep. Relieved of all anxiety concerning Emily,

1. *'The billows on the ocean . . .'*: From Burns's song, 'Deluded Swain, The Pleasure' (1793).
2. *Mr. Hull's well-known house*: Columbia Hall was owned by Caleb Hull and was the first hotel in Lebanon Springs, NY.

her thoughts reverted to the friends she had left at Eton; hovered about Mr. Redwood with an undefinable interest, and finally concentrated on Charles Westall. All the circumstances of her brief intercourse with him passed in revision before her; and she dwelt on each particular over and over again, as a miser counts his treasures—the cherished recollections of memory gave place to the (perhaps unbidden) visions of hope, and all at last faded away like the bright tints of the evening cloud, and she sunk into profound repose.

Deborah's weariness prevailed over the force of long habit, and neither she nor her protégées awoke till a late hour in the morning, when, in compliance with Ellen's persuasions, she ordered breakfast in her room: after partaking it with her usual appetite, she left her less enterprising companions, and sallied forth to reconnoitre the premises, and to try the effect of bathing on her rheumatism.

Neither Ellen nor Emily felt any disposition in the present state of their minds to remain at Lebanon. Emily's affections, released from the captivity of an imaginary duty, had bounded forward to their natural destination; and Ellen was impatient to accelerate her return to Mrs. Harrison, to whom alone she could unburthen her heart; but they both knew that Deborah had resolved to remain at the springs for some days, and that her resolution once formed, was quite as immutable as the laws of the Medes and Persians.[3] They felt too, that after the great inconveniences the good woman had endured, and the essential services she had rendered them, there would be a species of ingratitude in opposing her wishes. Ellen had not a nature to resist the persuasion of such a motive: the gentle Emily never resisted anything, and they both prepared to appear with the best grace they could before the gay and the fashionable, under the conduct of Miss Deborah. Emily's life had been too retired and humble to expose her to any mortification from the appearance and manners of her chaperone, yet she shrunk with natural timidity from the possibility that her history might be known, and that she might therefore be exposed to the curious gaze and free remarks of strangers. But Ellen encouraged her with the assurance, that as they were all strangers, there was no clue to the discovery that she was the little runaway Shaker, and having made her doff her Shaker dress, and put on a simple mourning frock which she had provided for her, she remodelled her hair—formed some becoming curls on her temples—and imparted such a worldly tastefulness to her appearance, that the simple girl confessed herself so completely metamorphosed, that she hardly recognized her own image.

---

3. *as the laws of the Medes and Persians*: Once a law was put in writing in the ancient Persian government, it could not be repealed.

CHAPTER XX.

As neatness and simplicity were the presiding graces at Ellen's toilette, its duties were very expeditiously despatched. Happily for her, since she did not possess the gifts of fortune, the loveliness of her face and figure made her superior to her favours or arts, at least so thought Deborah, as well as more competent judges, for when she re-entered after her perambulations, she said (the only speech of hers on record that betrays any *femality*,) she did not believe the United States could produce two girls 'prettier to look at.' Ellen felt some consternation when she added, that 'though she was not much of a dresser, she liked to rig out suitably to her voyage; and as she had observed by the ladies she had met, that Lebanon was a dressy place, her young folks should not be ashamed of her.'

She then proceeded to unpack her trunk, and drew from its stores a 'lutestring changeable,'[4]—a manufacture of the olden time, in which the colours were skilfully combined, to produce a constant alternation from one hue to another; the fancy of Deborah's youth had been orange and purple, and as it was her pride and boast that she never altered her apparel in subservience to the whims of fashion, the 'changeable' that had remained through all chances and changes unchanged, and always "like a robe canonical, ne'er seen, but wondered at,"[5] was once more dragged forth to the light of day, and its antique and unbending dignity exposed to the levity of modern gossamer belles.

Ellen watched Deborah with dismay, while she drew on the closely fitted sleeve, and laced the formal waist, and adroitly placed her gold beads over her 'kerchief, that their light might not be hid. After her first and brief sacrifice to the graces, turning to Ellen, she said, with a complacency that her young friend could not but pity, "Now I think I am fit company for anybody—what do you say, Ellen?"

"Fit company for anybody you always are, Miss Deborah," replied Ellen, "without any outward adorning—but I think your dress admits of one improvement;" and while she made an effort to restrain the smile that in spite of her hovered on her lips, she persuaded Deborah that a lace shawl, which she dexterously threw over her shoulders, improved her appearance. Deborah assented, and the dinner bell ringing, our heroine, with the courage of a martyr, slipped her arm into one of Deborah's, while Emily, in happy ignorance of the ludicrous antiquity of her friend's costume, took the other. Thus they entered the dining room, where the company was already assembled, and having taken their seats, were precisely at that point of momentary silence that precedes the general onset. The rustling of Deborah's silk

---

4. '*lutestring changeable*': A dress made out of a type of glossy silk which gives the illusion of changing colour.
5. '*like a robe canonical, ne'er seen, but wondered at*': A variation on a line from III, ii of Shakespeare's *Henry IV Part I*.

attracted some observation, but it was not till she moved to the head of the table, and took possession of a seat that had been reserved for a gentleman who usually occupied it, while Ellen and Emily slid into vacant chairs on each side of her, that every eye was fixed upon the novel group. Deborah's figure, in her usual apparel, was rather grotesque, but not sufficiently so to provoke or excuse laughter—she would have looked between Ellen and Emily like the gnarled oak, somewhat scathed by time and accident, but still respectable in its hardy age, whose firm protection the tender vines had sought, and bloomed around it in all the freshness of youth and beauty. But the yellow and purple changeable was irresistibly ludicrous. Some lively girls who sat near the head of the table began a titter: the infection was caught by their neighbours, and all, even grave matrons and staid old gentlemen, were compelled to turn their faces, hide them with their handkerchiefs, or outrage all breeding, violate all decorum, and laugh outright. Poor little Emily, not discerning the subject of the mirth, and seeing it was directed towards the part of the table she occupied, believed herself the subject of it, and half frightened out of her senses, averted her head to conceal her blushes and her tears. Deborah's sagacity was at fault for a moment, but the truth suddenly flashed across her mind, and involuntarily rising and turning to Ellen, "Am I their music?" she exclaimed; when seeing that Ellen too—for the truth must be told—had lost all command of her risibles, and had joined the laughers, her astonishment expressed, 'And thou too? This is the unkindest cut of all;'[6] and she would have probably said something equivalent to it, but the attention of the company was diverted by a bustle at the door; and Mr. Redwood entered, leading in Mrs. Westall, and followed by Miss Redwood attended by Charles Westall.

Deborah's tall figure, standing erect at the head of the table, first caught Mr. Redwood's eye, and to the surprise of the company he exclaimed, "Miss Deborah!—my old friend—God bless you, I am glad to see you, and Miss Bruce—my dear Ellen," he said, advancing with the greatest cordiality, and shaking Deborah's hand heartily, and kissing Ellen's, "This is delightful, to meet you again—and so unexpectedly!"

Deborah forgot her irritation, in her sudden pleasure, and returned Mr. Redwood's greeting with all her heart. "I thought, sir," she said, "that you were halfway to Boston by this time."

"I was halfway there, Miss Deborah, but my courage failed me:—I found my strength and spirits unequal to enjoying the society of Boston. I have not philosophy enough to resist its allurements, so I turned my face

---

6. *'and thou too? this is the unkindest cut of all'*: References to the famous lines from Shakespeare's *Julius Caesar*, 'Et tu Brute?', spoken by Caesar in III, i, and 'The unkindest cut of all' from Antony's speech in III, ii.

CHAPTER XX.

homeward, and have been guided hither," he concluded, looking at Ellen, "by my good genius." Ellen, disconcerted by the unexpected appearance of the party, could not command words to reply to Mr. Redwood, or to return Mrs. Westall's polite recognition.

Mr. Redwood observed her embarrassment. "We are keeping our friends standing," he said; "Let us pass on, Mrs. Westall, my daughter I believe is at the lower end of the room." Then, lowering his voice to Ellen, he added, "we shall see you immediately after dinner."

Deborah looked after Mr. Redwood as he walked away, and shook her head: "He is dreadfully changed, Ellen, since we left him—poor man, he is not long for this world."

Ellen had noticed that his face, as the glow of surprise faded from it, reverted to a sickly, ghastly paleness: but at this moment a subject of stronger interest occupied her mind. She ventured a timid glance towards that part of the room to which Miss Redwood had turned on seeing her: there appeared to be some delay about the arrangement of the seats for the newcomers. In the meantime Miss Redwood was still standing with her hand in Westall's, and receiving the compliments of a gentleman in the uniform of a British officer, who had just approached from the table. Ellen fancied she saw—for the feelings that made her heart at that moment throb almost audibly have a wonderful effect on the vision— she fancied she saw a mingled expression of impatience and joy on Westall's countenance, and a moment after she heard him coming towards her with rapid steps.

The dread of observation—the fear of exposing those emotions that every delicate woman instinctively conceals, restored to her at once her self-command, and when she gave Westall her hand, she simply evinced the frank pleasure that became the reception of any friend; and she preserved her self-possession in spite of Deborah's exclaiming with her usual bluntness, "Well now, Mr. Westall! it does a body's heart good to see the face of a friend in a strange land, and especially yours, and looking so joyful too."

"I shall like my face the better all my life," replied Westall, "for speaking such plain truth: it would be but a poor index if it did not make the pleasure of this unexpected meeting intelligible. Miss Bruce, I rejoice to see," he added, in an undertone, "that you have been successful in your benevolent mission—but my mother is beckoning to me—farewell till after dinner."

So important an event as the arrival of a celebrated beauty at a watering-place, effected a complete diversion in favour of Deborah's changeable—and the regard shown to her by Mr. Redwood shielded her from the ridicule of the company.

After complimenting by her keen relish a variety of viands[7] within her reach, Deborah turned to observe how her protegées fared. "I am glad, Emily," she said, "to see you have an appetite; but Ellen, child, what ails you? You eat as people eat in dreams, that is to say, you don't eat at all: you must be more nice than wise, not to find something to suit your palate on this table, where there is such a fulness, and all fresh too. Take a piece of the chicken, Ellen—it is a nice chicken for this time o' year—by the way, I must find out how this young Mr. Hull feeds his chickens—try a piece, Ellen—" Ellen declined it. "Well then, take a piece of the lamb, child. I can assure you it is a firstling of the flock, tender and fat; or if you don't fancy lamb, let that gentleman help you off the dish next him—what do you call it, sir?"

"Ragout, madam."

"Well, I never heard the name before, and I can't tell now any more than when I ate it, whether it's fish or flesh, but for a new-fashioned thing it's very pretty tasted—the fare is excellent. I have ate a little of all, and I freely give it my recommend. Come, Ellen, don't split peas any longer, but take a little something—do."

Ellen continued, however, obstinately to refuse Deborah's solicitations; and her attention being soon engrossed by the pies and puddings which she appeared to deem worthy successors of the meats, Ellen was relieved from her persecutions, and permitted for a short interval to chew the food of sweet and bitter fancies—a kind of food that had quite spoiled her appetite for any grosser elements.

The unforeseen meeting with the Redwood party had suggested to Ellen's mind hopes and fears—resolutions and irresolutions. It must be confessed that there was something in the expression of Charles Westall's face, and in the tones of his voice, that conveyed to her heart an assurance of consolation for any evils that might await her. Love insinuates its language through the eyes, and in the modulations of the voice, but those alone whose senses have been touched by the magic herb of Oberon[8] can comprehend it—to all others it is like the 'harmony of immortal souls'[9]—they cannot hear it. Who could have imagined that Ellen had deduced from her brief interview with her lover the absolute certainty that she had nothing to fear from the arts of Miss Redwood! Who could have imagined that it strengthened her resolution to await the reversion of Mrs. Westall's kindness, and the development

---

7. *viands*: Articles of food.
8. *the magic herb of Oberon*: A reference to Shakespeare's *Midsummer Night's Dream*, in which Oberon uses a magical herb to make his wife Titania fall in love with Nick Bottom.
9. *'harmony of immortal souls'*: A variation on a line from V, i of Shakespeare's *Merchant of Venice*.

of her own history! But so it was. Certain that his attachment to her had not been shaken by Caroline's artifices, nor his mother's distrust; she was willing to leave all the rest to time and chance; or, rather—for we are doing injustice to the religious habits of her mind—to the kind Providence that had thus far watched over her.

Ellen dreaded coming in collision again with Miss Redwood: she trembled at the recollection of the unaccountable, mysterious hatred which Caroline had expressed at their last interview; but after a little reflection she arrived at the tranquillizing conclusion, that the éclat[10] that would attend Miss Redwood on the scene where they were now to play their parts, would render her quite indifferent to so insignificant a personage as herself; and in the shelter of her humility, she hoped to pass without observation or envy. She resolved to forego the pleasure of Mr. Redwood's society, to make the more difficult sacrifice of Westall's, and in short, to seclude herself as much as possible in her own apartment.

Ellen learned from the remarks of the persons sitting around her, that Miss Redwood's fame had preceded her arrival. "Poor girls!" said a good-natured looking old gentleman, who was surrounded by his nieces, to whom he addressed himself, "You may hang your harps upon the willows now, or play a requiem on them to your departed glory—this southern luminary will quench your light. See, my poor little Anne, your military beau has fallen within the sphere of her attractions already."

"I could not, in reason, uncle," retorted the young lady, "expect such a light material as Fitzgerald to resist Miss Redwood's solid attractions; give up your old-fashioned whim, uncle, of leaving a modicum to your relations to the seventeenth degree—banish all," she continued, glancing her eyes sportively around upon her companions—"sisters, cousins, all—all, but faithful Anne. Make me your sole heiress, uncle—add golden spurs to my armor, and Fitzgerald the prize, I will not fear to enter the lists against Miss Redwood."

"That's a brave girl, Anne, and a good-tempered girl, too," replied her uncle, patting her cheek. "I like a girl that can lose an admirer, and bear a joke about it: you are ten times prettier, Anne, in my eyes, than Miss Redwood. I would not exchange your good-humoured dimples for all her beauty. I observed that as she entered the room something crossed my young lady's humour—she flashed the fires of her bright eyes towards this end of the table, and 'the angry spot did glow on Caesar's brow.'"[11]

There was a fat lady sitting next the speaker, blowing away sturdily with her fan, and waiting impatiently for her turn to pour forth. She was one of those busy people, whose minds seem to be a sort of alms-basket, into

---

10. *eclat*: A brilliant sensation or lustre of reputation.
11. *'the angry spot did glow on Caesar's brow'*: From I, ii of Shakespeare's *Julius Caesar.*

which they collect odds and ends of information that belong to everybody's affairs but their own. After saying that she fancied anyone who thought Miss Redwood was not amiable would find himself greatly in error, she detailed, with the air of consequence with which she felt herself invested by the possession of such important particulars, the news she had picked up about the Redwood party, in which, as our readers will observe, there was the usual proportion of truth that obtains in such rumours.

"An express," she said, "had arrived the day before to secure rooms for the party. They had been detained a long time in a miserable hovel in Vermont, in consequence of a terrible wound which Mr. Redwood had received when he was wrecked on the lake, or overturned in his carriage, she was not sure which, but she understood the account was in the newspapers at the time. Poor Miss Redwood had suffered shockingly. Her friends had been apprehensive that her life would be sacrificed to her fatigue and confinement with her father. Her life, at the time of the accident, had been saved by the young gentleman who was with them; and it was believed, indeed," she added with a simper, "she might say it was certain they were now engaged, for Mr. Redwood, who had withheld his consent on account of the young man's want of fortune, had lately become interested in Mr. Westall, and all now was going on smoothly."

"What trumpery! What nonsense!" Deborah repeatedly ejaculated in an under-voice, as the narrator proceeded, when Ellen, frightened lest she should take up her testimony, whispered a caution, which she had the prudence to heed.

Someone asked of the lady informer the source of her information. She said that "a particular friend, who had left the springs that morning, had shown her a letter from a lady in Charleston, who had seen a letter which had been received from Miss Redwood."

"Your information, madam, is doubtless authentic," said the old gentleman, affecting a credulity which he was far enough from feeling; "but I am quite happy to observe, that the apprehensions of the young lady's friends concerning her health were groundless. She is a perfect Hebe."[12]

"Oh, that may well be, sir—young people recover surprisingly; but it is sure that Miss Redwood remained with her father night and day for weeks—how could she help it? The people, you know, so far in the country are quite barbarians."

Ellen, perceiving that it would be utterly impossible for Deborah to suppress her indignation much longer, proposed withdrawing from the table, and Deborah assented, loth to retreat without giving battle.

---

12. *She is a perfect Hebe*: The Greek goddess of youth.

CHAPTER XX.

As they left the dining-room, the British officer, who had taken his seat next Miss Redwood, (and who was the same Captain Fitzgerald of whom she had made such honourable mention in a letter to her grandmother,) said to her, "In the name of heaven, who is that ancient oddity? I saw your father address her as he came into the room."

"She is a Vermont woman—a demi-savage, that we met in our travels."

"So I imagined—she looks like a Yankee militia major, dressed in his mother's wedding gear; but that pretty girl with her, who seems to belong to another age and country, who is she?"

"The one in black, you speak of?"

"Pardon me—she is an innocent-looking little concern enough, but I spoke of the other, who is, as Hamlet says, 'far more attractive metal.'"[13]

"Oh, she is—I don't precisely know—she is a connection of the old woman's—at least a sort of dependent on her."

Captain Fitzgerald observed that for some reason or other his inquiry had been displeasing to Miss Redwood, and a firm believer in whatever impeaches the virtue of the female sex, he remembered the cynical rule that forbids a man to flatter one woman in the presence of another. "I should not have noticed the young lady," he said, "but there has been such an absolute dearth of beauty here since my arrival! Upon my soul, Miss Redwood," he added, with a prudent depression of voice, "I should have forgotten what beauty was but for a certain bright image indelibly stamped on the tablets of my memory. This young lady had one indisputable charm; she was your herald—the morning star that preceded the sun—O but what could have induced a civilized being to come to a watering-place under such auspices?"

'My evil genius,' thought Caroline, and she said, "I think I heard they were going to visit the Shakers in the vicinity. They have some connections there—I fancy they have merely stopped here, en passant, for their dinner; but really," she concluded, shrugging her shoulders, "I know nothing about them: one can't, you know, fill one's head with the affairs of such people."

Mr. Redwood had observed, with a feeling of impatience, Captain Fitzgerald's devotion to his daughter: he had been waiting for a pause in their conversation, which was conducted in an undertone, to remind her 'that she had not,' as he said, 'yet paid her respects to Miss Bruce, and their good friend Deborah.'

"Shall I have the honour of conducting you to the drawing-room, Miss Redwood?" asked Westall, who had been long watching for an opportunity to follow Ellen.

---

13. *'far more attractive metal'*: A variation on a line from I, ii of Shakespeare's *Hamlet*.

"Thank you—no, I must first go to my room and dispose of my riding-dress; but I will be obliged to you to make my apologies to the Vermontese, as they will probably be gone before I have an opportunity of seeing them. Come, Mrs. Westall, shall we find our way to our apartment?"

"Excuse my mother, Miss Redwood," said Westall. "You will not," he added, turning to Mrs. Westall, "risk losing the pleasure of seeing our friends?"

"Certainly not—I will first go with Miss Redwood, and then return to you, Charles."

"Do not put yourself to any inconvenience on my account, Mrs. Westall—the attendance of my servant will do just as well as yours."

Mrs. Westall felt the insulting implication of Miss Redwood's reply. She had been blinded by her self-love, and her next strongest passion—her ambition for her son. Miss Redwood's sudden and exclusive devotion to Fitzgerald had done more towards enlightening her mind on the subject of the young lady's merits, than all their previous intercourse, and she left her with a feeling that prepared her to see Ellen in the most favourable light.

CHAPTER XXI.

"Il y a dans l'esprit humain deux forces très distinctes, l'un inspire le besoin de croire, l'autre celui d'examiner."[1]
Madame de Stael.

OUR readers will pardon us for deferring their curiosity (if indeed they have any), while we give a brief expose of the different states of feeling which the several members of the Redwood party brought with them to Lebanon. After Ellen's departure from Eton, Mr. Redwood, no longer having any strong inclination to protract his stay there, made arrangements to recommence his journey immediately. He took leave of the Lenox family with sincere regret, and left them such demonstrations of his gratitude as impressed them with the belief that his generosity was unbounded.

He travelled very slowly in obedience to the advice of his physician; but notwithstanding his caution, and the most vigilant devotion from Charles Westall, he found his health daily diminishing, and he proposed to relinquish the long-projected visit to Boston. The springs in August offered a more tempting theatre than town. Caroline was all acquiescence and sweetness, and the travellers proceeded to Lebanon.

After Ellen left Eton, and during the journey, Caroline redoubled her assiduities to recover her lost influence over Westall. "Scarce once herself, by turns all womankind;"[2] she affected every grace, she pretended to every virtue that she believed would advance her designs. Mrs. Westall, a willing dupe, believing at least half her pretensions, and hoping the future might verify the rest, was a most devoted auxiliary; and Mr. Redwood began to indulge sanguine expectations that he should realize his dearest hopes—he augured well[3] from Caroline's serious efforts to win Westall's affections, and in spite of his experience and habitual despondency, he hoped everything from Westall's influence over her.

---

1. *'Il y a dans l'esprit . . .'*: From Madame de Staël's *De l'Allemagne* and can be translated as 'In the human mind, there are two very distinct forces, the one inspires the need for belief, the other for examination.'
2. *'Scarce once herself, by turns all womankind'*: From Pope's 'Epistle II: To a Lady' (1743).
3. *he augured well*: He had good expectations.

There is no limit to the power of a strong and virtuous attachment, but that Miss Redwood was not capable of feeling for anyone, and certainly did not for Westall. When she first saw him, his fine exterior and refined manners had pleased her—accustomed to the gallantries of admirers till they had become quite indispensable, and having no other subject to try the power of her charms upon, she played off her little coquetries on him, without any other design than to produce a present effect. Afterwards the matter assumed a graver cast—her vanity—the pride of beauty, wealth, and station, became interested in the contest with Ellen—and subsequently still stronger motives stimulated her rivalry, and made success important.

Never was there a man who had less of the coxcomb than Westall, but he could not choose but see the net that was spread in his sight.[4] To an indifferent observer of the effect of Miss Redwood's efforts, it would have been plain that 'the lightnings played on the impassive ice,'[5] but she did not so interpret Westall's frequent abstractions and studied politeness; for vanity dulls the keenest perceptions, and is itself at least as blind as love.

When the party arrived at Lebanon, Mr. Redwood's first impulse at the unexpected sight of Ellen was sincere pleasure; Caroline's, alarm; Mrs. Westall's, regret; and her son's, unqualified delight.

Ellen persisted in secluding herself almost wholly in her own apartment: she resisted the solicitations of Mr. Redwood, who could not voluntarily forego the pleasure of her society, the only pleasure of which he now seemed susceptible; she studiously avoided meeting Westall, except in the public rooms, and she had always some pretext to decline the walks he proposed, and the rides he arranged to include her.

Caroline, who seemed only to notice her by a freezing bow as they sometimes met in their passage to and from the eating room, really watched every movement, and after balancing all the motives that she believed could operate on Ellen's mind, she came to the conclusion, that her rival had abandoned the field. This somewhat abated her own ardour—the devotion of a host of admirers, who were crowding around her for recognition or introduction, and the highly seasoned flatteries of Captain Fitzgerald, gave her a distaste to the tame civilities of Westall, and not three days had elapsed before she was vacillating between the gratification of her pride and resentment, and the pleasure of granting the suit which Fitzgerald was already pressing upon her.

---

4. *Never was there a man who had less of the . . . but see the net*: In Vol. II of the first edition of the novel (1824), this line is misplaced, appearing at the top of page 150 rather than the top of page 149. The printing error has been corrected in the present edition.
5. *'the lightnings played on the impassive ice'*: A variation on a quotation from Pope's poem 'The Temple of Fame' (1714).

CHAPTER XXI.

Deborah was the only member of either of the two parties who was quite satisfied and tranquil; but she was determined, as she said, not to come so far and spend so much time and money without having her 'pennyworth of pleasure.'[6] The affair of the changeable had caused her but a momentary vexation; the only indications that she remembered it were, that she had carefully refolded and restored it to her trunk without one word of comment, and that she never again appeared in that ambitious array. If ever a shadow obscured Deborah's good nature, it was as fleeting as an April cloud. The notice of Mr. Redwood and Westall, which they seemed proud of bestowing, was a warrant for her respectability. And though the town-bred young ladies thought her quite terrible, and their beaus pronounced her a monster, the lovers of the picturesque admired her figure as she strided through the rooms, staring about her with fearless curiosity, with her holiday work (her knitting) in her hands. She was sometimes seen surrounded by a group of boys, relating to them a revolutionary story with all the animation of personal experience; and her little auditors (for boys are natural belligerents) would warm with the spirit of their fathers, and long to 'fight their battles o'er again.'[7] She even attracted the notice of the French Ambassador, who made many inquiries of her in relation to the mode of agriculture and domestic economy of our common farmers, and seemed so satisfied of the accuracy and intelligence of her replies, that he condescended to record them in his note book.

But Deborah's stable mind was quite unmoved by attention or neglect. She inquired everybody's name, and learned something of everybody's history. She sometimes mingled in the crowd, and took part in the conversation, and sometimes stood aloof making her own observations. In short, she went up and down wherever she listed with lawless independence; and her sagacity, simplicity, and good nature always obtained her sufferance, and sometimes procured her attention and respect.

This was the posture of affairs when our female friends on entering the parlour one morning in their way to the breakfast room, were encountered by the Armstead party. Miss Campbell sprang towards Ellen, exclaiming, while her fine face witnessed her sincerity, "My dear Miss Bruce. I am delighted to find you are not gone from Lebanon. I should have died with uncertainty and impatience the last five minutes, but that I most opportunely met my friend Charles Westall, at whom I have been speering questions

---

6. *'pennyworth of pleasure'*: A quotation which appears in a letter from Sir Thomas More to Henry VIII on 5 March 1534.
7. *'fight their battles o'er again'*: A variation on a line from Dryden's ode 'Alexander's Feast' (1697).

about you, which he answered as patiently as if he had been bred in the Socratic school—and, to do him justice, he asked as many as he answered. But how comes it," she added, hardly allowing Ellen time to return the kind greetings of the other members of her party, "how comes it that you have not mentioned our meeting, and the fortunate incident that broke the ice of ceremony, and made us friends at once? I have thought of nothing else since, at least it has given an agreeable hue to all my other thoughts: you hesitate—you were too modest to proclaim your own heroism. Oh, my dear Miss Bruce, the days are past when one might 'do good by stealth, and blush to find it fame'[8]—this is the age of display—of publication. However, thanks to my generous interposition, you have lost nothing on this occasion by your modesty. I have told the whole story to Mr. Westall—every particular of it with a suitable number of epithets and exclamations, and have had the pleasure of hearing him put all his ohs and ahs in the right places, and with the right emphasis, and conclude with a 'just like Miss Bruce.'

"But here," she continued, seeming at least not to notice the deep blush that suffused Ellen's cheeks, "here comes the eighth wonder of the world—the beautiful Miss Redwood—and we common mortals must fall back to gaze on her."

Caroline entered leaning on Mrs. Westall's arm, her father was beside her. Captain Fitzgerald joined them as they came into the room, and they passed near the window at which Westall and the ladies were standing. Fitzgerald recognized Miss Campbell in a dubious inquiring manner, which expressed, 'Do we meet as friends?' And her cold bow, replied unequivocally, 'as strangers.'

Caroline turned towards Westall—"your mother and papa," she said, "have settled it that we take our drive to the Shakers after breakfast. You are no laggard, and we shall depend on your being ready—and do be so good as to get a direction from Miss Bruce to her aunt, the elect lady."

"Your aunt the elect lady!" exclaimed Miss Campbell.

"No," replied Ellen, quite unmoved by a stroke that was meant to mortify her, "I have no aunt among the Shakers, neither, if I understand their order, is there any 'elect lady.'"

"Oh, I was mistaken then," said Caroline, "It is this Miss Allen's aunt, that I allude to—perhaps," she added, still addressing Westall, "you may persuade her to go with us as pioneer: she must be quite familiar with the curiosities of the place, and possibly she may favour us with an introduction to some of the gifted brethren."

---

8. *'do good by stealth, and blush to find it fame'*: From Dialogue I of Pope's *Epilogue to the Satires* (1738).

Poor Emily blushed and trembled as every eye turned on her, and edging herself behind Ellen, she whispered in all simplicity, "Do tell her I can't go."

"My dear Emily, Miss Redwood knows you cannot go."

"Afraid of being reclaimed," said Caroline, enjoying the confusion into which she had thrown the simple girl. "Nevermind, child, we shall do very well without you—I will trust to luck for a chance to quiz some of the old broad-brims."

"Caroline," said Mr. Redwood, "we shall lose our places at the breakfast table by this delay. Do you go with us, Westall?"

"The ladies must excuse me; I have an engagement after breakfast."

Miss Redwood bit her lips with vexation, and then turning to Captain Fitzgerald, "have you, too, an engagement?" she said.

"No engagement but on the field of battle could supersede your commands, Miss Redwood," replied the gallant captain.

"Then you will occupy the vacant seat in our carriage?"

Fitzgerald bowed his delighted assent. Mr. Redwood asked Westall, in a whisper, if his engagement would interfere with his giving him half an hour after he should return from his ride? Westall replied, "certainly not;" and they made an appointment to meet in the course of the morning.

Westall, true to the moment of his appointment, tapped at Mr. Redwood's door, and was admitted. He found him extremely pale, and somewhat agitated. "You are not, sir, I fear, as well as usual, this morning," he said, "your ride has fatigued you?"

"I am as well as usual," he replied, in a melancholy tone, "but my health is every day becoming worse: disease would do its work soon enough, but there are other causes that accelerate my decline:" he paused for a moment.—"Westall, I am about to repose a confidence in you that I never knew any other man, your father excepted, worthy of:—I have a weight on my mind from which you only can relieve me;"—he paused again, and seemed embarrassed. "It is a delicate subject. I hoped—I expected that you would have first spoken to me upon it, but you may have your own scruples—I know not—I am lost in conjectures—at any rate my frankness demands an equal frankness in return.

"Charles," he continued with a firmer voice, "it has long been my favourite, almost my only project, to give my child to you—to obtain for myself a virtuous son—to secure to her a safe and happy destiny. Your father's generosity impaired your inheritance; Caroline's will supply its defects—my daughter loves you—I do not commit her delicacy in saying so—the sentiment does equal credit to her head and heart—how long it will endure delay on your part I cannot say: she is a flattered and somewhat spoiled beauty—and this Fitzgerald is laying siege to her."

At this moment Westall almost wished he had a heart to give to the daughter of Mr. Redwood, but he did not hesitate as to the course he should pursue: after saying he was certain Mr. Redwood had misunderstood his daughter's sentiments in relation to him, he made a manly avowal of his attachment to Ellen, and related, with such reserves as a lover would be apt to make, the events and conversation of the morning of her departure from Eton.

Mr. Redwood was quite unprepared for this communication, for though his acquaintance with Ellen Bruce, and his vigilant observation of Westall, had shaken the dominion of his long cherished dogma of the selfishness of his race, and though he had of late much inclined to believe there were principles that might modify and control this selfishness; yet it seemed to him utterly incredible that a young man without fortune, without patronage, and with talents to generate ambition, should forego the brilliant advantages of an alliance with his daughter, for the sake of pure love, such as he had deemed only existed in romances and poetry, and was almost too obsolete to obtain a place there.

He received Westall's disclosure with an intense interest. Admiration for his young friend, and bitter disappointment at the utter defeat of his own projects, struggled for the mastery: he remained silent till Westall said, "You may deem my hopes presumptuous, sir, but you cannot, I am certain, think them dishonourable to me."

"Dishonourable! No, my dear Charles—my only wonder is that you have fallen in love with a poor little girl, who has nothing but the best heart in the world to give you—dishonourable! Would to God my youth had been rectified by the principle that governs yours."

Memory and conscience were busy, and sent their witness into Redwood's pallid cheek. "Westall, I am a miserable man—life has no attractions—no consolations for me—death no repose. I had a deep thirst for happiness—my spirit soared above the vulgar pleasures of the world, but I have fettered—wasted—degraded it; and now I suffer the fierce pangs of remorse for the past—of despair for the future. Westall, there is a misery for which language has no expression, in approaching the grave with the consciousness of having lost the noble ends for which life was given.

"Had I been borne along, as thousands are, like a leaf upon the waters, and left no trace behind, I should have comparative peace; but"—he folded his hands upon his breast—"I have dispossessed this temple of the divinity for which it was formed, I have destroyed the innocent—contaminated the pure—and my child—my only child—the immortal creature whose destiny was entrusted to me, I have permitted to be nursed in folly, and devoted to the world without a moral principle or influence!"

CHAPTER XXI.

The wild melancholy of Redwood's countenance, and the import of his language, alarmed Westall:—"Let me beseech you, sir," said he, "to be more composed—your strength is unequal to the agitation of your spirits—you know not what you are saying."

"Not know what I am saying," he replied, with a bitter smile: "Oh Westall, I am wearied with the dreary solitude of my own mind—the spirit of your father, young man, is in your face—his gentleness in your heart: I must have your sympathy, your aid—if indeed relief is possible. I have sought relief here," he continued, drawing a Bible from beneath his pillow; "this was the gift of your sweet Ellen. At midnight and in secrecy I have explored its pages—and I believe its record is true—at least I am inclined to believe it; but when the evidence of its divine original forces its way to my convictions, the arguments and the ridicule of infidelity recur to my mind, and the habits of skepticism hold it in suspense. And if it be true, its decisions are against me—its promises are all to the pious, the upright, and the benevolent."

"And is there no promise to the penitent?" asked Westall. "Believe me, this book contains the provisions of a father for his children; and there is no condition of the human mind, no modification of human destiny, which they cannot reach."

"Do not, Charles, make me the dupe of my necessities; do not send the light of hope into my mind, to render the darkness that shall succeed more horrible. Of what avail can be that penitence into which we are scourged by the fear of the future? Charles, I have already gone too far with you for halfway confidence, and I have no longer any motive for reserve. As I draw near the limit of life, the opinion of my fellow men, which has ruled me with despotic control, is reduced to its real insignificance. I ask your patience, while I relate to you some events of my life, of which there is now no record, but that which is written as with the point of a diamond on my conscience."

"You are wearied already with the exertions of this morning," said Westall, with instinctive delicacy. "Had you not better suspend our conversation for the present?"

"No, my dear friend, nothing will refresh me so much as unburthening my heart to you.—I have now nerved myself to the effort, and I feel equal to it—I may never again."

He then proceeded to relate the circumstances of his life with which our readers are already acquainted. His narrative was often interrupted by emotions too strong to be repressed; and as he concluded, he said to Westall, who had listened in breathless silence, "You now perceive, Charles, what reason I have for remorse."

"But why," asked Westall, stimulated by a governing feeling of compassion to suggest something that might alleviate Mr. Redwood's misery, "why this deep remorse? Your life has been stained but by one criminal action, and that committed in the thoughtless period of youth."

"Ah, Charles! Do not soften matters to me now—that one action has cast its dark shadows over every period of my life: say you one criminal action? What call you my total neglect of my daughter? What that cold indifference to the happiness of the human family which has permitted me to lock those talents in my own breast, which might have been employed for their benefit?—What kind term will you bestow on my cold skepticism? What on my useless, daring speculations? No, no, my friend," he added, impetuously, "you must not—cannot flatter me now—it is too late—I have learned truly to estimate the barrenness, the misery of that life which has no higher objects of pursuit than those that perish in the using. I must endure the effects of that folly which passes by the pure fountains of happiness in the path of life, and of that selfishness which makes a dreary desert of the world.

"I was made for something better than a man of the world. This consciousness, which has never forsaken me, has sharpened the sting of conscience, and has made me probably suffer more and enjoy less, than most men would have done in my circumstances. Do not reply to me now, Charles. You are in no state of mind to give me the counsel and aid I so much need. I perceive the compassionate interest that I have awakened, and am grateful for it. Once I should have scorned it, but now it is balm to my hurt mind.

"With my present feelings, Westall, you will not be surprised at my anxiety to make all the amends in my power to my daughter for my neglect of her. I am not blind to her faults—they are, alas, too glaring not to be seen; but I hoped everything from her youth and the influence of your character; and I thought, and still think, that she has a deeper interest in you than I believed her capable of feeling in anyone. But that is all past—it was my last dream—you have chosen well. I cannot boast my principles—but Ellen suits my tastes; and feeling her loveliness as I have felt it, I cannot now but wonder that I ever should have indulged the extravagant expectation that you would fix your affections elsewhere. Charles, your sweet friend resembles the only person I ever truly loved: resembles her in her face and figure, and still more in the gentleness and purity of her character. Oh, had I possessed such a child! poor Caroline! The world would wonder, Westall, if it knew that the beautiful idol to whom it renders homage is the object of her father's pity—of his remorse—but I forget your interest in my perpetual recurrence to my own anxieties.

"You must persuade Ellen to give up her scruples in regard to her mother's restrictions; there can be but one rational opinion about them.

CHAPTER XXI.

She was doubtless some sentimental deluded young creature, whose tenderness for her offspring induced her to devise this innocent little artifice to keep her in ignorance of her parentage."

Westall had too entire a sympathy with Ellen to regard the matter in this light, but he declared with sincerity, that though on her account he trusted that her long cherished hopes might not be disappointed, as far as related to his own feelings, the result would be a matter of perfect indifference.

"No parentage," he said, "could confer honour on Miss Bruce—none could touch the essential dignity of her character."

Mr. Redwood smiled at his enthusiasm; but he respected it. He entreated Westall to give him as much of his time as possible; 'he knew,' he said, 'that it would be a sacrifice to him, but he believed that sacrifices were neither difficult nor painful to those who were habitually disinterested.'

Mr. Redwood expressed the greatest anxiety in regard to Fitzgerald's attentions to his daughter. He said he had learned that this gentleman was a younger branch of a noble family, turned into the army to seek his fortune in military life, for which he had no other qualifications than a fine figure and handsome face—and that moreover he was distinguished among the officers of his regiment for his dissipated habits.

These were certainly sufficient grounds of alarm; and they increased now to a frightful degree the harassed and troubled state of mind which seemed to be hastening Mr. Redwood to the grave.

At one moment he resolved to leave the springs immediately, and the next was convinced that he was unequal to the effort. Westall remained with him until summoned away by the dinner bell; he then left him somewhat tranquillized, and with the resolution that he would spare no efforts to minister to the peace of his mind. Such was the benevolent interest he felt in him, that he would have compassed sea and land to inspire him with a just hope and a quiet resignation.

CHAPTER XXII.

"Call you this a quiz?" said my uncle, "in my day it would have been called a lie."[1]

Plain Dealer.

Miss Campbell valued herself on never feeling or doing anything by halves—she had taken a decided liking to Ellen—with her cordial admiration there mingled a little of the pride of a discoverer, a complacent sense of the merit of having first felt Miss Bruce's attractions, and asserted her claims. She attached herself almost exclusively to her, and Westall was delighted to observe after dinner that Ellen, instead of retiring immediately to her own room as usual, accompanied Miss Campbell and her party to the drawing-room. Miss Redwood observed that he was following them—she beckoned to him and said, "be good enough to tell Miss Deborah, that during my ride this morning I met her neighbour Martin. I stopped him to inquire after the Lenoxes. He told me they were all well excepting old Mrs. Allen, who is very ill, and afraid she shall not live to see her grandchild."

Westall went most unwillingly to deliver a message which must hasten Ellen's departure. Fitzgerald had overheard the communication, and looked at Caroline inquisitively.

"A ruse de guerre,"[2] she whispered. "It is such a bore to meet that giant, Miss Debby and her suite at every turn, that I have tasked my invention to get rid of them."

"Oh, a quiz,[3] admirable—skill against ignorance—the only mode of warfare with savages. 'Pon honour, Miss Redwood, I cannot imagine how you have survived your exile among those barbarians. The condition of society in these northern states is quite terrible—insufferable to those whose felicity it has been to live where the natural distinctions of rank are preserved."

---

1. *'Call you this a quiz? . . .'*: This passage does not appear in William Wycherley's 1735 play *The Plain Dealer*. It might be taken from an English periodical of the same title that was published twice weekly in 1724 and 1725, or from a more obscure work with the same title.
2. *A ruse de guerre*: A stratagem intended to deceive the enemy.
3. *a quiz*: A practical joke or hoax.

CHAPTER XXII.

"I assure you, Captain Fitzgerald, I was excessively annoyed. I found it quite impossible to make those people feel they were not my equals."

"Your equals! Good heavens! Had the animals 'organs, senses, affections, passions'![4] Would to heaven," he added, lowering his voice, "Miss Redwood would consent to go where the eye and the heart will confess that she has no equal."

"That would be heaven, indeed!" replied Caroline, turning her eye on Fitzgerald with an expression that authorized his most daring hopes.

"Yes, heaven," he replied, "not a puritanical heaven of liberty and equality, but a place where beauty, rank, and fashion, are far above this plebeian fog—a place worthy of you, Miss Redwood, where there are queens, and subjects, and worshippers—love and loyalty."

It is impossible to say how long the Captain would have continued his battery, had not his fluency been suddenly checked by one of those provoking interruptions to which all lovers are liable. Mrs. Westall, to whom Mr. Redwood (too ill to appear at dinner) had consigned his daughter, tired of playing solitaire while her fair protegée was all eye and ear for Fitzgerald, and deaf and dumb to everybody else, took the liberty to remark that all the ladies except themselves had retired from the table, and rising at the same moment, she proposed to Caroline an adjournment to the drawing-room.

Miss Redwood would rather have deferred the movement, for she dreaded encountering Deborah. "Come with us," she whispered to Fitzgerald, who stood with deference awaiting the ladies' departure: "if we are obliged to meet the old amazon, heaven help us! We shall need all our combined skill to parry her downright questions."

"As your auxiliary, Miss Redwood," replied Fitzgerald, proceeding towards the drawing-room with the ladies, "I fear nothing: but upon my soul, without a divinity to inspire me, I should never muster courage to encounter one of these question-asking Yankees. I had rather march up to the cannon's mouth."

"Thank heaven," said Caroline, casting her eyes around the drawing-room, and ascertaining that Deborah was not there, "we are safe for the present. If you will open the piano for me, Captain Fitzgerald, I will play the air you were asking for this morning."

Captain Fitzgerald arranged the piano—Miss Redwood took her seat at it, and Mrs. Westall left her and joined Ellen, who was sitting on the other side of the room in an animated conversation with Grace Campbell.

---

4. *'organs, senses, affections, passions'*: A variation on a line from III, i of Shakespeare's *Merchant of Venice*.

"Your fair friend, Mrs. Westall," said Miss Campbell, "has certainly made a conquest of Captain Fitzgerald—a conquest that I suspect will lead very soon to an amicable treaty."

"Appearances justify your opinion, certainly," replied Mrs. Westall; "and provided Mr. Redwood ratifies the treaty, I know no one that will interpose, or even feel an objection."

"I don't know," said Miss Campbell, "I have no particular admiration for Miss Redwood: but I declare to you, I think she is too young and too beautiful to be sacrificed to a mere fortune-hunter."

"She is heartless," replied Mrs. Westall, "and therefore fair game for a fortune hunter."

Charles Westall noticed that his mother spoke with uncommon asperity; but her gentlest tones had never delighted him so much, as an expression that indicated a state of feeling which he had long hoped that her own observation and reflections would produce without his interference. He perceived that she was completely alienated from Miss Redwood, and that the reaction of her feelings was all in Ellen's favour, and with a very pardonable filial enthusiasm, he mentally congratulated himself on always having believed that his mother's good sense and good feeling would finally rectify her opinions.

Probably Ellen's thoughts had received a direction from Mrs. Westall's observation; but suddenly recalling them to the point whence they had started, she asked Miss Campbell 'if she thought Fitzgerald was really in love with Caroline Redwood?'

"In love!—Oh my sweet innocent, in what blessed ignorance of the present generation you must have lived. In love—no, believe me there is no love extant, unless it be," and she glanced her laughing eyes with most provoking significance towards Westall, "unless it be on the shores of romantic lakes, or in such sweet sequestered vales as you describe that in which your friend Mrs. Harrison resides. Fitzgerald in love!—his device is a golden arrow—his motto, the old proverb—'without Ceres and Bacchus, love is cold.'"[5]

"Shame on you, Grace," said young Armstead, "you are a most ungracious girl. You should adopt the mode of some pretty simpering fair ones of my acquaintance who imitate bereaved widows, and always speak of their late lovers as they do of their deceased husbands, with a 'poor dear' prefixed to their names. 'Poor dear Fitzgerald' would be a becoming mention of one of your most devoted worshippers."

---

5. *'without Ceres and Bacchus love is cold'*: Originally from *Eunuchus* by Roman playwright Terence (c. 185 BC to 159? BC), this quotation was later explained in *Adagia* (1500) by Desiderius Erasmus (1466–1536). Essentially, it means 'without food and wine love is cold.'

"It was to the golden trappings of the idol that Fitzgerald bowed, William: his sacrifice was like the priests of Baal, the fire came not near it."

"You may carry your analogy still farther, Grace; for to your praise be it spoken, there was 'no voice, nor answer, nor any that regarded.'"[6]

"I deserve no praise for that," replied Miss Campbell, while a smile betrayed that she was not displeased to have it known that she disdained the flatteries of Miss Redwood's admirer: "I deserve no praise for seeing through that soulless creature—a mere parade-day officer, who dishonours the uniform worn by so many heroes. You and I, William, were brought up in the old school, nursed in Anglo-American prejudices, taught to believe that all virtue, valour, genius, were of British birth and growth: experience has abated some of the articles of my creed, and softened others. I have seen many an American shop-boy, many a gawky young farmer, who had more cleverness than such a British officer as Fitzgerald: more knowledge, more of everything that is essentially respectable."

"You are so enlightened, Miss Campbell," said Westall, "you should disabuse some of your fair countrywomen of their prejudices."

"It is impossible, utterly impossible. Such an enterprise would be as rational as a crusade against artificial flowers and ostrich feathers. So long as these red-coated gentry shall play the most elegant game at chess or whist—hand a lady to the dinner-table in the most graceful manner—carve the dish next her *secundum artem*,[7] and in short, perform all the little etiquettes of society with unparalleled grace, they must remain the favourite ornaments of our drawing-rooms—our fair ladies will overlook their little irregularities in morals; and rational and virtuous men, like you, Mr. Westall, and my cousin William, (you do not merit the compliment from me, Will, but I put you in to make the party stronger,) such men must yield to them the precedence."

"Oh, Grace!" said Mrs. Armstead, "little did I ever expect to hear such a philippic[8] against anything British from the lips of one of your grandfather's descendants."

"My dear aunt, you mistake me if you imagine that I mean to limit my criticisms to our foreign military beaux—no, unfortunately we have a large class of native productions that have equal claims to a polished exterior, and essential good-for-nothingness. If my dear grandpapa could take

---

6. *'no voice, nor answer, nor any that regarded'*: In this quotation and the preceding reference to 'the priests of Baal', Sedgwick alludes to 1 Kings 18, in which Elijah challenges the priests of Baal to prove the existence of their god by asking him for fire for a burnt offering. The priests of Baal prayed to Baal from morning until noon, but no fire appeared.
7. *secundum artem*: See note 6 on p. 32.
8. *philippic*: A scathing attack.

a peep into my heart at this moment, he would be quite satisfied with the loyal affection I bear to the land of his birth; and I flatter myself that the old gentleman, belonging as he doubtless does now to the universal nation of the good and happy, would rejoice that his descendants are all Americans, and only attached to the parent land by the indissoluble ties of respect and of affection. I do not believe that we, 'love Caesar less,' but we certainly 'love Rome more.'"[9]

"Well, my dear Grace," replied Mrs. Armstead, "I am glad to find that if you have caught the national enthusiasm, the epidemic of the day, you are not a traitor to England."

"So far from it, mother," said young Armstead, "that I will hazard a prophecy, that within six months from this fifteenth day of August, our cousin Grace will be the wife of an Englishman."

"You are a false prophet, Will."

"Time, not you, Grace, must pronounce that decision; and I call this honourable company to witness that I rest my prophetic fame upon this prediction."

By a natural train of thought, Mr. Howard, whom Ellen had seen devoted to Miss Campbell when they met at the village inn, occurred to her mind, and she asked Grace 'why he was not still of her party?'

"He was suddenly summoned away," she replied, "by letters from home:" and, to avert observation from her rising colour, she looked out of the window.

"I stand to my prediction, Grace," whispered Armstead, "in spite of your treacherous blushes."

"Mr. Westall," exclaimed Miss Campbell, "you were inquiring for Deborah, here she comes with the little Shaker."

"For mercy's sake, Miss Campbell," said Ellen, "do not let Emily hear you call her so. The poor child has been frightened to death since Miss Redwood's address to her this morning made her an object of notice. Her story is now, I am told, though fortunately she does not know it, in everybody's mouth."

Westall met Deborah at the door, and drew her aside to communicate Miss Redwood's message. Emily entered the room alone, and looking fearfully around her.

"Poor little timid, distressed thing," said Miss Campbell, "she looks like a lamb that has strayed from the shepherd into a company of wolves."

Ellen advanced towards the bashful girl, and drawing Emily's arm within her own, she led her to a seat, where she was sheltered from observation.

---

9. *'love Caesar less'... 'love Rome more'*: From III, ii of Shakespeare's *Julius Caesar*.

CHAPTER XXII.

Westall qualified the information he reluctantly communicated to Deborah, and urged that one day's delay could not be of consequence. She, however, with her usual promptitude, determined to leave the springs the next morning, and immediately announced her determination to her companions, without deeming it necessary to avow the cause of it.

A bright beam of pleasure shot from Emily's eyes. Ellen's turned involuntarily towards Charles Westall, and one brief glance contradicted all her well-maintained reserve and scrupulous silence.

Loud exclamations expressive of disappointment from all the Armstead party, and, louder than all the rest Miss Campbell's, attracted a momentary attention from Miss Redwood. She paused in the midst of the successful performance of a favourite march, and exchanged a significant nod with Fitzgerald; she then struck the notes with a stronger hand, but she could not drown the unwelcome sounds of 'Do, Miss Bruce, stay one day longer'—'Oh, Miss Debby, one day cannot make any difference—just one day.'

But Miss Deborah, affirming that it had all along been her intention to go within a day or two, remained inexorable, and the young ladies left the drawing-room to arrange their affairs for their departure.

Mrs. Westall followed Ellen to the stairs, and detaining her there till her companions had passed up, she said, "If my feelings or wishes have ever done you injustice, forgive me, Ellen—believe me, there is now but one other so dear—so interesting to me as you are."

Ellen faltered out, "I am very grateful," and turned hastily away, leaving Mrs. Westall quite satisfied with the significance which her glowing cheek and moistened eye gave to her scanty expression.

Ellen had scarcely reached her own apartment when Miss Campbell came running to her quite out of breath: "Suspend your packing operations, my dear Ellen," she said, "and sit down and listen to me for a moment, I cannot be ceremonious with you—I have the greatest favour to ask of you—and you cannot, must not deny me. Will you remain here for ten days as my guest? I bar a negative. Now do not make up your mouth for any excuses till you have heard me out. You told me this morning that your old friend, Mrs. Allen, no longer needed your services, and that you were only going this roundabout way to Vermont, because you had no other way of getting to Mrs. Harrison. Now my aunt is going to Boston—she has a vacant seat in her carriage—Lansdown is but a few miles off the direct route, and my aunt says nothing will delight her so much as to take you to Mrs. Harrison. She bids me tell you that Mrs. Harrison was an acquaintance of her mother's, and that you must not refuse her an introduction to her."

Ellen's decision vibrated between a strong inclination to remain, and a natural reluctance (which even Miss Campbell's extreme cordiality could not remove) to receive such favours from persons nearly strangers to her.

While she deliberated, and Grace Campbell urged her request, they were interrupted by a servant who brought Ellen a note.

"This note, whoever it comes from," said Miss Campbell, "will, I trust, induce you to decide to remain. You seem now as much puzzled as poor Launcelot Gobbo[10] was with the opposing counsel of the fiend and his conscience. Conscience is on my side, I am sure."

"And the note, too," said Ellen, refolding it; "and now if Miss Deborah will relinquish her right to me, I will throw away all squeamishness, and gratefully accept your invitation."

The note was from Mr. Redwood, and contained an earnest entreaty that Ellen would defer her departure for a few days. It was written hastily, was almost illegible, and concluded thus: "I once meditated an injury against you—it is now my earnest wish to repair the fault of that intention—my life is fast ebbing—do not refuse the last favour I can ever ask of you."

The note Ellen rightly believed was the fruit of Westall's intervention, but he could not have dictated the purport of it, and her delicacy was satisfied, now that she had a motive to remain independent of her lover. The ladies proceeded to Miss Deborah's apartment, and she, having heard the proposed arrangement, acquiesced with her usual rationality.

She seated herself on her trunk, and resting her elbows on her knees: "Not but what I am loath to part with you, Ellen," she said, "for the Lord knows," and she brushed a tear from the corner of her eye, "nobody ever wanted to leave you yet; but then there is reason in all things—you have taken a long journey, all for those that's neither kith nor kin to you, and now that you are happy among your mates, it is but fair you should have a play-spell: besides, it would be rather tough for our poor old horse to draw us all over the hills, and he should be considered too—to be sure I calculated to walk up the hills, but then I have come to that time of life when I had rather ride than walk—so all is for the best."

"We can all say 'amen' to that, Miss Deborah," said Miss Campbell; "you are a perfect philosopher. I am delighted—Ellen looks resigned—and your little Emily there most provokingly happy."

"Well," replied Debby, "contentment is a good thing, and a rare—but I guess it dwells most where people would least expect to find it.[11] There's Ellen Bruce, she has had troubles that would fret some people to death, and yet I have seldom seen her with a cloudy face."

---

10. *Launcelot Gobbo*: A character from Shakespeare's *Merchant of Venice*.
11. The conversation about the virtue of contentment, which begins here and continues to the top of p. 256, seems to have been widely held up as a model of morally sound writing, for it was reprinted several times in periodicals, digests and conduct books over the course of the nineteenth century.

"How do you account for that, Miss Debby? I am curious to get at this secret of happiness; for I have been in great straits sometimes, for the want of it."

"Why, I'll tell you. Now. Ellen, I don't mean to praise you"—and she looked at Ellen, while an expression of affection spread over her rough-featured face. "The truth is, Ellen has been so busy about making other people happy, that she has no time to think of herself; instead of grieving about her own troubles, she has tried to lessen other people's; instead of talking about her own feelings and thinking about them, you would not know she had any, if you did not see she always knew just how other people felt."

"Stop, stop, Deborah, my good friend," said Ellen; "you must not turn flatterer in your old age."

"Flatterer!—The Lord have mercy on you, girl; nothing was farther from my thoughts than flattering. I meant just to tell this young lady for her information, that the secret of happiness was to forget yourself, and care for the happiness of others."

"You are right—I believe you are right," said Miss Campbell, with animation; "though I have practised very little after your golden rule."

"The more's the pity, young woman; for, depend on't, it's the safe rule and the sure; I have scriptur warrant for it, beside my own observation, which, as you may judge, has not been small. It's a strange thing this happiness: it puts me in mind of an old Indian I have heard of, who said to a boy, who was begging him for a bow and arrow, 'the more you say bow and arrow, the more I won't make it.' There's poor Mr. Redwood, as far as I can find out he has had nothing all his life to do but to go up and down and to and fro upon the earth, in search of happiness; look at his face, it is as sorrowful as a tombstone, and just makes you ponder upon what has been, and what might have been; and his kickshaw of a daughter—why I, Debby Lenox, a lone old woman that I am, would not change places with her—would not give up my peaceable feelings for hers, for all the gold in the king's coffers: and for the most part, since I have taken a peep into what's called the world, I have seen little to envy among the great and the gay, the rich and handsome."

"And yet, Miss Debby," said Grace, "the world looks upon these as the privileged classes."

"Ah! the world is the slave of its own fooleries."

"Well, Miss Deborah, I have unbounded confidence in your wisdom; but, since my lot is cast in this same evil world, I should be sorry to think there was no good in it."

"No good, Miss!—that was what I did not and would not say. There is good in everything and everywhere, if we have but eyes to see it, and hearts to confess it. There is some pure gold mixed with all this glitter; some here that seem to have as pure hearts and quiet minds as if they had never stood in the dazzling sunshine of fortune."

"You mean to say, Deborah," said Ellen, "that contentment is a modest, prudent spirit; and that for the most part she avoids the high places of the earth, where the sun burns and the tempests beat, and leads her favourites along quiet vales and to sequestered fountains."

"Just *what* I would have said Ellen, though it may not be just *as* I should have said it," replied Deborah, smiling. "You young folks like to dress everything off with garlands, while such a plain old body as I only thinks of the substantials. But here am I preaching while Emily, as busy as a little bee, has packed everything and tied every bundle and box; her heart is already halfway to Eton. I wish it was as short a journey to my old limbs as it is for your young spirits, Emily. Now don't redden up, child, like the sky at sunset: true love is a creditable feeling, and I hope you know it to be so now that we have sifted that Shaker chaff out of your mind. Come, Miss Campbell and Ellen, we will go on to the piazza, and leave Emily to the company of her own thoughts."

The young ladies followed Deborah to the piazza. Mr. Redwood and his daughter, Fitzgerald and Westall, were sitting at one extremity of it. Deborah proposed joining them; but Ellen begged they might remain where they were. "I cannot," she said, "voluntarily inflict my presence on Miss Redwood. I never approach her that she does not shrink from me as if I breathed a poisonous influence."

"Or rather," said Miss Campbell, "as a condemned spirit shrinks from the healthful air of morning. She is not worth heeding, Ellen: it is the folly of her haughtiness, or perhaps,"—and she looked at Ellen with an arch smile—"there has been some rivalry in the case; she may have detected too soon the 'fair speechless messages'[12] that pass between certain eyes and yours. Do not colour, dear Ellen; Miss Debby says truly, it is a 'creditable feeling.'"

"Spare your raillery, Grace; this is no subject for it. There is no rivalry in the case, I assure you. Whatever my feelings may be, you perceive that all Miss Redwood's are now exclusively devoted to Captain Fitzgerald; and yet her dislike towards me, or rather hatred, for I must give it that harsh name, has no relenting. I never approach her—I never pass her, even in her happiest moods, that her brow does not contract, and every feature becomes rigid, with an expression that it would seem impossible for so young and beautiful a face to wear."

"Pshaw, Ellen!" said Deborah; "the girl is whimsical, and her whims are no more worth your minding than the freaks of a fretful child. Come along with us. I must see Mr. Redwood once more, and sorry am I it's the last time, for he suits my fancy better than many a better man."

---

12. *'fair speechless messages'*: From I, i of Shakespeare's *Merchant of Venice*.

CHAPTER XXII.

Ellen seemed still reluctant, when Charles Westall joined the ladies with a request, as he said, from Mr. Redwood, that they would consider his inability to come to them, and favour him with their company. The ladies acquiesced, and Miss Campbell took Deborah's arm, on the pretext that she could not accommodate her quick step to Ellen's lagging pace.

This benevolent manoeuvre gave Westall an opportunity to satisfy his impatient curiosity as to Ellen's decision in regard to her departure, and when they reached Mr. Redwood, the speaking animation of his countenance evinced how much he was delighted with the result of his inquiry. Miss Redwood stood with her back to the company, apparently entirely engrossed in settling with Captain Fitzgerald the comparative beauty of the liveries of half a dozen servants who stood at the spring below them.

A faint gleam of pleasure lit up Mr. Redwood's pale and desponding face as Ellen approached him; he took her hand. "Miss Deborah," he said, "is very good to consent to leave you." Caroline turned suddenly round, and darted a look of eager inquiry at Ellen. "And you, my dear Miss Bruce," he added, in a low voice, "are very kind to grant my poor request."

"Caroline, Miss Bruce remains a few days longer at Lebanon; I hope you will do everything in your power to prove that her stay is not a matter of indifference to you." Caroline bowed—she looked absolutely pale. "Your favourite book, my dear Ellen," continued Mr. Redwood, "asserts, I believe, that it is more blessed to give than to receive; if so, I shall be the cause of great happiness to you, though not in a mode most flattering to my own pride."

Every word that her father uttered increased Caroline's agitation; it was too apparent to escape observation, and for once the same thought flashed through Fitzgerald's and Miss Campbell's mind—the same thought, but it produced a very different effect. 'Good heavens,' said Miss Campbell, mentally, 'does the foolish girl really fancy that her poor father, who is so fast going where there is neither marrying nor giving in marriage, is projecting a love match with Ellen, or that she will marry a half-disembodied spirit!' 'Ah,' thought Fitzgerald, 'the girl is keen-sighted, she foresees a match—these second marriages make horrible havoc with fortunes.'

Mr. Redwood charged Deborah with many kind remembrances to his Vermont friends, and she, really affected at the thought of parting from him forever, and always unobservant of forms, turned hastily away without saying a word to Caroline. Suddenly recollecting herself, she returned. "Goodbye to you, Miss Caroline," she said, "the Lord bless you, and make you a blessing and a comfort to your father, which he much needs; and don't," she added in a whisper, "don't do anything to fret him, for his life hangs as it were by a cambric thread; and oh, now I think of it," and she checked herself as she was again turning away, "I thank you heartily for remembering John Martin's errand to me, it was very thoughtful of you—and I assure you, Miss Caroline, though my memory is something broken, I never can forget a kindness."

Mr. Redwood was evidently gratified with the good nature which led Deborah to magnify a trifling courtesy. "My dear Caroline," he said, "I am glad that you have had an opportunity of obliging Miss Deborah—where did you see John Martin?"

"Oh, I have not seen him at all," replied Caroline, making an effort to shelter her mortification by a careless laugh. "Only a quiz upon Miss Debby, papa—a merry thought of mine, which I know you will forgive, since it has led to an indefinite postponement of Miss Bruce's departure. Captain Fitzgerald, you promised to show me the setting sun from the hill—a pretty view I am told—have you ever seen it, Miss Campbell?—Farewell, Miss Deborah."

Miss Redwood walked away with Captain Fitzgerald with apparent unconcern. This was not the first time that Caroline had shown in pressing emergencies a perfect self-command, though on slight occasions she was a very child in exposing every shade of passion.

"I hope all you good rational people," said Mr. Redwood with a sigh, "will remember that my child is but eighteen: and now, may I beg a few moments' private conversation with Miss Bruce?"

"A few moments, certainly," replied Miss Campbell: "Come, Mr. Westall, I challenge you to a turn on the piazza, and we will see which bears privation with most magnanimity."

"Do you believe the old gentleman is really going to make love to Miss Bruce?" asked Grace Campbell, as she turned away.

"Not on his own account, I fancy," replied Westall.

"Ah, I comprehend—but depend on it, a love cause is better in the hands of the principal than the most eloquent agent."

And so it proved; for though Mr. Redwood frankly avowed to Ellen the disappointment of his own hopes, and though he urged her with all the energy of strong feeling and the most affectionate interest, to waive her scruples—though he begged, on his own account, that before he died he might have the happiness of seeing the two persons in whom he felt the strongest interest united; it was not till Westall, availing himself of an opportunity that occurred in the evening to plead his own cause with the irresistible zeal of true and well-requited love, that Ellen gave her promise—that she would write to Mrs. Harrison—lay the case before her, and abide by her decision.

CHAPTER XXIII.

"Thou I find
Hast the true tokens of a noble mind,
But the world wins thee."[1]

Crabbe.

Miss Campbell and Ellen rose by appointment on the following morning at the dawn of day, that they might witness the departure of Deborah and Emily. As they all stood on the piazza, awaiting the arrangement of the baggage in the chaise, Deborah drew Ellen aside:

"Look here," she said, undrawing a bag, and discovering one corner of a packet, "here is the identical money you refused to receive from Mr. Redwood; he sent it to me last night for a marriage-portion for Emily: it is true, child—God bless him—it is true—he has given it, and I have taken it with a thankful heart and a prayer (as in duty bound) that the Lord would return it to him a hundred fold, in something better than silver and gold. I shall keep the present a secret till Emily's wedding-day, which I'm sure is not far off; and Ellen," she added, after a moment's pause, "I'm thinking that another wedding-day is coming among our friends. Now, what do you look down for? If there is anybody in the land might hold up their heads with a good grace, it's you; for, to my notion, there is not a nobler man in the 'varsal world, view him in what light you will, than this same Charles Westall."

"But, Deborah," interrupted Ellen. "I am not"—

"Engaged—I know that"—

"Ma'am, your chaise is ready," said the servant.

"Coming in a minute. I know how it stands, Ellen, pretty nearly; for last night, when I got this packet from Mr. Redwood, my heart was so full I thought I could not sleep till I had told you. I looked in your room—you was not there; I came on to the piazza—you and Mr. Charles Westall were standing by the door yonder; while I was hesitating whether to go back without interrupting you, I heard a few words, just enough to give me a

---

1. *'Thou I find . . .'*: From Crabbe's 'The Frank Courtship', which appears in *Tales in Verse* (1812).

little insight into the business. I thought it fair to tell you; and besides, I wanted to charge you not to be notional; for a girl of your sense, Ellen, you are apt to be a little notional, which is not your fault, but comes of your living with Mrs. Harrison, and reading too many verses, which are apt to make girls dreamy."

"Miss Debby," cried Emily, "everything is ready, and the sun is rising."

"Coming child, coming. One word more, Ellen—" and here Deborah paused, for the first time in her life at a loss how to express herself. She drummed with the butt end of her whip on the railing, made figures with the lash on the floor, knit her brow, bit her lips, but did not speak till spurred by a second call from Emily; and then the tears gushed from the good creature's eyes as she said, "Ellen, you are rich in nothing but the grace of God; the best riches I know: but then there's neither quails nor manna nowadays, and one must look a little to the needful. When my father died, (a thrifty, prudent man,) he left me fifty pounds lawful. It has been in good hands, and has run up to between two and three hundred. I have enough for myself besides, Ellen, laid up for a wet day, so that is all to be yours. Now don't speak, but hearken to me—besides the money, I have a nice store of table linen for you, and some coverlets, and feather beds."

"Oh, Deborah, Deborah!"—

"Say nothing, child—I can't bear it. I won't be gainsayed. Goodbye, Ellen, the Lord bless you, child, and all that care for you,"—and she strided across the piazza without giving Ellen time to open her lips; shook Miss Campbell's hand heartily as she passed, took her seat in the chaise, and the moment Emily had taken a hurried leave of Ellen, she drove off, followed by the blessings and prayers of her grateful young friend.

The two ladies stood silently gazing after the old chaise as it slowly descended the hill. After a few moments, Miss Campbell turned suddenly round, and observing that the tears were streaming from Ellen's eyes, "Who would think," she said, "that Miss Deborah would call forth such a sentimental tribute; and yet I could find it in my heart to cry heartily too, for sure I am, I never shall look upon her like again."

"She deserves every tribute," replied Ellen, "that can be paid to genuine worth. Under her rough exterior she bears a heart that angels might joy to look into—full of all honest thoughts and kindly affections."

"Yes, I believe you; and now, dear Ellen, though more than half an angel yourself, I am going to expose a heart to you that has no such high qualifications; so get your hat and shawl, and we will stroll into some of these woods, far out of the sight and hearing of the 'world's people.'"

The two ladies ascended the hill above the spring, and leaving the highway, took a footpath that indents a beautiful grove. They soon reached a place of perfect seclusion, and seating themselves on a rock, they remained

CHAPTER XXIII.

for some time silent; Ellen awaiting Miss Campbell's communication, and she with some embarrassment picking the leaves from a branch she had plucked in her way, and strewing them about her: at last, throwing away leaves, branch and all, she said, "I hardly know, Ellen, whether to be most ashamed or proud of myself, on account of the confidence I am about to repose in you. It seems so like the girlish prating of a Miss in her teens; after our brief acquaintance to unveil to you the state of my heart, when even I myself have not yet dared to take one calm survey of it. But there is a charm about you, Ellen—an 'open sesame' that unlocks all hearts—you have touched the master-spring of mine, and it must be shown to you as it is, with all its light and all its darkness: believe me, you will find it 'o'er good for banning, and o'er bad for blessing.'"[2]

"Well, dear Miss Campbell, do dispense with any more preparation; I have already felt such sweet and kindly influence from this unknown country, that I long to explore it."

"Will you pay my frankness in kind, Ellen? Nevermind—do not blush; I see you belong to the sentimental class, who never tell their love, and I will be generous and tell you all; and, perhaps, you will be just and tell me—all that I have not already guessed.

"To begin then with the beginning. I might almost use the concise style of a certain ludicrous personage, and say, 'I was born, and up I grew'[3]—but that there were circumstances that occurred in our family, in my youth, which affected my character and relations in life. My father was a lawyer, a man of talents, and rising rapidly in his profession, when he was carried off by the yellow fever, then raging in our city. I was but a month old when he died. My mother took refuge among the Moravians[4] in Bethlem. The sudden death of my father blasted her happiness and hopes; and the fatigue of removal, so soon after her confinement, threw her into a decline; she languished two years, and then followed my father. The Moravian sisters had attended to all her wants with exemplary devotion. My helpless infancy had interested their kind hearts; I was exclusively attached to them, and as my aunt Armstead was then engrossed with a plentifully stocked nursery, and I had no other near female relative, my friends were easily persuaded to permit me to remain under the care of one of the sisters of Bethlem.

---

2. *'o'er good for banning, and o'er bad for blessing'*: From Sir Walter Scott's *Rob Roy* (1817).
3. *'I was born and up I grew'*: This quotation also appears in the American writer Lydia Howard Sigourney's 1858 novel *Lucy Howard's Journal*, but the original source has not been identified.
4. *the Moravians*: See note 9 on p. 34.

"When I was ten years old, my uncle Richard Campbell, who was my guardian, came to see me; he was then, and still is, a bachelor; he is a merchant, and has amassed a large fortune, all, as I am told, in a very regular way of trade, and by the faithful application of every maxim in poor Richard's almanac.[5] He was my father's eldest brother; had courted in his youth a very charming young girl, who preferred and married his younger brother, a poor, helpless genius. This disappointment inclined my uncle Richard to distrust our whole sex, one of them having made such an erroneous calculation as to the main chance, and he is said never to have jeoparded his fortune by offering to participate it with any other lady. His younger brother, and successful rival, abandoned his country and went to England, in the hope of carrying his literary talents to a better market than he could find for them at home. There he had small successes and great discouragements; and, after struggling a few years, he died, and left his wife unprovided with everything but three or four children, rather an unproductive property you know. She preferred remaining in England to returning, to be either a dependent on her friends, or a reproach to them; and with the aid of occasional remittances from my good aunt Armstead, and some little remnant of her father's estate, and with faculties of industry and economy in her situation deserving of all praise, she contrived to subsist and educate her family respectably. Her eldest son is said to be a genius, a painter by profession, and a man of sense; but of him more anon.[6]

"My uncle Richard preserved towards the poor widow of his brother the resentment of a mean mind; and there is, as far as I know, no reason to believe that in all her embarrassments he ever extended to her the slightest aid. As I told you, when my uncle first saw me I was ten years old, a little prim miniature old maid, dressed in the formal fashion of the Moravians, as staid in my deportment, and as precise in all my movements, as the good ancient maiden who had formed me after her own model. In short, I was my uncle's beau ideal. He was just then meditating a selection of someone of his young relations to inherit his property—of someone who, by the hardest slavery, the slavery of the mind, the complete subjection of the will, might deserve the rich inheritance he has to bestow. Most unfortunately for him and for me, his choice fell upon myself: unfortunate for both, for if there ever existed two beings who had not one principle of affinity, they are my uncle and myself. He is a conceited bigot in everything, from his religion down to his particular mode of tying on his neckcloth; he is ignorant of everything but how to get and how to keep money: in short, dear Ellen, for his character is not worth the drawing, the breath of intellectual and moral life has never been breathed into him."

5. *poor Richard's almanac*: Poor Richard's Almanac, published annually from 1732–1758, was one of Benjamin Franklin's most popular writings.
6. *of him more anon*: More will be said of him shortly.

CHAPTER XXIII.

"And is this the uncle, Miss Campbell, whose fortune you are to inherit?" inquired Ellen.

"The same, my dear—and do not suspect me of ingratitude. I have faults enough, Heaven knows, but ingratitude is not one of them—a good word, a kind look, were never thrown away upon me; but I owe my uncle nothing. He selected an heir because he chose to control his property as long as possible; and he selected me because he fancied that I should prove an obedient machine, a meek subject to his will."

"You must have convinced him of his mistake long before this," said Ellen; "how have you retained his favour?"

"Oh, he is completely enlightened, my dear; but luckily for my worldly prospects, he prides himself on never changing his purpose. But I have gone beyond my story. He took me home with him, placed me at a public school, where I had companions of my own age, and I soon lost the quiet deportment that had been the effect of the law of imitation, and all the orderly virtues that had been produced by careful pruning and training. I was like a plant transferred from the cellar to the genial influences of air, sunshine, and showers. My uncle had scarcely announced his decision to the world, and pronounced his infallible opinion of my merits, before I was transformed into a gay, laughing, romping, reckless child. Figure to yourself, my dear Ellen, such a child with all the uproar and misrule that follows in her train, introduced into the house of a sober citizen, a priggish old bachelor, with as much pharisaical exactness in the arrangement of his household and furniture, as if his salvation depended on preserving the mutual relation of chairs and tables.

"His servants were always in my interest, for I was generous to them to the extent of my ability, and they contrived so to shelter and excuse my faults, that my uncle endured my residence with him for two years; then on one unlucky, or rather lucky day, since I may date from it my escape from thraldom, as I was returning from school with a troop of my young friends, I met old Dickey, a blind fiddler, who used to patrol the streets, led by his dog, who was the familiar friend of every child in the city. We were near my uncle's door; I was in the humour for a frolic, and thoughtless of the consequences, I invited Dickey in, pressed my companions to follow—we ejected the chairs and tables from the parlour, and in five minutes were dancing as merrily as ever fairies tripped it over a green. In the height of our mirth, my uncle entered to witness the horrible sacrilege to which his immaculate parlour was devoted. Children, Dickey, dog, and all, were instantly sent packing. I followed in their train, full of resentment at the indignity that had been offered to me by such treatment of my guests, and heroically resolved never to enter my uncle's house again. I went to my aunt Armstead's and poured my wrongs into her kind bosom. She, no doubt, saw that my folly surpassed my uncle's severity, but she is the most indulgent being in the world—she had an excessive partiality for me, and without reprimanding me very severely, she took the prudent resolution to go to my uncle, and represent to him the absolute necessity for his own comfort, as well as my prosperity, of placing me under female surveillance. She proposed taking charge of me herself, and in pleading my cause she paid such deference to my uncle's will and whims, that she obtained her point without much difficulty—indeed, I believe, if the truth were known, the quiet angels in heaven were not more rejoiced to be rid of the rebel spirit and his misguided followers, than my uncle was to be relieved from me and the little mob that was forever at my heels.

"In my aunt's family I have lived in indulgence so unbounded, that it would have been ruinous to me, but for the salutary influence of those domestic affections, which next to the control and regulation of principle, are certainly the best security for virtue. I could sketch my own character, my dear Ellen, but I am afraid I should not much like to look at the picture. I have had what the French call *grand succés*[7] in the world, and yet I am more than half wearied with it—at least when I am beyond the siren sounds of pleasure, I can feel an anchorite's contempt for it. I have been at the very head of society in Philadelphia—I may say it to you, because it is evidently no merit in your eyes; you care for none of these things. I had rivals who excelled me in every particular attraction of a fine lady—many that were far richer than I could hope to be, some that were far handsomer than my glass, my vanity, or even my flatterers told me that I was—some that I felt to be far wittier, and some that I knew to be much more accomplished—but I united more than anyone of them all. I had not beauty enough to be that most insipid of all creatures, a mere belle—nor literature enough to fall into that unhappy class, the blue stockings,[8] the terror of our city beaux, the dread of our fashionables—nor sufficiently brilliant expectations to throw me into the vulgar class of the fortunes; but I had enough of each to attract the votaries[9] of every class—I have been surrounded by admirers, and yet I have walked among them with an unscathed heart till within these few weeks; and now, my dear Ellen, be kind enough to look the other way, for though I have not all your sentimental reserve, I have a little maidenly pride, of my own, which I would rather not discourage.

"You noticed the gentleman who was with me when I first had the happiness to see you—he is an acquaintance of a few weeks standing,

---

7. *grand succés*: Great or huge success.
8. *the blue stockings*: Women who profess interest in intellectual or literary pursuits.
9. *votaries*: The devotees.

and yet, shall I confess all to you—he has made himself perfectly indispensable to my happiness."

"That may be," said Ellen.

"Yes, my dear, and I suspect there are some who live and act more by rule than I do, who find that such things are. I despise and distrust as much as you can, the idea of love at first sight, and all the folly connected with it; but my late experience has made me a little superstitious in regard to the old orthodox doctrine that 'matches are made in heaven.'"

"But why so? If the account your cousin has given of Mr. Howard is a just one, (and your cousin seems not to be an enthusiast,) there is nothing supernatural in his winning your affections, and certainly there is nothing extraordinary in his reciprocating them—reciprocal I am sure the attachment must be."

"Certainly, or you would never have heard mine aforesaid confession. Howard and I understand each other, but there are obstacles in my way that he does not understand.

"I have always been interested in the character and destiny of my cousin Fenton Campbell, the eldest son of the aunt of whom I spoke to you, who resided in England. From the accounts we have received of him, he inherits his father's genius with the good sense of his mother. He has already attained some distinction in his profession, and has long been the support of his mother and sisters. My aunt Armstead and I have taken especial pains that every account of his thriftiness should be poured into my uncle Richard's ear: and two years ago, when I had mortally offended my uncle, by doing something he had forbidden, or not doing something he had commanded, I forget which, I entreated my aunt to seize the favourable moment to urge Fenton's equal claims to mine, and his superior merits, and to induce my uncle to make a will which should divide his fortune equally between us."

"That was indeed generous, Miss Campbell."

"No, my dear, not particularly generous. I was moved to it more by my impatience under my obligations to my uncle than by any more disinterested motive."

Ellen's animated countenance evinced that she admired the magnanimity that spurned a self-delusion, and Miss Campbell proceeded—

"My uncle was persuaded: he announced his resolution to me, which, as you may imagine, I received with very provoking nonchalance; and he wrote to Fenton, and promised him, that provided he would come immediately to this country and fix his residence here, he should inherit the half of his estate. Fenton returned a very calm expression of his gratitude, but said it was entirely out of his power to perform the required conditions, as his mother was in a declining state of health, too feeble either to endure a voyage, or to be left by her son. He particularly requested that his mother might not be informed of his uncle's generous intentions in regard to him, as nothing would distress her so much as to be in any mode an obstacle to the prosperity of her family. This letter of Fenton's of course deepened my favourable impressions of him, but it had quite a contrary effect upon my uncle, who thought that no folly could surpass the giving the go-by to such a chance of fortune. Poor slave of mammon![10] He could not forgive Fenton for not forsaking all other duties, to bow down and worship the golden image he had set up. My aunt Armstead wrote to him repeatedly and urgently to come over for a few months to conciliate my uncle, and confirm his wavering mind, but no motive could persuade him to leave his mother. My uncle suspended his arrangements: his displeasure against Fenton prevented a decision in his favour, while the frequent accounts he received of the young man's diligent application to his profession kept alive his wish to deposit a part of his fortune in his prudent hands.

"Thus matters remained till about six months since, when we received the intelligence of my aunt Campbell's death. My uncle Richard renewed his proposition to Fenton; he accepted it, and three months ago arrived in Philadelphia.

"I have not yet seen him. My aunt Armstead removed to her country place in Jersey the week before his arrival. Cousin William tells me that the old gentleman has taken surprisingly to Fenton, attracted by the gravity of his manners, which William imputes to his laborious sedentary life, and to his grief for the recent loss of his mother, whom he most tenderly loved. So far all is well—but now, dear Ellen, come the cross-purposes. My uncle has taken it into his wise head to institute a partnership concern between Fenton and myself; and on the very day of Fenton's arrival in this country, he announced by letter his supreme will to me in much the same terms he would employ to convey his orders to a supercargo. Three months ago this would have been well enough; for I have had a sort of indefinite purpose to keep myself fancy free till I could see this cousin of mine—nothing else, I believe, has kept me single so long."

"So long!" exclaimed Ellen, smiling.

"Yes, my dear, 'so long;' for you must know I am on the verge of three-and-twenty, an age *un peu passé*[11] in the world of fashion, and quite unknown in the lives of heroines, for excepting lady Geraldine, the most spirited of Miss Edgeworth's characters,[12] and whom (heaven bless her for it!) she has made, I think, to arrive at the mature age of two

---

10. *mammon*: Wealth or profit.
11. *un peu passé*: A bit past one's prime.
12. *lady Geraldine*: A character in Edgeworth's novel *Ennui* (1809).

and twenty, I do not remember in all romance, a single heroine that had attained her majority."

"But you surely do not seriously mean, my dear Miss Campbell, that any such motive would influence your marriage?"

"My sweet little methodistic Ellen, I am very much afraid it would; depend upon it, one cannot live altogether in the world and not be of the world: but let me go on with my story, and you will find that I am in danger of a romantic folly that would be more appropriate to your innocence and sweet simplicity."

"My cousin, instead of coming immediately to my aunt's, remained in the city. I was a little piqued at his delay, for I thought it would have been much more natural and disinterested for him to look after us than to remain hanging about my uncle. In the meantime, as Heaven decreed, William Armstead brought home with him his friend Howard; he was a Bostonian; that prejudiced me in his favour, for I like the eastern people particularly: they have not, perhaps, the air of fashion, the flexible graces that flourish at the south, but they have great intelligence, high cultivation, and above all, a manly dignity of manners, a simplicity and naturalness, an elevated tone of moral feeling, a"—

"Do you speak of a class or an individual?" asked Ellen, archly.

"Both, Ellen, both—a noble class, and a most worthy representative of that class. But to proceed. We were in the country. Howard might not have fancied me elsewhere; but there all that is good and ethereal in my nature rises superior to every artificial influence, 'the malt's aboon the meal'[13]—moonlight—rural walks, and all the appliances and means of love came in aid of our mutual liking; and, before we parted, we were fast approaching the last interesting scene in the love drama—the exchange of mutual vows. At this critical moment Howard received letters that obliged him to leave us for a few days; he is to be here tomorrow, and it was partly from the wish to have such a friend as you near me at this important juncture, that I so earnestly entreated you to remain at Lebanon. There is a pitfall before me: I am certain that if I fill up the measure of my iniquities by refusing obedience to my uncle in the matter of his nephew, I shall incur his everlasting displeasure and the penalty of disinheritance."

"That," said Ellen, "can be of little consequence, since you do not incur the penalty by any violation of duty."

"Of little consequence! Would to heaven, Ellen, I were as unsophisticated as you are; or that I had never been 'clasped with favour in fortune's

---

13. *'the malt's aboon the meal'*: From the Scottish song 'Fair Ye Weel, My Auld Wife', which appears in Volume 2 of *Ancient and Modern Scots Songs* (1776), edited by David Herd (1732–1810).

tender arms.'"[14] An unwonted seriousness overspread Miss Campbell's face as she added, "I certainly am not selfish. I disdain the vulgar distinction of wealth; but who can escape or evade the force of habit, accustomed as I have been to the ease and indulgence of fortune, to the power it confers, and the deference that attends it? How shall I encounter toil and submit to privations? How shall I bear the neglect of those who have courted my favour, who have felt honoured by my slightest attention?"

"By rising to an elevation they can never reach, Miss Campbell," said Ellen, affectionately taking her hand. "If you love Howard, if he deserves your love, he is worth this sacrifice."

"Upon my word, young ladies, talking of love and lovers before breakfast," spoke a voice behind them, which made both the ladies start, and turning round they perceived William Armstead approaching them with a letter in his hand. "I have been looking for you, cousin Grace," he said, "this half hour, and have at length traced you to this place: who would have expected to find you sentimentalising in a shady grove—and before breakfast too? You are leading Grace quite out of her element, Miss Bruce. Grace, I have a letter here for you from our worthy uncle, which, if I mistake not, will contain matter of fact that will dispel all your morning fancies; and I have a piece of news for you too."

"Has Howard arrived?" exclaimed Miss Campbell.

"You need not blush, Grace, because your tongue is obedient to your heart. No—Howard has not arrived, but Fenton has."

"Fenton," replied Miss Campbell in a disappointed tone, and the colour retreated from her cheeks as suddenly as it had appeared. "Oh, William, I could almost wish you the fate of Ascalaphus[15] for bringing me such news."

Miss Campbell broke the seal of her uncle's letter, and ran her eye hastily over it; and as she read half to herself and half aloud, her companions caught these broken sentences—'take it very ill I get no advices from you'—'Fenton more punctual, but says nothing as to the business in hand'—'two for the divisor, don't like that'—'will have neither subtraction nor division to my capital'—'obey orders, marry Fenton, you shall have the sum total'—'disobey, and you are a cipher the wrong side of the figure.'

Miss Campbell's indignation mantled into her face and sparkled in her eyes, and she tore the letter to fragments and scattered it to the winds— "Mean, sordid being!" she exclaimed; "and he thinks I will traffic with

---

14. *'clasped with favour in fortune's tender arms'*: A variation on a quotation from IV, iii of Shakespeare's *Timon of Athens*.
15. *Ascalaphus*: In Greek mythology, Ascalaphus had a rock placed on his chest and, later, was turned into an owl by Demeter for telling that he had seen Persephone eat the pomegranate seed. Alternatively, in *The Iliad,* Ascalaphus was killed in battle.

my affections as he does with his merchandise! No, let his silver and gold perish—I will marry whom I please, and when I please!"

Ellen, with the impulsive sympathy of generous feeling, pressed the arm into which hers was locked; and Armstead said, "Spoken worthy of yourself, my dear Grace; but consider well and warily before you take a step which cannot be retracted. You are a woman of sense, and you know it is one thing to wish to attain a difficult summit, and quite another to reach it. You are a woman of prudence—a woman of the world, and you know that the visions of youthful love bear a very faint resemblance to the realities of life. You know, dear Grace, that it would be at least as difficult for a fashionable woman like you to play love in a cottage, as for a camel to go through the eye of a needle[16]—consider well, cousin, consider well, before you take an unchangeable resolution."

"I have considered, William—have I not, Ellen?"

Ellen smiled without replying, for she feared that her friend's hasty resolution had been somewhat quickened by resentment against her uncle: luckily the warmth of Grace Campbell's feelings at the moment prevented her noticing the half-incredulous expression of Ellen's face.

"I have considered, William," she repeated, "and if your friend will take my unportioned hand, Fenton shall be welcome to all my uncle's paltry wealth—he shall see that I despise it, and the world shall know that I disdain its splendour."

"And you, my dear Miss Campbell," said Ellen with enthusiasm, "will have the secret consciousness of having acted right and nobly."

"Ah, thank you, Ellen, for your prompting. I am apt I believe to forget *secret* feelings. I have been a gallery picture, you a sweet little cabinet article; but times are changing with me, and you will teach me better."

"I am thinking, Grace," said Armstead, "how Howard will relish these changing times, it would be a disappointment to find him not as magnanimous and disinterested as yourself."

"Howard not disinterested! Your friendship grows cold, William."

"Not at all—we may as well look truth in the face, cousin, though it should come to us through the medium of friend or lover—love matches among people who have lived in a certain style, you know, are getting to be quite obsolete—we are beginning to regard them as only becoming boys and girls—only suited to the infancy of society."

"I know not whether you are sarcastic or serious, William."

"Perfectly serious," rejoined William, "and as serious in my opinion that Fenton Campbell is to the full as disinterested as Howard."

---

16. *as for a camel to go through the eye of a needle*: William here alludes to Matthew 19: 14, in which Jesus says that it would easier for a camel to pass through the eye of a needle than for a rich person to enter heaven.

"Impossible! We have all been mistaken in Fenton: he is a cold, calculating Englishman—his servility to my uncle proves it. It was unworthy any man of spirit to be the bearer of this letter to me."

"Come, Miss Bruce," said Armstead to Ellen, "hasten your friend's pace, she will work herself into such a holy indignation against poor Fenton before we reach home, that she will not be able to receive him with common civility. Come, my dear Grace, forget your displeasure—look again like yourself, if it is only to let Fenton see the gem sparkle which he has forfeited."

In vain Armstead continued his efforts as they approached the house to dispel his cousin's gravity: he reasoned, he rallied, but all in vain—the fear he had insinuated into her mind in relation to Howard, had taken complete possession of her: she blamed herself for the frankness of her communications; and for a few moments at least, she would have rejoiced to have been even as destitute as Ellen of extrinsic attractions.

Conscious that the agitation of her mind unfitted her for meeting her cousin with the indifference and calm civility which her pride prompted her to assume towards him, she approached the door of the parlour, where Armstead told her that his mother with Fenton was awaiting her, with a slow and reluctant step.

"Come in with me, Ellen," she said, as her friend was turning away, "I always do better in company than alone; but as she reached the threshold of the door, she hesitated, and turning to Armstead, said, "Do you, William, go in and invent some apology for me, I will meet Fenton at breakfast—it will save us both useless embarrassment."

"Pshaw, Grace! Don't behave like a child," replied her cousin, and at the same instant he settled the mode of procedure by throwing open the door, and saying with affected formality, "Miss Campbell, allow me to introduce you to my cousin Fenton—my sometime friend Howard."

Grace forgot for once whether she was in company or alone, forgot everything but the surprising certainty that Howard and Fenton were the self-same person—every trace of displeasure vanished from her face, unmixed delight shone in her brightened eye and glowing cheek, and without noticing the joyful expression of her aunt's face, the ludicrous twist of William Armstead's mouth, or the sympathy that moistened Ellen's eye, she gave Fenton her hand, and in virtue of his being friend, lover, or cousin, one or all, permitted him to devour it with kisses.

"Come, my dear mother, come, Miss Bruce," said William Armstead, "I believe we may trust to the good faith of our friends to make their compact without witnesses." And as he followed the ladies out of the room, he turned, and with a very wise and cautionary shake of the head, said, "beware, cousin Grace, beware a 'cold, calculating Englishman!'"

"Well, William," asked Mrs. Armstead, "how have you contrived to keep Fenton's secret so long? You ought to have told me—you surely might have trusted me—you know I am no babbler."

"I know, dear mother, 'thou wilt not utter what thou dost not know.'"[17]

"Oh for shame, Will! I cannot possibly comprehend of what mighty consequence it could be in the first place to devise this secret—and then to keep it."

"Ah, there it is; and this question would have arisen in your mind long ago, and in spite of any resolution to the contrary, some significant look or word would have betrayed our ambush before we had effected our purpose."

"Still, Mr. Armstead," said Ellen, "I think your mother's question is a rational one—certainly this artifice does seem a little juvenile and romantic in a man of five-and-twenty; and a man too of Mr. Campbell's gravity of manners."

"If it seems to *you* romantic, Miss Bruce, it must need explanation; and I am certain that the explanation will satisfy you, that Fenton has been sufficiently rational, and you, my dear mother, that in keeping his counsel, your son has been only prudent." Armstead then proceeded to say that his cousin had long had the most favourable impression of Grace's character, partly the consequence of the young lady's letters to his mother, which were often accompanied by generous gifts, always offered in the most gracious manner; and partly the consequence of the zealous affection with which his mother had mentioned Grace in her letters to her sister-in-law, and to her nephew; and finally, as he reminded his mother, of her having (notwithstanding her surprising talent at keeping a secret) betrayed Grace's agency in the alteration of her uncle's will.

Here Mrs. Armstead interrupted her son to say 'that it was very fortunate she did make that communication; for in a private letter which she received from Fenton at the time, he had declared that, without the knowledge of that circumstance, he never would have accepted his uncle Richard's proposition.'

"No doubt, dear mother, you had excellent reasons (as who has not in a like case) for telling the secret, and abundant consolations for having told it; but allow me to finish my story. Fenton, with all these prejudices in Grace's favour, arrives in Philadelphia; is introduced to my uncle, and favourably received. He learns our absence from the city, and determines to follow us immediately; he calls the next morning to take leave of my uncle, and is informed by him, with his usual grossierté,[18] of the contents

---

17. *'thou wilt not utter what thou dost not know'*: From II, iii of Shakespeare's *Henry IV Part I*.
18. *Grossierté* [modern French, 'grossièreté']: Roughness or rudeness.

of the letter he had written to Grace. Fenton knew enough of his cousin to believe that she would be as averse from giving her heart, as Falstaff was his reasons,[19] on compulsion; and when I arrived, most opportunely, in Philadelphia on the day he had received this pretty piece of information from my uncle, I found him in a web of such doubts and difficulties as you sentimentalists, Miss Bruce, are apt to weave about yourselves.

"But we sentimentalists," rejoined Ellen, "since you insist on placing me in that class, are not apt to expose our difficulties to the profane eyes of scoffers."

"No—and so my cousin would probably have lost himself in a labyrinth, from which no device of human ingenuity could have extricated him, had not some expressions that fell from my uncle revealed to me the secret of his perplexities. I went immediately to Fenton, disclosed to him my discoveries, and suggested the scheme which has succeeded so happily. My uncle Richard knew the young people were together, and believed that all was going on well in obedience to his orders—the complete retirement of my mother's place protected us from observation, and my lofty cousin has been wooed and won in a manner most flattering to her own, and to Fenton's pride."

---

19. *as Falstaff was his reasons*: Rephrased, Grace would be as reluctant to give her heart as Falstaff was to give his reasons. Falstaff is a character who appears in four of Shakespeare's plays: *Henry IV Part I*, *Henry IV Part II*, *Henry V* and *The Merry Wives of Windsor*.

CHAPTER XXIV.

"God's holy word, once trivial in his view,
Now by the voice of his experience true,
Seems, as it is, the fountain whence alone
Must spring that hope he pants to make his own."[1]

Cowper.

SOME days glided away, while the gay society at Lebanon presented nothing to the eye of a casual observer but a brilliant surface of pleasure. But we claim to be among those gifted personages, who, like the *Diable boiteux*,[2] are permitted to penetrate below the surface, to visit secret retirements, to dive into the depths of hidden thoughts, to explore their recesses, and to discover them to the curious eye. Availing ourselves of our prerogative, we beg our readers to quit with us the thronged piazzas, the dancing hall, the lively coteries that fill the public rooms, and take a peep into the respective apartments of the individuals we have presumed to introduce to their notice.

And first, as entitled to our chief interest, is Ellen—who, in spite of the beseeching looks of Westall, and the raillery of Grace Campbell, persisted in secluding herself in her own room.

"What romantic whim have you taken into your head, Ellen?" said her friend, who had followed her from the breakfast-table one morning. "Come, my dear, you must not shut yourself up in this cell any longer—I bring an absolute requisition for you from my aunt Armstead, who has ordered the carriage to carry us all to see the Shakers, and ramble about the hills in the neighbourhood, to spy out the beauties of the land. Fenton will take his portfolio with him, and while in sketching nature, he is paying his devotions to his first love, I shall be at liberty to give you a lecture upon your duties."

"Well, Miss Campbell—I will go with you."

"Thank you, my dear; but pray do not look as if you were going to the stake."

---

1. *'God's holy word, once trivial in his view . . .'*: From Cowper's poem 'Hope' (1782).
2. *Diable boiteux*: A reference to the French novel *Le Diable boiteux* (1707) by Alain-René Lesage (1668–1747).

This was the day on which Ellen expected a reply to her letter to Mrs. Harrison, and she could not conceal, and dared not explain the reluctance with which she consented to an arrangement that must retard the time of her receiving it. She tried to evade Miss Campbell's scrutiny, by saying, with a forced smile, "Such a frail creature as I am may well feel dread of a lecture on my duties; but you may perhaps lessen it by telling me what those are that are to be the subject of your preaching."

"Kindness to your lover—frankness to your friend, Ellen. There is poor Westall turned off with the 'fezzenless bran'[3] of commonplace civility, and I, who have poured all my love-lore into your ears, am obliged to make out the history of your heart as well as I can by the index of the changeful cheek—sometimes deadly pale, and then lit up by a glow that seems the shadow of your thoughts, so quickly does it brighten and fade away. You see, my dear, mysterious as you are, I have noted and comprehend the signs of the times."

"Believe me, my dear friend," said Ellen, taking Grace's hand affectionately, "I have a reason for the suspension of my intercourse with Westall—for my reserve to you, a day or two will, I trust in heaven, end this mystery; and when I am absolved from the necessity of any farther reserve, you shall know all."

"God speed the happy hour, my sweet Ellen, and show me that you have reason, even in your madness."

The ladies were interrupted by Mrs. Westall, who appeared at the door with her workbox in her hand, 'come,' as she said, 'to sit the morning with Miss Bruce.'

"Miss Bruce is engaged to ride with me, and I hope you will do me the favour to change your purpose, Mrs. Westall," said Miss Campbell, "and occupy a seat in my aunt's carriage, which we want very much to have agreeably filled."

Mrs. Westall assented readily to the polite request, and while she went for her hat and shawl, Miss Campbell said, "Your good mother elect has taken you mightily into favour of late, Ellen. Straws show which way the wind blows. I overheard her yesterday zealously stating your claims to gentility to the Elmores of New York—a point, you know, of infinite moment in the judgment of the daughters of a *ci-devant*[4] barmaid."

"And was Mrs. Westall able to establish my right to the favourite epithet 'genteel?'"

---

3. *'fezzenless bran'*: 'Fezzenless' is possibly a derivative of 'fezzed', meaning to be furnished with a fez or cap. 'Bran' can mean class or quality. Together, 'fezzenless bran' can mean the 'hatless type', implying uncouthness.

4. *ci-devant*: Former.

CHAPTER XXIV.

"The password with certain people—yes, my dear, perfectly, I believe; for, after hearing her statement, one of the young ladies observed that her mamma said she 'was sure you was genteel from the first moment she saw you, you wore such particularly fine lace, and a real camel's hair; those,' she said, 'were mamma's criterions for knowing a lady, they were so lady-like.'"

"Oh, what would mamma have said," exclaimed Ellen, "if she had known that I was indebted to the generosity of Mrs. Harrison for all my lady-like qualities?"

"I can't say, my dear, for the inquisition of the young ladies was suddenly interrupted by Mrs. Harris, a relation and dependent of the Osmer family, who rests her fame on her patrician blood, and who, therefore, had another, though perhaps not quite as absurd a criterion by which she would graduate your rank; 'Pray,' she said, 'Mrs. Westall, can you tell me the maiden name of Miss Bruce's mother? I once had a very distant relation who married a Bruce.' Mrs. Westall seemed a little embarrassed—said she did not know; and Mrs. Harris turned to Caroline Redwood, who sat next her, and said, 'you, Miss Redwood, can probably inform me something of Miss Bruce's parentage.' 'I, ma'am!' exclaimed Miss Redwood; 'indeed I know nothing of Miss Bruce: I believe her parents are dead:'—and her immovable colour, Ellen, for once did move, and she was so pale for a moment, that I really thought the girl was going to faint. Is it not very strange she should have shown so much emotion on the subject?"

"Yes, very strange; but nothing from Miss Redwood can ever surprise me," said Ellen.

Miss Campbell looked on Ellen for a moment earnestly, and then said, with a little hesitation, "The old woman's curiosity is natural enough, and I should like to gratify it. Do tell me, Ellen, your mother's maiden name?"

"I cannot tell you, Miss Campbell—do not ask me," replied Ellen, with a trembling voice.

"Forgive me, my sweet friend," exclaimed Grace Campbell, recovering her usual frank manner, and throwing her arm around Ellen's neck and kissing her pale cheek; "forgive my silly curiosity—every shade of it has passed away. I care not what mine the diamond comes from, so long as I know by every test that it is a diamond of the first water. Come, put on your 'real camel's hair,' it is a cool morning, and my aunt is waiting for us."

The ladies joined Mrs. Westall in the passage, and they proceeded together.

"Where is your son this morning, Mrs. Westall?" asked Grace Campbell; "He hardly deserves an inquiry, recreant knight that he is."

"Oh, say not so, Miss Campbell; he is detained from us by a painful duty; he has scarcely left Mr. Redwood's bedside for the last two days—poor man: Charles thinks him declining rapidly."

"There is no doubt," replied Miss Campbell, "that he is sinking very fast. I saw him yesterday sitting by his window; I observed he had the ghastly paleness of death; and though he bowed to me with his usual courtesy, not a muscle of his face moved."

"I hope," said Ellen—"I believe he is not as ill as you imagine; he suffers from extreme depression of spirits."

"Yes," said Miss Campbell; "but this very depression aggravates his disease. He is, as far as I can learn, in the very depths of nervous misery. I heard his insensible daughter say to Fitzgerald yesterday, that she expected her father would come out a Methodist at last, for she never went into his room that she did not find him with a Bible in his hands."

"A Bible!" exclaimed Ellen—"God be praised!"

Miss Campbell caught the fine expression of Ellen's upraised eye—"What a little enthusiast you are, Ellen. You would make an admirable lay-preacher; but in the present rage for division of labour, it is not proper to preach and practise too; so you shall practise and I will preach: shall we unite our talents for the consolation of Mr. Redwood?"

"I should rejoice in any vocation that could administer consolation to him," replied Ellen.

"No doubt, my dear," said her lively friend; "but pray keep your holy zeal to yourself, for here comes Fenton, a sworn disciple of Gall and Spurzheim,[5] and we shall have him exploring your head for the 'organ of veneration,'[6] and your heart for its correspondent qualities; and then I am afraid I shall find to my cost that he is without the 'organ of adhesiveness'[7]—that, I suppose, may stand for constancy in your *bump* metaphysics, Fenton?"

"Yes, my dear Grace; and if I do not possess it, finely developed too, I will sacrifice my theory to experience, like a true philosopher."

Miss Campbell was about to reply, when her aunt said, "You forget we are waiting for you, Grace. Fenton, hand Mrs. Westall to the carriage. Give Heaven all due thanks, Mrs. Westall, that you have not a pair of lovers on your hands."

"I should be in a much more grateful humour if I had," replied Mrs. Westall, looking kindly on Ellen.

---

5. *Gall and Spurzheim*: Franz Joseph Gall (1758–1828) and his pupil, Johan Gaspar Spurzheim (1776–1823), popularised the personality theory of phrenology.
6. *'organ of veneration'*: According to phrenology, the organ of veneration is located at the top of the skull, the degree of protrusion of which supposedly corresponded to the individual's degree of worshipfulness or respect of what is good.
7. *'organ of adhesiveness'*: Located at the middle posterior of the parietal bone, the organ of adhesiveness was thought to determine one's degree of emotional attachment in relationships.

Ellen would have comprehended Mrs. Westall's meaning without the interpreting glance that beamed on her from Miss Campbell's eye, and she sprang into the carriage after her friend, her heart quite lightened of one burden that had pressed sorely on it.

In the meantime Westall, abstracting his mind as far as possible from his own deeply interesting concerns, was performing his benevolent duty at the bedside of Mr. Redwood, whose decline was indeed more rapid than even his friend, who knew the feverish state of his mind, could have anticipated. At times, fixed in the gloom of deep despondency, his mind seemed cut off from all communion with the external world: his appearance was that of a man suffering from the frightful images of a dream—his fixed and glassy eye—the drops of sweat that stood thick on his livid brow—his fixed posture—his clenched hands—his whole attitude and expression betrayed utter despair. At these moments all Westall's efforts to arouse him seemed not to make the slightest impression on his senses—but, suddenly, he would turn his eager eye on his young friend, and listen to him as if the sentence of life or death was on his lips, while Westall set forth the arguments for the truth of our religion with which his familiarity with its evidences furnished him, and suggested its hopes and consolations. There were intervals, too, when Redwood felt as if he had attained a living fountain—as if his spirit was forever emancipated from the bondage of doubt and despondency, and peace was commanded on his troubled mind; but these intervals were short: "Ah, Westall," he would exclaim, "I am afraid to trust myself. I know not how far my mind is enfeebled by disease. I know not how far my faith and hope may have their source in the strong necessity I feel for present relief. The objects of sense are becoming dim to my sight—the cold shadows of death are settling about me: my dear Charles, in this frightful state, can I calmly investigate the evidence of the truth of a religion which promises pardon to the penitent for the past—resurrection and immortal life for the future?"

"But, my dear sir," replied Westall, "there have been men, in intellectual power the first of their species, who in the full vigor of their faculties, with the aids of learning and leisure, have calmly pursued their honest inquiries, and have received our blessed religion as the rule of life—the victory over death."

"True—true, Westall; but names have now no authority with me. I have been too long their dupe and victim. Oh, how in my folly I have admired, and praised, and almost worshipped those daring leaders of our sect, who lived fearlessly, and braved undaunted the terrors of death! Now I see nothing in what seemed to me their philosophic fortitude, but an obstinate vanity, a pride of opinion, a self-deifying, that made them render homage to their own consequence, when they should have sought the God of their spirits.

"Westall, I shudder at the thought of such a death as Gibbon's, Hume's, Voltaire's[8]—if their indifference to the future was unaffected, what a voluntary degradation to the level of the brute creation! If pretended, what mad audacity!"

"But surely," said Westall, "there is honest skepticism in the world. There are minds so constituted, or exposed to such unhappy influences, that unbelief becomes a condition almost irresistible."

"Yes—it may be so," replied Mr. Redwood; "it must be so—but for my own case, I have no such flattering unction. Humbling as the confession is, Charles," he added, (taking up the Bible which now was almost always in his hands,) till within this last month, I have never read this book with seriousness—never but from idle curiosity, or to find exercise for my ingenuity, or food for my ridicule: and now I would give worlds for one year, nay one month of the life that in my folly and madness I have cursed as a weary burden imposed by arbitrary power, that my mind might be opened to the light which has dawned on it from that book—my heart reformed by its rules—renewed by its influence."

"God grant you, my dear sir," said Westall, fervently grasping Mr. Redwood's hand, "not one but many years to be blessed with its efficacy. But for the present let me entreat you to dismiss all agitating thoughts, and to make an effort only for that resignation which is the first principle of our religion, and which will certainly produce inviolable repose."

The conversation of the gentlemen was interrupted by the entrance of Miss Redwood, who came to make her usual morning visit. She lingered longer than usual, and inquired with more particularity into her father's symptoms. She entreated him to send to town for a physician—examined the vials on his table, and expressed her fears that everything was not going on right. Her father observed a good deal of agitation in her manner—he thought it indicated unusual solicitude, and he was touched by it.

"My dear Caroline," he said, "all might perhaps go right if you would come and help my kind friend Charles to nurse me."

"Lord, papa, I would with all my heart: I should like to do anything—everything for you; but you know I am no nurse, and sickness is so frightful."

"Frightful, indeed, Caroline; but a child's tenderness might, I think, deprive it of half its terrors."

"Well, dear sir," whispered Caroline, slipping a letter into her father's hand, "grant the petition this letter contains, and I will stay day and night with you for a fortnight to come."

---

8. *I shudder at the thought of such a death as Gibbon's, Hume's, Voltaire's*: Edward Gibbon questioned Christianity in his *Decline and Fall of the Roman Empire*. David Hume (1711–76) regarded belief in a superior divine being as infantile. Voltaire (1694–1778) was a critic of the Roman Catholic church and a Deist.

CHAPTER XXIV.

Mr. Redwood took the letter, and detained Caroline's hand, though she was evidently impatient to withdraw. Westall rose to leave the room. "Stay, I entreat you, Westall, and you, Caroline—one moment's patience, my child—I anticipate the contents of this letter. Charles must be the bearer of my answer to it: you should have no reserves from him, Caroline, for after I am gone he must be your protector till your marriage transfers that duty to another."

"I hope, sir," replied Miss Redwood, with a look of anxiety and displeasure, "that I shall be permitted to choose my own protector."

Westall walked to the extreme part of the room to relieve Caroline as far as possible from the embarrassment of his presence, while her father read the letter, which contained, as he expected, a declaration of Captain Fitzgerald's love for his daughter, and respect for himself, written in good set terms, and according to the most approved formularies, and concluding with the modest request, authorized by Miss Redwood, that Mr. Redwood would consent to their immediate union.

"Is it possible, Caroline," said Mr. Redwood, laying his finger on the last request in the letter, "that you authorized or approved this?"

"Yes, sir."

"And you would desert your sick—your dying father, to go off with this fellow—a stranger—a fortune-hunter—a profligate!"

Caroline's colour deepened at every additional epithet her father bestowed on her lover: she flashed an indignant glance on Westall, as if she would have said 'an enemy hath done this;'[9] and commanding her voice as well as she was able, she replied, "You are very unjust, papa: your mind has been set against us; and you forget that if Captain Fitzgerald or I had deserved your cruel suspicions, we should have taken a very different course; if your fears are well-founded, a short time may leave me at liberty to bestow my hand and fortune when and where I please; but I neither expected nor wished that liberty. Fitzgerald, whatever you may think, is a man of honour; and I am sure he is sincere, when he says in his letter that next to my affection, he desires your favour."

"No doubt, no doubt—my favour and its consequences; but he shall have neither—Westall, tell him so," added Mr. Redwood, raising his voice above his daughter's, who was giving vent to her feelings in hysterical sobs; "tell Fitzgerald I will never consent to his marriage with my daughter; tell him that I am a dying man, but let him found no hopes thereon, for I am resolved, that if my daughter ever marries him, she shall forfeit her fortune."

"And who," said Caroline, recovering perfectly her self-possession, "who shall receive it? The smooth pious Ellen Bruce—or the kind friend Charles Westall—or perhaps some missionary or tract society?"

---

9. *'an enemy hath done this'*: From Matthew 13: 28 (KJV).

"Oh Caroline, Caroline!" exclaimed her father, in sorrow more than in anger, "God forgive you." After a moment's pause, he added in a voice faltering from extreme weakness, but thrilling from the earnestness which deep feeling gave to its tones, "Oh my child, give me your confidence for the few days of life that remain to me—think no more of this man—he is not worthy of you—he is not worthy the trust of any delicate woman: give to my last hours, Caroline, the consolation of a voluntary surrender of your feelings and judgment to mine."

Caroline made no reply.

"Speak for me, Westall," continued Mr. Redwood, raising himself and leaning his head against the post of his bedstead, "Speak for me, I have neither voice nor strength."

"It is unnecessary, sir," said Westall, and he turned an appealing look on Caroline, as he added, "Miss Redwood will not, I am certain, resist what you have already said."

"And who, or what, sir," asked Caroline, her spirit rising from the control of her better feelings, "has given you a right to interfere in my private concerns?"

"Your father."

"My father, sir, cannot delegate his rights nor my obedience."

"But your father, Caroline," interposed Mr. Redwood, "can make your obedience a necessity—go, Westall, and make my decision known to Fitzgerald."

"Permit me, sir, at least," said Caroline, "to be the bearer of your message. It should, I think, be tempered by some friendliness in the messenger."

"Go, then, child—and if you have no regard for me, respect yourself; open your eyes to the real views of this man, and dismiss him forever from your thoughts."

Caroline deigned no reply, but left the room, her face indicating the determination of an imperious spirit.

"Oh Westall, Westall!" exclaimed Redwood, "from what misery I might have saved myself and my child by the timely performance of my duties to her."

He seemed for a few moments lost in sorrowful reflections, and then starting up, he asked Westall if there were yet no letters from Mrs. Harrison.

Westall, whose ear had been quickened by his impatience, said he trusted there was a letter at the office, for he had just heard the horn of the post-coach as it descended the eastern mountain.

"Go, then, dear Charles, and get the letter—the warrant for your happiness; and God grant that I may see the best blessings of his providence resting on you before I die."

CHAPTER XXIV.

After a long interview with her lover, which was spent chiefly in listening to passionate declarations of disinterested affection, which she more than half believed, Miss Redwood retired to her room in great agitation of spirits and summoned her servant. When Lilly appeared, she received a communication which rendered it necessary that she should make new arrangements of her mistress's baggage—trunks and bandboxes were emptied on to the bed, chairs, and floor, and from the chaos of fine clothes, the mistress and maid proceeded to make such selections as their taste and discretion dictated.

Neither the principal nor agent seemed to possess the calmness necessary to the execution of these sudden preparations. Indeed it was difficult to say which was most flurried with her own individual purposes and expectations. Lilly, on sundry pretexts, went often out of the room, and always returned in a humour to deserve the pettish rebuke which she received from Caroline. But the rebuke was no sooner given than retracted; for Caroline, afraid of the consequences of provoking the girl, conciliated her by some petty gift—some olive-branch symbol, which mistresses and maids both comprehend. Those only who understand the momentous and intricate details of a fine lady's wardrobe, will believe that the remainder of the day was consumed in packing a trunk of ordinary dimensions.

Caroline then proceeded herself to arrange her dressing-case: after having stowed away compactly its usual apparatus, she enclosed the treasure rifled from Ellen in a sheet of paper, carefully sealed it, and then placed it in the dressing-case. She laid in her purse also, locked it, and gave the key to Lilly.

"Now, Lilly," she said, "I believe everything is ready. I trust in heaven we shall return tomorrow; but if we do not, we have secured everything of value." Miss Redwood looked at her watch; "It is time to go," she said, hurrying on her hat and shawl: "Do you, Lilly, drag the trunk to the farther staircase, you'll find a man there ready to receive it—then return and take the dressing-case in your own hands—remember, girl, my purse is in it, and I had rather you should lose your own soul than that anything should happen to it—but stop, let me see, cannot I take it myself: just tuck it under my shawl—no one will observe it."

Lilly gave the dressing-case to her mistress: "But Lord bless me, Miss Caroline," she said, "it makes you such a figure—just look in the glass."

Caroline looked, but for once her appearance seemed to be a secondary object.

"I will take it myself, Lilly," she said, "It's nonsense to stand here deliberating about it. I shall only carry it to the door, and then give it to Captain Fitzgerald."

Caroline opened the door—Lilly laid her hand on it. "Now, Miss Cary," she said, beseechingly, "do give in to me for once. It will look so unbecoming for the captain to be seen carrying your dressing-case—Lord help us, such a footman's job!"

"Hush, girl, I must go"—

"You may go, Miss Cary, but for goodness' sake give me the dressing-case—why I shall whip down the hill, across the fields, and be at the carriage before you."

"Take it, then, you fool," said Caroline: and she resigned the dressing-case, and turned hastily away. She stole along the passage with the silent tread of a culprit: when she came to her father's door a pang of remorse, probably aided by an emotion of filial feeling, checked her footsteps, 'He looked so terribly sick this morning,' she said, mentally—'Good heaven! should I never see him again.' She lifted her hand to knock for admittance, when she was arrested by a voice that alarm just raised above a whisper—"Miss Redwood! my dear Miss Redwood! What are you doing?—For heaven's sake no more delay." The thought of her father vanished from her mind—she bounded forward—gave her arm to Fitzgerald, and they passed together unobserved out of the house.

The last ray of summer's long twilight was not quite lost in the shadows of the evening, and the fugitives prudently selected the most unfrequented road, by which to descend to the plain below, where a carriage was in waiting for them.

The poets say, 'the course of true love never doth run smooth,'[10] and so thought Miss Redwood, when halfway down the hill she and her companion were encountered by Ellen and Westall. Westall had, early in the day, obtained possession of the looked-for letter from Lansdown, and having awaited Ellen's return, till patience had had her perfect work, and would work no longer, he had sallied forth in the expectation of meeting the returning party, as he did at no great distance.

They had been delayed by an accident that had lamed one of their horses, a circumstance that afforded a pretext to Westall to propose to the young ladies to quit the carriage and walk up the hill; and he, leaving Miss Campbell with her natural escort Fenton, proceeded with Ellen, and for a very good reason had preferred, as lovers are apt to do, without any reason at all, the most retired road.

As soon as they were removed from observation, he produced Mrs. Harrison's letter, and Ellen was attempting to read it by the feeble light, when they were met by Miss Redwood and Fitzgerald. Fitzgerald internally

---

10. *'the course of true love never doth run smooth'*: From I, i of Shakespeare's *Midsummer Night's Dream.*

cursed the unlucky encounter, and Caroline drew her bonnet closer; but any apprehensions they might feel seemed quite unnecessary, for Ellen did not raise her eyes from the letter, and Westall only noticed them by slightly touching his hat, being at the moment too much engrossed with his own affairs to have any suspicions excited in relation to theirs. They therefore proceeded unmolested to the place where the carriage was stationed, a servant let down the steps, and Fitzgerald was hurrying Caroline into it, when she started back, exclaiming, "Good heavens! Lilly is not here—I cannot go till she comes."

The servant who had brought the trunk, on being inquired of, said that the girl had left him with the declaration that she would follow immediately. "Then," said Caroline, "there is no alternative—we must wait—I cannot and will not go without her."

It certainly was not Fitzgerald's cue as yet to cross the will or whims of Miss Redwood, and he submitted with the best grace he could assume. A servant was sent back to the springs to hasten the faithless girl, and returned after an interval that had seemed to the anxious and impatient lovers interminable, with the perplexing information that Lilly was nowhere to be found.

Caroline was in despair, and Captain Fitzgerald, impatient at her manifesting a degree of feeling which he deemed out of all proportion to the importance of the occasion, could scarcely curb his displeasure while he urged the necessity of their proceeding immediately.

"We are mad to delay thus, my dear Miss Redwood," said he; "You are, no doubt, missed before this time: that meddling fellow, Westall, will be sure to tell your father that he saw us: our plans will be counteracted—my happiness sacrificed. The girl is doubtless detained by some trifling accident; or if by her own fault, her insolence shall be chastised tomorrow—for tomorrow, my dear Miss Redwood, we shall, beyond all question, return."

"Think you so—are you sure of it, Captain Fitzgerald?"

"Absolutely sure—it cannot be otherwise."

"Then order the coachman to drive on," said Caroline, sinking back into the carriage in a state of mind ill suited to the errand on which she was going.

In vain Fitzgerald essayed to soothe, to argue, to flatter her into her usual spirits. Her imagination pictured a dying, unforgiving father: the beseeching, pathetic tones of his voice, to which in the morning she had refused to listen, rang in her ears like a funeral knell: she was now tortured with the fear that Lilly had been treacherous, and now with the possibility that the secret of the dressing-case might be accidentally revealed; and when she arrived at the place of their destination, a village inn a few miles from Lebanon, her feelings were wrought up to a pitch of excitement little short of frenzy.

Fitzgerald ascertained that the pastor of the village was absent, but that fortunately there had just arrived at the inn an itinerant clergyman, who, to use his own homely phrase, was '*candidating* about the country,' and though a very inferior member of a most respectable body, he was regularly licensed, and was therefore legally qualified to perform the marriage ceremony. Some time elapsed before Miss Redwood became so much tranquillized that Fitzgerald deemed it prudent to expose her to the observation of a third person.

She at last yielded, partly to the influence of her lover, and partly to the propriety—the now inevitable necessity—of controlling her feelings. The clergyman was summoned—he took his station—appointed to the parties theirs, and then drawing a hymn-book from his pocket, he said, 'It would be pleasing if the gentleman and lady would commence the present solemn exercise by singing a hymn.'

"Singing a hymn!" exclaimed Fitzgerald: "Is that a necessary part of the marriage service in this country, sir?"

"Oh no, sir, not necessary, but very suitable. I don't know what the custom may be here in York state, but in Connecticut it is quite customary to close a marriage opportunity with a singing exercise. I thought, upon the present interesting occasion, it would be best to begin with the singing, as the young lady looks a little flurried, and might not be able to unite with us after the solemnity is concluded."

"We will dispense with the hymn, sir," said Fitzgerald, smothering an imprecation on the whole body of puritanical parsons. "Please to proceed to do your office, and with all possible brevity."

The clergyman, however, had quite too much respect for professional details to comply with the last injunction. He began with a dissertation on the happiness of the married state; he then proceeded to an exhortation to the faithful performance of its duties, and closed his prefatory 'exercise' with a prayer, which it is to be feared failed to produce devotion in the parties.

The prayer finished, he began the service that was to bind Caroline indissolubly to Fitzgerald, when the whole party was startled by loud and reiterated knocking at the outer door.

Fitzgerald's conscience foreboded evil: he quitted Caroline's side and sprang towards the door to turn the key; but no key, no bolt, no means of fastening were to be found. He returned to Caroline; she was trembling excessively; he took her hand, and whispered, "For heaven's sake be composed—what should we fear from an interruption?" And then addressing the clergyman, he said somewhat sternly, "Proceed, sir, to your duty."

But the good meek man was not at all qualified for so energetic a measure, and while he hesitated, the noise in the passage increased. The

CHAPTER XXIV.

intruder had made good his entrance, and was in altercation with the landlord. The declaration "I must see them, sir, and that instantly," reached the ears of the lovers, and was directly followed by the throwing open of the door and the appearance of Charles Westall.

"Why this impertinent intrusion, sir?" said Fitzgerald, advancing to Westall with an air of defiance.

"This is no time, Captain Fitzgerald," replied Westall, quite unmoved, "for us to bandy insults; our quarrel, if we have any, must be deferred; my business is with Miss Redwood, and admits of no delay. Miss Redwood," he added, turning to Caroline and taking her hand, "I beseech you to return with me to your father. I have left him in a state that precludes all hope of his life; that precludes, I fear, the hope that he will ever recover his consciousness."

"Then of what use, sir, can Miss Redwood's return be?" interposed Fitzgerald.

"Of what use!—I appeal to you, Miss Redwood: your father may be conscious of your presence; an act of duty and affection may soften the anguish of the dying hour; it may, Miss Redwood, be a source of consolation for yourself, which, believe me, you will need."

"I will go with you, Mr. Westall," replied Caroline, in a faltering voice, and she threw on her hat and shawl which were lying beside her, and offered her arm to Westall.

Fitzgerald thrust himself between Westall and Caroline, and seizing her arm, turned fiercely to Westall, "Stand off, sir!" said he; "I have a right to Miss Redwood. Miss Redwood, you have plighted your faith to me; you cannot—shall not leave me till the priest has done his office."

"Captain Fitzgerald," said Westall, "you need not apprehend any interference with your rights: matters have gone too far between you and Miss Redwood to be retraced: all that I ask—all that I wish is, that you will not attempt to deter her from doing an imperious duty, which omitting to do will disgrace her eternally."

Fitzgerald was softened by the admission of what he feared would be a contested right; he relinquished Caroline's arm, and permitted Westall, without any farther opposition, to lead her to his carriage.

Westall then returned for a moment to Fitzgerald, to beseech him to take all feasible measures to prevent the publicity of the evening's expedition; if not prevented, he thought it might be deferred till Miss Redwood had left the springs, and she thus saved from the disgrace to which a lady is always exposed by a clandestine affair. He then left Fitzgerald to take such means as his own prudence should suggest to effect this desirable purpose, and proceeded with Caroline, as expeditiously as possible, to the springs, where they arrived between twelve and one o'clock. Caroline fortunately did not encounter any person on her way to her own room, whither she went to await the summons which Westall promised to send her as soon as he could ascertain her father's present condition.

It may be necessary to account for what appears to have been very impolitic haste on the part of Caroline and her lover. The threatening symptoms of Mr. Redwood's increasing illness, certainly warranted the natural hope of Fitzgerald, that Miss Redwood's parent did not possess the gift of immortality, which impatient fortune-hunters are apt to attribute to rich old fathers—and the constant and even growing favour of the beautiful daughter, authorized the confident expectation which the gallant captain indulged, of a successful termination of his campaign; when, lo! one of those adverse accidents, which happen alike in love and war, occurred to frustrate his plan of operations: this was none other than the receipt of a letter from his commanding officer, containing an order to rejoin his regiment; and the information that the regiment was ordered to a station in the West Indies.

The captain perceived, at once, that in this exigency a *coup de main*[11] was the only mode of extrication from his embarrassments. He immediately informed Miss Redwood of his recall; but as he knew that the young lady had set her heart on a voyage to Europe, he prudently deferred to a subsequent opportunity the communication of the appointment of his regiment to the West India station. It had become necessary to make a premature application to Mr. Redwood: Caroline, as has been seen, unable to resist the pleadings of her lover, consented to be the medium of it. Mr. Redwood's decided answer precluded the hope that he would change his mind. It was impossible for the captain to await the lingering termination of his sickness, and the hackneyed procedure of a clandestine marriage was the last and only resort.

Few fathers are inexorable, and nothing, as Fitzgerald thought, was more improbable than that Mr. Redwood, with a spirit subdued by a mortal sickness, would withhold his forgiveness from his only child; and, in the very worst supposable case, (for which Caroline had provided by the arrangement of her baggage,) the affairs of the heiress might be committed to an agent.

Thus had the captain, after a survey of the whole ground, with the prudence of a skilful officer, provided for every contingency but precisely that one which for the present suspended his victory.

---

11. *a coup de main*: A sudden, surprise attack.

CHAPTER XXV.

"Breaks not the morning's cheering light
Forth from the darkest hour of night?"[1]
Young Lady's Scrap-Book.

WE must now return to relate the incidents that had occurred while Caroline and her lover were pursuing their clandestine expedition. Ellen and Westall were left slowly retracing their way to the springs, and poring over Mrs. Harrison's letter. Whatever might have been the excellent old lady's epistolary talents, Westall certainly thought her letter a *chef d'oeuvre*[2] when he read the following passage:

"I have no hesitation, my beloved Ellen, in giving you a decision on the subject you have referred to me. You have borne your probation with unremitting patience, and I am sure your fortitude will be equal to the issue, whatever it may be. I see no reason for delaying one moment to penetrate the mystery of your birth. I have, as you well know, admired and encouraged your fidelity to the letter of your mother's dying injunctions; and I do not see that you depart from its spirit now. The box was not to be opened till you had arrived at the age of twenty-one, except in case you should previously make a matrimonial engagement. The engagement made, you were at liberty to explore the box: but your own delicate scruples (which I perfectly approve) induce you to defer your engagement till you ascertain what bearing this long dreaded, long desired secret may have on your history. Though I am convinced that whatever discovery you may make will not affect the wishes or decision of your lover, yet you are right to leave him the liberty which you reserve to yourself.

"I do not ask for riches or honours for you, my dear Ellen, but my earnest desire is, that you may have sprung from virtuous parents, whose memory you may cherish with an honest pride, and to a reunion with whom you may look forward with eager and well-founded hope: whatever may be

---

1. *'Breaks not the morning's cheering light . . .'*: The source of this quotation is unknown.
2. *chef d'œuvre*: Masterpiece.

the event, do not delay to inform me of it; remember that I must weep or rejoice with you—that the light which shines on you, will send its cheering ray to my old heart; or if there must be clouds in your heaven, that they will overshadow me too—for we have the same horizon."

Mrs. Harrison's advice was most acceptable and most gratefully received, as advice always is when it happens to coincide with the strongest inclinations of the heart. When the lovers reached the house, they heard the bell ringing which announced the tea hour, and perceived that the company was thronging to the tea-room.

As they ascended the steps of the piazza, Westall said, "Let us improve the present opportunity, Ellen—the east parlour is vacant, and for a short time at least we shall be in no danger of interruption there. I will order candles while you go for your treasure."

Ellen assented—left him, and reappeared in a few moments with the box in her hand; her cheeks were alternately deeply flushed and deadly pale. Westall understood too well the source whence her feelings flowed to attempt to check them. Ellen tried to unlock the box, but she could not—she shivered with emotion. "Do you open it," she said, giving it to Westall, "for I cannot."

Westall as he took the box from her, perceived that her hands were as cold as marble. "Had you not better defer this, Ellen?" he asked.

"No, no. I am prepared for anything now," she replied, sinking on her knees before the table on which Westall had placed the box.

Westall turned the key, and disclosed to her eager eye the interior, containing nothing but a small miniature-case.

The bright glow of expectation faded from Ellen's cheek. "Oh my mother! my mother!" she exclaimed, in a voice in which bitter disappointment and tender expostulation mingled.

Westall took her clasped hands between his—both were silent for a few moments: he then said, "My dear Ellen, do not distress yourself thus—have not your fears vanished with your hopes? This unforeseen result pains you, but is it not better, far better, than much that you have apprehended? And severe as your disappointment is, Ellen, will you not be consoled by the devotion of my life to you?"

Ellen only replied by laying her head on her hands and weeping bitterly.

Westall proceeded to urge every consolation which the stimulated tenderness of a lover could suggest, but Ellen was deaf to all that he said. It seemed as if she had been that moment torn from the bosom of her mother, and was left alone in the universe.

"Oh, it *was* then an artifice," she said: "Caroline Redwood spoke the cruel truth. I could have borne anything but this," she continued, with an impetuosity that startled Westall—"for this I was not prepared."

"My mother! Must I never vindicate—must I never speak your name!"

Again and again she took up the box, examined it without and within, and dropping it, exclaimed, "Oh, my mother, is this all?"

There was something so sacred in Ellen's grief—something so touching in her brief expressions, and in the indescribable language of her beautiful countenance, that even her lover, whose heart vibrated to every pulsation of hers, was compelled to silence.

Mechanically he took up the miniature case, and passing his eye over it, he perceived a fragment of paper adhering to the edge of it, on which was written, in a delicate female hand, "From my ———" the remainder of the sentence had been torn off. It occurred to Westall at once that there might have been some foul play, and he was on the point of suggesting his conjecture to Ellen, when they were both startled by someone tapping at the door, and then impatiently opening it.

"Pardon my intrusion," said Miss Campbell, instinctively shrinking back, and then advancing, "my errand admits of no ceremony—Mr. Westall, you must go immediately to Mr. Redwood, his servant has been anxiously looking for you—he says his master is extremely ill, and sends to entreat you not to delay a moment to come to him."

"I cannot go now," said Westall, insensible for the moment to any suffering but Ellen's.

"You must go," said Miss Campbell, with an imperative decision which indicated that she had more reason for her urgency than her words expressed; and Westall whispering an entreaty to Ellen that he might be permitted to see her again in the course of the evening, left the ladies to witness a scene of more remediless grief than Ellen's. Miss Campbell remained for a few moments an embarrassed spectator of Ellen's emotion: it surprised and affected her the more, because there was in Ellen's ordinary manner such an instinctive shrinking from the display, or the exposure of her feelings. Grace was not, however, of a temper to remain for any length of time a silent or inactive observer of a friend's sufferings, and after a few moments she kindly passed her arm around Ellen, and said, "What rude storm has assailed you, my dear Ellen?"

Ellen made no effort to reply, and after a little pause her friend added, "Though you will not let me feel with you, you must permit me to think for you, Ellen—you are exposed to intrusion here. Let me go with you to your room—I will stipulate to make no demands—no inquiries—only suffer me to remain with you till you are more composed."

Ellen returned the pressure of her friend's hand in token of her acquiescence, and taking up once more her box with a heart-bursting sigh, she retreated to her own apartment with Miss Campbell; and there, after having recovered from the first shock of her disappointment, she rewarded the delicate kindness and affectionate interest of her friend, by confiding to her the few particulars of her long cherished hopes, and the final utter demolition of them.

And now we must leave her, listening to such consolation as the inventive mind of her friend could suggest, while we follow Charles Westall to the apartment of Mr. Redwood, whom he found walking to and fro in the greatest agitation, supported by his servant.

At the sight of Westall he sunk into a chair, exclaiming, "It is all over, Charles—she has gone—she has left me to die here—gone without one parting word—misguided, miserable girl!"

The recollection of his meeting with Miss Redwood darted across Westall's mind, and he comprehended at once Mr. Redwood's emotion and the language he held.

"Impossible, sir!" he said, "she cannot have gone without leaving some explanation—some communication for you—go Ralph, and find Miss Redwood's servant, and bid her come here."

"Find Lilly!" replied the man, "I might as well look for the wind that blew yesterday, Mr. Westall; Lilly has gone faster one way than Miss Caroline has the other."

"Lilly gone—and not with her mistress? Do you, then, Ralph, go yourself to Miss Redwood's room, and look on her dressing-table; she may possibly have left a letter there for her father."

"And of what avail, Charles, if she has?" asked Mr. Redwood—"what explanation can soften the terrible truth? But go, Ralph—go."

The man obeyed, but not till he had whispered to Westall, "Keep a steady eye on master: the fever betimes mounts to his head, and then he is raving."

The man's apprehensions seemed quite superfluous, for excepting a few rational exclamations, such as "Poor—poor girl!" "Oh God, thou art most just!" "Charles, this last blow is too much for me!" Mr. Redwood remained silent till the servant returned, holding in his hand a large packet, which he said 'might be for master, though there was no writing on the top of it.'

Mr. Redwood snatched it from him and broke the seal. As he unfolded the packet, a miniature rolled from it on the floor, and Westall picked it up. The image of the only relict in Ellen's box was still vivid in Westall's mind, and it was not strange that he should have instinctively compared the dimensions of the miniature with the case in Ellen's possession, and hardly conscious of the several links in the chain of his thoughts, he turned the miniature to examine the back of it. The upper part of the paper that had been pasted over it, was torn off, and on that remaining was traced in the same handwriting that was on Ellen's fragment, "beloved husband to his faithful Mary."

CHAPTER XXV.

A faint light dawned on Westall's mind, when his attention was withdrawn by a sudden exclamation from Mr. Redwood.

"In the name of heaven," he said, "what does this mean? How did Caroline get possession of these papers?" and he held up the certificate of his marriage with Mary Erwine, and the letter directed "to my child." "Oh Charles," he added, "my head—my head;" and he pressed both hands to his head as if his thoughts were bursting it. "Oh memory—memory!—think for me—tell me what these mean?"

"Be composed, sir, I beseech you," said Westall, in the calmest tone he could assume: then opening the letter, he glanced his eye rapidly over it, refolded it and paused; he could not speak: his first impulse was to fly to Ellen and tell her that Mr. Redwood was her father. The fearful wildness of Mr. Redwood's eye still fixed inquiringly on him, recalled him to the present necessity. The discovery must be first made to him; and Westall lost every other consideration in his anxiety to make the communication in such a way as not to destroy the equipoise of Mr. Redwood's mind, which seemed now utterly unable to sustain any additional excitement.

He still hesitated—it appeared that Mr. Redwood understood his apprehensions, for, grasping his hand, he said, "Speak quickly, Charles, while I can comprehend you."

"Be patient, sir—be calm, I entreat you," replied Westall; "There is a blessing—an unspeakable blessing in reserve for you—this letter is from Mary Erwine—from your wife to her child."

"To her child, Charles!—you perplex me—you disturb me; she had no child."

"Yes, Mr. Redwood," replied Westall, almost choking with his own emotions, "her child, and God be praised, that child lives—lives to love and to bless you."

"What is it you mean, Westall? explain yourself," said Mr. Redwood, covering his face with his hands.

Westall described, as concisely as possible, the condition in which he had found the box left by Ellen's mother; and he read aloud some passages of the letter which placed, beyond the possibility of doubt, the fact that Mr. Redwood's wife left a child, and that that child was Ellen Bruce.

Westall did not deem it necessary to allude to the mode by which these testimonials must have passed into Caroline's possession.

Mr. Redwood listened in breathless silence, till Westall had concluded. Not an exclamation, not a sound escaped from him, save the audible beating of his heart. After a few moments he uncovered his face, a smile passed over it as wild and transient as the flashings of lightning on the dark cloud. "Send for Ellen," he said, the effort to speak slowly and calmly too apparent in his voice: "Do you stay with me, Charles—I must not be left alone: the light burns dimly here," he added, pressing his hand to his head.

"Do not send for her now," said Westall, "give this night to tranquillity—to happy anticipations. Tomorrow you will be better prepared to see her."

"Tomorrow! Now or never, Charles; send without one moment's delay."

Westall took out his pencil to write a note to Ellen. Mr. Redwood stopped him: "No, my dear Charles," he said, "go yourself—the poor child will need some preparation—she will need your support. I shall do well enough—I am better—much better, now."

Westall went and returned with Ellen, in a space of time that seemed brief, even to Mr. Redwood. Ellen was as pale as marble; but a celestial joy shone in her face—she sprang towards her father: he rose, stretched out his arms to receive her, and folding her in them, they wept together.

After a moment he started back, and gazed wildly on Ellen. "Ellen Bruce *my* child?" he said—"Is it not all a dream? Speak to me, Ellen—call me father—forgive me in your mother's name."

Ellen's resolution forsook her: alarmed, trembling, and weeping, she sunk on her knees; her father shook his head, and would have stooped to raise her, but, utterly exhausted by the conflict of his feelings, he leaned on Westall's shoulder. A single look from Westall roused all Ellen's energies; she sprang to her father's aid, and assisted Westall to lay him on the bed.

"He is insensible for the moment," whispered Westall, "but he will soon recover his consciousness, and then, my dear Ellen, his life—more than life, his reason, will depend on your fortitude and calmness."

Westall then gave into Ellen's hand the miniature, the certificate, and the letter—the last she kissed again and again—poured over it a shower of tears, and not daring then to trust herself to look in it, she placed it in her bosom.

She then took her station beside her father, and watched with inexpressible anxiety every variation of his changeful countenance. He soon recovered sufficiently to speak, but his words confirmed their worst fears; for they were the ravings of delirium. He laughed and wept alternately—he called on Ellen—on her mother—on Westall; but most frequently and with most impetuosity, he demanded Caroline. He seemed to imagine that she was on the brink of a precipice, and to feel that he vainly sought to rescue her.

So much did his madness appear to be stimulated by this fancy, that after a short consultation, Westall and Ellen determined that an effort should be made to induce Miss Redwood to return immediately, to try what effect her presence might produce on her father. Ralph was sent to ascertain, if possible, the destination of the fugitives; and having succeeded in insinuating himself into the confidence of one of Fitzgerald's agents, he returned in a short time with the information, that they might probably be found at a village inn, at no great distance from the springs.

CHAPTER XXV.

Westall's next care was to determine to whom he should apply to undertake so delicate an embassy, and while he was deliberating, Ellen said, "Go yourself, I beseech you, Mr. Westall. Ralph and I can do everything here; and you, and you alone can persuade Miss Redwood to return—to return," she added, with a faltering voice, "before it is too late."

"Alas! my dear Ellen," replied Westall, glancing his eye at Mr. Redwood, who, after a paroxysm of raving had sunk on his pillow, pale and exhausted, "it is, I fear, already too late."

"Oh, do not say so—it may not be—" said Ellen, and she, bent over her father with a look of great anxiety; then turning suddenly to Westall, "We may at least," she said, "save Caroline from the disgrace that must fall on her, if it is known that she has deserted her father in this extremity."

"Generous being!" exclaimed Westall, "you shall be obeyed; but I cannot leave you here alone."

"Ask Grace Campbell, then, to come to me—but no," she added, looking towards the bed and observing that her father was sinking to sleep, "perfect quiet will be best—now go, and God speed you."

Westall departed, admiring with enthusiasm (as lovers are wont to admire the virtues that belong to the objects of their tenderness) the self-command of Ellen, and the generosity with which she could forego at this crisis of her life the indulgence of her sensibilities, to consider how she might preserve the honour of one who had so relentlessly inflicted suffering on her.

The moment Westall left her, Ellen sent the servant into an adjoining room, that she might avoid the risk of breaking her father's slumbers by the slightest noise. Hour after hour she sat on his bedside, gently chafing his icy hands, wiping the cold dew from his forehead, and noting every breath he struggled to inhale, and every convulsive motion of his distorted features. At length his feverishness abated—he ceased to be restless—the firm grasp of his hand relaxed—a gentle warmth was diffused throughout his system, and his respiration became quiet as an infant's.

Ellen raised her hands and eyes in silent and devout thankfulness, and withdrawing from the bed, she took from her bosom her mother's letter, and opened it with a mingled feeling of awe, of apprehension, and of tenderness.

Could it be otherwise? It was the record of the wrongs of her departed mother first to be learned in the presence of her dying father. Repeatedly she fixed her eyes on the letter, but they were so dimmed with her tears, that she could not distinguish one word from another. At last an intense interest in her mother's fate subdued every other feeling, and she succeeded in reading the letter which will be found in the next chapter.

CHAPTER XXVI.

"Methinks if ye would know
How visitations of calamity
Affect the pious soul, 'tis shown ye there!"[1]

Southey.

"My Child—If the injunction is obeyed with which I shall consign to my friend the box that is to contain this letter, long before you behold it the hand that now traces these lines will have mouldered to dust—the eye that now, as you lie on my bosom, pours its tears like rain upon your sweet face, shall weep no more forever; and the heart that now throbs with hopes and fears for you, my love, shall have ceased to beat with mortal anxieties and mortal hopes.

"Sweet innocent—gift of God—image of immaculate purity—thy mother would preserve thee, an unsullied treasure for the riches of Christ's kingdom—a stainless flower for the paradise of God: thy mother would shelter thee so that the winds of heaven should not breathe unkindly on thee. But this cannot be. Thou must be exposed to the dangers of human life, solicited by its temptations, and pierced by its sorrows—and thy mother, thy natural guard and shield, must be from thee. Thy mother can do nothing for thee—Said I nothing!—God forgive me. I can do—I have done all things—I have resigned you to Him whose protection is safety—whose favour is life. I have believed his promises—I have accepted his offered mercy; and in faith, and nothing wavering, I have committed my orphan child to Him. And now, though thy path should be laid through the waters, they shall not overwhelm thee, and through the fire, it shall not kindle upon thee.

"My child, I am now to account to you for a resolution, which, should it please God to preserve your life, must materially affect your future destiny.

"I beseech you to permit no unkind thoughts of your mother to enter your gentle bosom. Remember that if I deprive you of your rights, degrade you from the station in which you were born, and remove you from honours

---

1. *'Methinks if ye would know . . .'*: From *Roderick, Last of the Goths* (1814) by English poet Robert Southey (1774–1843).

and riches, it is that you may become 'an heir of the kingdom;'[2] remember my motive—read the brief history and unhappy fate of your mother, and you will not—must not blame her.

"My father's name was Philip Erwine. He was a Scotchman by birth, the only son of a rich and respectable family. He was educated for the church, and preparing to enter life with the most happy prospects, when they were forever clouded by a clandestine marriage, which the world deemed imprudent, and his father unpardonable, with a portionless, obscure girl, whose maiden name, *Ellen Bruce*, I have given to you. My grandfather discarded his son from his home and his affections, and only cherished the remembrance of this one act of disobedience. Oh my child, the pride of this world is cruel tyranny.

"My father subsisted for some months on scanty remittances secretly made him by his mother; but she died soon after. My grandfather married again—had more children—and my father, thus cut off from all hope of a reconciliation, emigrated to America. My parents were strangers in a strange land, and obliged to meet the evils which the poor and friendless must always encounter. My father, nursed in the lap of indulgence, sunk under privation, and became utterly spiritless and dejected. My noble mother, with an 'inborn royalty of mind'[3] that makes the trappings of earthly distinctions seem poor indeed, endured all her trials without a murmuring word, or even look. She made incredible exertions for the support of her family, and maintained an outward cheerfulness, while her heart was sinking with the consciousness of having been the cause of my father's calamities. Her health and life were the sacrifice. I have since heard my father confess that when he laid her in the grave, he was first roused to a sense of my wants and his duties.

"He left New York, the scene of his sufferings, and fixed his residence in a village on Long Island Sound. There he obtained a comfortable living by teaching the children of some gentlemen whose summer residences were in the vicinage. Whenever he was compelled to be absent from me, I was left in the care—the vigilant, maternal care, of the kindest-hearted woman in the world, who afterwards married a Mr. Allen, and went to reside in Massachusetts. I was the constant companion of my father's solitude—the consolation, he called me, of his exile. All the treasure of his heart was lavished on me: I was the refuge of his affections, and nurtured with a thoughtful tenderness that quite disqualified me for the indifference of a selfish world—quite unfitted me for the rude storm that has since assailed me, and before which I have fallen.

2. *'heir of the kingdom'*: A reference to James 2: 5 (KJV).
3. *'inborn royalty of mind'*: From 'Ode for Music' (1769) by Thomas Gray (1716–71).

"My father was a good man: adversity had made him an humble Christian: still he possessed the pride natural to the human heart, and I, his only child, was the object of all that pride. Yes, my love, he was proud of thy mother's beauty—that fatal beauty that has been the source of all my griefs— that beauty which is now perishing by disease, and soon will be quite effaced by death. Thank God, I was never proud of it: in my simplicity, I was ignorant of its value and its danger.

"My father would sometimes bewail for me the loss of distinctions, which were no loss to me, for I had never known them; and in the joyous independence of childhood, I could frolic away his sadness, and prove to him, by the contentment of my spirit, the vanity of his desires.

"I had just attained my fourteenth year when I lost my father. I pass over that period of my life. My support—my defence was taken from me—the world was all before me, and I would gladly have turned back and laid me in my father's grave. Thank heaven, my child, there is a misery you cannot feel!

"My father did not leave me without a provision. Tender as the parent bird that plucks the down from its own breast to feather the nest for its young, he had practised the severest economy—deprived himself of every, the least indulgence, that he might reserve his small earnings for my sake.

"Mrs. Allen, to whose guardianship my father had left me, sent me to a boarding-school to acquire some slight accomplishments, which she hoped, with the solid instruction I had already received, would qualify me for a teacher, and thus secure to me the means of permanent independence. I had been one year at school—my education was finished, or rather my small means were expended, when a Mrs. Westall came with her husband from Virginia to visit her northern friends. Though some years older than I, we had been playmates in our childhood. She remembered with kindness our youthful intimacy. My youth and loneliness interested her husband's benevolent heart: he invited me to accompany his wife to the south, and promised, if I became dissatisfied with my home in his family, to obtain for me among his rich neighbours an agreeable situation as a teacher.

"Now, my child, your mother claims your pity, your sympathy, your forgiveness, while you read the record of an indiscretion that casts her into an early grave, and condemns you to orphanage.

"The day after our arrival at Mr. Westall's plantation, I had stolen just at sunset into the garden with my friend's little boy, Charles Westall—the thought of this child throws a bright gleam across the track of memory, and I pause to dwell on it as the traveller in a desert lingers to pluck a sweet and solitary flower. Scarcely less a child than himself, I was the favourite companion of his sports. He had chased me through the walks, and having caught me, he made me kneel on a turfed bank, that he might, as he said, crown me his queen. He pulled the comb from my hair, and was weaving knots of honey suckles and rose-buds among my curls, when we were startled by the rustling of the branches of some high shrubs behind which we had retreated. We both looked up and perceived a gentleman, a stranger, gazing intently on us.

"Little Charles sportively drew the branches around me, saying, 'this is my Mary, my queen—and nobody shall look on her till she is crowned.'

"'Such a nymph,' said the stranger, 'should have a guardian angel and a sylvan veil.'

"These were the first words I ever heard from your father; this was the first time I ever saw him, and from this moment he was never absent from my thoughts: wherever I was, in society or in solitude, Henry Redwood's voice rung in my ears; his image was forever before me. Look, my child, at the picture which you will find with this letter: look on these eyes—the lofty brow—the mouth—and then imagine what this face must have been when kindled with the inspiration of the living spirit.

"I was young and ignorant—artless and unsuspicious— constantly exposed to the charms of his genius and accomplishments—to the fascinations of his tenderness—and if I had ever doubted (which I did not) that he was all that he seemed, his being the friend of Mr. Westall would have quieted my fears.

"Here I have paused to look over what I have written, and I blush at my own inconsistency. I blame myself, and yet I seek a justification in my child's eyes; this is natural, for, alas, the heart is deceitful. But I will do so no more—I will tell the simple truth, and trust to my child's heart to plead for her mother.

"Not many months elapsed before I married Mr. Redwood clandestinely, and without much scruple or reluctance. Every sentiment of duty and propriety was lost in the fervour of a first attachment, and in the fearless confidence which youth and love inspired.

"He urged the necessity of secrecy, and assigned many reasons for it. I received them implicitly, or scarcely listened to them, for I had cast the care of my honour and happiness upon him, and my affection was unclouded by a single doubt or anxiety.

"Soon after our marriage Mr. Westall died suddenly—the kindness of Mrs. Westall detained me with her for some time: I then left her to take charge of the children of a Mr. Emlyn, whose plantation adjoined that of my husband's father. Our opportunities of meeting, though somewhat diminished by my residence with strangers, were still frequent, but they exposed me to suspicions and remarks that made me miserable.

"The last time I saw my husband I confessed my anxieties to him. I even hinted my expectation of your existence; that I believe he did not understand, and I had not courage to explain myself. I observed that he felt unusual emotion at parting with me, and the next morning I received the information that he had gone on a tour of pleasure to Europe, to be absent one or two years. With this intelligence, which almost deprived me of my senses, your father sent me, by mistake, some letters that had passed between him and one of his friends, from which I discovered, that while he felt some tenderness for me, he regretted that he had encumbered himself with an insuperable obstacle to his advancement in the world.

"He was the world to me—and I found myself worse than insignificant to him. Every fibre of my affections was clasped around him, and I was thus in a moment rudely torn away: poverty I had never dreaded—calamity in any other shape I could have borne—but I merited the chastisement. I also discovered from these fatal letters that your father was an unbeliever; not merely that he rejected the truths of revelation, but that he could even treat a future retribution and the hope of immortality as childish illusions.

"Oh, how then in the bitterness of my sorrow and disappointment did I blame myself that I had so long forgotten my Christian duty, and had looked upon my husband's indifference to religion (for his unbelief I never suspected) as what was to be expected in a young man. My child, I deserved my fate—I was born of a Christian mother, watched and guided by a Christian father—religious principles were deeply rooted in my heart; and yet for a while every thought of duty was suspended—every affection was melted into one deep, absorbing passion—my whole existence was resolved into one sensation—alas, this it is to love!

"As soon as I became sufficiently tranquil to think of the future, I took a resolution to go to Philadelphia, without any very definite purpose but to hide myself from everyone who had ever seen me, and to escape from a scene where every object renewed my anguish, and where I was no longer capable of performing the duties I had undertaken.

"Oh that terrible journey!—I was alone and unprotected, and so young and so wretched, that everybody noticed me, and I had such mortifications and trials to endure! But I will not make your heart bleed by relating them—why should I? They are past forever.

"The journey was fatiguing to me—my sorrows preyed on my health, and before I reached Philadelphia, I was seized with a nervous fever, which obliged me to remain at a German settlement. I recovered partially from it, but it left my mind in a state of alternate apathy and insensibility, which rendered removal impossible. I hired a lodging in a very poor German family, where I awaited my confinement. I was careless about my life, and took no thought for my health, which ordinary attention might perhaps have restored, but long fastings and sleepless nights, when my weary spirit knew no rest, have wasted my strength; and now I would give worlds for a little space of that life which my wilful neglect and my guilty despair have destroyed.

"Your birth awakened me to a new existence—breathed a new spirit into me—created ties to life; and from the first moment I folded you to my bosom, I would have accepted existence on any terms; no condition, however deserted and neglected, has now any terrors for me. All other feelings and desires are extinguished in the pure flame of maternal love, and for you, my child, alone I would live.

"But it cannot be—a terrible cough racks my frame—the fires of consumption are kindled on my cheek, and every day I see and feel the steady and sure approach of death—I weep over you, and the kind creatures that are about me weep to see me, and the long silent watches of the night I pass in praying for you.

"In my still solitude, when thou wast sleeping all unconscious on my bosom, I have heard a voice saying unto me, 'leave thy child with me.' I have obeyed the voice—I have resigned you to the protection of that good Being, who in tender compassion has declared himself the orphan's God.

"And now it is deeply impressed on my mind that I ought to do something to preserve my lamb from the danger of wandering from the fold of the good Shepherd. Your father, by deserting me, has forfeited his right to you. When I am no longer in the way of his worldly prospects, his heart may be touched with compunction for the wrong he has done me; you might awaken a parent's feelings, and he might invest you with your rights.

"All this might be—and what would you gain? The unwilling sufferance— the scanty favour, it may be, of a proud and selfish family; for such, from the confession of your father, are his connections. But for this shall I expose you to the danger, the almost inevitable certainty, of alienation from the Christian hope?

"It must not be—I behold something in your innocent face—the emblem of heaven—I feel something in the soft touch of your little hand that appeals to your mother's heart to direct your course in the path that leads to the mansions in our Father's house.

"I have at last taken an immovable resolution to keep your existence a secret from your father, and to preserve from you, and from everyone, the knowledge of my connection with him till you are of an age when you will be secure from his influence—when your character will be formed by wise and Christian care.

"You must not, my child, think hardly of me for keeping you so long in ignorance of your parentage—I dare not leave anything to hazard— the very young do not know how to choose good from evil, and Heaven preserve you from the hard school of experience in which your poor mother has been taught!"

Here there occurred a blank in the letter; and the remainder scarcely legible was as follows:

"Since writing the above, I have been too weak to use my pen. In the meantime my kind, generous, best friend, Mrs. Allen, has complied with a request I sent her, and come to me from her distant home. Ah, how has she grieved to find me so sick, and in this mean lodging; but I have not suffered from its poverty, and I chose it that I might not diminish the pittance I have saved for you—the remnant of the liberal supply my husband sent me at his departure.

"I have found in this humble dwelling all the kindness I needed, and I have enjoyed an inward peace that springs from the reflection that I have for you, my child, sacrificed earth to heaven.

"Mrs. Allen remonstrates with me. I see that she thinks I have been so long lonely and sorrowful that my mind is not quite right, but she is mistaken—I am sure she is mistaken. She tells me that I may involve you in many embarrassments—she suggests a thousand difficulties that may occur, but I cannot consider them now—I cannot go back to the world—my thoughts are all the other way.

"She does not oppose me any longer, but has most solemnly promised to fulfil my wishes, though she still calls them strange and singular. She says I am young—I am young in years, but in the last twelve months I have grown very old. Oh, to the wretched, hours are years, and weeks are ages!

"She begs me to be governed by her discretion, but I cannot.

"She knows not—no one knows—how to look upon the troubled and vanishing dream of this life, till the light of another falls upon it. No one knows how mean everything that is transient and perishable appears to me—how insignificant the joys, nay even the sufferings that are past, as I stand trembling on the verge of that bright world of innocence and safety, where I hope to appear with the child God has given me.

"My last prayer will be for you, my child—and for your father—God have mercy on him!"

Every word of this letter which may appear very long and tedious to an indifferent reader, sunk deep into Ellen's heart. It seemed to her as if the book of Providence was unsealed and open before her, and as the bright light fell on the path by which she had been led to the present period of her existence, 'Oh my mother!' she exclaimed, 'hast thou not been with me a guardian spirit, to lead me by the way which was disclosed to thy prophetic eye?'

Her emotions were deep and indescribable—stronger than any other were gratitude to her mother, and admiration of the courage and single-heartedness with which she had renounced the world for her.

'I might,' she thought, 'like Caroline, have been the slave of the world—the victim of folly: I might have followed my poor father through the dark and dreary passages of unbelief, but for that good part which my sainted mother chose for me.'

A thousand reflections crowded on her mind: but gratitude for the past—her own bright hopes of the future—every other feeling was soon lost in an extreme solicitude for her father's recovery.

She knelt by his bedside—But there are feelings too sacred to be drawn from their silent sanctuary—there are services too hallowed to be described. They are seen in secret, and rewarded, as Ellen's were, openly.

We must now recur to Caroline, who, on re-entering her own room, was startled by the spectacle of her dressing-case—the lid open, and packet and purse gone. She seized the dressing-case, emptied out every article it contained, in the vain hope that in some corner the treasure might lurk, but fruitless was the search, and she dropped it and burst into tears.

"Oh," she said, "had the wretch taken anything else—my money—my trinkets—anything but this—the loss of this may ruin me."

While she was thus bewailing her calamity, she heard a gentle tap at the door, and on opening it Ellen appeared. Caroline started back, and said haughtily, "Has Westall sent you to me, Miss Bruce?—I could have dispensed with this favour."

"No, Miss Redwood," replied Ellen, advancing into the room with an air of dignity and gentleness, "I have come here on my own errand—Caroline, your"—here for the first time there was a slight tremulousness in her voice, and after a moment's pause, she added, "*our* father"—

"You have it then?" shrieked Caroline.

"Yes," replied Ellen, "I have it—Providence has restored to me my right; but you, Caroline, have nothing to fear from me—let the past be forever forgotten. Our father, Mr. Westall, and myself, are all that know where these precious documents were found: and is not the secret safe with us? We are the persons most concerned for your honour—are we not? Forget the past then, and regard me without fear or distrust."

Caroline was touched with Ellen's generosity, and deeply mortified, for the moment at least, at the wrong she had done her.

"I never meant," she said, as soon as she could command her voice sufficiently to put the words together, though in the most embarrassed and stammering manner, "I never meant, Ellen, to keep those papers from you forever. I do not believe I should have kept them so long, but I thought that you could not suffer from the loss of that which you were ignorant you possessed; and I knew that when papa discovered you were his child, he would care nothing for me. It was uncertain, you know, for a long time, which of us Westall preferred, and though I have since felt a perfect indifference for him, I did then wish—at least I should not have disliked his addresses, and I was sure if papa knew all, he would throw his influence into your scale, and then Charles Westall would have no reason for preferring me, as, your rights acknowledged, your fortune would be equal to mine, and that I could not but think very unfair, as nearly all papa's fortune came from my mother, and yours, you know, was quite pennyless."

Self-justification is the natural tribute, even in the most hopeless circumstances, to the law of rectitude written on the heart. Lame and impotent as was Caroline's attempt to justify herself, Ellen replied without appearing to notice any of its inconsistencies.

"You have not," she said, "rightly judged me, Caroline. If you could have imagined the joy—the gratitude I have felt this evening, you would not, I am sure you would not, have deferred my happiness. My mother's name is vindicated—sanctified my faith has always held it; but it is now beyond the reach of suspicion or imputation. You know not, Caroline—how should you know!—the dreadful solitude of living without a natural tie to your fellow-creatures. You know not the exquisite sensations I have felt this night, even amidst afflicting fears, beside *my father's* bed."

Ellen's emotion checked her utterance for a moment: she then added, "Caroline, it is best that we should understand one another perfectly. Your mother's fortune is as entirely yours as if I had never had an existence. I have not the right, and, certainly, I have not the wish to interfere with your inheritance in the smallest degree. All that I covet, is an equal share of our father's affections; your confidence I hope to win; your sisterly affection I will try to deserve."

After a short pause Ellen added in conclusion, "There is one arrangement, Caroline, which, if I insist on controlling, you must not think I too soon assume the rights of an elder sister. It is my wish that our relationship should remain a secret for the present."

Caroline looked astonished. Ellen, without seeming to notice her surprise, proceeded, "in the present state of my feelings, I wish particularly to avoid observation and remark. The avowal of my engagement with Mr. Westall, and your friendship, will give me a right to share with you the care of our father. Should he not recover, the secret shall never be divulged—it is enough that I know it—for worlds I would not cast a shadow over his fair name."

In assigning her motives, Ellen had avoided any reference to what she knew must be Caroline's wishes on the subject. Caroline felt this delicacy to her heart's core; she was subdued by the pure goodness of Ellen; she felt the influence of the holy principle that governed her sister's mind, and penetrated with a poignant contrition like that which made the Egyptian king exclaim, 'Truly, I have sinned against the Lord your God and against you;'[4] she sunk

---

4. *'Truly, I have sinned against the Lord your God and against you'*: A variation on Exodus 10: 16 (KJV).

on her knees—the pride and haughtiness of her soul were vanquished—she stretched out her arms with an almost oriental abjectness. Ellen raised her and clasped her arms around her. It may not be too much to say, that the beautiful sisters were a spectacle at which Heaven might rejoice; for they seemed to embody penitence and perfect love.

"Oh, Ellen!" exclaimed Caroline, as soon as she could speak, "is it possible that you will not, after all, triumph over me? Can you forgive my slights—my insults? Can you forget the wrong I have done you?"

"All is forgiven—all forgotten," replied Ellen; "Think no more of it, Caroline. Let us now think of nothing but how we shall best minister to our father's restoration; for this we will unite our hearts and efforts. Let us go together to his room."

"Yes, I will go—I will do everything you ask of me, Ellen," said Caroline; "but first tell me, for I never can speak on the subject again, first tell me where those papers were found. Did Lilly give them to you?"

Ellen could not satisfy Caroline's curiosity to know the particulars of her servant's unfaithfulness. She could only inform her that the packet had been found in her apartment. The truth was, that Lilly, during her northern summer, had formed too intimate an acquaintance with 'the mountain nymph, sweet liberty,'[5] and had conceived too strong a friendship for her to be willing ever again to leave her dominions.

She had, too, in imitation of her mistress, been carrying on a snug love affair of her own with the servant of a West India planter, then at Lebanon. Miss Redwood's clandestine arrangements were the signal for the execution of Lilly's plans, and they afforded an insurance from the danger of immediate pursuit—the only security she needed.

Lebanon is a border town, and the boundary line of New York once passed, and Massachusetts entered, Lilly was assured of the protecting hospitalities of the people of her own colour; and it had even been hinted to her, that in case her retreat was discovered, the white inhabitants would be very backward to enforce her master's rights.

Thus encouraged, Lilly availed herself of the propitious moment of Caroline's departure, subtracted the purse from the dressing-case, and not wishing to encumber herself with any superfluity, she left the dressing-case, and in her haste left it open, and made good her retreat.

What particular grounds there might have been in this instance for the intimations given to Lilly, we cannot say; but it must be confessed, that our northern people are quite careless of the duty of protecting slave property, and that they manifest a provoking indifference to the rights and losses of slave-holders. Indeed, so notorious is their fault in this particular, that their

---

5. *'the mountain nymph, sweet liberty'*: From Milton's *L'Allegro* (1645).

southern brethren seldom run the risk of an irrecoverable loss by exposing their servants to the danger of an atmosphere infected with freedom; and those among them who possess the greatest abundance of these riches, which emphatically take to themselves wings and fly away, prudently make their northern tours attended by white servants.

The sisters found their way through the dimly lighted passages to their father's apartment. Westall met them at the door; he perceived, at a single glance, that all was right between them.

"Thank Heaven," said he, "you are both here; your father has just pronounced your names."

"Is he conscious?" whispered Ellen.

"I do not know; but he seems quite calm and refreshed."

Caroline and Ellen approached the bed together. Mr. Redwood looked at them with an expression of surprise and inquiry, and a slight convulsion agitated his face. They both bent over him and kissed him. He joined their hands, clasped them in his, and raised his eyes—peace, gratitude, and devotion spoke in them. He said nothing; he seemed to fear the effort to speak. After a few moments he relinquished the hands of his children and closed his eyes. Tears stole through his eyelids, and a sweet serenity overspread his countenance.

"This is heaven's own peace," whispered Westall; "the world cannot give it—the world cannot take it away."

CHAPTER XXVII.

And as the morning steals upon the night,
Melting the darkness, so his rising senses
Begin to chase the ignorant fumes that mantle
His clearer reason.[1]
Tempest.

Heaven hath a hand in these events.[2]
King John.

THE night and its afflictions, which we have just faithfully recorded, passed away, and joy came with the morning. Mr. Redwood's condition was already much amended. He experienced, to its full extent, the restorative power of happiness. His disease had been more moral than physical, and it yielded to moral influences.

Without superstition one might have believed that Ellen possessed a 'healing gift,' so beneficent was the effect of her vigilant care. She was constantly at her father's bedside, ministering to his mind and body, and performing all those tender and soothing offices which the sick so often feel to be more efficacious than the most skilfully compounded drugs.

She never left her father's room but for the purpose of renovating her strength and spirits by a few turns on the piazza with Westall. If her lover ever thought that her filial duty abstracted her too much from the reciprocation of their mutual feelings, (a natural jealousy, for a man is never satisfied without expressing what a woman is content with feeling,) he was quite consoled when, during these brief interviews, he listened to the detail of her feelings in relation to himself—of her hopes and misgivings; in short, to that whole history of the heart which is such delightful music to the lover's ear—and such very dull music to every other.

---

1. *'And as the morning steals upon the night . . .'*: From V, i of Shakespeare's *The Tempest.*
2. *'Heaven hath a hand in these events.'*: The quotation is inaccurately attributed to Shakespeare's *King John*; it actually appears in V, ii of *Richard II.*

Ellen communicated to Mrs. Westall and Miss Campbell the discovery of her parentage. Both, as might have been expected, received the intelligence with inexpressible delight: all human happiness must be qualified, and that of the two ladies was considerably abated by Ellen's injunction to temporary secrecy, and by her passing without the slightest notice over the particulars that led to the discovery. After Ellen had concluded her communication, and had received the embraces and congratulations of her friends, Grace Campbell's smiles triumphed over the tears with which they had been conflicting, and she turned to Mrs. Westall and said, "Well, my dear madam, I suppose you and I must put down all of mother Eve within us, for no evil spirit will enter this paradise that Ellen has conjured about her, to devise ways and means to relieve our curiosity."

"And my dear friends," said Ellen, "I am sure you will be content to endure that curiosity which could only be relieved by an evil spirit."

"Oh, I don't know—at any rate, I had rather not be tempted," replied Miss Campbell. "But, my dear Ellen, as we are not permitted to see the ring or lamp—the magic means, whatever they may be, by which you have attained the happy finale of your fairy tale—do gratify me in one particular—suffer me to produce a grand sensation once in my life—allow me to proclaim you Ellen Redwood before the world and in the presence of your disdainful sister?"

"I cannot."

"And why not?"

"Because my sister is no longer disdainful, but kind and affectionate; and besides, my dear Grace, you know that I have a rustic aversion to notoriety; and more than all that, our arrangements are already made. Should my father continue to convalesce as rapidly as he has done for the last four-and-twenty hours, he will be able to leave here on Thursday next, one week from this day—the day appointed for the departure of your party. Caroline and Fitzgerald are to be married, quite privately, in my father's room, on Wednesday morning, and are to proceed immediately to Canada; and I am to resign the place your aunt kindly offered me in her carriage, and, with your leave, Mrs. Westall, am to occupy that which Caroline vacates in our father's."

"A most delightful arrangement," exclaimed Mrs. Westall.

"A delightful arrangement to you, ladies, doubtless," said Miss Campbell; "but I confess I do not feel particularly flattered that Ellen should sever herself from our party with so much nonchalance, and form her exquisite plans without the slightest reference to us."

"You have not heard all our plans, my dear Grace," replied Ellen, with slight embarrassment; "we have been compelled by the necessity of the case to form them hastily: my father has expressed a wish that Caroline and

I should be married at the same time; to this I could not consent; my duty to Mrs. Harrison—my affection for her, forbids it. My father is willing to make an effort to go to Lansdown, that he may see my beloved friend, and express his gratitude for her maternal kindness to his child."

Ellen hesitated, and Miss Campbell said, "This is all very pretty and very proper, but still there is no consolation for my self-love."

"You have not heard Ellen out, Miss Campbell," interposed Mrs. Westall; "the most agreeable part of all these arrangements is yet to come; a part which, in right of Charles Westall's mother, I have already been consulted on. My dear Ellen, I will take pity on your girlish reluctance to come to the point, and just tell Miss Campbell, in direct terms, that your wedding is to be celebrated at Lansdown, on the first day of September."

"Since Mrs. Westall has helped me on so far, my dear Grace," said Ellen, "I will come to that point to which all this preamble has tended, and in as direct terms as Mrs. Westall's, beg the favour of you to persuade your aunt to accommodate her progress to our snail's pace, in order that I may have you for my bride's-maid."

"Thank you, thank, you Ellen. Now *I* can perceive that your arrangements are all delightful. Persuade my aunt!— Bless her, I can persuade her to anything; and if I could not I would poison the horses—bribe the coachman to turn the carriage off some of your northern precipices—anything for the pleasure of seeing you married to Charles Westall." After an instant's pause Miss Campbell added, "In romance all the business of life ends with a wedding, but in real life that seems to be the starting point. Now, as I am a little worldly in my views, I should like to know, Ellen, whether you and Westall are going to set up housekeeping in the Harrison mansion, and live upon love and verses, as Miss Debby would say?"

Ellen assured Miss Campbell that she had no such romantic views, that on the contrary all due respect had been paid to their temporal affairs. She informed her that on account of Mr. Redwood's health, they were to pass the winter in Virginia—that in the spring they were to return to New England—that Mr. Westall was then to form a partnership which had long been projected with an eminent lawyer, and enter upon the business of his profession.

"My prudence is quite satisfied," said Miss Campbell, when Ellen had concluded: "and now, my dear friend, tell me, are you never to appear as Ellen Redwood?"

"My father insists on my bearing that name from the moment we leave Lebanon."

"That is as it should be," said Miss Campbell—and the ladies separated.

Fitzgerald, who had felt himself at the mercy of events which he could not control, passed a week of impatience and anxiety: but a week 'though it may be tedious, cannot be long,'[3] and the day arrived that was to assure his right to Caroline Redwood. There were some indications that it might not have been impossible to persuade the young lady to retract her engagement, but it seems that her friends did not deem it expedient to interfere, for they never spoke to her upon the subject.

Ten o'clock was the time appointed for the marriage ceremony, and at that hour Fitzgerald led Caroline into her father's apartment.

Ellen, Westall, and his mother were there, awaiting them. Mr. Redwood was sitting on his easy chair, his health and spirits obviously and surprisingly renovated. He had summoned all his fortitude for the occasion; but he shuddered when he saw his daughter come into his presence for the last time, and thought of the probable destiny to which he was about to resign her. She had never looked so lovely as at this moment—the events of the preceding week had softened her heart, and touched her beautiful face with a moral expression.

Mr. Redwood received Fitzgerald with politeness, rather chilled by extreme reserve. He drew Caroline to him, and put his arm around her—"My dear child," he said, "before the clergyman is admitted, I have somewhat to say to you. We have already exchanged forgiveness—mutual it should not have been, but that you made it so, for my parental faults met with their just retribution in your breach of filial duty—that is all past, and we will forget it if we can.

"Caroline, I have made Ellen acquainted with your generous wish that a large portion of your fortune should be conveyed to her; but Ellen is a nice casuist, and she has convinced me that I have no right to make any disposition of a property which descends to you from your mother."

"Oh Ellen!" whispered Caroline to her sister, "will you not allow me to make some atonement to you?"

"My dear Caroline," replied Ellen, "if I needed an atonement, your kindness and confidence are an ample one—that I have accepted—I can accept no other."

"My small patrimonial inheritance," resumed Mr. Redwood, "has been increased by the legacy of an uncle, and though my fortune is still moderate, it is quite adequate to my own wants, and to Ellen's very moderate desires. Captain Fitzgerald, my dear Caroline, must pardon me, if I avail myself of my right to remain your steward during my life. The income of your fortune shall be regularly transmitted to you, wherever your husband's destiny may take you. God grant that the restoration of peace to his country may enable

---

3. *'though it may be tedious, cannot be long'*: From a 1759 essay by Samuel Johnson in no. 71 of *The Idler*.

him to perform his promise to resign his commission, and come and reside among us."

After a brief pause, Mr. Redwood continued, "I am now going, my dear child, to bestow on you an inestimable treasure;" he put into her hands the Bible he had received from Ellen; "this your sister gave to me with prophetic benevolence—she knows that her purpose has been accomplished—the dark shadows of unbelief have passed from my mind forever—the terrors that threatened to annihilate my reason are vanquished—the life-giving truths, and immortal hopes of that book have translated me from darkness to light. My friends," he added with increased energy, "you know not what it is to endure the evils of life with the horrible belief that the grave is the place of final extinction—of eternal death: neither can you know," and a divine joy seemed to illuminate his countenance, "neither can you know the rest of my wearied spirit— the gratitude I feel to the blessed Redeemer—the resurrection and the life."

He was silent for a moment and then said, "Receive my blessing, my child, and remember that it is my last injunction that you make this book your guide."

Caroline, deeply affected, knelt before her father—Ellen sunk on her knees beside her, and clasping her arm around her sister, she raised her tearful eyes to Mr. Redwood, "severed—strangers," she said, "as we have been on earth, we may yet be a family in heaven."

"God grant it, my children!" responded her father fervently, and for a few moments he bent his head in silence over his daughters; he then raised them, gave Caroline's hand to Fitzgerald, and Ellen's to Westall.

The clergyman was summoned—the nuptial ceremony performed—Caroline received the farewell embraces of her friends, and left them forever.

We fancied we had finished our humble labours, when by a lucky chance a letter, written by Deborah Lenox, and addressed to Mrs. Charles Westall, ———, Massachusetts, fell into our hands. As it was written nearly two years subsequent to the date of these memoirs, and contained some interesting notices of the personages that figure in them, we immediately transmitted it to our printer. It was sent back with a respectful request from the compositors of the press (those accomplished orthographers) that the spelling might be rectified. In reward of their patient toil in our behalf, it has been deemed a duty to gratify their fastidiousness, and Deborah's epistle has been reluctantly re-written—letters have been transposed, subtracted, and added, and we believe its orthography is now quite perfect. In no other way would we consent to alter it, for we respect the peculiarities of our honest friend, and are willing to have the sibyl *with* her contortions.

"Eton, Vermont State, 20th July, in the year of our Lord 18—

"MY DEAR ELLEN,

"I guess you will be surprised to see my pot-hooks and trammels, and puzzled enough you will be to read them; but I could not let so good an opportunity pass without letting you know that the Lord has spared our lives to this date, and that all your friends at Eton are well, except the minister, who enjoys a poor state of health.

"The reason you do not receive a letter from sister Lenox by this opportunity, is, that she does not know of it, on account of her having journeyed to New York to meet George and his bride, who we hear, though she has the disadvantage of being born and bred at the south, is as likely and prudent and notable a woman as if she had the good fortune to be brought up in New England, which leads a reflecting person to consider that it is best to lay aside their prepossessions, and to believe that there are good people everywhere. I did not expect George would have got over his disappointment so soon; but he has acted a rational part, for it stands to reason that a man can find more than one woman in the world to make him happy: that is to say, if he can't get cake, he had better take up with gingerbread.

"But before I go any further, I ought to finish giving you the reasons why you must put up with a letter from such a poor scribe as I am, instead of receiving one from any of the rest of the family, who all write, Lucy and all, coarse hand and fine, very nicely. The girls are busy, excepting Lucy, preparing tea for our grand visitors. James's wife, kindhearted little soul that she is, has gone to fix off Peggy; and Lucy is at the knitting society, which has lately been established in aid of the pious youth at the Cornwall school, and foreign and domestic missions. So you see, my dear Ellen, I e'en have to put my hand to the plough.

"You and I never did a better *chore* than getting Emily back among us: it would gladden your heart to see her old grandmother, who is truly a new creature, and owns, like Job,[4] that she is more blessed at the end than at the beginning. Emily makes a first-rate wife, which I take to be partly owing to her having learnt many prudent and prospering ways among them Shakers; and I do think if they could be prevailed on to turn their settlement into a school to bring up young folks for the married state, they would be a blessing to the world, instead of a spectacle to show how much wisdom and how much folly may be mixed up together.

---

4. *like Job*: In the biblical book of the same name, Job loses all his belongings and family, and undergoes a period of testing by God. At the end of the book, Job has his wealth restored to him double-fold, and he establishes a new family.

CHAPTER XXVII.

"Little Peggy came here this morning, with a basket of new-fashioned early beans, a present from Deacon Martin to me: the deacon and I have had a strife which should have the first beans, and he has won the race; and by the way, I do not believe you have heard about the deacon's marriage, which has made quite a stirring time here at Eton. You must know that a few weeks after the deacon lost his wife, he felt so lonesome without a companion that he came to sister Lenox to recommend a suitable one, and she directly spoke a good word for Peggy's aunt Betty, who is, as it were, alone in the world, and though a poor body, she comes of a creditable stock in the old countries; and what is more to the purpose, her walk and conversation among us has been as good as a preached sermon—that is to say, a moral discourse. Well, the deacon was quite taken with the notion, for Betty is a comely woman to look to yet, though well nigh on to fifty, and he went directly to lay the matter before some of the church-members, and they made strong objections to the match, on account of Betty's so often breaking the third commandment,[5] which comes, I suppose, of her being brought up in Old England, where they are by no means so particular about teaching the youth their catechise as with us. The deacon, however, had set his face as a flint, and there were consultations about it, till at last two of the brethren agreed to go and talk to Betty on the subject, and make her promise that she would put a tight rein on her tongue.

"Betty promised everything they asked; but you know when a body always goes in the same track it makes a deep rut, and it is next to an impossibility to turn out of it; and so, while Betty was talking with them, every other sentence was, 'God help us, gentlemen,' and 'God bless your souls, I'll do my best,' and so on; and they came away more dead set against the match than ever. But Martin went on in spite of them, and married her; and except in the matter of the third commandment, there is not a more exemplary deacon's wife in the state than Betty makes.

"But I shall never come to the end of my letter, if I go on at this rate. I find that the older I grow, the more I love to talk; and somehow or other I always did love, above all things, to hold discourse with you, Ellen. To go back then to my last starting point. I emptied out Peggy's basket, and went to open the door for her, and what should I see but a fine coach with a noble span of horses turning up to our gate, and who of all the people in the world should be in it but Mr. Fenton Campbell and his wife, Grace Campbell that was!

"I did not know her at first glance, for she is dressed in deep mourning for her uncle Richard Campbell, who has died lately; sorry enough, I

---

5. *breaking the third commandment*: In Exodus 20: 7 (KJV), the third commandment is 'Thou shalt not take the name of the Lord your God in vain.'

dare say, to leave all his other accounts to go to his last one. However, the moment she smiled one of her own beautiful smiles, as bright as the sun at mid-day, I knew her, and she sprung out of the carriage and was on the door-step at a bound, and shaking both my hands, just with that warm-hearted way of hers, she came in and sat down, and directly we fell to talking of you, and our tongues went as spry as that old woman's, who, as a humoursome gentleman said, had hers fastened in the middle that it might run at both ends!

"Peggy's ear is always nailed the minute she hears your name, and she kept drawing closer and closer to us, and at last the poor thing began to cry; and then Mrs. Campbell made some inquiries about her, and when she heard her story, and learned that you wished Peggy to go and live with you as soon as her aunt would spare her, and that her aunt had given her consent, and that Peggy was only waiting for an opportunity, and was all on tiptoe for it, she just spoke a word to her husband, and then told Peggy that if she would be ready in the morning, she would take her to you. I thought the child would have gone clean out of her wits with joy: her eyes, the blind one as well as the other, looked as if they would have danced out of her head; she clapped her hands, and whirled around, and fell on her knees, and kissed Mrs. Campbell's gown—poor thing! she is too feeling a creature for this world; and I am thankful she is going to you, Ellen, who know all about feelings, and can temper hers.

"I don't well see where Mrs. Campbell will stow the child away, for her carriage is filled with all sorts of notions, and a large kind of pocket-books which they call portfolios, and which Mrs. Campbell says are filled with her husband's drawings, for they have been to the Falls, and to Quebec, and so on, and you know painting is his fancy; and I judge it takes a great deal of room to draw such large lakes and rivers on. However, she has determined of her own accord to take Peggy, and I always find your real noble-minded people can contrive a way to do every kind action that turns up in their path.

"Mrs. Campbell had not heard a word of the death of Captain Fitzgerald and his wife, till I told her about it: and I declare, Ellen, it was a teaching providence to me when I heard it; and I could not but think of the time when I saw them at Lebanon, so young, so blooming, and so handsome, stepping over the earth with a step so light and so lofty, that it seemed not to be in all their thoughts that they must ever lie down under the cold clods.

"Poor young creature! I am sure, when she was flaunting away here at Eton, I never thought I should have wet my old eyes for her; but for all, I did cry like a child when sister Lenox received your father's letter, telling all about her death and that her last words were to beg them to send her little girl to you, and ask you to make her like yourself.

CHAPTER XXVII.

"The dealings of Providence are sometimes mysterious; but he that runs may read this dispensation. However, Ellen, as it would not be pleasing to you to have anything cast up against your sister, especially since she is dead and gone, I will say no more upon this head; only to observe, that if this child lives to grow up under your training; the world will see that a woman's being beautiful and rich need not hinder her from being wise and good too: and it seemeth to me, that though God respecteth not the outward show, the more beautiful the temple is the more fitting is it for a dwelling-place for his Spirit; and I think it would be a pleasing and an edifying sight to see the perfection of earth and the beauty of heaven built up and fitly framed together.

"Often, when I am alone, and considering, my thoughts turn upon you, Ellen, and upon all that happened before your sister went off to them West Indies, which have proved her death; and thinking upon you brings to mind some passages of Scripture, which have been remarkably acted upon in your life; and first, in the sixteenth chapter of Proverbs and the seventh verse, Solomon says, 'when a man's ways please the Lord, he maketh even his enemies to be at peace with him'—and in the New Testament Scriptures it is written, 'be not wearied with well doing'[6]—'overcome evil with good,'[7] and so on. Now, in my view, these texts appear as a kind of history of what passed between you and Caroline; and it is a comforting thing to see such a plain agreement between the book of experience and the book of God's word—that is to say, to see a Christian's life a scripture proof.

"Caroline's behavior, at the upshot, was a satisfaction to me in many ways, and especially as it helped to build me up in the doctrine I have always maintained, namely, that there is no soil so hard bound and so barren but what, if you work upon it long enough, you may make it bring forth some good thing at last; not that it will equal that soil which is warm and rich at the start, and is from the beginning diligently opened for the sun of God's grace to shine in upon it, and the dews of heaven to nourish it—a soil like—I must write it out—like your heart, Ellen.

"You need not to have said so much in your letter about your gratitude for my offer of the hundred pounds, feather beds, and so forth, for I knew you did not despise it, and that it was true, as you say, that you only refused it on account of your house being entirely filled with Mrs. Harrison's furniture, and your sister's handsome presents.

"Your worldly condition, Ellen, seems to me to be conformable to Agur's prayer—'Give me neither poverty nor riches'[8]—a prayer that

---

6. *'be not wearied with well doing'*: A variation on Galatians 6: 9 (KJV).
7. *'overcome evil with good'*: From Romans 12: 21 (KJV).
8. *Agur's prayer—'Give me neither poverty nor riches'*: From Proverbs 30 (KJV).

everyone professes to approve, but, I am sorry to say, I have observed but few whose conduct bears out the profession.

"Before I finish my long preachment, I wish to send my compliments to Mrs. Harrison, who I hear looks ten years younger since she went to live with you; and my duty to Mr. Redwood, who I hope, now he is so happy, won't take Mrs. Fitzgerald's death very deeply to heart, since we must all have criss-cross lines in this life.

"In conclusion, my dear Ellen, I have only to say, that as your light has shone brightly in adversity, I pray it may shine on in prosperity, making glad many hearts long and long after death has closed the eyes of

"Your old friend,
"DEBORAH LENOX."

Appendix A:

Sedgwick's Preface to the 1850 Edition

The 1850 edition of the novel included both prefaces – the original one from 1824, followed by this new one.

PREFACE TO THE 1850 EDITION.

No reader can be so fully aware of the defects of the following pages as their writer—certainly no one half so sorry for them. But whatever they are, I am consoled by believing that they do not offend against religion or sound morality, and that they are true to the condition of society in New England, and to the individuality existing there which I attempted to describe. The book may seem very dull to the reader of the brilliant novels with which the press is teeming. I confess that I cannot judge its merits. To me it is endeared by the memory of the glowing sympathy of the beloved brother who first incited me to literary labor, and whose approbation (heightened doubtless by affection) gave me as keen enjoyment as I ever derived from it.

The description of the religious community of the Shakers may have a permanent interest for those who are curious in investigating the history of the human mind, as developed in the infinite varieties of religious faith. Only an imperfect knowledge of this community can be obtained from reading their few books. I had an advantage from long residence in their neighbourhood, from frequent opportunities of personal observation, from a kindly intimacy with some of their members, who, in common with the whole Society in Massachusetts, professed an allegiance to my father in requital for some civil immunities his intervention procured for them. It was my intention to describe them truly, without exaggeration or false colouring, but I had the mortification to find that my best friends among them, "the Elder Sisters," were dissatisfied with my representations. It is not easy for a philosophic, or even an impartial observer, to satisfy those who tenaciously and enthusiastically hold to peculiar modes of faith and worship. It is difficult to perceive the accuracy of a landscape painting if we have not stood at the painter's point of sight.

The Shakers regard their Mother Anne as equal to Jesus Christ. Both, in their belief, were human beings in whom the fulness of the Godhead dwelt—to use their own language, "God was manifest in them, in the female as well as in the male." With these high claims for their founder, they mistook language by which no disrespect was intended, for irreverence and derision; and to them the modes of speech, the usages, the assumptions—what, in short, may be termed the costume of the community—was profaned by its exhibition in the person of Reuben Harrington, a hypocrite and apostate. The Elders, as the organ of the Hancock Society, addressed a letter to me, shortly after the publication of "Redwood," expressive of indignant and wounded feeling. This document was accidentally destroyed. I deeply regret its loss, as I should be very glad to do them the justice to place their own contemporaneous comment before the public. At the time, I made such explanations and apologies as a sincere regard and respect for them dictated, and they magnanimously forgave me.

On revising the book, I see no reason for any material change. What then seemed to me true, now appears so. The sister, a woman of rare gifts, in the general acceptation of the phrase, whose history, under the name of Sister Susan, I have told substantially as she related it to me, has long since passed to the reward of a self-sacrifice, a holy self-denial that places her among the Christian saints, no matter by what earthly sectarian designation named. The followers of Mother Anne have now maintained their Society in its integrity and good order for more than sixty years. That it is thus preserved by a sincere faith, and sound morals, cannot be questioned, for the tendency of false pretension and bad morals is inevitably to dissolution. There can be no mistake as to their actual condition, as they exist in the midst of a suspicious, keen-sighted, and vigilant population, where there is something like an atmospheric pressure on every side, and at a period, and in a country of constant mutations, where old faiths are every year dissolving, and new ones every year forming.

Appendix B:

Significant Revisions for the 1850 Edition

Sedgwick's new preface for the 1850 edition of *Redwood* (see Appendix A) reads more like an addendum to the first preface than an entirely new one. Whereas the 1824 preface addresses several aspects of the novel, including the Shakers, the 1850 preface focuses exclusively on the depiction of the Shakers. Despite her announcement in the new preface that she sees 'no reason for any material change' in the new edition, there are in fact dozens of revisions that involve adding, deleting or changing anything from one word to several sentences. After charting all the differences between the two editions and further analysing the changes in wording and phrasing, it became clear to me that Sedgwick had at least one larger goal (besides correction and modernisation of spelling and punctuation) when revising the novel for the 1850 edition: to soften her criticism of the doctrines and practices of the Shakers.

As the passages in the following chart demonstrate, at least eight of the revised passages in the text of the novel itself render its depiction of the Shakers less critical and less extreme:

Wording in first edition (1824)	Wording in revised edition (1850)
Ch. V: 'the charm of the elder sister's power was dissolved'	'the charm of the elder sister's power was weakened' (Susan's power as a Shaker elder is not so easily dismissed.)
Ch. V: "'Resist to the death,'" exclaimed Susan in a voice of authority. "It is a strong temptation, child...."	"'Resist the devil and he will flee from you,'" exclaimed Susan in a voice of authority. You are under a strong temptation, child...." (Because she only quotes scripture [James 4: 7, KJV], Susan is absolved of seeming personally to prefer Emily's death to her marriage.)

Ch. VII: 'Justyn Allen, the father of Emily and Edward, was born in Connecticut, whence while a minor he emigrated with his father's family to the state of New-York. There he and all the rest of the family, with the exception of his mother, were, for a short time, under the dominion of Anne Lee, the founder of the Shaker society: by the charitable deemed an enthusiast—by those of severer judgment, an imposter. At her first appearance in this country, she made many converts from amongst the respectable class of farmers. Her dominion however over the Allen family was of short duration, and after a few weeks of wild fanatacism, the father and children returned to the half-distracted mother, to lament or deride their delusion. Susan Allen, the youngest child, alone remained constant to her new faith, which she had been the last to adopt, and which had been endeared to her by difficult sacrifices.'	'When "Mother Anne," the founder of the Shaker community, came from England to this country, the Allen family who then resided in the western part of Massachusetts, were, with the exception of the elder Mrs. Allen, for a time under her dominion. After a few weeks of wild fanaticism they returned to their ordinary life, lamenting or deriding their delusion. Susan Allen, the youngest child, alone remained constant to her new faith, which she had been the last to adopt, and which was endeared to her by the costliest sacrifice a woman can make.' (Here the authenticity of Anne Lee's claims to have been the second coming of Christ are not derided, the damage done to Justyn Allen's wife by his temporary Shakerism is omitted, and Susan Allen's sacrifice of a married life is cast in more admirable terms.)
Ch. XV: 'from all parts of our union—all are shocked or disgusted by some of the absurdities of the Shaker faith, but none have withheld their admiration. . . .'	'from all parts of our union; if they are displeased or disgusted by some of the absurdities of the Shaker faith, and by their singular worship, none have withheld their admiration. . . .' (Here people are displeased rather than shocked by the Shaker faith, and their 'singular worship' bears some of the disgust, rather than their faith alone.)

Ch. XV: 'they believe it (or affect to believe it) to be a spiritual blessing. . . .'	'they believe it to be a spiritual blessing. . . .' (No self-deceit is suggested on the part of the Shakers; they merely hold this belief.)
Ch. XVI: 'The Shakers preserve all their austere formality in the disposition of their dead: the brethren and sisters are laid in separate and parallel lines, as if they contemplated the same restrictions in the other world which they impose here: each grave is designated by a rough hewn stone inscribed (with ostentatious humility) with the initials only of the name borne by the person who reposes beneath it.'	'The Shakers preserve all their austere formality in the disposition of their dead; each grave is designated. . . .' (Here there is no imaginative speculation as to what the dead Shakers may be thinking, which makes the description less jocular and more objectively accurate.)
Ch. XVI: 'independently, promptly, and secretly. Her mind was tempest-tost, and while the sore conflict lasted, reason threatened at every moment to abandon the helm. Much cause as she had to distrust Harrington's integrity, she did not on this occasion doubt the sincerity of his kindness. Her mind was engrossed. . . .'	'independently, promptly, and secretly. Much cause as she had to distrust Harrington's integrity, she did not on this occasion doubt the sincerity of his kindness. In the confusion and agitation of her mind, she did not look behind. Her mind was engrossed. . . .' (Here Emily is confused and agitated, but not near insanity, which softens the effect that the Shakers have had on her and shifts some responsibility to her for not looking back before absconding with Reuben.)

Ch. XVI: 'Emily, though she groaned aloud as the door closed after the elder sister, suffered her to depart without any farther communication. She passed the remainder of the day in severe struggles; but finally, at the close of it, she came to the supper-table. . . .'	'Emily sprang after her as she closed the door, and grasping her gown, held her fast for a moment, still doubtful, irresolute, then clasping her arms round Susan's neck—"Will you," she sobbed, "will you always love me?" "Yea, dear child, and always pray for you." Emily retreated to her room. Susan's last gracious words comforted her, but she passed the remainder of the day in severe struggles; finally, at the close of it, she came to the supper-table. . . .' (The addition of the touching dialogue significantly softens the portrayal of Susan, indicating that she will sincerely love Emily, regardless of Emily's decision.)

EU Authorised Representative:
Easy Access System Europe Mustamäe tee 50, 10621 Tallinn, Estonia
gpsr.requests@easproject.com

Printed and bound by CPI Group (UK) Ltd, Croydon, CR0 4YY

21/10/2025

01980710-0002